DEEPER

BRITNEY JULY

DEEPER

DEEPER

Editor: Erica Russikoff

Cover Design by: Mary at Books and Moods

Proofreader: Zahra J

Interior Formatting / Design: Britney July

To the girls who stan with taste ;)

PLAYLIST

Imported – Jessie Reyez & 6LACK
Paint – Travis Garland feat. JoJo
U Did That – Teairra Marí
Often – The Weeknd
Moment – Victoria Monét
Falsetto – The-Dream
Feature – Jay Park feat. Cha Cha Malone
Easy (Remix) – DaniLeigh feat. Chris Brown
BEST ON EARTH – Russ feat. BIA
the valley – Miguel
dRuNk – ZAYN
Available – Justin Bieber
The Canvas – SiR

In my Veins – Jesse McCartney
Under the Influence – Chris Brown
On a Wave – Tinashe feat. Drake
Stan – 6LACK
Superstar – Usher
A Muse – dvsn
Triggered (Freestyle) – Jhené Aiko
Kiss it Better – Rihanna
Devotion – Tone Stith
imagine – Ariana Grande
Rumors – Sabrina Claudio feat. ZAYN
Deep – Summer Walker
Natural – ZAYN
Nobody – Selena Gomez
Scripted – ZAYN
Try – Nelly Furtado
Yours – Jesse McCartney
Peaches – Justin Bieber feat. Daniel Caesar + GIVĒON
Adore – Prince

This is art, babe
Play your part, babe
Then we all get paid.

– MIGUEL, "THE VALLEY"

1

ENTERTAINER

I didn't even want to go to the concert.

It was Victoria's twenty-fifth birthday, and she was having an otherwise shitty life. She all but swore this would be the pick-me-up she needed to get out of her rut. As a makeup artist for modern women, and some semi-famous, she was currently going through a bit of a dry patch. And a concert for some British guy was going to be the glue to piece her life together.

I let her believe that.

This wasn't just any concert. It was for her beloved Zander Khalil. We were eighteen when she first started obsessing over English boy group So What, and right away it had always been about Zander for Victoria.

I never got into So What, the boys in the group ranging from our age, to a year older, or a year or two younger. Even still, their fans were a bunch of screaming preteens—albeit some teens, too —who weren't wise enough to catch on to their clandestinely coded dirty song lyrics. They made cliché pop music that held no true meaning.

No, at eighteen, if it wasn't hip-hop and R&B, I wasn't

hearing it. Especially nothing sugary and manufactured from a bunch of preppy White boys from the UK.

Okay, they weren't *all* White. One look at So What and Zander immediately caught my eye. You couldn't *not* notice Zander Khalil right from the beginning. His mother was British-Indian, and his father was British-Pakistani. With his bronze skin, dark eyes, always perfectly styled ebony hair, and full lips, there'd always been something...dazzling about Zander, I could admit. Something alluring and arousing.

Zander was the first to leave So What after four years and three albums to go solo. After two number-one albums filled with sensual and more than suggestive lyrics, it was safe to say he'd ditched his boy band image. He made music when he wanted and how he wanted, but never did he actually perform any of it on the road. Hence why this little concert was a big deal. After four years of being on his own, Zander Khalil was finally going on tour.

And I just had to be there.

It wasn't a nationwide tour, just four cities. According to Victoria, the point was to test the waters, to see who was interested in hearing him perform live. After tonight here in LA, he was set to do another show in Atlanta, and then New York, and another in Houston. His other shows were sold out, leaving Tori to believe he'd announce his *real* tour soon.

I grimaced, becoming even more impatient as we stood in line to get into the venue where Zander was set to perform. Victoria and I'd come to this place, The Warehouse, tons of times before, only then we were supporting our favorite rapper and R&B songstresses, or dancing during their club nights where DJs would play their sets.

Zander's sound wasn't pure R&B, but it was urban enough to where he wasn't clean-cut pop either. His debut single, "The Sound," was about a night of intense sex. The lyrics had been kinky and erotic enough to let us know then that Zander wasn't about to beat around the bush. He sung about sex openly and honestly, and I had to give him his props.

When the intro came on and he was heard whispering into the mic, "Let's go to bed," it was our first warning of what was in store for his debut.

The chorus to "The Sound" played in my head, and there was no use in denying its heat or whether it would be a straight hit.

You and me on mattresses
Between the sheets
Going round for round
The way your body shakes
You scream my name
I love to hear the sound

His voice was honestly heaven-sent.

I stared at the Zander poster taped to the brick wall a few feet ahead of us, taking in his dark brooding eyes and the way he seemed to gaze right at you. Maybe if he wasn't currently testing my patience, I would've swooned at the handsome image. Instead, I scowled and wished he'd show up already.

"He just needs to sing 'The Sound,' and then I'm out," I told Victoria.

Tori wasn't hearing me. "That's *all*? Girl, I need 'The Sound,' 'Taste It,' and 'Bad Side.' Plus, you know how 'You for Me' gets me in my feelings."

I should've called off sick.

"Yeah, I know," I said.

Truthfully, I didn't see the hype. Zander was a known hermit, a big reason his career was where it was—just okay—and probably the main reason his high-profile relationship hadn't worked out.

First, there was his longtime girlfriend from back home, Ishani Chopra. And then, after he left So What, he got caught out and about with popular up-and-coming actress Jolene "Jolie" Jones, abruptly ending things with Ishani in a very asshole way. He and Jolie were on and off for a year or two before she finally moved on.

Losing luscious-lipped, big emerald-green-eyed, gorgeous blonde Jolie had been the biggest fumble of his career according to some gossip blogs. That really got an eye roll out of Tori. "He's more than who he's screwing," she'd sworn.

According to Victoria, he *still* followed Jolie on all social media platforms. Tori wasn't a fan, but I was sure that had more to do with jealousy than anything.

"I just hope he shows up," I said as I checked the time on my phone: 10:33 p.m. He was over an hour late. Meaning, we had to wait even longer to be let in.

Victoria groaned. "Bianka."

Most people called me *Bia*; whenever Tori brought out my full name that meant I had really irked her nerves.

I rolled my eyes. "Leaving it alone. Happy to be here."

At least Zander sounded good live from what I'd seen of his So What concert days and early solo performances on YouTube.

"You just don't know how ready I am for Zander to show the world what he's made of," Victoria turned and said to me. "I swear, in the original So What days, everyone only ever cared about Teddy, and don't get me started on those annoying-ass 'Veddy' shippers."

While I hadn't paid that much attention to So What, I did notice that Teddy Sykes was always the most adored member of the group followed by Vernon Smith, and the rest of the boys: Oliver Davies, Jac Taylor, and formerly Zander.

"Zander's *always* had the best vocals," Victoria went on. "Ugh, and that vein that bulges when he hits those high notes? I have fantasies about it. I've even masturbated to it."

I blinked a couple of times, unable to believe she'd disclosed that information. We weren't exactly shy about letting each other in on our relationships with our boyfriends or our sexual conquests, but to know she diddled herself to Zander—well, I guessed it wasn't surprising. She probably named her battery-operated boyfriend after the guy.

"I feel like there are some things I shouldn't know about you, Tor."

My best friend wasn't at all ashamed. She'd more than likely go straight home after this and give herself some release after finally seeing Zander in person. Her love for Zander was so fierce, so intense, you'd have to pry her cold, dead hands off of him to get her to stop. And even then, it would be impossible, her fingernails went right to the bone she was so entranced by and attached to him.

To have an infatuation like that, a love like that, was something I'd never experienced, with a partner, or a musician, or an actor. In some ways, while I pitied her coveting, I envied it all the same.

I couldn't even blame her for fantasizing about Zander; after the last asshole I'd dated, it had been months since I'd experienced an orgasm. Truth be told, I was a little more than frustrated because of it. You could masturbate all you wanted, but nothing beat a good fuck.

I gathered my phone and checked Zander's Twitter page for the tenth time, finding he still hadn't sent any tweets since that afternoon.

The show started at nine, didn't he know that?

Even though the show had been announced a couple of months ago, it was still hard to believe this was happening when The CelebriTea posted about Zander finally being ready to perform a few days ago.

I went back and reread over the online gossip blog's post, checking for signs of a hoax.

The CelebriTea

Your Source for All Celeb News

May 25

ZANDER KHALIL READY TO TAKE THE STAGE

Say it ain't so?! Could we be getting an extra five weeks of summer? Known shut-in Zander Khalil has been spotted out and about in LA this week prepping for a comeback. The heartthrob has finally decided to grace the stage on his first solo four-city mini tour, possibly hinting at a much bigger tenure in the future.

"He's so ecstatic!" his rep claims.

The twenty-five-year-old sultry alternative R&B singer, best known from English pop group So What, went solo after four years with the multi-platinum selling boy band.

When his debut single "The Sound" shot to number one on all the charts across the globe, many believed Khalil was set to take the world by storm as a one-man show. But after releasing his debut album *Exposed*, and a slew of late-night talk show appearances and award show performances, Khalil went back into hiding.

Only, he wasn't done there. One year after the release of *Exposed*, Zander was back for more with his sophomore effort *Damage Control*, filled with even more steamy bedroom ballads and hits than his debut.

———

I stopped, unable to read any further. Looking around me at the bustling crowd anticipating the show, I only half saw the appeal surrounding Zander. In my eyes, he was just a pretty boy with a pretty face. There was nothing else beyond that. There was nothing...*deep* about him. He just didn't give.

I tucked my phone away and hung back, waiting impatiently.

The Warehouse was an average-sized venue than most, and due to Victoria's anxiousness and determination, we'd been waiting a little longer than necessary as she had us arrive extra early to get our current spots at nearly the front of the massive line. The venue took up most of the block, as parking was across the street and cost fifty bucks. Tori was wise to Uber us to the show.

Night had fallen upon us and everyone was buzzing to be a part of Zander Khalil's first show. Cars drove up and down the street, a few stopping to let other attendees out to get their place in line. All around me the feeling of excitement and eagerness could be felt through the air. A few girls even had signs and posters to wave around. Hopefulness practically radiated off of my best friend as she bounced from one foot to the other. If she had to, Tori would probably wait all night for Zander to show up.

She'd gone all out, in the event that she possibly got to meet him face-to-face. She'd chosen to wear a lace black bustier with black canopy jeans and matching Vans. It was sexy and casual against her makeup and ponytail. The nice peek of her cleavage was a bonus.

Since I didn't want to be at the concert, I merely opted for a large *Damn.* T-shirt and a pair of my favorite Jordans. Aside from pulling my bundles up into a ponytail, I didn't bother to put on makeup or accessories. This was Victoria's crush, not mine.

"Tickets, come get ya tickets! Don't miss out on the hottest show of the year!"

A couple of scalpers were making their way back up the block, trying to sell last-minute tickets to get inside. The marquee over the entrance lit up with Zander's name, illustrating that the show was sold out. It wasn't a surprise; as soon as his tickets were live, fans rushed to buy them while they still could. Tori had been generous enough to purchase hers and mine online months ago when the news first broke about Zander's tour.

The scalpers, one tall and skinny, and the other short and stubby, looked like the predictable loitering type who would sell any and everything to those desperate enough. This was LA; everybody was selling something.

"Need an extra ticket, baby?" Skinny asked as he approached me, winking. "Call up a friend and make it a party."

Frowning, I said, "No. I don't even want the one *I* have now."

"Bia!" Victoria chastised me, shielding me from the scalper. She waited until he was on to the next group of people before she spoke some more. "Girl, that attitude of yours is your worst trait, I swear."

She was always saying that.

I clung closer to the wall of the building, wanting to be inside already.

As if to aggravate me more, someone was playing Zander's music loudly from their phone. The sound of "Taste It" had me scowling.

"*Girl, let me taste it,*" Zander crooned over a smooth melodic beat, "*I like when you're impatient. This time ain't no waitin'. Stop that hesitatin'. C'mon, let's get faded. C'mon, let's get naked. C'mon, let me taste it—*"

A ghostly silence swept through the crowd, followed by hushed murmurs. A look over and I saw why. Slowly, coming up the street was a Black Badge Cullinan. Through the windshield I spotted two nondescript men up front, and as the vehicle passed us by, I noted the side windows were so black I couldn't see if there were any other passengers.

Finally. It had to be Zander. Now, at least, the doors would finally open.

Right on cue, up ahead I spotted the line moving and security letting people in.

Victoria released a squeal as she bounced in place. I had no choice but to be happy for her; seeing her all geeked made the mood infectious.

Once inside we hit the bar and Victoria ordered herself a pink vodka lemonade while I opted for a simple Coke. Tori's tickets secured us a good spot front and center by the stage. Zander would have no choice but to notice Victoria this way.

We stood at our place and I took in the room, noticing how quickly it filled in and how crowded it'd be once everyone was inside. Before long, the air would be hot and sticky at most with this capacity. Loud chatter greeted my ears as well as a sight of dozens of faces and camera flashes.

The spotlight on the stage in front of me held my attention the most. I wasn't a fan of Zander by any means, but of what I'd heard of his vocal abilities, I couldn't complain too much.

At least homie could sing.

"You're *so* pretty!" A woman's voice turned me around to find a fan standing beside Victoria gawking at her. "I love your makeup. Who did it?"

Bashful, Victoria blushed. "Thank you. I do it myself."

The woman's eyes enlarged. "Do you do it for other people? I'm getting married in a few weeks and my girl decided to up and move to the A." The woman made a face at the scenario. "*This* is actually supposed to be a treat to take my mind off of all the shit I still have to do for our day."

"Heard you," Victoria responded. She soon looked down her person and came up and frowned. "I didn't bring any cards with me, but you can take down my number. Actually...let me show you my Instagram page."

Tori and the woman began scrolling through Tori's professional IG before the woman took her own phone out and followed Tori online and accepted her number. When the woman went back to her own friend group, Tori faced me and grinned.

"A wedding, Bia!" she gushed at the opportunity.

Maybe she was right, maybe this night *was* the pick-me-up she'd needed.

In another minute, I squeezed her close and snapped a selfie to post online.

Time ticked by and my legs began to ache from just standing around.

"Any day now," I muttered to myself.

Being so close, Victoria nudged me with her elbow. "Patience."

We'd long since bypassed our patience era of the evening. A smooth hour had passed since we'd been let in and Zander still had yet to make an appearance.

What was the hold up?

I was just considering going for a restroom break when a man appeared on stage. He eyed the crowd and I watched as trepidation spread across his face at the sea of us before him.

Narrowing my eyes, I looked on with bated breath.

The man peered off to his left, at someone off stage in the back, before facing the audience once more. He ran a hand through his blond hair and cringed. Fine worry lines creased his pale forehead as he began to frown.

I watched as he took a deep breath and began to speak into the microphone clutched in his hand. "Folks, I'm sorry to inform you that tonight's show has been cancelled. Zander Khalil won't be performing."

A collection of incredulous "Whats" rung from the crowd behind me.

The man held his hand up as if to pacify the mounting

tension. "I'm sorry. Our talent for the night is just unable to perform and the show is off."

"Is he postponing?" someone demanded to know.

The man rubbed his neck. His skin was turning red under all the scrutiny. He was just the unfortunate messenger. "Look, I wish I could tell you more, but that's all I got."

His words ignited rage amongst the fans who were expecting to see a show.

Victoria turned and looked at me and I could see her broken heart in her eyes.

Her pretty face crumbled. "Maybe something came up."

She was disappointed. She'd never been to a So What concert, and to support Zander solo was a big dream and goal for her.

And now he was cancelling the show way past the last minute?

No, fuck that. I didn't stand for over four hours just to be easily dismissed by some pansy-ass recluse who owed Victoria and everyone else a performance.

"This is bullshit!" someone hollered from the crowd.

Got that right.

"BOO!" another person shouted out.

"Teddy wouldn't do this," someone else snapped.

Around me people were pissed and upset, but none of it hit me like seeing Tori's frown sink deeper.

"I'm going to use the restroom. Meet you out front so we can just go?" I asked as I leaned in to be heard over the chatter.

Victoria bobbed her head. "Deal."

I gave her a firm hug before departing for the restroom.

What a waste of a night out.

After finally getting in to the packed restroom, I quickly used it and washed my hands. The more I took in the situation, the more irked I became.

"He seriously hasn't toured since he left So What," a woman was saying to her friend as I passed them on my way out of the room.

Her friend snorted. "He's such a flop."

While I didn't mind studio versions of songs, I knew the rush it was to see your favorite singer live. To see them in their element. To hear their live vocals and emotion emit in front of you.

Zander was a rare vocal talent. I had no doubt he'd be good solo versus the backing of his old pop group. If he ever showed up to perform.

Out front the crowd had dispersed all over the sidewalk and security was everywhere. I craned my neck left and right to spot Victoria and I couldn't find her.

Shit.

Up and down the street vehicles were driving by and fans were crossing the road to get to parking, or into cabs or rideshares.

The sight of a black SUV caused me to pause in my search for Victoria.

The Cullinan.

For a moment, I put Victoria on the backburner as I marched farther up the sidewalk. The man from the stage, who I was assuming was the manager of the venue, was busy trying to calm down the fans before a riot broke out. Security was nearby in case someone attacked the poor guy. It was only a matter of time before the police showed up.

No one noticed me cut around the building. The Cullinan hadn't kept going up the street; it had turned and driven down the alleyway beside The Warehouse. Tinted windows, driving slowly, arriving at the venue? It had to be that R&B-singing son of a bitch.

In the darkened alley, the pavement was glittery from random shards of broken glass, and a repugnant odor hung in the air from the nearby dumpster. That mixed with the stench of nicotine and weed was a sheer warning to go back. There was a parked car by the side of the building by a side-door exit, but it wasn't the Cullinan.

Pausing, I looked over my shoulder, seeing people passing by up at the mouth of the alley. There was a great distance from the front to the back, a journey from safety to blatant risk. I could turn back now and just let it go. This was probably a *really* bad idea, but damn if my soaring temper didn't drive me ahead.

Fuck Zander Khalil.

Something in my gut told me to keep going, that the side-door exit wasn't the only one to the building, and that Cullinan wasn't just a random luxury rider passing through.

A gust of wind sent me going forward, keeping my head held high until I was at the opposite end of the alley rounding the corner.

And just like that, I smirked. The Cullinan was parked behind The Warehouse. At the back of the building there was a set of stairs leading up to the back exit. No one was around, and oddly, back here, the night was quiet with only a faint whisper of the chaos from the people at the front of the building. There were a couple of other cars, probably belonging to the staff, but I just knew that Zander was in the Rolls-Royce.

I wasn't usually this bold and reckless, but for my best friend —who really was having a tough time—I'd do anything.

I marched over to the vehicle and knocked on the dark tinted window, scowling at it, hoping he could see how pissed I was. The glass was hard against my knuckle and only my reflection greeted me from the surface.

"I know you're in there!" I snapped. "Show your face, you coward!"

I wanted all the smoke with Zander. He had hurt Victoria, and disappointed so many people tonight. And not to mention, wasted *my* time.

After a minute of unanswered knocks on the window, I felt tempted to key the car. *Really* tempted.

Whistling blew through the air and I whirled around to find those two scalpers from before.

The skinny one flashed me a grin with a mouth full of dirty teeth. The heavy set one looked on impassively.

It was late. The spotlight from the luminescent floodlight

hanging off the side of the building shone down ironically on the scene I was in.

Fear didn't register; I was too annoyed for the night.

"We got some fine action right here, Brennan," Skinny spoke first, advancing closer. He was wearing an Iron Maiden T-shirt with some cargo shorts while his friend, Brennan, was in a gray hoodie and black shorts. Neither looked intimidating, even with Skinny crossing over to me.

I backed up against the Cullinan. If Zander was inside, *he* was getting one heck of a show.

Skinny came to a stop right in front of me, taking his time to blatantly check me out as his green eyes ran all over me. "You wouldn't pay for a ticket, but what will you buy?"

Was that a line?

Victoria liked to say I was impulsive and reckless, and had major attitude issues. Needless to say, she was the friendly and bubbly one as she liked to put it, and I was the mean and chill one.

"Not interested," I let him know as I took a step further against the Rolls-Royce.

Skinny snarled, sizing me up once more. "Too bad."

Did I have an attitude? No, bad energy could be returned as far as I was concerned. If they thought they were going to have their way with me, they had another thing coming.

I didn't think before swinging and punching him square in his face.

Skinny released a scream as his hands rushed up to conceal his bleeding face. He shot me a mean look. "You bitch! I think you broke my nose."

Brennan snickered, remaining back as he watched on.

Either Zander was an asshole, or he wasn't in the car. Deciding on the latter, I walked around Skinny and headed for the alley to get back to Victoria.

Wet and sticky fingers curled around my arm, yanking me back before I could leave. Skinny's bloody grasp on me was tight.

Despite his build, there was strength there as malice hung in his eyes.

"Where do you think you're going?" he asked.

I jerked away. "Want a black eye with that nose?"

A switchblade materialized in his hand and he flipped it open. "What was that?"

Oh shit.

I froze, petrified at the sight of the weapon. My heartbeat began to speed up as goose bumps littered my skin.

Shit. Shit. Shit. Don't panic. Don't panic. Don't panic.

Mentally, I tried to assess the situation I was now in.

Screaming seemed like a totally stupid and redundant thing to do. Could I kick the knife out of his hand?

I tried to will my feet to move so I could get in a stance to attempt to kick Skinny's wrist. Anything to wipe that sneer off his red-coated lips.

CLANG.

The loud snap of a door shutting drew our attention to our right.

He threw his cigarette over the railing, the reddish-orange cherry still glowing as it hit the ground. Smoke billowed from his lips as he remained standing on the first step, staring directly at us. When he spoke, there was no missing his accent. "Is there a problem?"

Of course.

Zander fucking Khalil.

2

GOOD GUY

The scruff on his golden jaw, the studded nose ring, those piercing deep dark eyes. There was no mistaking it.

Zander was here, live, and in the flesh. He was cloaked under a black hoodie with black jeans and red shoes. The hood was pulled up, obscuring his face from being seen unless you were looking at him head-on. Not quite conspicuous, but incognito enough to get the job done.

Skinny hesitated, taking a step back.

Zander began to descend the stairs, but before he could even land his foot on the second step, the back door exploded open. He didn't even flinch as three men rushed out. One, the driver, had the car keys dangling in his hand, and the other two big beefy-looking men had to be security.

The scalpers took off back down the alley, abandoning me with the threat of authority coming their way.

One security guard, a tall light-skin man who was nothing more than a wall of muscle and ink, seized me while the other, White, bald, and void of tattoos, hung back protectively covering Zander.

Zander angled his head to see me, his eyes measuring me out silently, making me feel exposed. "Dax, she's in a T-shirt."

His accent was thick, much more prominent than his singing voice.

Under the brim of his baseball cap, Dax assessed me, not letting his guard down. For a guy who was snarling at me, I had to admit, he was kinda fine.

Dax backed off and went to secure the alley while the other guard reluctantly let Zander come over to me as the driver went and got in behind the wheel.

Zander was tall—not as huge as his Herculean bodyguards, but a smooth six-foot. Standing in front of him, he instantly dwarfed my five-six. What's more, he held a loud presence. I could *feel* him even as he stood a foot away from me.

Once more he read me over. His eyes lingered on the bloody handprint on my right arm before lifting to meet my gaze. "Are you all right, miss?"

With all the harassment tamed, I regained my resolve.

"Fuck you, Zander," I practically spat at him.

He narrowed his eyes, taking me in as if I were out of my mind. "Excuse me? *That's* your way of thanking me?"

"It's your fault I was in that mess. My best friend came to see you sing and you flaked on her, on *all* your fans, and I just knew that was you in that Rolls-Royce."

Zander blinked a couple of times, still confused. "It sounds like what you lack in manners, you also lack in self-control."

He was trying me now. "Fuck you, Zander."

He briefly closed his eyes and shook his head. "I'm sure there are much better things you can say with your mouth than disrespect."

My hand flew across his face before I could attempt to stop myself.

The loud sound of my slapping his precious face caused Dax to turn from the alley and the White guard, Mr. Clean, to advance close.

Zander simply held a hand up as his eyes stayed locked on me and both guards remained where they were.

Zander took a step closer, sizing me up. "Maybe I deserved that, but don't ever put your hands on me again."

I prepared to hit him again. "Is that a threat?"

"No," he said. "No one deserves to be subjected to abuse."

I hated how right he was in that moment.

The loud banshee-like cry of sirens blared in the air from up front, drawing all of our attention to the alley.

If things were bad up there before, I knew it would be worse by now.

"What's your name?" Zander prompted as he turned back to me.

"Bia—Bianka," I said.

"Get in the car, Bianka," he told me.

His tone, mixed with his accent, was hypnotic, but common sense pushed through. "What?"

Zander gestured towards the alley. "Let me drive you back up front safely. I don't trust the walk back. It's been an uncomfortable evening, yeah?"

How chivalrous of him.

Mr. Clean wasn't feeling the idea, however. "Zan, man, I'm not too sure about this."

"Terry, it's all right," Zander insisted. "I'm positive Bianka and I've come to an understanding about boundaries."

Right then, I wanted to strike him again. There was a gleam in his eye, seeming to dare me to respond.

"Get in the car, Bianka," Zander repeated.

He was so demanding, and as if he'd physically pushed me to do so, I turned and opened the back door. The black leather interior with the yellow trim was bold and majestic. A bumblebee came to mind as I climbed into the back, noticing that Zander was right behind me. Dax went around and entered from the other side. I was in the middle.

The ceiling took me by surprise. It was starlit, some sort of magical fabric that made it seem as if I were staring up at the night sky.

Whoa.

Terry got in up front in the passenger seat beside the driver.

At once I was engulfed in the scent of new car smell and pure testosterone. There was only so much space in the back seat. Dax had his legs together considerably, while Zander was sitting back manspreading, the material of his dark jeans brushing against my bare thigh. I was too aware of him.

Before I could let myself slip into anxiety at being surrounded by nothing but strange men, the Cullinan began rolling. We took off for the front of The Warehouse. Up ahead, the flashing red and blue lights along with the cacophony of sirens had everyone sitting up.

Terry chuckled, his bulky shoulders shaking. "Pay up, Dax, I told ya they'd flip."

Dax clicked his tongue, keeping his eyes out the window as we came to the end of the alley. "Whatever."

Four squad cars had shown up and people were rushing into the street to get to parking, or down the street either way to escape. A couple of women were in handcuffs, struggling to get free, and in the middle of the madness was the manager of the venue. He was speaking to a cop, a defeated expression on his face.

Nowhere in the chaos could I see Victoria.

"Where did you park?" Zander asked, unconsciously placing his hand on my knee as I reached for the door.

"I took an Uber with my friend, but I don't see her," I said.

I tried to climb over his lap, but Zander's arm shot up, forming a barricade. "It's crazy out there."

"So...?"

He looked at me quizzically. "Just call her first before you attempt to go out in that mess. We don't need you getting trampled."

I gathered my phone I suddenly realized I'd been clutching for a good ten minutes. I pressed the side button, but nothing happened. I pressed it again.

My fucking phone was dead. "It died."

Zander snickered, suppressing the urge to reprimand me. I could tell.

Again, I resisted the impulse to slap him.

"Does anyone have a charger?" I asked the entire car as I pushed Zander's hand away from my skin.

My question was met with silence. Of course.

"Can I borrow someone's phone?" I asked next.

Again, more silence.

"Well, let me out the car then," I snapped.

Zander sat up, leaning towards the driver. "Olson—"

The car lurched forward and Zander flew back in his seat, his arm once more coming across my chest protectively, as I wasn't wearing my seat belt.

"What the fuck?" Zander demanded to know.

Olson drove up the street, his eyes flickering towards the rearview mirror at the scene we were escaping. "I just didn't think you wanted to be spotted."

A look behind me as we drove away saw that the cops were too busy trying to tame the madness.

What must've been Zander's phone came to life in the pouch of his hoodie. He fished it out, finding a woman calling. The image was of a woman with the same bronze complexion as Zander and long raven-colored hair. In the photo for her contact, she was smiling, but it wasn't exactly pleasant. The caller ID read in all caps, *NAZANIN*.

Beside me, Dax winced as Zander grimaced.

"I wonder who's going to be worse to deal with now that you cancelled the tour, Naz or Paul," Dax quipped.

Terry glanced back at Dax and they shared a look before simultaneously answering, "Naz."

Zander paid them no mind as he shoved his phone back into his hoodie. "Whatever."

"What's the story you're going to tell Naz, man?" Dax wanted to know, obviously humored at the sight of Zander sinking down in his seat.

"That appears to be the million-dollar question, doesn't it?" Zander responded. He settled his gaze on me, speaking out to Olson once more. "Where are you going?"

"The hotel, sir," Olson replied. "Or anywhere you want to go; I just didn't want them to catch you at the venue."

"My hotel's not too far from here. It's literally like five minutes away. No funny business." Zander held his hand up in a scout's honor motion. His accent and the sleepy tone of his voice enveloped me in a weird sense of comfort. "You've been through enough tonight. Let's just get you somewhere safe to charge your mobile and call your friend."

"Zan." Dax wasn't convinced of this idea. "You've got way too much to lose than to risk this."

"So should I just drop her off at the side of the road?" Zander challenged.

"I mean..." Dax let the idea hang in the air.

Scratch that, he *wasn't* fine.

"Dax." Zander's tone read of annoyance and order. "Headlines read out: *Zander Khalil Throws Girl from Car and Drives Off*. On top of the shit show that's going to be cancelling the tour, you think that that would help us, yeah?"

Dax quieted down. But then, as if an idea popped into his head, he started to perk back up. "No one's around. I'm sure if you throw her a couple of—"

Zander silenced the whole line of conversation with just one look.

Whoa.

He was irritated, not with Dax and his asshole way of trying to get rid of me, but with something else, something that probably had to do with why he'd cancelled his tour.

I didn't feel too comfortable the farther we got from The Warehouse. The only thing keeping me leveled was the fact that Tori and I didn't live too far from downtown LA where the venue was nestled amongst all the popular businesses. Hemingway Park was a good twenty minutes away from The Warehouse, depending on the traffic. If shit hit the fan, maybe, just maybe, Victoria had gone home to wait for me.

Zander hadn't lied; less than ten minutes later we arrived under the portico of The Residence Hotel. A monstrosity of a structure that reached heavenward it seemed.

Terry climbed out of the vehicle first, going and taking a look around for cameramen or journalists perhaps before opening Zander's door. Dax was outside fast and together they cocooned us within the walls of their muscled bodies before ushering us inside. The bright lights and fresh cool air were a welcome contrast against the heat from waiting in line so long.

"Welcome back, Mr. Khalil," someone, probably the concierge, spoke nicely as we crossed the beige marbled lobby.

Instead of going towards the main array of elevators, we passed them until we were at a different set. A framed sign on the wall noted of this bank of elevators being for the executive suites. We entered a chrome elevator and at once Terry and Dax took their stance in front of the doors.

"You can go to your rooms," Zander instructed as he hung back against the railing.

Dax didn't turn around. "You sure?"

"You've done enough for the night. We're just going to charge her mobile and see her off."

Terry leaned over and pressed the call button for the twelfth floor before pressing a button marked *PH* for what was surely the penthouse suite, followed by a special code on the keypad below.

When the cab arrived at the twelfth floor, Terry and Dax reluctantly stepped off the elevator. Terry peered back with a protective gaze while Dax's knowing smirk had me raising my middle finger at him. The doors shut and my reflection was flipping Zander and me the bird.

Zander stood back, lifting his head towards the ceiling, imagining us as the elevator soared to the top floor. "Apologies for Dax; his only concern is taking care of me."

I rolled my eyes. "I noticed."

Ding.

We arrived and the door opened. I waited for Zander to step out first before following him past the lavish lounge spread set up just outside the suite.

Zander procured his key to the room and let me in first before coming in behind me and shutting the door.

Once inside, I paused, taking in the expensive layout. The entertainment area greeted me first, a cream-colored sectional complete with a coffee table in front of a wall of nothing but windows. The curtains were open, and since we were on the top floor, the night view of the city was a nice backdrop. Further into the room, in the corner, was a baby grand piano beside another large window.

Zander walked by all this and I followed him into the next room, where a large sofa sat. A flatscreen hung up on the wall in front of the coffee table. Zander made no effort to turn it on as he stepped past me and headed over to the end table by the sofa. The penthouse was like a whole apartment; there was a formal dining room table in the next room, and a kitchen area.

The suite was dripping in opulence. It was all enough to make me feel poor and extra ashamed of my little apartment in Hemingway Park.

"Here." Zander came and held out a charger. "iPhone, right?"

"Yeah." I accepted the charger and gathered my phone, ready for this nightmare to be over.

"You can go into the master bathroom and charge it while you clean up." Zander examined my arm. "I do wish those assholes hadn't run off."

I took my arm back, remembering it was him who put me in that awful situation. Him and his mysterious reason for cancelling the show.

Zander stood and reached back, grabbing the neck of his hoodie and beginning to pull it over his head. As he did this, the shirt he had on underneath rose, giving me a nice peek at his taut stomach.

He had a lower stomach tattoo. By the waistband on the right side of his jeans, tattooed were the words *I Dare You...* I couldn't help but snort at the phrase. I seriously doubted Zander Khalil had to dare anyone to suck his dick.

In fact, against my angst, I couldn't deny how gorgeous he was in person. From the accent, to his presence, to the smell of his expensive cologne. If I weren't so angry, perhaps I would've been a little bit starstruck, or maybe even fangirling.

Victoria would've been.

At the thought of my best friend, I went and slipped into the bathroom.

Oh come on.

It shouldn't have surprised me how nice the bathroom was, but the room screamed rich-rich.

I hate it here.

It was a full marble bathroom with a separate shower and tub area. There was even a private room for just the toilet. The his and hers sink offered plenty of counter space and even wall outlets. I plugged in Zander's wall charger and hooked up my phone before grabbing a fluffy, soft white washcloth. On the counter was a complimentary bottle of body wash and I turned the water on and washed my arm, ridding myself of the scalper's blood.

My only belongings were the clothes on my back, my cell phone, and my apartment key I kept in my phone case whenever I was going out and didn't want to carry a purse.

My phone buzzed, letting me know it was turning on and charging. The white Apple symbol another testament. Moments later my phone was glowing with alerts, missed text messages from Victoria, a few missed calls, as well as a voicemail message.

I called her back and she answered immediately. "Bia?"

"Yeah, it's me," I said.

On her end, Victoria breathed a sigh of relief. "Where the hell are you? What happened? One minute I was outside waiting for you, and the next, folks is fightin' and this girl maced this other girl. Everyone took off running when one-two pulled up. I tried to stick close to the building, but they were acting a fool and I didn't want to get run over."

It was time to play Two Truths and a Lie. Victoria didn't need to know I'd met Zander, the jerk who'd wasted her and everyone else's time that evening. "Ugh, I went outside after using the restroom. I thought that fancy car was Zander and I tracked it down, stupid I know, but I just wanted an explanation. Those scalpers cornered me, and thankfully, a nice guy came to the rescue."

"Bianka Brooke Leslie!" my best friend reprimanded me by calling out my full name. "Have you lost your damn mind? Do you know how many girls get snatched up in this city?"

I shivered to think what would've happened hadn't Zander shown up. I would've liked to think I was going to get the better of Skinny at least. "I know, Tori. I'm an idiot. Where are you?"

"At the McDonald's around the corner," she said. "I stuck to the plan."

The plan. It was something my mother had taught me when I was younger, that if we were ever separated, never to panic, that the first thing to do was make it to a busy place of business and call and wait.

"Good."

"So why didn't y'all stay around the venue and find me?" Victoria prodded.

"The police were there. He got spooked."

"Spooked? Uh-huh, what is he, a criminal?" Shit. Tori wasn't buying it. "Come on, Bia, what really happened? What, did Roderick text you or something?"

Roderick Jackson was my ex—my lying, cheating ex. The worst kind of ex, where the sex was good and kept you coming back, but the person attached to the dick kept you one lie away from catching an assault charge. Rod was big in LA, a club promoter, and he often rubbed elbows with rappers and ballplayers. Pretty girls came with that lifestyle, something I knew from the jump, but still, I expected Rod to be a man and keep it in his pants.

I'd forgiven him the first time he cheated, and the rest was a messy history of lies and heartache.

"No," I quickly denied. "This isn't Rod, just some nice, random stranger who had a hotel room nearby."

"He fine?"

Fan or no fan, there was no denying the truth about Zander Khalil. "Yes, Tori."

"You owe me," she said into the phone. "If I hadn't have dragged you out for the night you wouldn't be about to have nasty hotel sex."

My eyes rolled to the ceiling. Victoria had a thing about hotels, the anonymity and the pampering. One of her exes had money-money and would often book rooms for them to spend the weekends in. She said hotel sex made you wilder, whereas sex at home was too customary and domestic.

"Please," I told her. "I'm on my way home now that I know you're safe. Again, I'm sorry we got separated."

Victoria sighed. "I'm sorry Zander cancelled. I hope he's okay."

"Fuck him." Because for real. "You better be able to get a damn refund."

"Bianka."

There was no getting through to her. Zander could do no wrong as far as she was concerned. "Let me get this phone to charge some more. I'll call you when I get in, okay?"

"Okay."

"Get home safe."

We hung up and I checked my percentage, deciding six percent wasn't enough to take an Uber out of Zander's room just yet.

The sound of the piano greeted me as I stepped out of the bathroom. Out in the sitting area, Zander was at the piano, shirtless and barefoot now as he played with one hand and ate a peach in the other. On the dining room table was a bowl of the fruit, and it was fascinating watching him eat with one hand and play with the other.

With his shirt off, Zander's tattooed skin showed his love for the taste of ink. He had a sleeve on one arm and the makings of another on the other. His chest and his torso were bare, but really, I didn't mind. He had a broad chest and impressive arms.

Against my better judgment, my anger seemed to dissolve with every layer of clothing Zander removed.

But then I was right in front of him, where he seemed perfectly healthy and fine. He had no reason to let Victoria and his fans down. There was no reason he couldn't have performed tonight.

"Things okay?" he asked as he continued to play with his left hand.

"Yes."

"Good." His attention was back on the piano, playing with such a composed, nonchalant grace as if he'd been trained to play with one hand his whole life. "I'll text...*Terry* to wait with you until your ride comes."

Leaving was a top priority, but with my battery percentage, I could stand to hang back just for a little while. If anything, it bought me time to question the obvious.

"Why did you cancel?" I demanded to know.

Zander peeked up at me. "None of your concern."

So he felt entitled to let people down? "Fuck you, Zander."

He went back to the piano, back to his peach. "You know, I'm starting to fall under the impression that you don't like me."

"I don't." And now I never would.

"And yet you were in attendance for my show this evening." He snuck me a clever look, as if he'd said something grand.

"Because my best friend bought tickets and made me go with her. She and everyone else were excited to see your lazy ass."

A violent note came from the piano as Zander's left hand came down hard on the keys.

His eyes were ablaze as he glared up at me. "*Lazy?*"

"You don't perform because you don't want to put in the effort. You just throw together music videos and collabs to hold fans over until your next release. Real musicians, like Teddy Sykes, actually go out and do shows and perform for all the people who support them." I was being petty now, because another thing I knew about Zander was his little ongoing beef with Teddy.

When Zander left So What, there was bad blood amongst the guys. They'd felt betrayed and had been shading Zander ever since. Teddy was a good singer from what I'd heard, his style more rock than pop, but he wasn't touching Zander admittedly. Honestly, I thought Teddy's popularity had more to do with his Whiteness than anything, because vocally and artistically, Zander should've had the bigger fanbase.

My words set Zander off, and now he was pissed too.

On his feet, he came around the piano and stood in front of me. Those dark eyes of his bore into my soul, the anger within their depths magnified.

It felt good to upset him, to stand up for my best friend and the others. It felt good to knock him off his high horse, because fuck Zander Khalil.

"Fuck you, Bianka." His voice was soft, his thick accent blanketing his words poetically almost.

What was frustrating was that even when angry, Zander looked as handsome as ever. His full lips were pressed firmly together and his continued stare had me mystified.

Weirdly enough, the air started to shift between us.

"You know, it's a shame you aren't my biggest fan," he decided to say when he spoke again.

I folded my arms. "Why is that?"

Slowly, Zander smirked. "If you were mine, I'd fuck an apology out of you."

All of me halted in pure confusion. Heat rushed to my groin, and against my control, his words affected me. Part of me wanted to slap him, but another wanted to sit on his face.

Zander could tell as his eyes drifted to my T-shirt, blatantly imagining what was underneath it. "Are you ready to go?"

My phone wasn't charged enough to leave, but I had a feeling we both weren't thinking of a solid reason for me to stay. "No."

Zander took a step back and bit into his peach. "Make yourself comfortable."

The charge in the air was electrifying. It had been more than four months since I'd had sex. Despite all my annoyance for Zander, I couldn't pretend I wasn't attracted to him. I couldn't ignore the ping deep inside me telling me to mount him.

I took a step closer, and I couldn't say who made the first move, but all I knew was the taste of peach on his lips and the feel of his hot hands had me going weak at the knees.

My body melted into his as I reached up and raked my fingers through his thick hair. Zander kissed like he sang—raw, passionately, and intense.

Drunk. I could get drunk off of his kiss, his lips—*him*. Zander was that intoxicating.

He set his peach on top of the piano and in seconds was grabbing the hem of my shirt and pulling it over my head, exposing him to my black underwear. His eyes ran over me, his sticky touch causing goose bumps to take flight.

Instead of continuing to undress me, he left me in my panties and bra, going and reclaiming his peach.

"Get on your knees," he instructed.

While I wasn't against it, I preferred to go last. "You first."

Zander shook his head. "No."

Blinking, I tried to hold my composure. "Excuse me?"

"I'm not going to allow you to come yet, because you don't like me." He was eating his peach and grinning at me, and I hated myself for how terribly I wanted to fuck him.

I felt unsteady, needy—desperate for a release, and he knew. I could tell by the smirk on his face.

"Get on your knees, Bianka," he directed. "I want to see what we can do with that mouth."

For a moment, I paused, stuck. Giving head was something I liked to work myself up to with a person. Something I was completely prudish about. Every guy didn't deserve the pleasure of a nice little soul-snatching session.

But then...

Zander stood before me, a daring brow raised.

And suddenly I got the meaning of his tattoo.

He leaned close, uttering, "If you can handle it."

Game on. "Guarantee you by the time I leave, you'll be a fan of me."

I took Zander's peach and bit into it, finding it soft and ripe, the nectar dripping from my hand as I passed it back.

Lowering myself to my knees, I peered up at Zander as I undid his button and unzipped his jeans.

"That's a good girl," he marveled as he watched me. He didn't help me slide down his Calvin Kleins or his jeans. He stood there, waiting patiently, enjoying his peach.

And then Zander was free and I took a moment to admire what he was working with, pleasantly surprised. *Now this is a nice dick!*

"Do a good job and you'll be rewarded," Zander spoke from above me, interrupting my assessment.

I rolled my eyes, my lip curling up. "Stop talking and I'll make you come."

"Promises, promises," he mocked as he bit his peach where my mouth had been.

Smirking, I asked, "Think you're going to have the last word?"

Zander chewed casually, shrugging. "I will when I fuck you."

Something inside me lurched, *needing* to know what it would be like to go to bed with this man.

With my still sticky hand, I touched him, running my fingers down the thick length of him, covering him in nectar. I followed this path with the tip of my tongue, not once breaking eye contact with Zander. His velvety flesh was hot to the touch, a warm welcome as I took him into my mouth.

I wasn't sure what tasted better, his skin or the juices from the peach. Looking up at him watching me suck him, with his face contorted in desire, caused me to throb. I could've come just like that, high off the pleasure of pleasing him.

Zander knew this as he barked out, "Stop touching yourself."

My left hand was between my thighs as my right massaged Zander, assisting my mouth. I didn't want to stop sucking him or touching myself. This wasn't my first time, but it was truly one of the first times I was enjoying the experience.

Deeper and deeper I took him into my mouth, down my throat, trying to steal his soul. I honestly could've drained Zander twice if he hadn't have jerked away.

"Stop touching yourself, Bianka." His breathing was jagged and he hadn't come. Good, he was as unfulfilled as I'd been for the past four months.

His hand shot out and grabbed a hold of me, helping me to my feet. "In the bedroom. Now."

I hadn't stepped a whole foot away before a hard slap greeted my ass, causing a stinging sensation to ripple across my cheeks. The ache between my thighs increased as I whirled around to find Zander's gaze on me. Unapologetic. Unrestrained. Unmerciful.

"We're even," he offered by way of explanation.

I knew right then that this sex would destroy me, and I was ready for it.

In the master suite, I got out of my sneakers, undid my bra, and stepped out of my panties before crawling onto the bed. Behind me, Zander appeared in the doorway carrying a new peach. He abandoned his jeans and his boxer briefs at the foot of the bed before climbing on with me.

"Lie back," he told me.

I'd never tell him, but I liked being told what to do—at least by him. Something about his voice, something about the look on his face, I was more turned on than I had ever been in my life.

Zander crawled up to me, coming and pressing his forehead to mine before devouring my lips with his own. He soon broke the kiss, leaning close to my ear to whisper one more demand. "Don't come until I'm inside you."

This was part pleasure and part pain, as I felt ready to combust by the feel of his fingertips trailing up and down my body.

Zander bit into his peach, chewing and swallowing before holding it over my left breast and squeezing until sweet nectar dripped down on my nipple. He came forward and licked at it, teasing my tender nub before taking it into his mouth and sucking me dry of the juice.

I cried out, pressing my knees together, trying to keep my orgasm at bay.

Zander's teeth nipped at my skin. "Don't come."

Again, he squeezed the peach over my right breast, dousing me with more nectar before drinking it from me. When he knew how close this was making me, he reeled back and squeezed the peach down my belly, pooling the liquid inside my belly button. I watched as he lowered his head and traced his tongue along the line of nectar he'd made. He slurped it out of my belly button loudly, his tongue going around and around.

And then, as if to kill me, he lifted his head and winked at me. "Do you like me now, Bianka?"

I bit into my lip, not wanting to give in. Was this his game? Bringing me to the brink and withholding until I gave in?

Zander chuckled and descended lower on my body, going and squeezing the last of his peach over my naked bikini line. Instead of licking it up right away, to torture me, one by one he put his fingers into his mouth to rid them of the nectar first. "Mmm."

He got into a comfortable position between my legs, all of me on display for him to behold. He grabbed my left leg and pressed a gentle kiss on my inner thigh and soon did the same for my right leg.

I could take no more. I lifted my hips, impatient to meet his face, but Zander reeled back. There was that grin again, and I could hate to love it for the rest of my life if time let me.

Zander blew on me, his breath almost making her purr back.

Languidly, he licked the nectar from my skin before making his way to his real meal. My back arched and my head hit the pillow as I screamed out at the feel of his soft lips and tongue.

"Fuck!" I whined. "Oh shit! Oh shit! Oh shiiit!"

Zander watched me tiptoe closer to the edge as he tasted me without shame, with a well-trained patience. He bathed his face into me, taking his time. Making love to my most delicate place with his mouth.

His tongue on my clit sent a tingle to my spine as my body began to spasm.

I tried, I really did, to hold it back, but staring into Zander's eyes as he licked me made me unravel harder than I ever had before. I melted as a burst of ecstasy erupted inside of me, taking over my thoughts and senses.

Immediately, Zander stopped.

I wasn't supposed to do that.

Zander shook his head as he came from my legs and peered at me intently. I was still coming down from my high, clinging to my euphoria. I heard him rummaging around and a dazed look over found him procuring a condom from his wallet, watching me.

Zander *tsk-tsked* as he gazed down at me. "You have terrible manners, no self-control, and you can't take directions." He tore open the condom, his eyes fixed on mine as he soon rolled it on and came closer. "What are we gonna do with you?"

Ahhh.

I could feel the tip of him. He was dangerously close to entering me. To ending me. I was too greedy for more to be ashamed of my response. "Fuck me."

A smirk crossed Zander's face as his hot hands slid underneath my knees, pushing my legs up and further apart. "I intend to."

There was no time to prepare. One minute he was hovering over me, and the next he was inside me in one hard, powerful stroke. The feel of him had me wrapping my legs around his waist, locking him in place.

"Oh God," I whined at the blissful intrusion. He was inside of me, filling me, possessing me, and it felt *so* good.

With his hand around my throat, Zander came in for a rough kiss as he thrust into me in another fierce blow.

I moaned my apology into his mouth, but he wasn't satisfied just yet.

Slow and intimate weren't the words for what we were doing. I had never been wet like this before. I had never been dominated like this before. I had never been fucked like this before.

A sheet of sweat covered our bodies and we were slick with the nectar from the peaches. The smell of us, the taste of us, was prominent.

Zander picked up my hips as he continued to pound into me. It was better this way, deeper. He was relentless with his strokes. I was going to come again.

He'd asked me if I liked him now, and the last thing I could remember was screaming out, "Fuck yes!"

3

BACK TO LIFE

Mistakes are like leftovers, they're never as good as when they are new, fresh, hot—in the moment.

In the morning, I woke up in a bed that was not my own. In a place that was not my apartment. I didn't drink much, so there was no amnesia blissfully clouding my memory of Sunday evening. There was no confusion or deniability about my coming to Zander Khalil's hotel room and later having sex with him.

Like a balled fist, it hit me hard in the gut when it came to what I'd done.

I rolled over and that's when it became all too real.

Asleep, *naked*, beside me was Zander. My waking up hadn't disturbed his peaceful slumber. Looking at his gently closed eyes, I envied his thick lashes. Lashes girls often had to pay for. He was on his back, his arm resting on his stomach, and his hand with the elegant elephant tattoo was rising and falling with his breathing. And how the fuck did he look like this while sleeping? All lovely and precious.

I was a pretty woman, but an ugly sleeper, this I knew. Thank God I woke up first.

Also, my being up first provided a perfect escape route.

I crawled out of bed, thinking nothing of those peach-stained sheets.

Peaches. Who would've thought? I would never look at them the same way again. Before, I never was for the idea of mixing food and sex. The idea always made me feel sticky—I was currently a mess. Showering was a must before departing.

In the master bathroom I found my phone fully charged with a snarky text message from Victoria.

> Home now! Make sure you order room service and make HIM pay

The Residence Hotel was easily a five-star establishment. I bet their food was worth throwing on a fluffy white complimentary robe and eating in bed. Of pretending I was on vacation on some tropical island.

But the guilt was already starting to eat away at me. I could bullshit myself and say Zander didn't belong to Tori, that she had no real claim to him, but sleeping with her longtime crush was still pretty fucked up no matter how I tried to paint the picture.

I didn't text Victoria back; instead I treated myself to a shower. As I washed my body, I was flooded with scenes of the previous evening. Of Zander taking me to new heights I had yet to go on. It was hard to feel shame when the crime was so good. No, a true punishment would've been my not having an orgasm —*multiple* orgasms at that. I shouldn't have gotten to enjoy every moment of it. The guilt was still enough, though, to hold me down in place so that I wasn't floating on cloud nine like I had been in Zander's bed.

My body sang for him, verse after verse of moaning, a chorus of heavy sighs, a melody of need, and an encore of pleasure.

An old R&B song came to mind at the thought of it all, and soon I spent the rest of my time in the shower, and even washing my face and brushing my teeth with the gratuitous toothbrush, humming along to it.

I wrapped myself in a towel and grabbed my phone and walked out of the bathroom, almost smack-dab into Zander.

He was only wearing a black pair of drawstring sweats. His just-woke-up look was just as pretty as his sleeping look. Did he ever look awful? After our activity and my not going to bed with a scarf on or bonnet, I knew my leave-out and my bundles were a mess. Life wasn't fair. Zander's bedhead was nothing compared to mine.

Because staring was rude, and I was terrible at saying *hello*, I prepared to go and get dressed.

"Nice tattoos," I quipped as I walked on by for the bedroom.

"Nice skin," he said, making me turn and catch him watching me. Even his just-woke-up voice was appealing.

"*Skin?*"

"*You* don't have any tattoos," he pointed out as his dark eyes met my gaze, unashamed. "Your body is an empty canvas, and I enjoyed painting you."

His words were heavy and I didn't like how they made me feel. "What, do you write poetry too?"

"I enjoy art in all its forms, Bianka," Zander said matter-of-factly. "I think next to music, fucking would be my favorite."

"Sure you wouldn't say 'making love'?" I teased.

Zander shook his head, serious. "No. Fucking is just different. It can be raw, primal, aggressive, selfish—hard. It's you taking paint and throwing it at the wall and not caring about boundaries or constraints. Not worrying about the picture being pretty.

"To make love, you have to see the image, gently coax it out of your creative places as you take your time. It's art, too, but it's not like fucking."

Holy shit. "That was deep."

Zander gave a lazy shrug. "Just how I see it."

Seriously though. "I like that."

He got this naughty smile on his face. "How deep can you take me?"

His words were laced in sheer innuendo and I was glad there

was distance between us. If we were closer, my towel would be on the floor and he would be inside of me. I knew it, and so did he. I could practically feel his hands all over my body again, grabbing, squeezing, owning me. The object of his desire.

Zander released me generously. "Hold that thought. I'm going to go freshen up."

He slipped into the bathroom, and because he clearly heard me before, he started singing the lyrics to "Wet the Bed." He was taunting me, and a needy part of me wanted to be in that bathroom with him, or back in bed, going at it some more.

I struggled, but I snapped out of it and pulled myself together and quickly dressed. I was on my way to the front door when I heard him speak up behind me.

We were in the sitting room. The door was just across from me. My escape.

"Let me have Olson take you home if you're determined to go," Zander said.

"No, I'm going to get an Uber," I said.

Zander accepted this. "Let me wire you some money to take care of the trip."

"No," I shot him down again.

Zander didn't hide his disappointment in all my refusal. I knew, in a way, I was letting down all those female artists I listened to who advised you to take money from men, to "finesse" them. But my pride had always been too much to ever let the idea be okay with me. I guessed a woman in my position, about to go back home to a shitty, small outdated apartment, should've been willing to take the money, to maybe even suggest a much bigger amount, or even blackmail Zander into giving up more for my silence. But I had pride, and I could, and always had been capable of, take care of myself.

"It's not that much," I said, trying to let him down easier.

Zander let it go. "Can I have your number, to know you got home safe?"

This took me by surprise. Zander had a sweet side. "I'll DM you on Instagram and let you know."

Zander narrowed his eyes. "Humor me."

If his driver took me home, he'd know where I lived. If he had my number, he could contact me. It was important to cut all ties now and forever, so that no one could know what we'd done.

"Give me your number and I'll text you when I get in," I suggested.

Defeat caused Zander's shoulders to sag. He knew this tactic, this much more polite way of rejection. Still, he recited his number without missing a beat. "213-555-0112."

Doing my part in this play we were in, where I was pretending I was going to go home and text him, I typed his number into my phone. "Thanks." I looked up and caught Zander watching me, and I was glad he didn't touch me or try to. If he could undo me just by looking at me, I knew I'd let him have me on the floor if he touched me.

Suddenly, I laughed, to lighten the mood. "This is so awkward. I don't usually do this. I've never...done *this* before."

One-night stands were something I read about or watched in movies. I never was that adventurous in my life. I gave myself away in relationships only, something that made me an eternal "good girl" in Victoria's eyes. Not that she wasn't; her random romps weren't many to write home about.

Zander's lips twitched. "Me neither."

"I'm serious."

He leaned close, his nearness causing me to catch my breath. "I am too."

My first one-night stand was with Zander Khalil. And I was his first, too.

Why did that make me feel special?

That famous Sam Smith song started to play in my head and I felt tempted to ask Zander if it was in his as well.

"My privacy means everything to me. I hope you'll be discreet," Zander said gently.

"It never happened."

He rolled his tongue across his upper lip, his eyes drinking me in slow. "Oh, it happened, but only between us."

His level of flirting, of attention, was stifling. Leaving was imperative, but staying for another go at it—

I forced myself to walk up to the door and open it, going and seeing myself out. I peeked back at the singer behind me, the singer not hiding the fact that he'd been staring at my ass. "Have a nice day."

"You as well."

To smooth things over, just a little, I said, "I...I'm sorry I slapped you last night."

"Under the bridge."

It felt like we were ending better than we started. "By the way, my people call me *Bia*."

I turned, ready to go over to the elevator.

"Bianka." I turned around as he spoke up, defiantly using my full first name. "Thanks for coming out to my show." A light chuckle rolled off of his breath, and then there was that grin again.

A soft smile curled my lips up. "Fuck you, Zander."

He shut the door and I walked over to the elevator.

Fucking boy bands.

When I made it back to my apartment, I found a folded sheet of paper taped to the door. Instantly I grimaced as I snatched it off and read over its contents.

Due to a water leak, we will be shutting off the water supply tomorrow, Mon May 29th from 8 a.m. – 11 a.m. for repairs. Sorry for the inconvenience. –Management

Someone must've stuck it on my door sometime after I'd left for the venue with Tori. Even still, I crumbled the paper in my hand and shook my head, sick of this shit. The staff at my apartment complex was notorious for these last-minute and totally inconvenient notices. Thank God I'd missed that time slot and showered at the hotel.

Inside, I turned on my kitchen sink, the familiar sounds of pipes groaning and vibrating as the hot water supply came to life greeting me, as well as the stop and start of the water jetting out of the faucet.

I hated living here, but it was the most I could afford working one job *and* having a car.

After the water was back to normal, coming out in steady streams, I leaned against the counter in my bathroom, thinking. I debated with myself on whether or not to actually text Zander. I could wash my hands of the situation and be free of the whole event. But still, since Zander was nice enough to want to know of my safety, I did manage to send him a simple text message.

Home safe. Thx, Bianka

Pleasure meeting you...

There, it was done. And it was time for a nap.

I only accomplished gaining an hour of sleep before loud knocking at my front door woke me up. Dressed in an old T-shirt, I climbed out of my bed and left my bedroom to go and see who was over at such an offending hour.

Victoria.

She barged in with a quick hello and waited for me to shut the door behind her. "Bia!"

My best friend was her usual, perky, happy-go-lucky self. And like the kind girl she'd always been, she'd come over with doughnuts and coffee. I didn't like coffee unless it was iced, or filled with an unhealthy amount of sugar. Victoria took hers like a champ. She liked to say, "I like my coffee like I like my men: Black."

Zander had always been her exception.

Zander.

I busied myself with grabbing the box of doughnuts and placing it on my coffee table. We sat on my sofa cross-legged, facing each other as Victoria drank her coffee and sifted through her phone.

I grabbed a cruller and nibbled on it, thinking of ways to avoid speaking about the previous night.

Thankfully, Victoria wanted to talk, but not about me. "So, I know why Zander cancelled."

Swallowing, I faced her, curious. "Why?"

She scowled, disgust coating her brown features. "That bitch."

"What bitch?"

Victoria rolled her eyes and held out her phone, showing me exactly who she was talking about. On her phone, she'd opened up Instagram. Gossip page, The CelebriTea, was pulled up, and one of their recent posts was a repost of a certain blonde I recognized. The caption was messy: *Looks like #Jolie has a new boo. We see you, girl. #ZanderWho*

In the photo, Jolie was jumping on some guy with red hair's back, flashing the biggest smile on her face as he held on to her.

Victoria took her phone back and shook her head. "Fuckin' bitch."

I didn't get it. "He missed out on a major bag for *that*?"

My best friend deadpanned, looking at me as if I were slow. "Bianka. Zander acts like Jolie is the love of his life. The guy doesn't tweet or post on socials, but just a few weeks ago he tweeted that 'it was always her,' with an at."

"So...he's a simp?" How pitiful.

Victoria shot me a disapproving look, a *shut up and listen* expression as she continued to rant about the oh-so heinous Jolene Jones. "Anyway, she never responded publicly, and now she's posting pics with the next dude. Girl, fuck her."

But Zander had slept with me.

Had he still even cared?

"Maybe that's not the reason why," I tried to say. "Maybe… he's seeing someone else. I mean, who's Nazanin?"

Victoria gagged. "Eww, that's his sister."

"Oh, I just heard someone mention her name at the venue."

Tori settled back and drank more of her coffee as her eyes were glued to her phone, reading comments people had posted under the picture of Jolie.

While she read and liked comments, I gathered my own phone to see if it was true about Zander and his loving tweet.

Upon opening up my Twitter app, I found that Zander was a current trending topic. He'd issued an apology for cancelling his show and tour, and people were talking about it.

As I skimmed tweets, I saw that many were either in support of him or annoyed that he'd flaked.

My feelings were a mess, and I felt tempted to tweet out an offense towards Zander to keep up appearances, but I couldn't bring myself to do it.

"Well." Tori was looking at me now, eager to know my side of the evening.

I thought about it, I really did, about just coming out and telling her the truth. Seeing her hate for Jolie all but confirmed how she would turn on me if she knew. Mistakes were fun in the moment, but the consequences left in their aftermath were all too overwhelming.

"Well, I meant to just go home after charging my phone, but one thing led to another and we hooked up," I confessed, keeping it vague.

Victoria smiled, proud of me, accepting my sexual conquest. "How was it?"

An image of Zander taking me hard caused me to scratch at my neck and breathe out. "I h-had a good time."

"So you came?"

The first round, the second round, and okay, even during that last round when we were both winding down from our sexual high. "More than once."

Victoria's eyes lit up and she high-fived me. "Yes for female orgasms!"

I managed to loosen up and laugh. "Fuck yes to female orgasms!"

"Did you suck it?" she asked scandalously as she settled down.

My not meeting her gaze gave her the answer.

"Oh my God, Bianka!" she chastised me as she swatted at my naked knee. "You do not give your best sex to strangers. You know what, it's fine, you were in a hotel, and hotels were made for that life."

"This was my first one-night stand, give me a break," I joked.

She eyed me funny. "Did he at least return the favor?"

I felt myself grow hot. "Yes, and he could teach a class on it."

She softened up. "Well, what did he look like? Light skin, brown skin, dark skin, tall, short, buff, thick, skinny—what?"

I laughed at her inquisition. "He wasn't even Black."

Shit.

Maybe he should've been to keep up with the ruse.

Victoria's eyes enlarged and she was quick to set her coffee down. "Oh, dear God."

Like Victoria, I simply admired and dated Black men. This encounter was a first on many levels. But when it came to Zander, much like how Victoria viewed him, his racial background wasn't a big deal. He was attractive, talented, sexy, and fucked me better than anyone before him.

I got sad at that last fact. How could I tell Victoria that the best sex I'd ever had in my life was with a guy she was obsessed with? "Yeah."

"*What* was he? Besides delicious, I hope," Victoria prodded on.

Only Victoria. "He was...human, and that's all that matters." To give her a little something, I feigned confusion on the rest. "Maybe part Asian, I'm not sure, but he was fine as hell and confident. He carried himself in this way that he knew he was the shit, but he wasn't arrogant."

"Damn, hope you got his number." Victoria bit into a cream stick and was back in her phone.

I did have Zander's number, but I couldn't continue to text him or see him again. "Anyway, thanks for waking me up. I got some place to be and now I'm going to be cranky."

Victoria leaned back and looked upside down at the calendar on the wall by my ancient landline I didn't use. "Shit, it's that time of month already?"

My mood lessened as I nodded. "Yeah, I guess the sooner the better, huh?"

Victoria frowned, coming and throwing her arms around me. "I'll always be your family, Bia, don't question it."

Family. Such a tough topic for me, and Victoria knew why. She offered, as she often did, to come with me on my journey, but like I always did, I turned her down.

After she left, I got dressed properly, combed and fixed my hair, then got behind the wheel of my Nissan Sentra and drove twenty minutes south to Lindenwood, my city and origins, to visit my father like I did every other week.

I arrived and parked my car in the same spot I always did, out in front of the familiar powder blue house with the bright colorful flowers in the flowerbeds by the front porch.

Being home always made me fall back to before, of what I both loved and hated about this house.

I could've stayed in the car and rapped along to Wale for hours instead of turning off the engine and removing my keys from the ignition.

I climbed the same stone steps to the porch like I'd done all my life and went and knocked on the front door instead of ringing the doorbell, instead of using my key. I did this, like I always did, with the hopes that maybe he wouldn't hear me, that maybe he wouldn't come.

But like always, my father came and answered the door. His aging eyes that were turning blue took me in, and he forced out that same smile he always did whenever he first recognized me on my visits.

"Hey, Dad." I greeted him with a wave.

Five minutes later, per a sad tradition to keep in touch, we were in the dining room. Crayola crayons and markers were on the table as we sat across from each other coloring. He once mentioned the idea of using adult coloring books, but for me, I liked the fun the children's books provided. They made me feel young and free, capable of any and everything.

I'd been coloring with my father since I was a little girl. Times had changed, significantly, brutally, but somehow, unconsciously, we had this. We had coloring. It was the only way we could still love each other.

"How's the shop?" he asked me, keeping his eyes on his project.

I worked retail in Hemingway Park, selling clothes in a trendy clothing store called Angles that sold everything from casual and dressy, to designer duds and pop culture tees and handbags. It wasn't much, but it paid the bills and kept me out of Lindenwood.

"Good, I live for our discount," I said with some cheer in my voice.

"Hmm." He hummed back, concentrating on shading in what looked like a tropical fish. Unlike me, my father had gone ahead and purchased himself some adult coloring books to exercise his mind.

I couldn't help myself. My eyes began to wander around the room.

Pictures of my older brother and me littered the walls and I felt my stomach fill with a sickness that wouldn't go away.

You be Cain, and I'll be Abel...

It was ironic really. I'd never been into boy bands or pop music like that, but when we were kids, Pryor had been a huge fan of the pop group NSYNC. He had a cassette of their *No Strings Attached* album and later the CD of their *Celebrity* album. I could vividly remember all those times hanging in his bedroom, singing into his floor fan the lyrics of their catchy music. I had never liked the group for myself, but for Pryor. He was in love with NSYNC; he'd even had posters and pinups of the group, although he would never own up to it now probably.

Now here I was, having woken up in bed with an ex-boy bander.

"How's Pryor?" I got the courage to ask for the first time of the year.

"He's doing good, real good," my father told me.

He would know how my older brother was doing. They spoke; they were on the same page almost.

Resentment was a powerful force. My father resented me because I hurt his wife, his love, and my brother resented me because I got it right. I followed the rules and my mother didn't shame me. I was the black sheep of what was left of my familial unit. The living embodiment of anger and regret. My flesh was bound together by pent-up rage, and I just wanted to scream.

When the people you loved the most, your own blood, hurt you, there's no way anyone else could. There's no way anyone else could cause an inkling of damage. Because you're already fucked up with trust issues and problems.

I tried not to pity myself, because everyone's tortured when you think about it. And what makes your pain more important than someone else's?

Once upon a time, Katherine and Elijah Leslie raised two

loving and fully capable kids, Pryor and Bianka, in this home. They loved them equally and wholly and accepted them without question. It was real storybook.

And then Katherine was killed and nothing was the same.

Today was a shitty day, there was no getting around it. I always felt like shit during and after these visits.

Worse, I was a wreck with guilt. Victoria. She would resent me too. It was then and there while coloring in an image of a dog that I decided she could never know.

Fucking boy bands.

4

INSOMNIA

I couldn't sleep. Nightmares of a life previously lived plagued me. It was always the same, a joyful nuclear unit, a mother, a father, a son, and a daughter, happy as could be. Until an ugly evening where it was all ripped away leaving behind only three. Scratches from the mother's fingertips lingered on the skin of those she didn't want to leave.

It was always like this when I got around him. My father's distant way of handling me left me reliving every painful memory of how things used to be, and how terrible they were now.

When I'd gone to leave, I tried to hug him, tried to feel him somehow.

"I love you," I'd said.

He'd stopped me, in an almost nonchalant way. He held me at arm's length, taking a silent moment to stare at me, and then the floor. "You look so much like her, Bianka. So much like her." His voice was far away, even though he was right there with me.

My father didn't hug me goodbye. He patted my arm and let me go. Dismissing me from his presence, and his heart.

I'd come home, too sick to eat, too numb to focus on the TV.

Instead, I found myself crawling into bed.

Not even Victoria's supportive text message had been enough to save me from the oblivion of my father's rejection.

> Hope it went well. I'm here if you need me

When I couldn't sleep, I took to cleaning my apartment, anything to distract myself. I scrubbed my fridge, mopped my floor, vacuumed my living room, actually dusted all surfaces, and when everything was spotless, and I felt those memories slipping back over me like a black cloud, I gathered all my trash and made the run out to the dumpster in the parking lot. The cool night air against my sweaty skin was welcome, the goose bumps alighting my flesh bringing me back here in Hemingway Park, lifting me out of Lindenwood.

In my bedroom, I sorted all my dirty clothes to do laundry in the basement laundry room. Usually, I hated doing laundry on-site. The Lakeside Manor apartment complex was only six stories high, but the building was a good eighty years old—and incredibly ancient otherwise. I never felt safe doing laundry all the way at the bottom of the building. I barely felt safe living on the first floor after the first week I'd initially moved in.

As I rode the elevator to the laundry room with my first two loads, I let my fear distract me.

It worked for all of my first load, until I was back at square one. It was late in the evening, no one was around, and being in the cold basement by myself made me feel smaller than usual. My mind betrayed me, drifting back to my father and our biweekly visit once more. He'd said Pryor was doing real good. I hadn't spoken to my older brother in years, but I still loved him. How could I not? He was my blood, family, or, part of what remained of it.

I sat on the folding table, clutching my phone and debating internally if I should reach out or not. My fingers shook and my breathing became shallow as my stomach threatened to bubble over.

Worst case, he won't pick up.

I found Pryor's number, wondering if it had changed, and pressed the Call button.

The sound of it ringing caused me to close my eyes and hold my breath.

Only, the phone rang and rang, but he didn't pick up. The voicemail prompted me to leave a message, but he hadn't set up his own personal greeting, making this whole endeavor even more cold.

Not even a minute after I gave up calling, a text came through on my cell from Pryor himself.

> what do you want?

Sweat prickled my palms and I chewed on my cheek, unable to process his way of approaching me.

He didn't want to talk to me?

Still, with our father loving me in his own way, Pryor was my only lifeline left.

> I know it's late, but it's been a while

> So?

> How are you?

> I'm good. Why do you ask?

> Because we haven't seen or spoken to each other in years

> I liked it that way. You were always the favorite, best to stay at odds

> Come on, Pry, we're all we've got

> Sorry...but no thanks. I'd rather keep our distance. Don't call or text me again. I'm blocking you

A teardrop landed on my screen and I hated myself for breaking, for reaching out, for being so dumb, so lonely, so needy—so easy to dismiss. To say goodbye to.

My sadness was full steam, and I was raw. Rage and ruin. All of my heart nearly scattering to the floor as I fought the urge to vomit as tears stung my vision.

I wanted nothing more than for the roof to cave in and for all six levels to fall on me. And so I squeezed my knees to my chest, hanging my head and waiting for it all to crush me. I waited. And waited. And waited.

Until the buzzing of the dryer let me know my load was finished.

5

TIGHTROPE

A colorful arrangement of roses greeted me as I walked into work on Tuesday morning. The roses, a mix of dark and light pink, sat in a glittered vase on the service counter.

I had just spotted the card with my name on it when my coworker, Holliston, came out from the back room. She was carrying a box of new inventory to stock. Pop music from her playlist was playing throughout the store.

"Oh, hey," Holliston greeted me. She nodded towards the bouquet. "Those came for you yesterday."

"I see." I eyed the flowers, wondering who sent them.

Holliston set the box down by an empty display table. Her blue eyes flickered my way, as she nervously tucked a strand of her auburn hair behind her ear. "They're from Roderick."

Of course.

I snatched the card and read over his cliché ass handwritten note.

You're one in a million, girl – R

His gift wasn't lost on me. It was nice, especially after the day I'd had Monday. "Oh wow."

Holliston gathered her boxcutter and squatted down to open our new merchandise. "What's it say, '*Sorry for being an asshat*'?"

Leave it to Holly to keep it respectful and not truly cuss Rod out. "More or less."

"Gonna take him back?"

Before the concert, before Zander, maybe I would've allowed myself to fall for it.

I touched a petal of a light pink rose. "Nah."

"Good."

An acoustic song began playing and I watched as Holliston transformed into an even softer version of herself. She was closing her eyes and soaking in the lyrics.

I'm a little bit reckless
A little bit on the edge
Some kind of maniac
But I'm dyin' young tonight
Don't leave the light on
I know your heart's on the line
But I'm dyin' young tonight

The male singer's raspy voice really enveloped Holly under a spell.

"Who is this?" I had to know.

Holliston got back to stocking plain-colored T-shirts. "Teddy Sykes."

Jesus, there was no escaping the madness.

"Ah," I let out.

"Okay, judge me, but I'm a proud Whatter, always have been, always will be." Holliston's cheeks were bruising pink as she blushed at this fact.

"Girl, you good. Tori's been obsessed with them for years. Who's your favorite member?"

Holliston made a face. "Uh, duh, Teddy." She soon fished her cell phone from her back pocket and held it out, emphasizing its case. I came closer and peered at the glossy image of Teddy. He was at a microphone, his messy, unruly golden-brown hair with sun-streaked blond highlights was up in a bun as his brown eyes were peering out at the crowd. The crease in his forehead as he seemed lost in thought, made him look handsome admittedly. He was in a large gray T-shirt with the sleeves cuffed. One of his toned arms had an impressive sleeve of tattoos.

"Wow."

"Don't worry, I'm not one of those fans with the weird fantasies about Teddy and Vernon. After Teddy, I love Oliver the most. I support all the boys really." Holliston placed her phone back into her pocket. "I almost went to that Zander show the other night, but in hindsight, I'm glad I didn't. The jerk didn't even show up."

"Yeah, Tori and I went," I said.

Holliston shook her head. "Well, screw him, right?"

"He probably had a reason." Maybe. Hopefully.

Holliston paused, appearing thoughtful. "I don't know, he and Teddy have this weird beef going on so I'm Team Teddy, and maybe I'm biased on my annoyance towards anything Zander does because of it. He's a good musician, but he doesn't seem to want it like the others."

"In his defense"—*God, you're defending him now, Bia*—"they've been working since they were sixteen or seventeen."

Zander's career was a mystery really, and maybe *I* was now biased after going to bed with him.

Another song by who was surely Teddy Sykes came on, and by the repeated use of the word *darling* in the chorus, I could only assume that was what the song was called.

"I wish *he* would come to LA soon," Holliston said. "I'd for sure go to that show."

"Maybe he will." I took my place behind the counter and pitched Roderick's note in the trash.

Holliston sighed. "He likes perfect girls."

I frowned. "Then he would love you."

Holliston and I'd only been coworkers for a couple of years, but from what I knew, she was the epitome of a sweet girl. She was sunshine. A rare, bright, and gentle soul.

She was the one who was always calm and never got upset with the rudest of customers. When one of our coworkers called off, Holliston would offer to stay behind to fill their shift or would almost always come in.

Holly saw the best in people, which was probably why she had an on-again, off-again relationship with her asshole of a boyfriend Jake. He was just like Rod in the being-only-there-when-convenient department. Poor Holliston didn't see it though.

"Thank you, Bia." Holliston gave me a friendly smile before going back to work.

I busied myself with running the register and helping stock all new items, all the while sneaking peeks at the roses on the counter.

When I got off at five, I debated over bringing them home or leaving them. I shouldn't have cared. It wasn't an apology. Even if I knew it was bait, I was almost willing to let the gesture touch me.

In the end, I gathered the flowers and drove home, going and setting them on the tiny table in my kitchen.

They were pretty. Maybe I would call him. Or maybe I shouldn't have.

Knocking at my door pulled me from making the decision altogether.

Maybe it was Tori, coming over to hang out. After Monday's evening crying myself to sleep, I'd take any—

I opened the door and Victoria wasn't on the other side.

Roderick.

My gut told me to slam the door in his face, to run and hide and protect what was left of me. But inside this apartment was nobody but me, and I was tired of being so lonely. Rod was a familiar face, a welcome distraction from the bitterness of it all. He knew me, he loved me, or at least, he said he did.

His tall frame filled the doorway, his high-priced clothing making him instantly out of place as it always did, and his handsome brown face staring back at me caused me to go dumb and weak. He was clean, he smelled good, and I could just tell he'd gotten a fresh haircut.

"Hey," I let out, frozen in place.

Roderick took me in, licking his sexy full lips and bobbing his head, liking what he saw. "Hello, Bia, been a minute." He invited himself in and I found myself stepping back. His gaze surveyed the tiny space of my living room and then the kitchen across from it. "And I see you got my flowers."

"Yeah, I just got them today. It was very thoughtful of you, thanks," I said.

His soft hand was on my chin, lifting my head to meet his eyes. "You look good."

I took a step back. "Thanks."

Rod's response was a grin. "Listen, like I said, it's been too long. Let's hop in the whip and go grab something to eat. I wanna sit down and talk. I miss you, and I know you miss poppa."

While some of us could be confident with our low points of insecurity, Rod always thought highly of himself. As successful as he was, I couldn't exactly blame him.

Still, I hugged myself, unsure. "Rod—"

He held his hands up, appearing serious. "I fucked up before, and I see that now. You special, Bia, and I didn't really appreciate the gem that you are until I lost you. If you'll have me, I'd like to spend as much time as I can to make it up to you."

Did he mean it, or was he feeding me bullshit?

In his dark eyes, I saw what looked like sincerity. Call me a fool, but a part of me wanted to believe him.

"Okay."

Rod grinned, stepping to the side and gesturing out the door.

"After you." His eyes danced along my body, examining my T-shirt and jeans. "Unless you'd like to change."

This was Roderick; he only dined at the best.

A chime came from his pocket and he fished out his cell phone. His eyes were impassive as he read over his text and responded quickly.

Was it someone else?

"Are you even single-single?" I had to know.

A corner of Rod's mouth curled up. "Bianka, I know in the past I wasn't the best, but I know now to come correct." He held up his phone. "This was just business. I've got an event with a couple of rappers coming up and I'm RSVPing the location. I promise."

Hope was all I had, and so I went into my bedroom and put on a little black dress to join him for lunch.

In the parking lot, Rod led me up to the passenger door to his tricked-out Escalade. His eyes were on my body as he helped me inside.

Rod came and slid into the driver seat, flashing me a smile that felt safe. "Ready?"

Was I?

I crossed my fingers and held my breath, wishing for some truth.

He pulled up to a five-star restaurant and was generous as he slid the valet a Franklin. The place was extra nice, and he'd already made reservations as the host requested his name as soon as we were in the door.

Intimacy was the theme, as there were various rooms filled with only five or six tables each I could see. We were ushered to a room with large floor-to-ceiling windows, the outside view of the sunny day we were having setting a nice ambiance for our impending meal. The tables were small, square shaped, and seated only two each.

The white tablecloth, single candle in the platinum candleholder, the fine cutlery and wineglasses made a statement.

"I've been thinking about you these last couple of weeks," Rod told me. "I throw myself into my work and at the end of the day, I have nothing to show for it, no one to talk to, no one to take trips with, no one to share my life with."

He hung around bachelors, something that had been a prominent issue in our relationship. With all the women hanging around them, flirty and willing, Rod always had had a problem with saying no, with not going for something new.

"The grass isn't always greener," I responded.

He was quick to agree. "Heard you. I talk to my family and they even talk shit about my losing you. I'm thirty years old; that going out all night and partying shit has gotten old, Bia. Granted, it's my job and I've got obligations, but I know I don't *always* gotta be out there. Sometimes I feel like I'm out all night just to avoid coming home to no one."

Rod sounded sad and like he'd really seen the error in his ways. He was growing up.

"Yeah?" I challenged.

Rod didn't back down. "Yeah, I mean it. I'm done playing games and being that guy I used to be. I want something solid, something stable, something worth it, and I know that's you."

Hope made my heart anew and I couldn't stop myself from lightening up, from becoming less guarded.

It seemed as if Rod had finally, *finally*, changed for the better.

"Good afternoon, I'm Marion. I'll be your server for the day," a man with dark, floppy hair that was parted down the center came and stood at our table. His order pad was out of his waist apron and he was politely smiling from me to Rod. "Can we start you off with some water? Unless you're ready for drinks?"

Rod paid his pleasantries no mind as he skimmed the drink menu. "What would you say is your best wine?"

Marion rocked on the heels of his polished dress shoes. "I'm not big on wine, but I can show you our wine room. There's a wall of all our bottles. We might be able to squeeze you two in there."

Rod was intrigued as he stood up from his chair. He faced me. "You coming, Bia?"

I shook my head. "No, I'll just decide on what I want."

He came by me, caressing my shoulder before leaving the area with Marion.

It was when I sat up and gathered my menu that I noticed it. Across the table, Rod had left his phone.

Blinking, I tried to ignore it and focus on my search for my meal. It was all so redundantly fancy.

A tick went off in me and once more my gaze flickered over to the abandoned cell phone.

Could I trust Rod?

It had been four months since our breakup, but I still knew his passcode after countless times of catching him putting it in, *1130*, for his birthday, November 30th. I'd never been invasive or nosy before, but Rod was a habitual liar.

I chanced a look over my shoulder, finding Rod nowhere to be found. Marion was probably wowing him with the restaurant's wine spread.

I let out a breath, telling myself if I found nothing, I'd hear him out, if I did...

I grabbed his phone and punched in his code, not surprised it still worked.

Most of his apps, especially those linked to social media, held various notifications on them. Rod was a highly sought-after man.

My finger hovered over his text message app, questioning the sanity in doing something so intrusive. I thought of all the times he'd hurt me and I caught him in a lie and I went ahead and clicked on the app.

The screen brought up his most recent text thread, one that was anything but RSVPing a location. The contact's name was *Miami305.*

imy

You know I miss you too

Come show me

Handling some business right now. Ima slide
thru when I'm finished

Her next response was a nude topless photo while she wore skimpy underwear. She was a gorgeous woman, tempting, and he'd taken the bait with ease.

My throat started to close up on me. *Oh.*

I was just "business," Miami305 was his pleasure. Roderick had lied—again. This was just a means to get me back roped in; he hadn't any intention on cutting his side-pieces free. He just wanted me around, home in bed waiting up for him while he freely roamed the streets until he was good and ready for me.

Suddenly my stomach felt full and I was nauseous.

I left the phone on the table as I stood to my feet, beelining for the front door.

"Hey! Where you going?" Rod had a hold of me, he'd been on his way back from the wine room with Marion.

One look at me and he became concerned, Marion too.

"I'm leaving," I informed Rod, trying to stay strong and not cause a scene. It felt like *CLOWN* was tattooed to my forehead.

Rod stood back, dubious. "What's going on? I thought we were going to talk."

I stepped back. "Talk to Miami305."

Recognition was quick to take over Rod, and Marion sensing our lover's quarrel, was smart enough to walk away and help another table of his.

A muscle in Rod's jaw flexed as he released a breath through his nose. "Why would you do that?"

"Because you lied to me, just like you always do!"

"What? Was I supposed to cut everybody off when I wasn't

even sure what type of time you were on?" he shot back, defensive.

Was he serious? He'd made actual plans to go and fuck another woman as soon as he was finished getting back into my good graces.

Did I deserve this? Was I so awful that I deserved to be walked out on or walked all over? Was I so unlovable that this was my life?

As if my heart could break any further, I felt it tear deep in my chest. All I had ever done was try with Rod. I'd loved him as honestly and as affectionately as possible. And yet, there was always somebody else. He was too greedy to keep his dick in his pants. Too much of a coward to love me right.

"Fuck you, that's the type of time I'm on forever!" I shoved him away, going and making my way past the hostess podium.

Rod didn't follow and I didn't care. There was nothing that could cut me deeper.

With my pride and my heart even more severed, I got an Uber and went back to my apartment, alone.

6

TONIGHT

There wasn't much to do Friday night. After a long day at work, I came home and undressed and pulled on a night shirt, tempted to just lounge around and watch something online. Victoria had to work for the night anyway.

I was surfing Netflix when my phone rang. Probably Rod's next attempt of trying to get a hold of me, and *lie, lie, lie* again.

Never again. For the rest of my life, I'd be deaf to him. Lesson learned. Don't pull back the Band-Aid, because of course there's still a scar there; you're wearing a Band-Aid to begin with.

I rolled my eyes as I gathered my phone, ready to just block him once and for all.

There was no need. Roderick wasn't calling me. Zander was.

Immediately, I sat up in bed and did a double take. That same number, *213-555-0112*, from Monday, was calling me.

"Hello?" I picked up at the last minute, wondering what was going on.

"Hi," Zander said simply.

For a minute, I waited, thinking he'd say more. When he didn't, I felt myself smile. "Hi."

"How's your week been?"

Painful. "It's been...a week."

"It's funny, I know exactly what you mean. How are you today?" he asked. It was strange, but I could hear his smile in his voice.

"I'm swell," I told him.

"*Swell*? Is that sarcasm?"

"No, it's just a *me* thing." *Swell* was always my go-to whenever a person asked me how I was doing. It was dated, but it worked for me. "How are you, Zander?"

"Oh, I'm all right. A little lonely this evening," Zander confessed. "I wasn't Sunday."

No, he wasn't, and neither was I. "Right."

"Are you okay with what happened?"

The line of conversation was making me hot. Nostalgic of the other night. It felt like a dream, but Zander's call was a very abrupt reminder.

No one was around to hear me confess my sins to my coconspirator. "Yes. I-I really liked what happened. I *needed* that."

"I could still taste you when I woke up, you know." The sound of his voice sent a violent drum of need between my thighs.

He was back home and I was stuck in bed.

I reached down and found my spot, running my fingers over myself as I began to arch my back and come alive. "Did you enjoy your peach?"

"I fucking *loved* my peach."

My fingers worked harder and I sank deeper into my mattress.

"I hear you," Zander's voice whispered to me. "I know what you're doing."

I kept going, turned on by his tone. "Uh-huh."

"Can I see you again before I leave?"

My mood came to a halt at that request. "Excuse me?"

"I want to have you again before I return home."

"You're *still* in the hotel?"

"I needed a break. So, is that a yes?"

The first time, no matter how amazing, was bad enough. A second go at it would be intentional—who I was kidding? I hadn't been drunk the first time; it had been a very deliberate and sober decision.

"I'm not sure if that's a good idea," I said.

Zander clicked his tongue. "You won't come see me, I don't know where you live, I don't know your full name—you're making the idea of stalking you very hard."

His words made me burst into laughter. Like me, he had a dark sense of humor. "See, I oughta stay right here."

"Did you enjoy yourself the last time?"

"Yes, but...I feel bad about it."

"Why?"

"My best friend was the reason I came out. She'd hate me forever if she knew."

"I'm not looking to broadcast Sunday evening or tonight. Nobody has to know." It was in this statement that made me question the status of his feelings for Jolene Jones. If he were using this, *me*, to get back at her.

But then I told myself this was for his privacy, and my own good, because the media would be relentless.

"Zander..." Why was I hesitating? It should've been an easy no, but mistake or not, I couldn't deny how much I liked it, how much I enjoyed sleeping with him. How much a major part of me wanted to do it again.

"Are you going to make me beg you to come fuck me, Bianka?"

"Wouldn't hurt for you to try."

"I *need* you and I can't stand it." His tone was soft, low, vulnerable, all the things causing me to throb with want.

Maybe it was the fact that I was fresh and raw from a visit with my father, or maybe it was the fact that I, too, was alone that night, because for some reason, I caved. I'd like to think it was his accent, the needy, husky sound of his voice, and the fact I knew being in bed with him would make me feel good, better.

"I'm on my way, but first I gotta make a pit stop," I said.

"The code for the elevator is *4443*. Will you be taking an Uber?"

"Yes, and I'll pay my own way."

Zander sighed. "You're killin' me."

"That's the plan."

"What?"

My response was a laugh before I hung up.

This was wild. But for the first time in a long time, I felt excited. No one had to know, and unlike those clout-chasing individuals online, I had no desire to acquire fame or money from Zander.

After running a quick errand, I came home to shower. At least I was about to. Upon pulling back the gray and blue shower curtain, I found pieces of plaster in the tub. A look up saw that the aging brown spot on my ceiling was now a tiny hole where bits of the ceiling fell.

"You gotta be fucking kidding me." If it wasn't one thing, it was another.

I cleaned the ceiling pieces and carefully took a shower. As soon as I was out, I grabbed my phone and put in a maintenance request, reluctantly checking the box that allowed them to enter my apartment with their key since I'd be out.

It was yet another sign to leave, to go out and do something to make me feel good. After my shitty week, I deserved it.

And so, I did it. I caught an Uber to The Residence Hotel. The scene of the crime.

Inside, I walked with my head held high over to the private array of elevators. There was no lingering about in the lobby second-guessing this whole thing. There was no questioning it. I was on a mission.

When I reached the top floor, I felt butterflies in my belly as I climbed off the lift. Each step towards Zander's room felt heavier than the first. This was what one would call a liaison. An illicit affair. And I was appropriately dressed for the part.

I took a deep breath and released it before knocking on the door and sending an I'm here text.

Zander was eager to see me, because he was quick to answer the door.

Oh wow.

He was standing there in front of me sporting a dark green sweatshirt and black track pants. What caught my eye were the silver frames on his face. It was too much. He was already fine, but the spectacles took it to another level. He was on some otherworldly shit now.

Zander examined my attire. "What have we here?"

I twirled the belt to my trench coat. "Figured I'd stop and get something for your eyes only."

Zander leaned against the doorjamb. "Oh yeah?"

"Uh-huh." I pulled open my trench coat, exposing what I had on underneath.

I watched as Zander's eyes lit up and that devilish half grin took his mouth.

At first, I thought about showing up in a sexy negligee, but then I wanted to be silly, and instead I found a 2x Zander T-shirt and bought a pair of Vans to go with it. I wasn't wearing underwear, and I felt totally and completely free.

Zander's gaze was glued to the image of him on my shirt. He was smiling and I could tell he liked this. "I thought there'd be lingerie under there."

Giggling, I asked, "Disappointed?"

Serious again, Zander made room for me to enter the suite. "Bianka, I'm going to fuck you in that shirt."

I almost let him, right then and there. His accent made swear words sound even better.

"I thought we'd role play," I said as I strolled in and casually removed my coat. "I'll be your number-one fan."

Behind me Zander looked ravenous. Somehow his eyes even appeared darker. "You want to play?"

"What do your fans call you? Oh yeah, now I remember. Can I have your autograph, *Zaddy*?"

He blinked rapidly. "Autograph?"

I went and took the hotel pen from the table nearby. Leaning down, I pressed the pen to my foot. "Righhhht"—I trailed the pen up my shin, past my knee, and along the way it got caught on the hem of my shirt and I used it to pull my shirt up as I brought the pen past my thigh, exposing my nakedness underneath my tee —"here."

Zander released a breath through his nose as he came closer. "You're all I could think about all week. Let's take it to the back."

"Uh-uh, I came all this way for your autograph." With my hands on his shoulders, I urged him down.

Zander sank to his knees, peering up at me as he pushed my shirt up to my waist and accepted the pen. He was so close to me, to her, that I felt my knees getting weak.

Holy hell was this empowering, standing over him, looking down at him gaze up at me.

Zander kept his eyes on mine as he uncapped the pen. He slowly peeled his vision away to what was in front of him. It tickled when he started to write on my hip and by the grin on his face, I just knew he had written something slick.

In the floor-length mirror by the door I could see our reflection and what he'd inscribed on my skin.

Mine

I focused back on Zander. "Really?" I shook my head, loving the view of him kneeling down there. "If you're feelin' creative..."

Zander peeked at my nakedness before him and then returned to me. He ran his tongue over his upper lip, enticing me, making me anticipate its magic. "No."

"No?" I asked disbelievingly.

He stood to his feet. "Nope."

"What do you mean no?" I demanded to know.

Zander didn't respond, instead, he leaned down and picked me up, much to my surprise, before throwing me over his shoulder. He started for the bedroom and I couldn't stop myself from laughing.

This time when we fucked, I was on top, in control. I kept my Zander T-shirt on in the beginning, but Zander's hands were glued to my body underneath. He caressed my breasts, held on to my waist, pulling me into him, and he grabbed my ass. I liked it when he grabbed my ass the most, because I had more in the breast department, and sometimes I got a little insecure when out at a club or event. Zander didn't seem to care. He worshipped my body endlessly as I took the lead.

I set the pace and drove him wild. The tortured pleasure that was hanging on his face turned me on more. The sound of him moaning as I rolled my hips into him ignited my ego. When he groaned and let out a pained, "Fuck," I felt myself ready to burst.

When he grew impatient, he helped me out of my shirt and got more grabby, encouraging me to come. I was close, but I was fighting it.

"Come for me, Bianka," he insisted, going and thumbing at my clit.

"Wait, wait, wait," I begged.

I sped up riding him and one flick of his thumb sent me collapsing onto him in one loud scream of pleasure.

Chest to chest, breathing in sync, we were one. I didn't want to move. I didn't want to be out of this existence. His hands were still on my body and I decided that I liked them there, cradling me as I came undone.

"C'mere," Zander said after a while.

"What?" I asked.

He studied me and ran his tongue over his lips, leaving no room for confusion on what he wanted. "I'm not done with you yet."

I was still coming down as I got myself together and steadied myself on the headboard and sat on his face. His hands were on my breasts, massaging them gently.

Oh, sweet fuck.

Zander moaned with his mouth on me, enjoying this very erotic act we were a part of.

"Ugh," I let out, unable to imagine anything feeling this good as I rocked into him.

I was in no position to move as Zander savored every bit of me, beholding me with the purest look in his eyes. It felt like he was devouring my soul from my most sacred of places. And I let him.

In the end, I covered my face as I lay beside him.

"What are you doing, Bianka?" His voice was too dreamy as I felt him hover over me.

"You got me feeling all nasty."

His hands were on my wrists, removing the boundary of my shielding my face. "Sometimes it's good to be nasty."

Victoria was right: hotels made you more adventurous.

Sex with Rod while good, wasn't like this; this was somehow better, and I couldn't tell if it was the overpowering level of attraction I felt for Zander, or his apparent joy in pleasing me back. Rod was selfish. Sure, I would often come with him too, but there were the times that I hadn't, the times where he was only out for himself. He gave it up the best when he was trying to win me back, but once the dust had settled, he was back to his routine of just trying to achieve his own release.

If having sex with Zander twice meant anything, it was a sign that I could move on and find better than my ex.

"Where's my shirt?" I asked as I sat up and looked around for it.

"Relax," Zander said as he lay back. "No one's rushing you out the door."

There was a playful gleam in his eye. Lonely. He said he'd been lonely in this hotel room, bringing me back to Sunday night's cancellation and the posts Victoria showed me.

"Hey..." I fiddled with my hands in my lap. "Did...did this all start just so you could get back at Jolie?"

He didn't look away and he didn't get angry. "The only thing I was thinking about once you got in this hotel room was you that night. I was only trying to help you get cleaned up and charge your mobile. I didn't see myself sleeping with you until I was right in front of you and you looked like you were going to hit me again."

The same could be said for myself. "News broke about Jolie, and my friend thinks that's why you cancelled the show. I was thinking about how it sorta added up. Which is fine. I guess I can get it. At one point, if my ex called me right now with an apology...maybe I'd be with him tomorrow."

Zander was lying back with one arm behind his head while he ran the back of his fingers up and down my arm, staring up at me. "You'd go back to your ex tomorrow, huh?"

After this last time? Fuck no. "Exes are complicated. I went into work Tuesday and saw that he sent me a bouquet."

Zander pretended to snort. "I would've sent an edible arrangement."

I bit my lip and focused down on the sheets. "Yeah."

"And you would go back to him tomorrow?" Zander repeated, his tone clipped of emotion, his eyes watching me intently.

This side of him, the casualness of his approach, made me feel playful. "He's only the *best* I've ever had."

Zander's brows shot up. "Best?"

"Oh yeah, no one even comes close."

Zander didn't stop running his fingers up and down my arm as he kept staring at me. The empty expression on his gorgeous face let me know the effect my words were having on him.

When I couldn't take his silence, I allowed myself to laugh. "Oh come on, I'm kidding!"

His demeanor didn't change. "Ah."

"Do you really think I'd be here if you hadn't given me the best sex of my life?"

Zander wasn't pleased. "I'm hearing you say it, but I need to hear you *scream* it."

Oh. "What's—"

"What are you doing this weekend?" he cut in.

"Working tomorrow."

"Come home with me," Zander suggested. "I need to have you in my own bed."

I let out a dry chuckle. "I...I have to work."

"I'll compensate for the days you miss."

My eyes snapped towards his and I covered myself more, bringing the comforter to my chest. "No."

"Bianka."

Hastily, I tucked some hair behind my ear. "Why do you want me to go home with you?"

The loud sound of a phone ringing interrupted us and Zander didn't bother to go and answer it. He glanced down at nothing in particular, waiting it out, each ring probably echoing noisily in his head.

When it started up again and finally ceased, he glanced my way helplessly. "I'm having fun with you. I don't want to end it just yet. I've got complications that can wait until Monday, and it sounds like you do too. What's a weekend getaway going to hurt? To go away, recharge your batteries, sometimes that's very necessary. To be free for just the smallest moment in time can be essential."

"And with me?"

"I like our chemistry when we're in bed together. It's natural."

It was only two days. After coloring with my father, rejection from Pryor, Rod's still fuckboy bullshit, and falling into my usual small lonely hole, maybe I was vulnerable. Maybe it was the way Zander stressed my full name. The way he looked at me. The way he touched me. It was all so different.

There were plot holes in the adventure, but I told myself I could worry about it later.

I never got to be this selfish. I never got to be so free, reckless, and wild. An aching part of me was desperate to do this.

"Okay," I agreed with a shy, small smile.

I could end up regretting going away with him. The true mistake could've been turning him down and going home.

I wasn't quite sure of which, and I honestly didn't care.

7

SWEAT

Zander wanted to go straight to his house in Beverly Hills from the hotel. It wasn't until we were down in the lobby at the front desk that it hit me. An older couple entered the hotel and glanced my way, the woman pursing her lips with her face going sour at the sight of me before continuing on with her husband.

I was in a trench coat.

"I need to get some clothes," I told Zander once the room was handled.

Zander stood back, rubbing at his jaw, something he often did when he was thinking I'd come to realize. He was redressed in his sweatshirt and some jeans. He took in my outfit and soon left me to go and talk to Terry, Dax, and Olson.

Alone, I began to feel more self-conscious about my clothing, or lack thereof. Was I really about to embark on a sex-filled weekend fling with Zander Khalil of all people? As Tori advised me months earlier, I deserved some fun, I deserved to move on and find better than my ex.

Yet still, landing in bed with one of this generation's best male vocalists was one hell of an upgrade. Everything about this was unreal. Some fantasy romp you only read about on a Twitter thread, or some other online forum where people could make up bullshit so freely.

"Hey." Zander was back, and I couldn't miss the joy radiating from his person. He was truly living for this, being all free and spontaneous. "So, we're going to take the car and drive to my place ourselves. We'll stop and grab some clothes along the way."

Whatever obstacle landed in Zander's way he had a backup plan to see this through. He wanted this moment with me, this dream that only happened once in a lifetime. To feel wanted, that made me giddy inside.

Zander took my hand and led me out to where the Cullinan was waiting out front. He tipped the valet in exchange for his keys and he opened my door for me, gesturing to the front passenger seat. I climbed in and placed my bag on my lap, practicing easy breaths to get used to the situation.

Zander got in behind the wheel and it was so bizarre seeing him there, next to me, about to drive us somewhere. *Us*, that's what really tripped me up.

In the cupholder, his cell phone rang relentlessly, the image of Nazanin flashing. She was determined to get a hold of him, and Zander seemed content with screening her calls.

"Shouldn't you just answer that?" I suggested.

Zander shrugged as he got on the road and kept his eyes ahead of us. "She can wait until Monday."

"At least text her to let her know you're okay."

"Doing that would provide an open channel of communication that I do not want right now, Bianka."

He was going off the grid for the weekend to recalibrate his psyche. Easy for him to avoid all confrontation by just shutting everyone out. Me, I had to lie. I texted Holliston that I wasn't feeling well and wanted to take the weekend off before leaving a message on my boss's cell saying the same thing. Holly was sweet enough to just understand. When it came to Victoria, my best friend who I was totally backstabbing, I couldn't exactly lie any more than I already was. I told her the truth. That seeing my father messed me up, that being in those four walls of before messed me up—that the current shitty state of my life messed me up, that I was getting away for the weekend to just turn off my head.

And because Victoria was loyal and supportive, she wished me well and told me she was by her phone if I needed her.

It was enough to make me want to vomit. I did not deserve her.

Thinking over our text exchange, I decided to just come clean as soon as I saw her Monday. She would chew me out, and I would accept it. Zander wasn't hers, but there was no downplaying how fucked up this all was. Maybe, when she calmed down, she'd be up to meeting Zander still. I was sure if I asked, he'd be willing to meet his biggest fan.

For now, this weekend was all about escaping.

We hit a red light, the radio playing in the silence between us. In another second, Zander looked my way, a corner of his mouth curling up.

"What?" I asked, feeling myself loosen up and smile too.

He nodded at the radio and mouthed along to the famous chorus of Nas and Diddy's "Hate Me Now."

The irony, with me starting out an anti-fan and all.

"Fuck you," I said as I began to laugh.

He nudged me and we shared a grin. I definitely couldn't hate him *now*.

Zander drove to Larchmont Village, a quiet little low-key shopping district. Shop upon shop lined both sides of the street. He parked his ride in front of a store that sold wine, cheese, and spirits. It was later in the evening so some of the shops were already closed down for the night, as it was going on seven thirty.

I got out of the car and met Zander on his side, unsure about this venture. Where I was from, our neighborhood liquor store was straight to the point, this place was extra fancy, calling it "spirits" and offering cheese on the side to go with probably well-aged wine. In my trench coat and Vans, I felt like I didn't belong, which was no shocker, but still.

"You good?" Zander appraised me, studying my face.

I folded my arms, hanging my head a little. "Maybe this is all a little silly."

"Silly? We're just going to go in there and get you some clothes. Although one could argue what for," Zander teased, tugging on my coat.

I took a step back. "Is it expensive?"

Zander blinked, turning and examining the clothing store near the store that sold classy alcohol. The shop next to it was called Closet Babe, and judging by the fresh white paint on the building, the fancy font used for its name, and the two teen girls waltzing inside—one carelessly holding her cell phone with just her thumb and finger—something told me that even though this wasn't Rodeo Drive, it could potentially cost just as much.

"It's not crazy expensive," Zander said. "Doesn't matter, I'm buying."

I gritted my teeth. "No, you're not."

"Bia—"

"I can take care of myself."

Zander released a breath through his nose, practicing patience it seemed. He came closer to me. All traces of humor were drained from his face. "Are you judging me?"

I shook my head, taking a step back. "No."

"I'm not judging you either. Do you respect me?"

"I guess so, yeah."

Zander relaxed back. "I'm not judging you and I respect you. Why make this hard?"

"Money makes things weird. Some people, they give a panhandler a dollar and pity them."

Zander's expression softened up. "I don't think less of you in any of this, Bianka. Me giving you money isn't me trying to be disrespectful. I'm taking you away from your work for two days, let me pay you back your losses. In case you haven't noticed, I'm a fuckin' millionaire; it's not going to hurt me to spend a little on you."

"I don't want it," I said firmly.

"Your pride is amazing right now." Zander scratched at his neck and appeared thoughtful. "Fine, a compromise, I'll pay for your clothes, and you can buy me whatever item that I like. Fair?"

The place was probably pricey, and even if Zander ended up picking up more things for me, my buying one thing would be a lot for me. Still, it made me feel slightly better.

"Deal," I said.

Zander smiled as he caressed my cheek. "I think my next tattoo will be Xs."

"Xs?"

"You and me, and these *ex*changes. It's fitting, yeah?"

I felt myself loosen up. "Yeah, whenever you want me just send a text with an X."

A gleam passed through Zander's dark eyes and that half grin took his lips. "Are you feeling crazy?"

"Zander, *all* of this is crazy," I said.

The big, sappy grin on his face cooled my senses. "I'm going to wait out here five minutes. You go in there and ask to try something on."

I didn't get it, but when he made no move to follow me as I went over to Closet Babe, I let it go. I walked inside the shop, feeling completely overdressed in my trench coat.

Closet Babe was no different from Angles, I realized as I looked around at all the clothing arranged by color and pattern. Pop music was playing, and I recognized the sound of Ariana Grande instantly. Not my style of music, but I could hang as I meandered more into the shop.

"Hi!" a peppy blonde salesclerk greeted me as I walked by their service counter. "My name's Bailey. Need help finding anything today?"

She was so chipper she reminded me of Holliston. It used to be, where I could tell how long anyone had been working at a place by their demeanor. And then Holliston Simpson applied to Angles and threw me for a loop. I thought for sure after her first month she'd lose her perkiness, but after two years, the girl was *still* all sunshine and rainbows. Bailey seemed no different.

"No thank you," I told her politely.

The shop was fairly abuzz with other shoppers beyond those teen girls who'd entered before me. No one paid attention to the outsider in the trench coat. It was June, summer, and though the weather was winding down to a cool evening, it wasn't cool enough for my coat. The AC in the store made up for my heavy apparel.

Thankfully, I came to find, the prices weren't ridiculous. I plucked up a heathered red T-shirt with the words *Made in the 90s* on it in my size and grabbed a pair of denim mid-rise shorts to go try on.

The fitting rooms were in the back hallway near the restrooms, and even though they were all empty, I chose the room on the end closest to the three-way mirror.

I would've tried on my selections, but then I wasn't wearing underwear and didn't feel comfortable going commando in something that may not have fit.

Knocking on my door caused me to turn from the mirror in the room. A pair of men's black Converse sneakers could be seen under the door.

"Um, occupied," I said loudly.

"Open the door, Bianka," he whispered.

Zander.

I went and opened the door and he was quick to join me before locking the door behind himself. He was now wearing sunglasses, as if that could hide who he was on some Clark Kent shit.

Zander was so big and tall, and undeniably masculine. He looked ridiculous standing there in the dressing room with me. The tiny stall got even smaller with his massive figure now taking up space.

"What—" I wasn't able to get the question out before he backed me up against a wall.

Zander pressed his finger to my lips and peered into my eyes. "Can you be quiet?"

He wanted to have sex right here in the fitting room? The idea *was* crazy. Something I would never do.

Adrenaline rushed through my veins as I leaned forward and pressed my lips to Zander's, giving him my answer. He smiled as he kissed me back, pulling away to undo his jeans.

With shaky hands, I grabbed a condom from my purse, nervous.

"I've never done this before," I confessed.

Zander winked at me as he accepted it. "Me neither."

Another first for the both of us.

Zander picked me up and I wrapped my legs around his waist. My not wearing underwear provided him easy access to what he wanted. His lips were on mine and mine were on his. And then he was in me and my first thought was how much I missed the feel of him there. My mouth fell open and I felt myself ready to moan.

His warm hand covered my lips as he thrust deeper into me. "Shh. I know, I know."

The echoes of heels against the hardwood floor sounded out. People were heading our way.

"Yeah, I totally get what you mean. Justin is going to freak out when he sees me in this." A woman's voice was near us, right outside the door.

"He better." Her friend chuckled as they slipped into the stalls beside us.

Oh. Shit.

My heart raced as my eyes shot to the door, not feeling as discreet as I once did.

The sickest smile spread across Zander's face as he studied my trepidation and ate it up.

He pulled out of me slowly, watching me become undone at the sensation of him, before entering me again just as deliberate.

Ohhh.

My eyes slid to the back of my skull, and I seriously doubted just then I could keep my mouth shut. He just felt too good, too much, and yet I still wanted more.

Suddenly I didn't care who was near us or how reckless this was. I bit his hand, and when he pulled it away, I leaned down and brought my mouth to his.

We went at it in the fitting room and the moment wasn't lost on us. Our kisses were hungry, our hands were needy, and the connection was insatiable. It felt like I could always come with Zander. The attraction, the feeling, and the mutual yearning took me to the edge every time.

There was no shame for Zander when we finished and separated. He kept sneaking peeks at me as he adjusted and pulled himself together, like we had a secret no one else was in on.

He left first and I waited before going to the restroom and cleaning myself up. In the mirror I saw the biggest, corniest smile on my face and I couldn't even look at myself. *You just fucked Zander Khalil—again, Bia!*

"Once in a lifetime," I told myself at the opportunity I was in.

I smoothed out my hair and washed my hands before going out and finding Zander on the sales floor.

I wasn't sure what it was, but somehow my nerves were better. Zander could tell as he held me in his arms while I browsed tops, planted kisses along my neck as I looked at underwear, and held my hand as I poked at a clearance sale of jewelry. We weren't together-together, but as we shopped in Closet Babe, we were that annoying couple who couldn't be apart for one minute.

Zander picked out a white T-shirt with an embroidered Yin and Yang patch on the chest. It cost me seventeen dollars and forty-eight cents, which was nothing compared to the nearly three hundred dollars he spent on me. At the total he didn't bat an eye before pulling out a roll of money.

"You know, don't take this the wrong way," Bailey began as

she was folding and bagging my clothes, "but you look like Zander Khalil."

Zander smiled as he accepted his receipt and let her keep the change. "Why would that offend me?" he asked in his take on an American accent. "He's good-looking, right?"

"He's okay, a solid five at best," I spoke up casually.

Bailey eyed me funny at that blatant lie. "He's gorgeous. And you just sorta...I don't know, remind me of him."

"Well, I'm flattered. Thanks." Zander politely smiled before grabbing my bags and following me out of the shop.

"You should've told her who you were," I said once we were on our way to the Cullinan.

"Then it would've caused a spectacle," Zander said as he unlocked the Rolls-Royce.

I guessed it was safer than sorry. It wasn't like he was alone. The last thing either of us needed was to be photographed together.

Zander packed my bags in the trunk and another idea came over me.

"We need one more pit stop," I said.

He closed the trunk. "Where?"

"We gotta go to the hood," I told him.

Zander was confused. "The 'hood'?"

"I'm going to need some hair products if I'm going to make it through this weekend. And no offense, none of these bougie shops is touchin' the neighborhood beauty supply store."

"Okay."

I climbed into the back of the Cullinan to get dressed as Zander put in the nearest beauty supply store into his GPS.

"Was underwear really necessary to buy?" Zander asked as he began driving for what looked like a shop near Crenshaw.

"Underwear is essential, Zander," I said as I shimmied into a new pair of black mesh panties.

Zander snorted. "Not when you're not going to be wearing them long, they aren't."

"Oh, I'm not giving you any more tonight."

"Why is that?"

"If I keep putting this magnificent peach on you, you're going to get addicted."

Zander snickered. "Is that so?"

I caught his eye in the rearview mirror. "This shit is immaculate."

"You think so?"

I poked my head in between the driver and passenger seat. "It's not?"

Zander's grasp on the steering wheel tightened. "Easy, I may have to pull over and see about it."

I smirked as I finished getting dressed. "Mm-hmm."

Ten minutes later he pulled into a shopping complex and parked in front of a shop called J&K Beauty Outlet.

No matter what city you were in, or neighborhood, every beauty supply store was the same. Old Black hair model posters on the windows sporting the classic styles from ponytails to microbraids, to the occasional clothing each shop sold as well.

Something told me this was out of Zander's usual element, and for that I met up with him on the sidewalk and held his hand as we entered my type of world.

"Wow," he let out as we stepped inside and he took it all in.

On one side of the large open room was a section exclusively selling clothes, everything from old Baby Phat and Sean John to the newest stuff from Michael Kors. In the middle of the room was aisle upon aisle of hair supplies and accessories, and on the right side of the room from the front to the very back was mannequin head upon mannequin head of wigs. By the front counter I spotted an array of makeup tables and jewelry as well. Yep, nothing beat this.

"That's a lot of wigs," Zander noted as he followed behind me in my search for my essentials.

"Yeah, but the best type of wig to buy is a lace front, and I wouldn't buy mine in a store because they're not as good quality as the ones you can find online," I said.

Zander's eyes landed on my hair. "Is that what you're wearing?"

"Nope, these are bundles, or, hair extensions."

His brows furrowed, and he looked so incredibly cute when he was perplexed. "What's your real hair look like?"

We made it to an aisle that offered everything from scarves, durags, and bonnets.

I gathered my phone and found a picture of my last silk press and showed it to him.

A smile curved his lips up as he examined the photo. "I like this look. It's nice. I like natural Bianka."

"Uh-huh." I shoved my phone into my pocket and began debating between a scarf or bonnet.

"Ay, I see you!" a man shouted as he entered the shop with brown paper takeout bags with grease staining them. His eyes were on Zander and me.

Zander politely smiled back and lifted his hand to wave.

"Black is beautiful, my brother. Ain't it?" the man asked with a big, friendly smile on his face.

Zander observed me, a gleam in his eye. "Indeed it is."

I couldn't help but laugh at their exchange. My eyes landed on Zander's bronze skin and imagined my brown skin next to it. "Am I the first Black woman you've...hooked up with?"

Zander angled his head, looking deep in thought. "Yeah, I guess so."

Another one.

I bought my haircare items and tried my best not to laugh as the man who was dating the cashier made more silly comments to Zander about being with me. He kept congratulating him, and I caught the cashier appraising Zander like I'd won a prize as well.

This wasn't a big deal. It was only for the weekend. Nothing more, and nothing less.

The drive into Zander's gated community had me sitting up and taking it all in. The properties were spaced apart to where each resident had enough privacy to do what they wanted. The upkeep let me know the gardeners and landscapers must've made a real killing out this way.

"From the 'Wood to the Hills," I mumbled to myself. But I was just a mere guest; there was no way I could ever live in a place this nice for real.

Zander pulled onto a long driveway that led down to a massive mansion. At the wrought iron gate, he let the window down and punched in a code at the mounting keypad post protruding from the ground. The gate slowly swung open and Zander drove through and pulled in and parked by a row of other luxury vehicles near the front entrance.

"Are we alone?" I wondered, looking up and staring at his house. It was a Spanish-style villa with its tile roofs, stucco exteriors, and half rounded doors and windows.

"Yeah, I live alone."

Zander and I got out of the Cullinan and collected our stuff from the trunk. It was easy to forget Zander was a regular person knowing he was so famous and well-lived compared to most. Seeing him carrying his luggage and some of my bags to his front door where he let us in had me thinking it was all out of place. As if he needed a butler to do these things for him.

"I'll give you a grand tour later. I'm starvin' right now," Zander said.

"You have a chef?"

Zander snorted. "No, most days I cook myself."

"*You* cook?"

Zander leaned close, so close I thought he'd kiss me and was bummed when he didn't. "I bathe and dress myself too."

I narrowed my eyes. "Whatever."

The front foyer, along with the steps, held glossy white marble flooring. An impressive chrome light fixture hung high overhead as we entered the door. Oh to be a maid in this neck of the woods.

Zander showed me up to his bedroom, along the way, on the walls up the stairs, I took in framed photographs of his family. Pictures of younger Zander and Nazanin were enough to make me gush, and seeing his parents made me smile as well. Zander looked like his father, if only a shade lighter.

"What are your parents' names?" I asked as we made it to the top of the steps and Zander cut a corner and headed straight towards a set of double doors.

"Chanda and Imran," Zander answered as he opened one door to the master suite.

His bedroom was like a studio apartment. There was the king-sized bed with the cream-colored silk bedding, and there was even a private little sitting area complete with a love seat and a couple of chairs. Looking back at his huge bed, all I could think was how I couldn't wait to fuck him there. I could see why he had to have me here, because I wanted to have him here too.

Zander took me to the master bathroom that was connected to his room and I was awestruck. From the dual sinks, the glass steam shower, to the beautiful stand-alone bathtub, the place was a work of art. White marble appeared to be the overall theme of the house and it was in the bathroom that it really shined against the glass and black lacquer cabinets. Right there on the spot, I made a plan to soak in that tub before I went home Monday.

The whole time I was taking in Zander's private quarters, *he* was staring at me, watching.

"What?" I asked as I kicked off my shoes back in his bedroom.

He shook his head, going and running a hand through those thick ebony locks. "I'm probably about to fuck this up, but I just like that I haven't seen you once with your mobile out, recording me or snapping pictures. I didn't have to ask you to respect my privacy."

I wasn't offended or surprised he'd have this guard up. There was always somebody in LA trying to make it, trying to find a come-up. Even if I weren't trying to keep this low-key and away from Victoria, I still wouldn't have blasted it to the world.

"Let's go see what's in the fridge to whip up," Zander said. "Do you cook?"

"Not really."

Zander blinked, disbelief clouding his features. "No?"

"I can't cook, but I can feed you."

Zander looked away, trying to hide his grin, but it was useless. "I love peaches."

I giggled as we went down to the kitchen. "I do cook, just the same basic thing every time, though. Lots of baked chicken, and every once in a while I'll switch it up and bake some salmon."

"I love chicken," Zander said. "We'll have to take some out of the freezer so you can bake some tomorrow night."

"You want me to cook for you?"

"I want to taste your chicken."

I never cooked for Roderick because he treated himself like a king and went out to five-star restaurants instead.

Zander's kitchen was magnificent. There was even a window seat between one of the counters with a cozy fleece folded up for snoozing. The white marble island housed a sink and plenty of breathing room to whip up a meal if two cooks were in the kitchen because the counter space behind the island stretched the length of the wall. The kitchen followed an open-floor plan as directly across from us was the entertainment area, and next to it was the patio leading out to the backyard where a pool could be seen.

Zander put on some music and began hunting around for something to put together.

"Do you like spicy food?" he asked me.

I wrinkled my nose. "Not really."

Zander bobbed his head. "There's this dish I'd like to make for you Sunday. It's chicken karahi. It's a bit spicy, but it's so good. I don't make it as good as my dad, but I've heard I'm pretty close."

He looked like a shy little boy and I agreed to eat every bite of his spicy dish right then.

Zander took out some shrimp and just as he was rinsing them in a strainer a familiar song came on and I immediately stood from the window seat.

Too $hort's "Blow the Whistle" had me on my feet fast. "What?" I called out before commencing to dance to the iconic song.

I put my hands on my knees and shook my ass without shame to the beat.

Zander was frozen, watching me at the island. I had him mesmerized, and I wasn't sure why, but I liked the way he looked at me. He'd been all over the world and seen millions of women, but it felt like if he had performed at The Warehouse, he would've spotted me out in the crowd, and he would've only seen me. Like I was the only woman in the world to him.

It was silly to think this, to think that I was leaving any sort of mark on him, but there was no missing the way he'd slip and just watch me, like *he* wasn't the celebrity.

"Let me stop." I laughed as the song ended and a Prince record came on. I went over to the island and sat at a stool, relaxing and falling into the lyrics of "Adore." "What's your favorite Prince song?"

Zander's eyes flickered to mine. "'Insatiable.' Yours?"

I told myself to calm down. The way he was looking at me, it felt like he was answering for more than just his favorite Prince song. "'Purple Rain.'"

Zander nodded. "That's also a good one."

For a moment, I watched him work. In awe, and in denial. Was this real? Was I really *with* Zander Khalil at his *house*? He seemed so at one with himself as he went about preparing food, while I couldn't wrap my head around the reality of the situation. Where any minute felt like I would wake up back in my own bed, with the universe laughing at me.

But this was real. Very real.

Zander cooked this amazing garlic shrimp dish with a side of orzo—because he couldn't just be a good singer, no, he was a multitalented king.

We ate side by side at the island—he drank wine and I drank water, and we talked about music, which I loved hearing how passionate he was about. It was a shame he cancelled his tour, because now I *did* want to see him sing.

"What type of movies do you like?" he asked as he carried the dishes to the sink.

"I like dark theme movies, but a comedy sounds good right now," I said. With my belly full of delicious food, winding down with a lighter-tone movie sounded good.

"A comedy it is."

"What's your favorite comedy?"

Zander took me under his arm and walked us over to the entertainment area where we collapsed on the large sectional. "*Dude, Where's My Car?* was always my favorite growing up for some reason."

"I haven't seen that in forever, but to call it a favorite?" I had to look at him sideways for that.

Zander snorted. "What's yours?"

Growing up, Pryor and I would laugh our asses off watching one movie on repeat. "*Don't Be a Menace to South Central While Drinking Your Juice in the Hood.*"

Zander looked at me crazy and I laughed. We were definitely watching it.

Zander found *Dude, Where's My Car?* online and we snuggled up to watch both movies. Another thing about Zander I was growing to like, was how openly affectionate he was.

I guessed it was no surprise I fell asleep like that, there enveloped in his arms.

8

COMMON

In the morning, I was feeling domestic. After washing up in the master bathroom, I put on a new cami Zander purchased for me along with some matching satin shorts. Barefoot, I walked down to the kitchen and went about making Zander breakfast.

His fridge was decently stocked with fresh ingredients and equipped for the task. Zander hadn't lied; he really did cook for himself. There was no pork bacon or pork sausage, which led me to believe he didn't eat pork. I decided I could work with that and his apparent preference for almond milk over regular dairy. I got out everything I needed, along with the chicken I was set to bake later that evening to thaw before I commenced to cooking.

By the time I was preparing the pancakes, Zander came into the room. I'd been too engrossed in my prepping I hadn't noticed him get up.

He was shirtless now in some sweats, his hair disarrayed from his sleep. But because he was the flawless Zander Khalil, he even made messy hair look good.

Zander came over and gave me a little hug before going and sitting at the island. There was a joint tucked behind his ear. "I thought you didn't really cook."

"Who can't make pancakes?" I said.

"You'd be surprised," Zander said. "This really means a lot. The only person whoever really cooked for me is my mum, or sometimes my dad. So thank you, Bianka."

I felt special then. "It's nothing. I just hope you like it all."

"I'm sure I will. Do you smoke?" Zander asked before he stuck the joint in his mouth.

"None of the above."

This made him chuckle as he pulled a lighter out of nowhere and lit up. "One of my career highlights was being at some award show in Snoop Dogg's trailer with him and Rihanna sharing a blunt. Snoop has the best weed."

I bet if I asked, he would admit to knowing and meeting popular smoker Wiz Khalifa, too. "Whoa, did you try to collab with Rih?"

Zander shrugged. "Was too focused on the weed. Who knows, I could make a call for Z3."

"Z3? You've been recording?"

Zander waved his hand. "Here and there, little by little. I'm still playing with the whole tone, theme, and concept."

"I *love* concept albums. There was this trend on Twitter once about naming the seven albums that define you. For me, *Good Kid, M.a.a.d City*, and *To Pimp a Butterfly* have to be top three."

Zander took a pull from his joint. "Good choices."

"I'm really into music so it took me a minute to compile a solid list."

"Any R&B?"

"*Beyoncé*: self-titled is forever a mood."

"Bey is amazing," Zander agreed. He ashed his joint on a paper towel. "You're really into music, huh? What do you think of mine?"

Guilt caused me to focus on flipping my pancakes. "I'm not gon' hold you, I only know 'The Sound.' I was never into So What, and with my best friend constantly talking about you, I never cared to give you a try."

Zander's face was stoic as he took another drag. "Do you like 'The Sound'?"

"It's what made me respect and have faith in you as an artist. I may even go home after this and give you a fair and real listen."

Zander sat quietly and finished the rest of his joint and I finished my pancakes.

We sat together and I watched as he dug in. The sight of him smiling let me know he liked how everything tasted. He reached out and squeezed my knee, his warm, tattooed hand lingering briefly. What's more, he leaned over and kissed my temple.

Zander Khalil was very affectionate.

Together we cleaned the dishes in a comfortable silence when we were done. What I liked most about Zander was that I didn't have to try. There were moments where I would look over and catch my breath, still in shock to be in the midst of a celebrity, with *the* Zander Khalil, but there was absolutely no pressure to impress him or embellish who I was. Zander wanted me as is.

At least, for the weekend.

In his high-ceilinged living room, Zander sat at his piano and began trying to find a tune. He was freestyling, but those instants where he found a meter, he was good.

"You ever get a melody stuck in your head?" Zander played a note and angled his head to hear it better. He wasn't satisfied as he shook his head and tried another sound.

"Maybe a song or two," I said.

"I'm going to write a song about your body."

"Okay, John Mayer."

He smiled. "Fuck you."

Zander was frustrated, but he played well. His fingers danced across the keys, like a ballerina doing pliés and grand jetés. Everything about Zander was art—living, breathing, vibrant art incarnate.

"You'll get it, you sound good." I stretched, feeling listless suddenly. "I'm going to go soak in the tub."

I left Zander to his battle with his music and I went up to the master bathroom and drew a nice bubble bath.

His tub was big enough to swim in, with jets for added allure. It was tempting to go under, but I pinned my hair up and lied back to relax instead.

Not too long into my soak, Zander came to join me. He stripped down gloriously nude before coming and stepping into the tub. There was more than enough room for the both of us, but he came and lay back between my legs, as if he owned me and had every right.

I pretended to click my tongue. "You got all this room in this tub."

"I'm right where I want to be, though," he quipped.

His hair was shaved shorter on the sides and longer on the top, but not too long. I ran my fingers through his thick mane as he tilted his head back. He was up against me, and though we'd already slept together and crossed that fine line, nothing felt more intimate than this moment.

I wrapped my legs around him, locking him in place. "Mine."

Zander patted my thigh under the water. "Yes."

His concession put a smile on my face. Zander was spoiling me, making me awaken and realize I'd been starved of affection and attention. Rod loved the night life, the flashy clothes, jewelry, and cars, and not to mention the different women who came his way. He only wanted me when I wasn't there, but he wasn't willing to stay and be faithful and true. Because there was always someone prettier than me, someone more curvaceous, someone more willing to do any and everything.

But there wasn't another me, another Bianka Leslie.

Rod was right. I *was* one in a million, and it was his loss. After this weekend with Zander, when I was ready to go out there and try for real, I would use Zander as a model, a standard for how men should treat and value me.

Fuck your roses, Rod.

I almost felt tempted to text Victoria and Holliston my feat, my finally closing the curtain on the Roderick chapter of my life —but then that's where things would get tricky. I didn't want to have to lie any more than I'd already done.

"Okay, Q&A time," I announced.

"All right," Zander agreed.

You would think being Victoria's best friend I'd know everything about him already, but I didn't. Now I was finally curious, and why bother Wikipedia when I had the very person between my legs, against my chest, to provide me my much-needed info.

"Is Zander your real name?" I asked.

"In a way, yes. My full name is Saad Alexander Khalil. When we formed So What, management and the label decided that 'Saad' was too complicated—ethnic, so we came up with Zander instead."

I paused, unable to believe what he'd said. "That's shitty as fuck."

Zander cupped some of the water in his hand and soon let it spill back into the tub. "Indeed, it was."

"Which do you prefer?" I wanted to know.

Zander shrugged. "In a way, I sorta like how only family calls me Saad; it makes going home that much more intimate and special. It doesn't really matter in the end since Zander *is* my real name as well."

I liked the sound of Saad—it was beautiful, but after seeing and knowing his image for all these years, Zander would always be Zander to me.

"So, what do you do for a living?" Zander asked me.

I liked this being about him rather than me. "Nothing glamorous."

"So?" he challenged. "Before I got on, my mum worked at a hospice cleaning linen, and my dad was a tanker driver. I don't come from luxury."

Humble. He was humble about the working class. "I work

retail, at a clothing store called Angles."

"Yeah? Is it just a job or do you really love fashion?"

His words tapped into an old dream of mine. "Both. I used to want to be a designer. I just couldn't afford school when I moved out, so I settled for a clothing store. Sometimes I'll sketch an idea in my spare time, but it's just a pipe dream at this point."

Kid me used to inhale *Vogue* and *Essence*. They were my Bibles. In my old bedroom at home, I'd litter my walls with cut-outs of looks I loved, or taped together from different pieces.

Zander massaged my thigh. "Doesn't have to be. Can I see some of your sketches?"

Instantly I shot that down. "God, no. They're like my babies. I don't know about sharing them with anyone."

"You could trust me." He peered back at me, sincerity in his dark eyes. "I'd never judge you, Bianka."

"O-Okay," I decided in the end. Since he was wanting to know a vulnerable part of me, I thought it was only fair he do the same. "About Sunday night, why did you cancel? I just gotta know before I leave."

He sighed, and when it felt like tension was settling in, I massaged his shoulders. "Short version? I psyched myself out."

"And the long version?"

"You got a while?"

"I don't know about you, but I'm enjoying this bath."

Zander ran his hand up and down my thigh, taking a while to piece together where he wanted to start. There was so much I didn't know about him. So much I was willing to learn.

"So, like, this goes back to So What. One of the reasons I left was because of my anxiety. It started to get really bad performing and having all these people judge me and be so hateful. I could literally just be up on that stage singing my verse, or just goofin' off with the other guys and I'd get so much shit.

"People talked about me being Brown, and they attacked me for being Muslim at the time. I'm the furthest thing from pale. I could never blend in with those other guys seamlessly. After a while, I didn't feel like I belonged," Zander confessed.

Understanding tugged at my heartstrings. "And what did your management say?"

Zander sank against me. "They were really dismissive. It wasn't something they took seriously enough to protect me or speak out against. I was on my own."

I hated that for him. There was nothing worse than feeling utterly alone. I'd been there and it was an ugliness I wouldn't wish on anyone.

"It was hard to be under this spotlight where you're constantly being attacked. I didn't want to perform. I didn't want to be seen. It's one of the main reasons I haven't gone on the road on my own, and I've struggled with prepping myself to get in the proper mindset to move forward and kill it. Jolene used to tell me, or push me, to just go out there. This time I really was set to do it," Zander said.

"What happened?" I asked when he didn't go on.

"The day of the show, we'd gone and did a soundcheck and it went smooth. I felt good. That night, it was a complete one-eighty. I was in a bad space, nervous, anxious, inside my own head. And then Jo posted that picture of her and that guy and it really turned my stomach inside out. It fucked me up, ruined what was left of my mood. My anxiety was already at a high and I just couldn't deal with it. A part of me felt that maybe by the time I got there I'd change my mind, but I just couldn't. I *can* perform alone, but that night I felt alone. You know what I mean?"

I ran my fingers through his hair and leaned forward, pressing a kiss to his scalp. "I get it."

"It's a mental battle I'm trying to win, and that night I lost. I want to perform, I love my fans, and I love the feeling of being on stage. I just have to really take a moment and remember that these people coming to my solo shows are there solely for me. That I'm in a safe place. Once I can get that into my mind, I'm hoping the rest will fall into place."

Anxiety, I could only imagine, was no joke. To deal with it on such a massive level took a lot of strength and support. Suddenly I felt selfish for bashing him all these years, not to mention that night when he had his own issues going on.

"I'm sorry I misjudged you."

"It's okay. I gotta speak up more," Zander said. "Let it be known what I've got going on than just hiding behind shame."

I held him close, going and kissing his cheek. "You belong, Zander, you belong."

He ran his hand down my leg and squeezed briefly in a show of gratitude.

Zander had my full support. It was almost funny when I thought about the idea of the me-*now* going back in time talking to the me-*then* who had a sworn dislike of Zander.

"What was the other reason you left So What?" I wondered next.

"It just wasn't me. The music and image never spoke to me. I was growing up, but I wasn't allowed to put that in our music. We had to be clean. We were grown men, but the label and management acted like our fans weren't growing." Zander snorted, shaking his head. "Fast forward to today—Teddy can do a podcast and declare he's the 'king of beer,' and how he likes a little ecstasy, but *I* smoke weed and I get crucified."

Amongst the guys of So What, Zander still had a somewhat torn image. Some fans still bashed him for leaving, and were loyal to the remaining four. It did seem as though Teddy could do no wrong in the public eye.

"When we were recording, I wasn't allowed to use my full voice. I've naturally got a soulful tone. I wasn't allowed to do runs. I had to bury my soul. It didn't fit what they were trying to sell. After a while, singing became a tedious thing because I couldn't *be* myself," Zander went on.

"There was one So What song you guys had on your second album I heard and it was a little R&B, and that's when I first peeped that you had a little more to offer vocally. God, what was that song called? Oh yeah, 'Us or Not,' I used to low-key get down when Tori would play it in her car," I confessed with a shameful laugh.

"That's one of my favorites from our discography. Teddy Riley produced it. R&B is who I am, it's in my blood. I grew up on Usher, Ginuwine, Prince, Avant, Carl Thomas—like all the good shit. My vibe is based off what my parents would play. If I wasn't in the band, there's no way I'd be listening to fuckin' So What. So I left. And when I was finally ready to speak about it when I put out *Exposed*, I told my truth."

"And that's when all the bad blood started?" There was no missing all the shady tweets or comments thanks to Victoria.

"They think I'm a traitor for saying I didn't enjoy my time in So What, but I was the only person of color in the group. I had people attacking me from every direction. Of course, my experience differs from theirs. Take the lack of creative freedom and couple it with dealing with racism and islamophobia, I wasn't having a good time. Bad blood or not, those are my mates—my brothers for life. But to have them dismiss my feelings cut me deep. The only person who's never spoken against me, or spoken up for me is Oliver, but even we don't have a relationship now."

It sounded about White. Holliston was my only White associate, and while she got it, or tried to understand, there were many White people in the world who just didn't. Social media was the hub for dismissive White people who acted like speaking up against racism or injustice was a big inconvenience.

In a way, I sorta got it now. All the guys from So What were dealing with a sense of betrayal. The remaining four felt abandoned when Zander left, and Zander felt cast out when they didn't try to see things his way. What they really needed, was a sense of understanding and a good long talk. But something told me egos had gotten in the way a long time ago and it would be a while before the world got a So What reunion.

"You said 'when' you were Muslim, does that mean you're not anymore?" I asked.

"I gave up my faith years ago. It wasn't so much from all the hate. It was just a me thing. The religious aspect of it, I mean; some things will always be a part of me. I guess I just traveled the world, experienced different cultures for the little bit of time I was in other regions, and I just sorta grew out of it. The things I was taught or believed in as a child, I don't believe in anymore."

His words hit home. "I get it," I said softly.

"How so?" Zander wondered.

"My mom." I squeezed my eyes shut, feeling a wave of emotion I'd pushed back for way too long. "She was a cop. When I was a little girl, she taught me about defending myself, about being capable of fending for myself. She was a hero to me, this strong, beautiful force of a human, and I was in awe of her. As a kid, her being a cop was a simple thing, but then I grew up. I saw what the *bad* cops were like, how they severed families and lied irrevocably without punishment. I saw all that and I couldn't look at my mother the same. I couldn't understand how she could align herself with these people so willingly.

"She insisted that her purpose was different, her drive was different, but I just wasn't convinced. No matter the intention, I thought she was like this huge sell-out. She used to stress her goals to clean up and help our community in Lindenwood. It's a nice place where you can find roses in concrete, but when you get close to the gutter, it can eat you alive."

"I understand. Where I'm from in Slough it's like that. A lot of people are stuck in their ways, and some don't want to see you advance or go further than where they are."

"Exactly. There's a lot of crabs in the bucket in Lindenwood, but my mom was determined to help. Don't get me wrong, I loved my mom, but I didn't agree with her occupation anymore. We were still close, as mother and daughter, but when her job came up we'd argue.

"One day on the job, she was just getting a cup of coffee at a gas station in our hometown, and she walked in on an attempted robbery and they shot her." The pieces of the puzzle of my brokenness became clear and I hated it. "She died. Seeing my mom, a good woman, a good cop, who believed in the advancement and betterment of the world, of my city, get gunned down, it did something to me, Zander. I lost my faith in humanity that day she died. Because if a good person like my mom could get cheated, what good could there still be in this world?"

"Bianka." Zander sighed, peering back at me with wounded eyes. "Don't be pessimistic. Sometimes the only thing we can do is be strong in our greatest moments of turmoil. What about the family you've got left?"

"'Til this day, my dad hates me because I hurt his wife because she was proud of me and I stopped being proud of her. My brother hates me because even though my mom and I didn't always see eye to eye, she still loved me and complimented me because I was a good girl, I moved out, I got a job, I got a car, and I never caused any trouble. I got it right and Pryor did it all wrong."

"Pryor?" Zander repeated, curious.

"My older brother. We had a good upbringing, but Pryor was susceptible to peer pressure and often hung around a bad crowd. He got in trouble and got kicked out at eighteen. My mother didn't praise me or love me more, but she'd speak of me highly. Pryor acts like she loved me more, and because of it he hates me. He and my father get along still because I don't come around often. I'm not such a burden to them that way, which is why I'm in Hemingway Park."

"I'm sure they don't hate you," Zander tried to say. "Sometimes anger gets the best of people at the wrong times."

"No," I disagreed. "My father barely looks me in the eye, and I haven't spoken to Pryor in three years. Once a month, or every other week, I go to see my dad and we color in coloring books like we used to do when I was a kid. It's like we're desperately trying to get that old thing back, even though we can never reclaim it. My father asks generic questions about my day or work, nothing deep, nothing below the surface. He won't forgive me, and I've come to accept that."

Empathy was etched on Zander's face. "Do you think if you were in trouble and reached out, Pryor would come around?"

I shook my head. "I tried to call him the other day and he blew me off. Told me he was blocking me and he wanted nothing to do with me. It's not surprising, I guess. When we were kids and whenever someone would pick on me, he'd never step in to help. He used to even make fun of me for being bullied."

"Fucking bastard," Zander muttered, his body going stiff between my thighs.

I tried to be strong, to hold my chin up. To detach myself from it all. "I'm good now, better—I'm fine."

"Bianka."

I focused down at the water, telling myself not to care because who gave a shit? "I'm fine."

At twenty-five, I'd never broken a bone, never suffered from a serious ailment, but I knew the pain of a splintered heart. Outside of Victoria, I had no one. I was alone. I felt it every time my father rejected me and at the brutal distance Pryor had wedged between us.

I didn't know I was crying until I felt his hand on my face, wiping a tear away with his thumb. Zander concentrated on this task; his brows furrowed as he appeared thoughtful.

"I think that's enough bath time for the day," he said.

I agreed, having lost the joy in the moment.

Zander drained the tub before stepping out of it and helping me out next. We collected towels from the plush ottoman by the shower and headed back into the bedroom.

In his silk bed, Zander took me into his arms, as if to comfort me, to hold me. Somehow, when he was bathing my face in kisses, chasing those ugly tears away, my lips gravitated towards his, instinctively, naturally, rightfully.

It wasn't long before he was inside of me, connecting us into one. And for a moment, he paused, feeling what we felt. *Close.*

Zander groaned, releasing my name on a tortured breath. "Bianka."

Unlike the times before, he took me slow, caressing me gently, staring deep into my eyes, kissing me chastely, cradling my body and soul with a delicate sense of care. And I gave myself up to him, matching his tenderness with all that I had to give.

9

BETTER

I climbed out of bed, Zander's tattooed hand gliding across my skin. He did not want to let me go.

Once I was on my feet, I looked behind me to find him still asleep. After the most intense session of lovemaking I'd ever experienced, we'd drifted off. Now awake, I could see that the sun had gone down and the house was quiet. My belly rumbled and I placed my hand on my naked flesh. I was starved.

With Zander still asleep, I contemplated packing my things and leaving. I hadn't meant to break down like that. We weren't supposed to get *that* close. But we had, and he'd taken care of me without a hint of judgment.

My stomach growled once more and I knew I at least had to eat before making a getaway.

I quickly freshened up in the bathroom before slipping on a T-shirt of Zander's and heading down to the kitchen. Usually, I enjoyed listening to music while I cooked, but I didn't want to wake Zander. Though, he lived in a large house which questioned the possibility.

Still, I settled on turning on the TV in the entertainment area and allowed a rerun of *Psych* to play as I went about preparing the chicken breasts. I ransacked Zander's seasonings and marveled at his ability to *actually* carry more than just salt and pepper. After collecting what I would use, I seasoned the chicken and set it in the oven to bake. For sides, I grabbed a jar of vodka sauce and prepared a pot to boil for penne, and took out a bag of broccoli from the freezer.

I shut the freezer door and nearly jumped out of my skin.

Zander was standing in the room. In just a pair of sweats, he was studying me and the pans I had out.

"Geez," I breathed out, holding the frozen vegetables to my chest.

Zander came closer, assessing me as he did so. "What are you doing?"

I didn't get the question because I thought it was obvious. "Cooking?" I went back to the island and peered into the pot, finding that the water wasn't close to boiling.

"You don't have to do that. We could've ordered takeout."

We could've, but... "I promised I'd cook for you."

Zander raked a hand through his hair, once more gazing at the food. "I didn't think you'd still be in the mood."

I chewed on my lip and focused on opening the broccoli. "It's whatever."

"Bianka..."

"Not the best first impression, but then again, I'm on a roll," I tried to joke. I'd gone from damsel in distress to emotional wreck quite epically if I did say so myself.

Zander didn't find it funny. He was closer now. Right next to me, demanding I be brave and look at him.

"It's not 'whatever.'" His tone bordered on annoyed.

Finally, I looked at him, trying with all my might to brush it off. "This weekend is just supposed to be about sex. Not traumatic—"

Zander picked me up, effortlessly setting me on top of the counter to where we were eye to eye. His strength kept taking me by surprise. That and the way he was determined to get through to me.

"I'm not embarrassed or ashamed of showing you my pain, my past, or my loneliness," Zander said as he held my gaze. "So don't you be either."

It was different, his struggles, but I got his point in being vulnerable. He'd dealt with the whole world targeting him, while my whole world went up in flames the moment my mother died. He was alone in his torment, and I was alone in my exile.

I was a stranger to Zander, and yet he was here showing he cared.

"Understood?" Zander's hands slid up my sides, claiming my waist.

"Yes," I said as a warmth spread throughout my chest.

"Good." He came close, near my ear. "Dinner smells great."

Dinner was the last thing on my mind with Zander being so close, but somehow, I managed to pull myself together and focus. I sautéed the broccoli and boiled the penne while he watched TV. Every once in a while, he'd laugh, the spirit and energy within it echoing in my chest.

When everything was ready, we sat together at the island. Zander tried a piece of chicken and I awaited his reaction, hopeful he liked my dinner as much as he liked my breakfast.

I watched as he forked off a piece and placed it into his distracting mouth. A smile curved Zander's lips up as he finished chewing and bobbed his head. His dark eyes found me and his hand met my knee. "It's delicious. I love it."

I bounced with joy at his appreciation and dug in myself. It was late, but that didn't stop either of us from sharing a bowl of vanilla ice cream and curling up on the sofa to watch some thriller with Hugh Jackman. Zander's affection was never ending as I lay back against his chest, spooning him ice cream and reveling in his heat.

The cool sensation of his lips brushed against my temple and a delirious shiver skated down my spine. "How are you feelin', Bianka?"

Angling my head, I gazed back at Zander, finding him

watching me again. His heavy attention was enough to make me cease to breathe. It was dangerous how used to this a girl could get.

Leaning up, I pressed a quick kiss to his lips. "Better."

His arms wrapped around me and held me close and we continued the movie.

Better it was.

10

LET ME

"**Y**ou are such trash!"

My mouth hung open in blatant shock as I read over Zander's bold tweet again.

The man himself bore no shame as he stood in front of me. He was even suppressing a smile.

I shook my head, unable to hide my blush or stop myself from questioning when he'd been able to tweet it. The one thing I knew was that it was now Sunday. I wasn't sure what time it was, not that time had been essential all morning or afternoon. We spent the day in bed, in the tub, on a chair. We went at it like sex was a new discovery for us. I had never had so many orgasms in my life.

Even after an entire day I wasn't sure why Zander was standing there with his clothes on.

"Zandy," I said, being cute and annoying. I tugged on his drawstrings, giving him the eye.

For some reason, either his complexion or his whole vibe, black just did it for him. As he stood wearing a black T-shirt with his black sweats, he looked every bit of edible. There wasn't an inch of his inked skin that I didn't want to trace with my tongue.

Zander leaned away, causing me to pout. This made him grin at me, amused. "Stop that. I've got to get on dinner. I really want you to taste my chicken karahi."

"I will." My fingers curled around the waistband of his sweats as I grabbed a hold of them.

Zander didn't fight me as I lowered his sweatpants and freed him. He came closer, watching me with eager anticipation as I leaned close to take him into my mouth. All at once I felt him relax and give in as I planted a kiss on him.

"Shit," he let out in ecstasy as his head lulled back. His hand found my head and his fingers grazed my scalp in appreciation.

As much as sucking him was turning me on, I let it just be for him. A *thank you* for a nice vacation away from my normal life. Zander had been incredibly kind and sweet since we met, and I wanted him to know how much my opinion of him had changed. How much I was going to m—

"SAAD!"

A woman's voice shot through the air as a door shut loudly in the background outside the master bedroom.

"Fuck!" In lightning like movement, Zander yanked himself out of my mouth and away from me. He stood back, pulling his sweats up and coolly running his fingers through his hair as he let out a breath.

I wiped at my mouth and sat up. "Who is that?"

"My sister." He practically hissed as he searched the floor for something. He soon leaned down and hopped around as he shoved his feet into some Nike slides.

"Shit." I mirrored his swearing and scavenge for proper clothing as I was up out of the bed.

"Don't make me come find you!" his sister shouted.

Zander was dressed, but he lingered around, waiting on me to struggle into my bra and pull a T-shirt over my head. I put on a pair of shorts that I couldn't tell didn't match my top until we were out of his room on our way to the staircase.

It was when we descended the stairs that I first laid eyes on Nazanin Khalil. I *couldn't* take my eyes off her. She stood in the center of the foyer; her head raised up looking for her brother. And she was just as beautiful as he was. Dressed in a formal red jumpsuit, Nazanin appeared like a graceful model the closer we got to her. Her long dark hair fell like black liquid down her back and shoulders. Her svelte figure let me know she worked out on the regular to keep in shape. And her tall height made me feel smaller than I already did after taking in her expensive aura—as if the Chanel clutch in her hands and Christian Louboutin heels on her feet weren't indicative enough.

Her face, at first warm at the sight of Zander, cooled to an algid freeze when her dark eyes took in me behind him. Her expression fell awash in a cold mask as we came off the last step and kept our distance.

"There you are," she spoke up, carrying the same accent as Zander naturally. The only difference between the siblings was Nazanin's feminine features. She looked more like their mother while Zander looked like their father.

Nazanin faced me, intaking a breath through her nose as a judgmental brow raised. "And you're not alone."

I didn't need Wikipedia, or Zander, to tell me just then that of the two of them, Nazanin was the oldest.

Zander's hand found my back gently. "No, I'm not. Bianka, this is my older sister, Nazanin. Naz, this is—"

Sighing, Nazanin was quick to dig into her clutch. "Look, I'm not sure how much he's already paid you, but I've only got about five hundred in cash. That can't be more than your going rate."

Did she just—

Was she assuming I was a *prostitute*?

My face contorted in confusion and anger as I felt my body go into defense mode. "What the—"

"Naz!" Zander snapped in my honor. His hand came down on my wrist as he took a stance in front of me.

Nazanin faced her brother innocently. "What? I need to talk to you without your *friend* here."

"You got something you want to say to me?" I demanded to know, trying to get around Zander.

Gone was Nazanin's cluelessness, and back was her austere demeanor. "Do you want charge instead?"

I lurched forward, trying to get a hold of her, but Zander was quick.

"Nazanin!" he yelled loudly, on the verge of rage. When pissed, Zander looked decadent, sexy, dark, and his accent was much thicker.

None of this swayed my mood.

I broke free of his grasp and took off towards the stairs, all too aware that Zander was on my heels.

Back inside the master bedroom I decided to collect my things before I caught an assault charge.

"What are you doing?" Zander asked as he came in and shut the door behind him.

"Fuck you!" I shouted his way.

Zander blinked. "Do not yell at me, Bianka."

Like a scolded child, I conceded. Still, seething in an anger I couldn't tame, I went about grabbing all articles of my clothing and throwing them on the bed.

"Bianka." Zander was calm, and that annoyed me more.

"Good fucking bye, Zander," I said curtly.

He angled his head, silently staring at me. He didn't speak for a moment as he watched me gather more of my things.

"Where are you going?" he finally asked.

"Home," I shot his way.

"Why?"

I faced him, unable to believe he'd ask that. Instead of blowing up at him, I tried to be civil. "It's Sunday. The weekend is over and I'm going home now."

He rubbed at his jaw, appearing thoughtful. "Is that what you want?"

"What do you mean?"

Zander pocketed his hands and chanced coming closer to me. He took me in and then gazed at my clothes on his bed. "I mean, you're ready to just walk out that door and be done with this, yeah?"

I was pissed at his sister and now he had me confused. "That was the agreement."

"And things haven't changed?"

"What are you saying, Zander?" I wanted him to get straight to the point, because his surprise inquisition had me losing my angst.

"I'd like for you to stay. I'll handle Nazanin, but I want you to stay."

"What?"

"I don't want this to just be a weekend," Zander clarified.

"More?"

Zander stared me in my eyes, holding my gaze and meaning every word he was saying. "After the bath, the tempo changed."

Slow. It was slower.

"The first time I had you in my bed and it was slow. I already loved fucking you, but after going slow... I don't think I could ever get enough."

I opened my mouth and shut it. My head was swimming with words and feelings, and I felt totally conflicted suddenly. "So, you want to be friends with benefits?"

Zander shook his head. "No, I want *you*. You captivate me. You make me feel like I have to try, like beyond my image *I* have to impress you. You don't give a shit about my music or my money. You could literally walk out that door right now and not look back, and that bothers me a lot. I can't explain it, but I'd like to give this a real go."

His words caused me to take a seat on the bed and catch my breath. "I...I don't know what to say."

"Say you like me back, Bianka."

He liked me.

Of course he did. He wouldn't have invited me to stay for the weekend if he hadn't. But he liked me a lot, so much he wanted to be serious with me. Zander Khalil wanted me for more than just a weekend fling.

"I've never done this before," I let out softly, feeling shy as I looked up at him. "I've done things with you I've never done with anyone else in bed and out of it."

"And I don't want you to leave here doing those things with anyone else either," Zander confessed. "I want you to be mine, and I would be yours."

"But why?" He dated actresses; what did he want with a retail clerk who lived in a shitty apartment in Hemingway Park?

Zander came closer to where he was standing over me. "Because I like you and I want this with you. This, what we have, is art. Abstract art, where it doesn't follow the rules, where it doesn't make sense, but you can't stop looking at it, you can't turn away."

This poetic motherfucker. "And you like me?"

He crooked his finger and stroked my cheek. "It's not every day a girl slaps me."

I managed to laugh. Yeah, that was quite a start to...whatever this was that he wanted to build from.

"And you like me," I came to realize.

"Yes," Zander didn't deny. "I like you, Bianka."

It should've been all too easy to jump into a relationship with him, but I couldn't ignore all the glaring realities beyond his liking me.

"You're a celebrity," I said.

"And I'd much rather be home putting together a 1,000-piece puzzle than at some red-carpet event. I'm not into that. I couldn't care less about being a 'star.'"

It couldn't be that simple or easy for him. "What about Ishani?"

Zander blinked, taking a step back. "Careful."

It was a known fact that Ishani Chopra was sensitive territory for Zander, but still I had a right to armor up and ask all the big things now. "Hate to go there, but I don't want to jump in blindly and turn around and see you on TV with the next."

Zander backed off, pocketing his hands as his shoulders sagged. "I met Jolene at the American Music Awards where she was presenting. I took one look at her and couldn't take my eyes off her. Did I get her number? Yes. Did we start seeing each other soon after? Yes. It was new and it was exciting, and I got caught up.

"I fucked up with Ishani. I broke her heart and betrayed her deeply. I don't like talking about it. Being with Jo came with cameras. She's famous. I'm famous. It's a part of the reason I stay low now. The...*exposure* of it all, it's knackerin'."

It was completely messed up. No woman deserved the public humiliation of finding out their man was moving on with someone else before even letting her know. There was no excuse for what Zander had done. "That poor girl."

Zander's eyes shot to mine. "Yes, Ishani deserved better. It's not something to just brush off. I fucked up."

I hugged myself, so uncertain. An ugly voice in my head was telling me to run, that no matter how fine he was, and how good he fucked, it wasn't worth the risk. "I...I don't know."

Zander scratched at his head. "It was an awful thing, what I did to Ishani. With Jo, I never cheated on her. I learned from my mistake, Bianka."

I hung my head in my hands. "My best friend is obsessed with you."

"But I met *you*."

He was pleading with me to give this a try and my heart was so desperate I wanted to, too. "Zander."

He squatted down before me, peering up at me earnestly.

"I've got a lot to figure out tomorrow, but I know what I want here and now. I don't care about your past, I just care about your future, and if I can be in it."

My lips trembled and my heart jumped to my throat. To be wanted—wasn't that what everyone craved at the end of the day? Against all logic, I came to Zander's home and fell for him too. I was wholly attracted to him, completely curious about him, and shamefully eager to get into his music now.

"I want you, too," I admitted, unable to look him in the eye.

There was no coming back from this.

Zander came and leaned over me, his lips pressing to mine softly. "Thank you."

"But I do have to go home and face Victoria. It's the least I can do."

Zander stood back and nodded. "I hope that goes well."

"Me too."

Zander held his hand out. "Let's go downstairs and try again with Nazanin. I'll set her straight."

There was one more thing we needed to discuss before we faced whatever Nazanin had in store for us.

I took a deep breath and looked into Zander's eyes and said it, "For the record, I'm on the pill."

Zander froze, taking his hand back and studying me. "Oh...okay."

"We haven't been *safe* since after the bathtub," I went on. It had been the most intimate I'd ever been with a man, touching me far deeper than just sex alone. All morning and afternoon we hadn't stopped to use protection either, completely consumed in each other's bodies and the high our sex brought us. I'd never been that thoughtless before, and I wanted Zander to know this. "This isn't something I usually do."

Zander raked a hand through his hair as he blew out a breath. "I'm good, you know? I've been in the gym, and I went to the doctor so I could know I was good to go for this four-city tour, and potentially beyond, and I'm *good*."

"Me too." It was one of the first things I'd done post-Roderick. You could never be too sure with a cheater.

"Good." Zander came close and caressed my cheek. "I love the feel of you. Your body next to mine. My name on your lips."

An ache pulsed between my thighs and I knew we'd get carried away if we stayed upstairs any longer.

So, I was quick to stand up. "We better get back."

Zander snuck me a smile. "We better."

"How old is she?" I told myself maybe having a huge age-gap was the reason for her rudeness, although with age should've come wisdom and more poise.

"Thirty," he told me.

She was five years older than the two of us and she didn't look a day over twenty-one.

Nazanin was right where we left her, waiting impatiently now. "All's squared away, yeah?"

Zander held my hand, protectively. "Are you serious right now?"

Nazanin rolled her eyes. "You tell me, you sack off the grid for four days and turn up with this one."

"*This one* has a name." Zander's tone danced on agitated.

Nazanin wasn't backing down. "Right, Bianka. How lovely, will she be going now?"

"No," Zander said. "She and I are together."

"Oh, come off it," Nazanin scoffed. "Really?"

"Yes."

"And how did Terry and Dax let this—*Bianka* slip past them?"

"Doesn't matter how. What matters is she's here now and I'm with her."

Nazanin's nostrils flared, and though I could tell she didn't want to, she faced me and tipped her head in a how-do-you-do manner. "Apologies for my confusion earlier. My brother can be a bit reckless."

"Sounds like it runs in the family." I wasn't backing down.

Nazanin sized me up and smirked. "Cute."

Funny, it was about to get ugly.

"All right then, call Paul," Nazanin said as she returned to her brother.

"That can wait until morning," Zander groaned.

"No, I think you need a reality check. We've all been worried sick and I caught the first flight I could. Call him now."

Zander fished his phone from his pocket and quickly unlocked it, scrolling through his contacts.

"On speaker," Nazanin instructed.

Reluctantly, Zander did just that as the phone began dialing out.

The phone didn't ring long on the other end before it was quickly picked up. A man with an American accent answered. *"Zander?"*

"Hey, Paul, what's up?" Zander asked casually, all too aware that Nazanin was watching him.

"Oh, not much, just enjoying my Sunday evening. Hey, just one question, buddy."

Zander was confused. "Uh, shoot."

"At least tell me, did you wear a condom?"

"A *condom*?" Zander repeated.

"Yes, a condom—did you wear a condom when you fucked me? Because that's what you did by cancelling this tour and going ghost for a whole fucking week." Paul snapped into his phone. *"You just bent me over with no fuckin' Vaseline and stuck it to me raw!"*

Zander sighed, going and taking the phone off speaker before heading down the corridor to his office.

Nazanin stood back, a self-satisfied look hanging on her face. "Right then, he's going to come back down to Earth now."

"He was going to talk to him tomorrow," I spoke up.

With Zander gone, Nazanin didn't pretend to come off friendly. "It's better that he gets his shit together now rather than later."

"He's under a lot of stress and pressure."

Nazanin's hand grazed her collarbone. "I'm his sister. I know him more than anyone. He lashes out when he's overwhelmed, and he always needs someone to step in and pick up the pieces. That's why I'm here."

While I didn't know the details of his entire day last Sunday, from what I did know, Zander hadn't been reckless at all outside of cancelling his tour and show. "He hasn't done anything crazy."

Once more that critical brow rose. I got it then that *I* was where Zander was being reckless.

"Make no mistake, I *do* feel bad for you," Nazanin said with her best attempt at a sympathetic look. "Jolene pulled that stunt, and of course Saad decided to react. God knows men don't always think with their heads...up top." The sympathy morphed into pity. "It's a shame you were caught up in their war."

"It's not like that," I said.

She came close, looming over me. "You were *nothing* more than just a quick little fling, a mere distraction. Nothing more, nothing less. Why not be smart and cut your losses now and walk away with some dignity?"

I clasped my hands together to keep from hitting her as I fixed her with a polite smile. "You have your opinion, and I don't give a fuck. See how we both win?"

Nazanin took in a breath, caught off guard.

That's right, I bite too, bitch.

I went and waited for Zander in the entertainment room. The TV was on, but I wasn't the least bit caught up in whatever Lifetime movie was playing on screen. My head was elsewhere, against my better judgment, caught up on Nazanin's words.

She knew Zander's disappearing act was partially linked to Jolie. Zander admitted his ego being bruised by the sight of her with another man helped pushed him to not perform.

This didn't *feel* like a rebound thing—I didn't even see myself using him to get over Rod. My feelings were real, and I had never felt so vulnerable.

Zander was right, that time after our bath had changed the tempo.

We fucked without consequences, and then we made love slow.

And now here we were in the aftermath.

"Hey."

Zander came into the room with Nazanin begrudgingly behind him.

"Are you okay?" he asked as he assessed where I sat cross-legged on the sofa.

I managed a nod.

Zander opened his mouth, but Nazanin spoke up. "I'm starving. Could we go out to dinner, *alone*. I mean, it has been months since I've seen you."

Zander fixed his sister with a steel look that made her swallow and take a step back. "If you want to go out for dinner, Bianka will come too."

Nazanin pursed her lips and remained quiet.

While I liked him for taking up for me, I didn't believe in going where I wasn't wanted. "I'll stay."

Zander turned to me. "Bianka."

"Go, be with your family. I'll just find something here. I'm good, honest."

I could tell Zander was annoyed I backed off, but he didn't pursue the matter before leaving the room to get properly dressed to accompany Nazanin to dinner.

With a victory in her possession, Nazanin smiled wickedly before settling into the chair across from me.

We didn't speak. We just let the movie play as we both pretended to watch it. When Zander returned, dressed in a gray suit and a white unbuttoned dress shirt, Nazanin stood to go.

"I made reservations somewhere nice and simple. You don't deserve five-star right now," Zander said to his sister.

Nazanin scoffed before dramatically leaving the room, the echoes of her heels announcing her departure for the front door.

Zander came and pressed a kiss to my temple before reeling back and examining me. "I'll be back."

"Okay," I said.

It wasn't until after he left that I decided to just leave. What was I thinking? There was no way we could make this work. Da Vinci couldn't paint us a masterpiece.

Up in his bedroom I called Victoria as I started folding my clothes. It was then another dilemma hit me. I didn't have any luggage to take my things in.

"Hey." The sound of Victoria's voice both lifted my spirits and broke me down.

"Hey."

"What's up? You sound upset."

I couldn't do this over the phone. I owed her a face-to-face confrontation. "I need to talk to you tomorrow before I go in to work," I said.

"We can talk now if you want. You sound off, Bia." My best friend's concern was undeserving.

"I can't do this over the phone, Tori."

Her end was silent as she issued out a sigh. I imagined her shaking her head, coming to her own conclusion on what could possibly be wrong. "Why couldn't you just tell me you were going away with Rod?"

Closing my eyes, I cursed myself for not being stupid instead of selfish. "It's not Rod."

"Well that settles that. Call me when you get in and I'll come right over. I don't like how you sound."

"Promise," I swore before we ended our call.

Maybe it was best to just go home and call her over immediately. Or else I wouldn't be able to sleep with worry clouding my senses.

It was partially mean to just abandon Zander without a goodbye or explanation. But we were only fooling ourselves thinking we could go beyond this weekend. We had our time, and now it was over.

A text alert came through on my phone and I looked down to find Zander himself texting me.

> I didn't freak out b/c I was ashamed of you or havin you at my home. We were in the middle of somethin and Naz just popped up. I'm embarrassed she would think of you in such a negative light and assume you were there for money. I never want you to be uncomfortable in my presence or my home

Thank you

> Don't let this take away from the fact that we both want this

Zander let's be real

> I AM. I know what I want and that's YOU. Nothing's going to get in the way of that

Now my eyes were misty and I hated feeling so emotional. Everything was at stake and yet I was ready to risk it all.

Abstract?

Abstract

And I was his, and he was mine.

11

YOU CAN'T HIDE

I was in bed when Zander got in. He called out for me, but I didn't answer.

When he found me, I heard him sigh and take off his pants and jacket. He crawled into bed behind me and wrapped an arm around me. His touch was cold. The smell of weed and cigarettes filled my senses.

I let the scent wash over me as I pretended to be asleep. Not too long later, I was.

Usually, I slept in on the nights I was closing, but since I had to get back home to change and meet Victoria, I was up early Monday. Zander was still asleep when I got out of bed. I thought about leaving a note as I went into the bathroom to shower and brush my teeth.

It felt like running, but maybe I was. I couldn't get Nazanin and her rudeness out of my head. It wasn't fair to compare, but Zander was more coveted and valued on a much bigger level than Rod. My trust issues couldn't take another hit.

Don't psych yourself out of this, Bia, I told myself as I stepped out of the shower and wrapped myself in a towel.

And then, as if to really dissolve all trepidation that was plaguing me, Zander stepped into the room.

"Mornin'," his sleepy voice said to me.

He showered while I went back to the bedroom to towel off and get dressed. I put on my clothes and Zander gave me a free concert as he sang loudly in the shower. He belted out the lyrics to Prince's "Insatiable" and the corniest smile crept onto my face. Zander didn't need autotune, because he hit those notes impeccably.

How could I walk away from this?

For the first time in a long time, I felt good, happy, desirable.

Zander appeared in the bedroom, dressed in only a pair of jeans and a faded Ice Cube T-shirt. His hair was slicked back, but there was one rebellious lock freely hanging in his face. I wanted to go and coil it around my finger, tug on it and bring his mouth to mine.

"I'm sorry again, about last night," he told me. "These days, I only keep my family around me. They're very private, and Nazanin is very protective of me."

I could understand that, to an extent, but there was no ignoring the elephant in the room. "Why would she think I'm a prostitute?"

Zander hung his head, frowning. "I...I haven't always been the cleanest, the most rational."

"Okay," I said, waiting for him to go on.

Zander studied me, looking as serious as I'd ever seen him. "This...doesn't leave this room."

Sensing he was about to make a confession that could affect his career, I quickly agreed. "It won't."

"I mean it, Bianka."

"I promise, Zander," I swore.

He peered over at me. His eyes were cloaked in the shadowed depth he was pulling from. "I rocked out pretty hard when I first left So What. I could finally do what I wanted. Then when Jolene and I broke up it got worse. I partied every night. I got drunk. I got high. *Really* high." His eyes were on the floor again. "I wasn't at my best. I wasn't keepin' my nose clean."

I caught what he didn't say out loud. Cocaine. Coke. He'd used cocaine before.

"My best friend in the whole world is probably my younger cousin Rajaa. He was out there with me, and I should've been doing better by him. He's just this normal kid from Slough, and here I am leadin' him to hell. The industry people I was around at the time used to supply the drugs, and sometimes they had women around them, women who would offer up a good time for the right price. I never touched one. When I was hurtin' over Jolene I wouldn't even look at another woman.

"Rajaa was like eighteen at the time, and it was all so shiny and new for him, so he's dabbling here and there with the alcohol and just really havin' a good time. He didn't pay for strange either, but he got so careless he blabbed about what was going on to his brother, and he told somebody in my family, and they told someone, and Naz caught a flight out and did damage control."

"Is Rajaa okay?" I wondered.

Zander nodded. "He only would drink with me. *I* was the one doing more."

"Coke," I said it for him.

In shame, Zander bobbed his head as he fiddled with a ring on his hand. "I got my heart broken and I just wanted to numb the pain for a while."

"I'm not sure if I can do this," I told him honestly. "Like, this is already a lot as it is, but I can't get mixed up in any drugs. I could be your lover, but I can't be your therapist. I'm not a coping mechanism. I am a living, breathing being with a heart and soul."

I didn't like the weed or cigarettes, but at least those things were simpler and not as hedonistic as full-blown cocaine use. It was one thing to worry over infidelity, but to have to stay up all night being terrified over waking up next to a dead body? No, that life wasn't for me.

Zander's head snapped up. "I haven't touched it in a long while."

"What's a long while, Zander?" I needed to know.

"Almost three years. This was after our first breakup. Nazanin tore into me good and I dropped a lot of those people from my circle. I literally fly solo now. After that, Jo and I reconnected and gave it another go, and I never touched the stuff again."

"And your next breakup?"

"I had a terrible attitude, but I managed to keep clean."

"So if I were to walk out that door right now you wouldn't self-destruct?"

Zander was able to loosen up and grin. "No, because I'm not in love with you, Bianka. If I were, I think I'd be able to handle our splitting up. Jo and I broke up for a final time and I've been alone, managing, for almost a year."

It appeared Zander wore his heart on his sleeve when he loved. He had guilt over hurting Ishani, and with Jolie he had been prone to reckless abandon. Standing across from me, leaning against the door post, I was able to really look at him. His cheeks were full and while his muscular figure wasn't swollen and bulky, it was far from thin. There were some people I could just tell were on coke by their gaunt cheeks and skinny frames. Thinking back to his era pre-*Damage Control* when he was dropping singles and music videos, I had seen a few pictures of him where he was slimmer, way slimmer to a scary point.

"Have I scared you away?" Zander prompted.

"I'm just nervous, Zander. You come with a big lifestyle. You will go on the road at some point, and girls are going to throw themselves at you. I've been cheated on before and I stayed and I forgave one time, and the rest is just me with egg on my face."

"That's understandable, assuming we make it to that point where I'm ready to tour. Who's to say I won't be worried about you? You're a gorgeous girl and I'll be all over not knowing what's going on back here."

To that I had to laugh. It made sense that he, too, would worry about my cheating on him, but in comparison, the odds didn't add up. "Fair enough, but I'm serious."

"I promise if we give this a real, true go, I'll be faithful," Zander said. "If you love me, I'll be faithful. If you're in this with me, I'll be faithful."

His words were heavy, but they gave me hope. "Okay."

"Okay," Zander agreed. "And Bianka?"

"Yes?"

"I don't share," Zander said with some authority to his tone, a strong sense of finality.

I was getting ready to agree when his phone rang from the bedside table at the same time mine chirped with a text alert.

It was Monday.

"Duty calls, huh?" I sighed, not ready to get back to the real world just yet.

"I've got a meeting with Paul. There's no avoiding this mess I've made," Zander informed me. "I haven't seen him in a week, so I'm sure he's got some *colorful* things to say to me outside of our talk last night."

"Who's Paul exactly?"

"Paul Caan: the best manager in the biz. He gives it to me straight every time, and I just know he's about to have a field day with this tour thing. Wish me luck?" Zander grinned as he went to gather his phone.

I grabbed mine and found Holliston had texted me three times.

YOU MET ZANDER!!!

It's all over Twitter & Instagram. OMG

Bianka!!!

My heart dropped to my stomach.

No.

It couldn't be real.

"What the hell?" I heard Zander mumble in the background.

I paid him no attention as I went straight to social media, confirming the worst thing possible. On my Instagram app I pulled up the biggest gossip page, The CelebriTea, and sucked in a breath.

There it was. One of their first posts of the day was indeed a photo, no, *several* photos of Zander and me. We were inside Closet Babe together, and so was whoever had been sneaking and taking our pictures. They captured the moment Zander was placing a kiss on my neck, the moment he'd had his arms around me, and when we were holding hands while I looked at earrings. There was no mistaking who I was as my face was seen smiling as clear as day. And though Zander had been sporting black shades, those who were true die-hard fans could tell who he was by his tell-tale tattooed hands, hair, and face.

It had to have been that damn nosy cashier.

There was no time to be upset; I had to get to Victoria. If Holliston knew, there was a big chance Tori did too.

The caption even made my skin crawl as I tore my gaze away from those incriminating images: *Oops, looks like two can play at that game. Zaddy don' got him a baddie, y'all! Over the weekend #ZanderKhalil was seen out shopping with a new flame. The unnamed beauty and the R&B singer were in Larchmont browsing a boutique together. The two were all over each other, our source says. #NoMoreJolie for our man, Zan. He traded in the salt for some Lawry's. You know what they say, y'all #OnceYouGoBlack... ;)*

Zander came and peered at my phone after showing me his very own trending hashtag on Twitter.

"*Lawry's*?" He was confused.

An icky sensation ran through me and I couldn't shake it. The CelebriTea was a gossip page that often wove shade in their breaking news stories. What the fuck was up with that cheesy ass remark about going Black?

The mention only served to rile up nasty comments directed *my* way.

Even though I tried to hide it, Zander could sense my mood shift. "Bianka—"

"I've gotta go find Victoria," I said as I stood and forced interest in shoving my feet into my shoes.

There was still the issue of transporting my clothes from here to my apartment. *Shit.*

"Can I borrow a book bag? I just need to bring my clothes home," I said.

"Yeah." Zander eyed my clothes and then me. "Will you be using a rideshare?"

"Yes, I gotta get on that." I gathered my phone and pulled up my Uber app.

"Bianka."

"You know what I'm going to say."

Zander heaved a sigh. "Then borrow my Bentley. The tank's full of gas and you won't have to worry about paying or tipping somebody."

Had he just...? "Zander, I can't."

"Why not?"

"What if I steal your car?" He had more than a few, and he was a millionaire, so maybe this wasn't a big deal for him.

"What if I break your heart?" he challenged. "You could potentially steal my car, and I could potentially lead you on and break your heart. Neither of us knows how this could play out, but we just have to trust each other."

I hated how right he was in that moment. "Okay."

"Besides," he went on. "If I lend you my car, you're going to have to come back."

I was nervous about going and facing Victoria. I was terrified at the possibility of jumping into a full-on relationship with Zander.

But the funny thing was, the only thing that calmed me down in that moment was going and losing myself in his arms and finally bringing his lips to mine.

Zander held me against him, securing his arms around me, ensuring me that he wasn't about to let go. "I was waiting for you to kiss me." He stared down at me as I gazed up at him. "This'll blow over, I promise. There's nothing to see here, just two people figuring each other out."

"Can I call you *Zandy*?" I teased.

"You can call me whatever you like."

Being in his arms, staying with him felt tempting. But I couldn't be a coward. I had to talk to Victoria.

Zander lent me a Louis Vuitton travel bag and the keys to his black Bentley Continental GT. As I drove to Victoria's apartment, I felt weird behind the wheel of the luxury vehicle. If Zander and I went the distance—imagine that!—I wasn't sure if I could ever get used to his generosity. I believed in even exchanges, and I could never measure up to a millionaire. Not in this lifetime.

In the parking lot to Victoria's apartment building I tried calling first, but it was to no avail. I knew she was home because I was parked beside her Volkswagen.

"Shit, Tori." I sighed and gave up after the second attempt to call her. I *had* to face her.

I took a deep breath and got out of the car.

It was eleven in the morning. There was a chance Tori was asleep, but I knew that was honest wishful thinking.

I went and climbed the steps to her floor and walked over to her unit and knocked on the door, before standing back and waiting. I threaded my fingers together as my hands started to shake.

The door slowly opened and my stomach leaped to my throat and knotted up.

Before me, Victoria was in the doorway. She looked at me with a blank stare.

She knew.

"Tori..." I didn't know what to say.

A pained smile took her face as she lifted her attention to the ceiling, shaking her head in denial. "No fucking way."

"That's what I wanted to talk to you about."

"About what?" she wanted to know as she refused to let me inside to talk properly.

I wondered if she'd hit me, and if I'd take it on the chin and charge it to the "Girl Code."

"About Zander."

"About Zander," Victoria repeated, agreeing eerily calm. "About the one guy I've been obsessed with for the past seven fucking years. The guy *you* rolled your eyes at every time I brought him up? The one guy I was dying to meet?"

Her tone of voice, her coldness, ate at me. "I know, I know, I fucked up, and I'm sorry."

"Sorry?" That hate I'd feared the morning after I hooked up with Zander didn't surface, just betrayal. "Tell me the truth. Just when did you meet him?"

I swallowed as my vision drifted to the ground. "At the concert. I hit one of the scalpers in the face and he pulled a knife on me. Zander came outside to smoke and that's when we linked up. I was going to walk back up front on my own, but he insisted that he give me a lift to be safe." I looked up, finding Victoria engrossed in what I was saying. "It was chaos and I tried to get out of his truck to find you, but he wouldn't let me go. He didn't think it was a good idea. I wanted to call you but my phone was dead and Zander and his guards weren't about to let me use theirs. So we went to his hotel—"

"And you fucked him," Victoria cut in.

"Not right away." I cringed, because in a way, I had. "I was so mad at him for you, and his other fans, and I was snapping at him, called him lazy and compared him to Teddy. One minute he's just sitting there at his piano, and the next he's in my face... I don't know how it happened, but one thing led to another and we just collided." I clasped my hands together hard and loud, imitating the explosive connection Zander and I had found. "It was like everything I've never experienced, and I couldn't even call you up to brag because it was Zander fucking Khalil."

"You lied, Bianka." Victoria was hurt, shaking her head at the sight of me. "And you went back. That's what hurts the most. You should've just told me you met him and you hooked up."

There were no words. Because she was right. I could've told her from the start I'd met Zander. We could've linked up and it could've been her and Zander as an item, as a pair.

But why didn't I like that what-if? The possibility of not having Zander? Of never having started this thing we were trying out?

God. I *was* selfish.

"I'm mad, and I have a client to work on in an hour, so I can't talk right now." Defeat singed through in every word Victoria was saying and I was the cause.

"I'm sorry," was all I could say.

Stiffly, Victoria nodded her head before going inside and shutting the door.

Holliston was waiting on me when I entered Angles for my shift. A few shoppers were inside sifting through our selections while Holliston sat at the service counter. She took one look at me and had to do a double take before immediately making a beeline in my direction.

Zander was a big deal, and I wondered how long it'd be until people recognized who I was, and found me out.

"Oh my God," Holliston let out as she marched over in front of me. She was wearing a T-shirt with Teddy Sykes on it, and I almost asked if it were for my benefit or not. "How the hell...? What the hell...? Bianka."

This was going to be a long day. I got clocked in and put on my name badge and went about preparing to stock new arrivals and read the itinerary for the week's latest sales. Apparently, my coworker, Chekina, called off for the night and Holliston was willing to stay and work her hours. Really, that girl was a saint.

"So?" Holly asked me a couple hours into my shift when business was slowing down.

I propped my elbows on the front desk and hung my head. With Victoria pissed at me—at least, hopefully for the moment, all I had was Holliston. So I unloaded on her, telling her about the wait in line, my naïvely going behind The Warehouse to track Zander down, the scalpers cornering me, Zander stepping in, my slapping Zander, and the rest of our short history.

In the end, Holliston sat beside me so unjudging and open. I loved that about her. We came from two different worlds, her from a middle-class White family who were uber positive and nice, and me from a middle-class Black family that had torn apart the moment the matriarch died. I loved that Holliston tried to just get people and understand. I wasn't a complete pessimist, but next to Holliston's *glass-half-full* persona, I was definitely lacking.

"Wow," she said after I'd finished with the events at Victoria's doorway. Her blue eyes ran over me curiously. "So...do you think he has Teddy's number?"

A random and loud laugh escaped me. "Seriously?"

Holliston shrugged. "What? This is the rarity of all rare things. I have to ask."

"So, Jake is done-done?"

Holliston pouted. "No, we're figuring it out." She picked at her nails, shy about this fact. I wanted to tell her she could do better. Because she deserved better.

"Take it easy, Holl," I said instead.

Holliston gave me a bitter smile and gathered her phone. "I follow all the guys of So What on Twitter. I was on the trend page and saw Zander's name and that's when you popped up. Thank God no one's tagged you...yet. Oh wow," Holliston held her phone up and shook her head, "he's *still* trending. Apparently, some fans bumped into him at a radio station. He's about to be live with Kacey and Eddie of Viibe FM."

I'd just seen Zander, but like an addict, I wanted to hear his voice, to feel better about my sullen mood regarding my very disappointed best friend.

We managed to find the station, Viibe 104.2 FM, and joined in as the station was taking a break from playing music. I recognized notable DJs Kacey Slay and Eddie Heat in the midst of talking.

"*So big surprise right now in the studio today,*" Kacey was saying.

"*Big surprise,*" Eddie echoed.

"*We were just in here lollygagging when one of our producers popped in to tell us Zander Khalil is out in the lobby. You guys have no idea how fast my heart dropped,*" Kacey admitted with a laugh.

"*She literally grabbed her bag and pulled out a tube of lip gloss and a mirror—I kid you not. She never cares how she looks every other day, but today, nah, she had to get ready,*" Eddie said at her expense.

He laughed. Zander. I hadn't known him long but I recognized his laugh instantly. "*Well, it feels good to know that I make a difference. You do look lovely by the way.*"

Kacey ate up the compliment. "*Aww, see, thank you. I only try for the best.*"

"*There you go.*" Eddie groaned. "*We've got the one and only Zander Khalil on air everybody!*"

Someone at the station played an applause track and I could hear Kacey eagerly clapping along with it to welcome Zander in.

"*First of all, hello everyone,*" Zander said, speaking into the mic. "*And thank you guys for having me on such short notice.*"

"*Listen,*" Kacey responded. "*I'm a day one So What fan. I was at them concerts, okay? You can ask all my friends and family who my favorite member was, and they will tell you Zander Khalil. I'm the OG Zan Stan.*"

"*A what?*" Zander asked.

I loved how he didn't always enunciate his Ts. His voice was heavenly. *A wha?* he'd asked, making them all break into lighthearted laughter. I was happy they were easing him into the process of opening up.

"You call your fans 'Zandies,' and I just like to go by 'Zan Stan.' You know, because I'm unique," Kacey explained.

"Kace always gotta be a little extra, don't pay her no mind," Eddie teased next.

"It's cool, I like it," Zander insisted. *"You can be my number-one Zan Stan in my book."*

"Yass!" Kacey hooted into her microphone in victory. Really, I couldn't blame her. After spending some time with Zander, being his favorite seemed like a coveted position. *"Basically, I don't care what day it is, you're always welcome in our studio. Especially when I hear from our producers you've got some exclusive tea to spill."*

"I don't know about 'tea,'" Zander seemed to joke. *"That's a lot of pressure to deliver something juicy."*

"Definitely something juicy. You're one of the quiet ones, like, you're the epitome of the 'anti-celebrity.' There's never really any drama. You drop your music and you go."

"People think I've got this whole mysterious act goin' when it comes to that," Zander noted. *"And really, I just prefer to keep to myself and my family."*

"Usually you're good about that, but today you're literally a trending topic on Twitter, so I'm actually surprised you're here in person," Kacey admitted.

Zander hummed, and I could feel his energy shift to guarded. *"I've been trending for the past week, yeah?"*

"I mean, I saw some things. I'm not gonna lie. We heard there was an important announcement you had to share today. Can I ask if it has anything to do with what's trending?"

There was a pause and dead air hit the soundwaves.

All the playfulness was gone as they treaded on the messiness of the day's gossip: our being outed.

"For the record, you don't have *to tell us anything you don't want to,"* Kacey let it be known. *"Out of respect, we won't pry or make you uncomfortable."*

"*Hmm.*" Zander seemed to hum humorously.

"*Yeah, this is a safe space, and we respect your privacy,*" Eddie added.

Another silence befell the radio and I feared Zander was closing up.

But then he cleared his throat. "*You know...I don't usually like talking about my personal life—because it's my own space and peace, but now is as good a time as any to address something, and then we'll get into why I'm here.*"

"*Say what's on your mind, man,*" Eddie encouraged, sounding serious.

"*There's something going around in the media about someone dear to me. One thing about me is that I'm very protective of those close to me.*"

"*You're talking about the leaked photos of you and this mystery woman?*" Kacey asked to clarify.

"*Yes. Usually, I wouldn't address rumors, but there's stuff being said that's rubbed this person the wrong way, and that rubs* me *the wrong way. You got some blog takin' the piss and sayin' 'Oh, he's got himself a badd'e now who's put him on to Lawry's or whatever.'*"

His mockery of The CelebriTea's post made them all laugh and I found myself chuckling with Holliston as well.

"*Now you know us melanated people like us a little somethin'-somethin' with our food outside of just salt and pepper. No shade,*" Kacey said into her mic.

Zander chuckled. "*Absolutely, but like, it would've been fine if they left it there at the corny comment. But they didn't. There was this gross remark at the end about 'going Black' that just really triggered a lot of unnecessary hate. And she had to see that.*"

"*I hear you,*" Kacey responded. "*I've been caught up looking at the pictures, but I definitely agree with you. There's no need to put a spotlight* there *especially with how hateful social media can be.*"

"*That's where I'm at with it. To broaden my point, it's no secret I was in a popular boy band, a predominantly White group where I*" *was the only Brown one. I dealt with a lot of vicious attacks from fans and the media, and at the time, I just stomached it. With this woman, I'm not going to sit back and do the same thing, because I know how I felt when the world was targeting* me,"Zander said vehemently.

"You know, I'm glad you're bringing this up, because people need to hear this. There's definitely an unfortunate history with people of color in predominantly White groups, like you said, being harassed and ridiculed by fans," Kacey touched next.

"Exactly. This is often a reality for people in my position, and at the time, I bottled it up," Zander said. There was a pause as his words soaked the air, the heaviness in them bringing light to a major problem in the music world. *"But not today. Not for her. I just feel like..."* He seemed to take a moment to collect his thoughts. *"It's easier to pick on her because she's a Black woman, because essentially in the media they're easier targets.*

"No one's defending them but other Black women most of the time, and that defense goes unheard or taken seriously because obviously they're in the same group. I'm not going to stand by any media outlets singling this person out and being cute about it. She's not just *a 'badd'e,' she's a woman, and she's beautiful."*

"Aww," Kacey gushed. *"I like that. And judging by the pictures floating around she's very pretty."*

"Yes," Zander agreed, sending a violent amount of butterflies to my belly. *"She is."*

"To take it a step further, would you say you don't see color?" Kacey prompted.

Zander chuckled. *"I'm not going to be pretentious and say that. I acknowledge she's a Black woman, and she acknowledges I'm an Asian man. I'm not going to center my viewpoint of her on that. I didn't 'go Black.' She's not tradin' anything for masala or whatever."* He managed to laugh at the ridiculousness of it all. *"We're at different walks in life, obviously there's somewhat of a class difference, a cultural difference—but I'm willing to learn things about her and where she's at to meet in the middle. I'm not going to fetishize her, and this is me letting the media know that you aren't going to do that either."*

"*Ooh,*" Kacey purred into her mic. "*I'm lovin' this energy! I'm Latina, and I've definitely had guys in the past who've approached me with a 'Hey, Mami,' and it's just, like, really?*"

"*Exactly,*" Zander responded. "*It just makes it weird, to be honest.*"

"*I definitely feel you, man. Just to add on to what Kacey was saying about these pics, this new girl probably the baddest jawn we've seen you with,*" Eddie spoke up.

Zander came back to the mic on that one. "*See, that's another thing, I don't want you to put down my exes to build up this new woman either. I think we just gotta be respectful all around.*"

"*Ladies, if your man ain't pullin' up to a radio station to clarify some thangs in your honor, then be single,*" Kacey said, hyping up Zander's words.

"*Sheesh,*" Eddie said. "*Zander said I'm checking everybody today!*"

"*We're good, mate,*" Zander said, sounding serious. "*But tell me, do you have a lady in your life? ... Oh, you do. So, would you want anyone being rude towards her with sly little comments? ... No, exactly. Respect me and respect my lady, that's all I ask.*"

"*You say you're not usually this open and vocal, but I gotta say, I'm lovin' this side of you,*" Kacey applauded.

"*I prefer to be super private because I am protective of my space, especially after what I've gone through in the past. But I've learned if something is important to you, then you're going to guard it and keep it safe, and this person is definitely worth it.*"

"*Is this your way of also confirming this is your new boo?*" Kacey asked.

"*I mean, when I'm ready to properly name names and post pictures of my own, we'll get there. For now, don't be rude,*" Zander said. He took another deep breath, his spirit tangibly rising over the radio. "*Now, the reason why I'm here. I just wanted to address last Sunday and my cancelling the other shows. I owe my fan base and the venue the biggest apology. I feel bad about that, I really do."*

"People were saying you were over an hour late, and then just didn't show up out of nowhere," Kacey commented. *"Like, people were really pissed about it."*

"And that's understandable. I'd be upset too if I went out of my way to pay to see someone and they potentially just piss off."

"So, can I ask, what happened? What made you decide to just not do it?"

Zander took a second to think of how to word his issues.

Holliston blew out a breath, nervous and curious at the same time beside me.

"I've just been in my head a lot. It's sorta, like, an uphill battle. I've been dealing with anxiety since I was in So What. Back then, it was easier to manage because I was in a group with four other people and the spotlight wasn't just on me. I could hide within myself. Being solo feels like more exposure; a wall goes up and I psych myself out. I had plans to go on the road, and I think, honestly, I just jumped the gun and pushed 'enter' too soon, you know? Like, I got excited about the idea and didn't think it through enough.

"I once saw a tweet that sorta went, like, 'No one is built to know what a million people think of them.' Or something like that, and it's absolutely true. This life is already a mindf—k as it is being in the spotlight, and tossing in some hate makes it even harder," Zander confessed.

"So, is touring completely off the table?" Eddie asked. *"I know you have to get your head together first—because mental health should always be anyone's top concern before anything. Health is wealth."*

"Thank you. And that's where I am right now. I want to take a good second to breathe and mentally prepare before I jump into this, because I know I'm ready, and seeing the ticket sales, I know my fans are too, and I just am incredibly grateful for all those who've reached out in support of me and haven't jumped ship," Zander stated. *"I've been thinking about Z3 a lot, and I think it'd be better*

if I drop that later this year and then go on tour, make it worth it, make it long and memorable."

"Yo, that'd be fire! I still have your first two albums in heavy rotation. The synergy on Exposed *is just...beyond words, man."* Kacey sounded like she was in a daze, further making me want to hear Zander's first two albums even more.

"Thank you, thank you. Hopefully Z3 can be up there as well."

"Speaking of new music and Z3, what are you working on? Don't just be comin' up in our spot to put us in check, Zander," Eddie said with some sass. *"Sing us a little somethin', let us see you still got it live."*

"Uh, wow, right on the spot then, huh?" Zander laughed into the microphone.

"I'm just sayin', the people want to know what's the hold up, Mr. Khalil," Kacey egged on.

"Uh, um, okay. I've got something that's been tinkering around in my head. So, bear in mind this is a freestyle or whatever," Zander warned.

Eddie clicked his tongue. *"Just as long as the vocals are on point, we rockin' with you."*

"Can we make the room absolutely quiet?" Zander requested.

Someone in the room cleared their throat and all at once the air went silent.

And then I heard his voice, singing a capella:

Your body is a canvas
Baby let me paint the ways
Strokin' in slow motion, babe
Let's get on the same page
I'll sculpt your body right, girl
Makin' art all night
Could drown inside your watercolor, just think I might

Zander sang without flaw or error and then he stopped. *"Okay, that's all I've got."*

"Holy shit, was that off top?" Kacey asked.

"Yeah."

"Damn, I want the full thing."

"You guys can tell me if it's rubbish, it's okay, you won't hurt my feelings. I'm still working it out."

"Nah, I like it, I'm feeling the vibe. Do you write all your music?" Eddie wanted to know.

"I have a hand, yes, but full records not usually. This one I definitely want to write all on my own. The lyrics and the melody are inside my head, and I feel like I could write it all. It's definitely going to be a piano-driven ballad."

"This is a first for you to just take total creative control writing wise."

"I guess you can say I've got the proper muse."

I shut off the radio, unable to take any more.

I stood from the counter to stretch my legs and move, because I couldn't sit still with my mind going a million miles a minute.

"Definitely not a fling," Holliston announced from behind me.

"He just...defended me—*and* Black women, and freestyled a song he's writing for me." I couldn't breathe.

"Victoria will never forgive you at this rate."

Placing my hand to my rapidly beating heart, I willed it to calm down and not think too deeply on things. "Holy shit, he must really like me."

"The sex must've been crazy good," Holliston mumbled.

To that I was able to laugh. "God, what's next?"

"People are definitely going to write fanfiction about you two."

Honestly, God bless Holliston, because she was taking the load off so effortlessly. My life, if I decided to include Zander in it, was about to change, whether I liked it or not. I just hoped it wasn't a bumpy ride.

Customers were coming in in spurts, so we were back to business as I took control of the music and put on Zander's first album. The first track, "Exposure," was only over fifty seconds. It was nothing more than a series of cameras clicking and a menagerie of people—reporters, asking him questions. That track ended and bled into track number two, "The Sound." I really liked that song, especially after our weekend.

Not too long later my cell phone rang, flashing Zander's number and I excused myself to the back to sneak and answer his call.

"Hello?" I was even giddy to speak to him suddenly.

"How's my car?" he quipped.

"Sold it for 50k."

"That's a pity, it's worth a quarter of a million dollars."

My eyes nearly blew out of their sockets. I was *never* driving one of his cars again. "Of course."

He snickered in my ear, making me bite my lip. "How did things go with Victoria?"

My mood sank at the mention of my grief with Tori. "She's pissed."

"Give her some time. This is new and a fresh wound," he said gently.

I was going to give Victoria a couple of days before I tried again. With her being my closest friend, I couldn't lose her, not over a guy. "How was Paul?"

On his end, Zander sighed. "Fantastic. He told me to go out there and bleed for my fans, and so I went on the radio today."

"I heard, and thank you."

"It's nothing."

"When did you become a social justice warrior?" I teased.

"From the beginning of my career there's always been Black women on my team somewhere getting us right. I've heard a lot of conversations and asked a lot of questions along the way," Zander said. "Are you okay?"

"I didn't like that post, and I'm happy you said something for me." Especially since he never stood up for *himself* in the past. "In all seriousness, thank you, for stepping out of your comfort zone and standing up for me. For more than just me."

"You're always going to be protected around me, I promise. I'll always defend you, Bianka."

Outside of Victoria, I couldn't imagine anyone willing to take on the world for me. The fact that Zander did so easily meant more than I could say.

To keep my emotions in check, my mind drifted back to his singing. "And when you said you were writing a song about me, I had no idea you were serious."

"Do you like it?"

"Holy fuck, Zander," I let out. "I love it and you don't even have a chorus. I usually always wait for the chorus before I decide, but I love it already, I really do. In fact, we're playing your music right now in the store."

"I hear it faintly," Zander said.

"You should stop by sometime and gain me some cool points with my coworker. She's actually a big fan."

"Funny how that works out, huh? Everyone around you is a fan, and you aren't."

"I've since been persuaded otherwise."

Zander's chuckle made me hot, made me wish I were there with him instead of working. "Give it time. My fans can be damn near as good as the cops. They might find you. Zandies can be a bit obsessive. I didn't want to out you or say your name until I knew you were comfortable with me addressing you, *us*, in public."

He was respectful. "Zander?"

"Yes, Bianka?"

"I'm kinda, entirely, scared right now," I admitted.

The line was quiet for a while and I feared he was going to take a step back.

"Do you trust me?" he asked when he spoke up.

Did I?

Thinking about it, from our beginning, he stuck his neck out for me, sweetly stepping in with the scalpers, not letting me get potentially trampled in that chaos of the riot outside The Warehouse, and even now when he defended me on air. I didn't know where this could go and if it would last, but one thing I felt deep in my gut, was trust.

"Yes," I said.

"Then no matter what comes our way, I'm going to be with you, protecting you, so long as you're along for the ride."

12

STILL GOT TIME

It didn't blow up overnight. In fact, my identity was still a mystery a few days after news broke out.

There was a woman who had come forward, claiming to be me, and really, it was laughable at best. Fame was the deadliest drug of all.

What wasn't funny was the fact that Victoria and I still hadn't talked. I'd tried calling and texting her Wednesday, only to be ignored. An hour later she shot me a text.

> Sorry for the delay. I finally got a full schedule this week. Beyond BOOKED & BUSY. We will talk as soon as I get a min

As Friday evening rolled around with no word from her, I told myself to give her the weekend before meeting with her face to face.

Long after I got in from Angles, I sat curled up on my couch flipping through the TV, debating on ordering a pizza or not. Extra-large cheese sounded good. I once went through a phase of not eating red meat and swapped out my beloved pepperoni for cheese, and it became a quick fave.

I was about to sift through my Postmates app when my cell phone rang.

Zander was calling.

We hadn't spoken since Monday, which I understood since he had a lot of work to do for his upcoming album.

"Hello?" I picked up, anxious to speak to him after so long.

"Hey," Zander greeted me, his voice sounded chill and mellow. Maybe he was smoking. "I know I've been distant, and I'm sorry. I've been locked in the studio all week."

"You have a career, I get it," I said. "It's okay."

"I miss you," he said softly. "Is that weird?"

After spending a weekend together, and then the week after apart, I was missing him too.

"No, I've been listening to your music, watching videos and interviews all week. I miss you too."

"You like my albums?"

"Yes, *Exposed* was such a solid debut with no skips. I love *Damage Control* too, but *Exposed* is my fave of the two for sure."

"Any favorite records?"

The lyrics to one of the songs I was obsessed with came to mind and I closed my eyes and almost got lost in the vibe.

"Outside of 'The Sound'? I gotta go with 'Chill,' 'Make it Last,' and 'Freak for You.'"

I refused to fangirl over the guy now that I liked his music. I had some dignity about myself. I *still* didn't follow him on Twitter.

"Come over," Zander begged. "I want to see you."

Being playful, I said, "Nah, I'm good right now."

Zander clicked his tongue. "I thought you were my number-one fan."

"I said I liked your music now. I didn't say nothing about being a fan or your number one at that."

Zander sighed. "You still have my car."

"Oh, do I?"

"Bianka."

Clearly he was grasping at straws now. "Out of all the cars you have, you need to drive this one?"

"That's not all I want to drive."

My phone vibrated with a text alert and I put him on speaker to see that *he* was also texting me. I almost ignored it, but out of curiosity I checked our messages to find he was sending me an X. Just like I told him to do whenever he wanted to hook up again. Cute.

"Come get it." I hung up, feeling victorious.

He called me back immediately and I declined it. I couldn't make it easy for him, no matter how much a part of me wanted to go running back to the Hills to spend another weekend with him.

It wasn't a full ten minutes later when Zander texted me, wiping the smirk off my face.

7146 Frederick Blvd, Hemingway Park, CA 90255

Shit. He knew my address, at least, the address to my apartment building.

This time when he called, I picked up.

"Technology is a lovely thing, Bianka," Zander said to me.

Smart move. If I owned a fleet of expensive rides, I'd probably plant GPS tracking on them too.

"So, uh"—I cleared my throat—"I'm going to throw some pants on and swing by."

His husky chuckle made me squirm. "You do that, pack that LV bag as well. I hope you can spare another weekend."

"I work tomorrow night," I said. "I'm off Sunday, so maybe I'll come back."

"Maybe?"

"Too much of me and you'll OD."

"Well, I wasn't plannin' on livin' forever."

I couldn't explain how good it felt to be wanted, and not just for sex. After laying up and watching movies with him, I knew it was more. After trying to leave and having him hold me back, I knew it was more. After he stood up to the media and his sister for me, I knew it was more.

I took a shower and dressed in a simple T-shirt and jeans combo before packing his LV bag with overnight essentials. I left enough room in the bag to stow away a backpack so I could bring my items back home with me. It was in doing this that I realized that I was once again stranded at Zander's home in my driving his Bentley back to him. Somehow, we'd have to come to an understanding about my choosing to use a rideshare as opposed to using his cars. There was the chance he could drop me off, but I wasn't about to let him see where I lived.

Victoria was a freelance makeup artist for a popular cosmetic company, making more than enough money to afford her *much* nicer apartment on the north side of Hemingway Park. This was simply the best I could do. My shower was so old the tiles were nearly falling off the wall, not to mention the hideous support bar screwed into the wall. Rod used to try to do his best to not wrinkle his nose whenever he slept over.

Stop comparing him to Rod, Bia!

It wasn't fair, but still, from the pristine penthouse suite at The Residence Hotel to his own home, Zander was used to the finer things in life.

You're worth it, girl. Where you're from and where you live doesn't define you.

After a good mental pep talk and self-assurance, I gathered the keys to Zander's Bentley, went down to the resident parking lot, and climbed in behind the wheel.

Next stop, happiness.

It was the weekend, and traffic was a pain. It took an hour to get to Zander's gated estate in Beverly Hills where I used his pin to let myself inside. An hour spent in his car, listening to his music. The old Bia was quaking.

After reluctantly turning off the engine and shutting off "No Boundaries," I texted Zander that I'd arrived and he came out to greet me and help me with my bag. Ever the respectful gentleman.

"Hello," he said to me as he crossed over from his front walk to the parking area.

Looking up from grabbing his LV bag, I froze.

I—

Zander was wearing my shirt, or, the one with the Yin and Yang patch embroidered on the chest I'd bought for him. He probably owned a million shirts, far better and pricier ones, but he was wearing the twenty-dollar shirt I'd bought him from Closet Babe. I was more than sure he'd gotten the shirt to make me feel better about his buying me clothes. Still, he was wearing it.

I was proud of him in that shirt. The sight of it put me even more at ease. I would stop running, I would stop downplaying what this could build up to, and I would enjoy it for every moment that it was.

Even more, as Zander came over to me, I forgot about the bag and went and wrapped my arms around him, going and giving him a kiss. It was meant to be a quick peck, but quick wasn't our style. Zander's arms locked me against him as his lips returned to mine, letting me know how much he'd missed my company since Monday.

He smelled like cigarettes and weed, but he didn't taste like it. He'd brushed his teeth and rinsed with mouthwash before my arrival and I appreciated the gesture. I liked how together and orderly Zander seemed to be. How he even kept his nails trimmed and clean.

I just really liked Zander Khalil.

He carried the bag inside and accepted his keys as we stood in the foyer. The joy in his dark eyes as he glanced at me, taking me in, made me look away to hide my blush. Why were we so giddy?

Give us time, and we'd probably turn into one of those corny couples.

"I've got some takeout in the kitchen, you interested?" Zander asked after setting the bag on the bottom step.

"Yes, I'm starving."

I followed him into the kitchen where I saw he had takeout from famous local fried chicken chain Freddy's Fried Chicken. The smell of it made my mouth water. Freddy's had the best chicken, better than any of the international chains out there, not to mention their sides were bomb too. You could taste the soul in every bite.

Zander came up next to me, gesturing to the array of food he'd purchased. "I eat a *lot* of chicken."

Chicken was good, chicken was very versatile. "Fine by me."

"I didn't get to make my chicken karahi for you, but I will, I promise." The fact that he really wanted to cook for me made me happy.

"Can't wait."

"My butter chicken's pretty good too."

"I'll eat all your chicken, I promise."

Zander smiled, coming and planting a kiss on my temple. "Let's eat."

We unpacked the chicken and the sides at the island and ate together side by side. We were different in many ways, but I liked learning that we both liked the thighs the most, and wings were a close second. Chicken breasts were too dry when they were fried to me, which was why I mostly only ate them baked or diced in chicken alfredo. Zander mirrored my opinion as he told me he was that customer that made things difficult by requesting buckets of thighs and wings only.

"How are things with Victoria?" he asked me as we finished eating.

"We haven't spoken since Monday. She's busy with work, and I've been the same."

Zander squinted. "What's she even look like?"

"Tori's beautiful." I gathered my phone and found a recent

picture of us together and showed him. "She would've had you doing a double take."

Zander admired her photo and I watched as his eyes softened. "She's cute, but I don't think it would've worked."

That was the other reality, that even if I hadn't have slept with him, there was still the chance he wouldn't have met and fallen for Victoria. "Why not?"

Zander reached out, coiling his finger in my hair. "Because she liked me already, and *you* didn't."

I side-eyed him. "Bet it served your ego well having me fall for you."

The dirty look on his face gave me my answer. "You have no idea the pleasure it was bedding you that first night. I enjoyed it for the feel of you, but watching you *want* and *need* it after you hated me..." He closed his eyes and took in a breath through his nose before opening them. "That felt fucking good."

"Still," I said, getting serious again. "You have to meet her, because she's been a fan since we were eighteen, and I do feel guilty for that. It was her *birthday* weekend and...yeah, bad Bianka."

Zander's brows shot up. "Her birthday?"

I cringed and nodded. "Really shitty friend here."

Technically, she was the Gemini, and yet *I* was the one being two-faced.

"And she's taking it really hard?"

It probably sounded ridiculous to him. "There's being a fan, and then there's being a *stan*, that fine line of total obsession and devotion."

Zander's fingers traced the skin on the back of my hand as he angled his head. "Won't you be my stan?"

I leaned close, teasing. "No. Parasocial relationships don't interest me."

Zander tapped my hand. "That's too bad." He settled back and became serious. "We'll think of something to make it better. I don't want you to lose her over me, and I don't want to lose her as a loyal fan because she came out to see me and I feel terrible I didn't show."

Right, his attempt at making things better was his new album. The yet-to-be titled *Z3*.

"How's that going by the way?" I asked. "You've been in the studio every night this week."

"I love it." Zander lit up, and I could tell he was in his element during his creative process. "I could do ten songs a night if I wanted."

I nudged him. Curious. "How's that one for me going?"

"'Canvas' is finished," Zander told me.

"Can I hear it?"

"Absolutely not." He turned away from me and began gathering our leftovers to store in his fridge. "It drops next Friday, though. I went to the studio Monday and I found the melody and wrote the lyrics. Tuesday I laid down my vocals, and they mixed and mastered it yesterday. We want it to be the lead single for Z3. Paul thinks it's really good."

I narrowed my eyes. "You wrote a song about *my* body, and I can't hear it before the rest of the world?"

Zander hung his head as he shut the refrigerator. "I'm nervous, Bi."

A nickname—although I really liked hearing *Bianka* from him. I didn't let this distract from the fact that he was being really stingy.

"Please don't go cliché and quote Erykah Badu and tell me how you're an artist and are 'sensitive about your shit,'" I mocked.

Zander focused on throwing out the trash. "Well, I am."

Unbelievable. "I guess you won't be seeing your inspiration until next Friday then, huh?"

Zander looked up at me, eyeing me funny. "Bianka."

I folded my arms. "Zander."

Shit. He really was nervous about this song, despite being happy to be creating new music, previewing some of it for me, about me, was something that made him shy.

Before I could give in, Zander yielded and gestured out of the room. "I have a cut on my mobile, but... Let's go hear it live."

I led the way to his living room. Right away, I noticed on top of the piano was a notepad and upon closer inspection, in Zander's sharp handwriting, I could make out a building track list for his album. At the top of the pad he'd scrawled *Z3*, and then by asterisks he written down several song titles.

* Canvas
* Trial & Error
* War
* I Never

"Nosy, nosy, nosy." Zander materialized behind me, coming and snatching the writing pad away from me.

"Sorry," I let him know.

He snuck me a look. "Bear in mind this is my *first* song I've written on my own. There's still time to get someone on my team to step in and perfect it, but I just thought that it was good by my sole hand since I know the source material so close and personal. If it's terrible, Bianka, just—"

"Zander." I placed my hand on his arm. "Just shut up and play."

After heaving a sigh, Zander sat at the piano and let his fingers flow across the keys. The melody was solid, confident, and strong as he played. For a while, that was all he did, building himself up to sing to me what he'd written so intimately. When he opened his mouth and let out the first note, my breath got caught in my throat and remained there until he was finished.

Your body is a canvas
Baby let me paint the ways
Strokin' in slow motion babe
Let's get on the same page

I'll sculpt your body right, girl
Makin' art all night
Could drown inside your watercolor, just think I might

'Cause when I make love to your body, it feels like I'm drawing
instead
Feels like I'm at my easel, when I'm with you in bed
Illustrating every shade of you, I gotta confess
Darlin' you are my canvas, every time you undress

Ain't nobody in this gallery
It's just me and you
Baby I am the artist
And you are my muse
Inside these walls is a masterpiece
And you are Mona Lisa

'Cause when I make love to your body, it feels like I'm drawing
instead
Feels like I'm at my easel, when I'm with you in bed
Illustrating every shade of you, I gotta confess
Darlin' you are my canvas, every time you undress

Blending myself inside of you
This is more than sex

'Cause when I make love to your body, it feels like I'm drawing
instead
Feels like I'm at my easel, when I'm with you in bed
Illustrating every shade of you, I gotta confess
Darlin' you are my canvas, every time you undress

Picasso. Van Gogh
Take off your clothes
Let's create a show

He played a mini solo of the instrumental after he was finished, taking my breath away even more.

Oh wow.

There were no words for the beautiful melody he'd sung to me. The lyrics. The metaphor. The meaning. The depth.

Zander sheepishly looked at me beneath his thick eyelashes. "The studio version is much better, I swear. When the other sounds come in, it really takes it to another level. Paul thinks it's the perfect comeback—"

I crossed the distance between us, straddled his lap, and kissed him with all that I had.

Dressed in just Zander's Versace robe, I sat next to him on his daybed out by the pool. I was still coming down from our tryst in his bedroom. I couldn't even hold a glass of water we'd come to find out after we came down to the kitchen on our way outside.

Staying true to Zander's lyrics, we'd made passionate love in his bed. My fingers got lost in his hair, my lips were locked in against his, and he caressed me so gently and intently, I almost had my orgasm just from that alone. I decided then and there that slow was my favorite tempo between us. It felt more raw, intense, and vehement.

After, he held me against his chest, whispering, "This is art, Bianka."

Indeed it was.

I also thought it was music. Our bodies were the composers to our sweet, silent symphony. An orchestra of two.

Zander sat on the edge of the daybed while I lay on my side beside him. He was enjoying a bottle of water as he looked out at the pool.

This was a peace I could never get tired of.

"I know we're just finding our footing in this thing we're doing—"

"*Dating,*" he cut in.

"Right. But if you ever tattoo your face, I'm out." There were way too many people doing that these days, and while it was clear to see Zander loved tattoos, I just could not look at him if he put ink on his beautiful face.

Zander laughed. "Already promised my mum I wouldn't."

Good. "Points for Mama Khalil."

Zander chuckled and reached over, cupping my knee and patting it. "I'm debating on leaving it at my sleeves. I miss the feel of it." His eyes ran over my legs. "You ever think about a tattoo?"

I shook my head. "Nah, I preferred piercings."

"You don't have any."

"My body hates me," I confessed. "I got my nipples pierced at eighteen and my body just rejected them."

"Rejected?" Zander repeated, confused.

"Like they never healed. I did the sea-salt soaks and everything, but they didn't adapt. The day after my one-year anniversary, I took them out to shower and in that ten-minute interval one closed. I kept the other in for another year before finally giving up. Then last year I got my nose pierced and it wouldn't cooperate either. I gave that up like three months later. If I did get a tattoo, the thing would probably get infected out of spite."

Zander frowned in pity. *He* had a perfectly fine nose ring and a few piercings in his ears, and yet I sat defeated. My mother had pierced my ears when I was two, but I hardly wore earrings due to the lengths of my bundles. It was sorta pointless really.

"What did housekeeping say about the peach stains on your sheets back at the hotel?" I wondered.

Zander blushed, his bronze cheeks seeming to glow with radiance. "*That* was interesting. I had an excuse ready, but they must be used to that kind of thing because she didn't bat an eye. She didn't look me in mine either, but she didn't make a fuss."

I couldn't imagine being a maid and all the sordid things they must've discovered the morning after.

The night went on and at the thought of the upcoming week,

I sat up and faced Zander some more. "What's your game plan to pump people up for your new album and tour?"

"Paul says I need to be more active on social media," Zander said. "I'm going to tweet more and interact more. We're already brainstorming the 'Canvas' video. He was thinking of a rapper jumping on it."

I held my hand up. "It's fine on its own."

Zander was bashful. "Really?"

His first album had one collaboration with Ariana Grande, and I could admit she was good, her vocals mixed with his were worth gold, but on his second album he had two features that didn't quite fit him. "If you do a collab you should stick with a singer, but not on 'Canvas.' You can sell that on your own. If it does really good, then maybe find a rapper, could be Wale since he's amazing with metaphors and poetry."

"And singers for the album?" Zander was full-on listening to my every word, really interested in my general input.

"Like one or two at the most, one male and one female. If I had to pick, maybe Sevyn Streeter, Chloe Bailey, Layton Greene, Arin Ray, The Weeknd, or Miguel."

Zander bobbed his head. "I'll keep them in mind. Another one I've been wanting to work with is Luke James."

Immediately I perked up at that mention. "Yass!"

Zander peered off into the distance, seemingly in thought. "Paul's thinkin' big names and I'm not trying to do numbers for the sake of doing numbers. I want to be able to look at this project and be proud because it's genuine and pure."

I nudged him. "Hey, *you're* a big name, too."

He peered up at the sky. "Barely."

"Zander," I scolded him, unable to believe he thought so little of himself.

He came back to me, calm, whole, grounded. "I don't really want 'fame,' but like, the admiration of my art, you know? The spotlight and the charts and all that, doesn't really appeal to me. I just want people to hear my record and feel connected or inspired.

I want to be respected as an artist above anything. I do really like Sevyn, and of course Miguel and The Weeknd are amazing. I'll give those others a listen."

I was happy he cared about my opinion versus his manager's. "You know, I was thinking," I paused, nervous, "I know you're you, but maybe once a week on a Saturday, or *Zaturday*, you could drop a cover on your YouTube account to get the fans buzzing. You've got such a good voice and you love singing; I think they'd appreciate hearing you take on songs you love and that touch you. Plus, it's humble and down-to-earth."

Zander didn't take offense to the suggestion. "What should I cover first?"

I bit my lip. "Prince, 'Insatiable.' The shower edition may be my favorite version, but I'm sure you could do it justice out of the water, too."

His fingers moved across my skin, his thumb swirling in circles. "I want your honest opinion all the way through this, Bianka."

Truthfully, I'd been thinking about the weekend cover videos all week. I was honestly surprised he wasn't against it. It seemed once musicians got too big they never did covers.

I was late in becoming a Zandy, but I was very much anticipating Z3. "I'm happy to be your eyes and ears on this."

He stood, holding his hand out to me. "Let's go work on tomorrow's cover then, yeah?"

I took Zander's outstretched hand and stood, joining his side on the walk back inside the house.

I was terrified at the idea of loving him, I would admit, but wherever the ride took us, I was down for it all.

13

NATURAL

It was Paul's idea before he even met me.

With Zander's new single set to debut on Friday, he was in need of cover art for the song's artwork. Paul suggested I pose for the album art, *nude*. Since the song was about my body, what better image to use than my naked torso?

It took a bit of convincing on Zander's part Sunday night before I agreed to accompany him to a photography studio Monday afternoon after I got off work. In the end, it worked out perfectly since I got to drive my Sentra to his house and was in control of my coming and going.

While I was willing to do the shoot free of charge, Zander insisted and pulled strings to where I would be paid a thousand dollars for the time it took to get the right look. He wanted extra shots of me to use for the album booklet to the physical CD of Z3. A process he was completely into and hands-on about.

Zander promised me a closed set, and after I came out of my dressing room in just a silk robe, I found only the photographer, her assistant, the backdrop I'd shoot against, and Zander in the large spacious room. The bright lights were on and waiting for me to take my place in front of the white screen. In my dressing room, I'd put on a minimal amount of makeup and tousled my hair. I was as together as I would ever be.

Anxiety filled my belly as I approached Zander and the photographer. Mentally, I coached myself to go through with it. I was in the best shape of my life—I *looked* good naked, why not show it off anonymously while I still could? I had an amazing brown complexion. I loved my medium hue, why not embrace and flaunt it? I was young and pretty, why not immortalize this moment forever in a photograph?

Blowing out a breath, I was finally ready to step in front of the camera and disrobe.

"Nervous?" Zander came over to me with the photographer, an older woman who gave me a gentle smile. "This is our photographer for the day, Sam Wilson, and that's her trusty assistant Natalie. Sam's one of the best in town. I specifically asked for her because I figured a woman would make you more comfortable."

I appreciated the effort, because it was a little easier to do this with a woman taking my nude photo than a man. Almost like going to the doctor for a physical checkup.

My eyes cut to Zander as my heart filled with nothing but admiration for him. I could respect him forever after this day. He wanted me paid and comfortable—he in no way was taking advantage of me, making my trust so easy to give up.

"Nice to meet you." Sam stuck her hand out for us to shake properly in greeting.

I took her calloused hand in mine and shook and offered up a smile. "Nice to meet you, too. I'm Bianka."

"Looking forward to shooting you today. Zander is in charge of the shoot and he already has a vision for you," Sam said to me, pulling Zander close and squeezing him.

"Sam's going to shoot you and someone on our design team back at the office is going to do the Photoshop to finish it off."

Okay, I wasn't flawless, but I had to ask, "*Photoshop?*"

"I want, like...a stroke of gold paint spelling out the title of the song." Zander took a step back and examined me, his eyes envisioning my nudity under my robe. "I think I want you for my album cover, too. The title for Z3 popped into my head last night."

"What?"

Zander flashed me that mischievous half grin of his. "*Abstract.*"

Abstract, I mumbled the name to myself. "I like it."

"Sounds good to me," Sam agreed. "Are we ready to—"

Knocking sounded in the background, loud and demanding as the doorknob jiggled rapidly.

Sam peered towards the door across the room as Natalie went and answered it. In seconds, a man breezed into the studio, sizing up the tiny assistant before coming our way.

"Why is the door locked?" he asked Natalie before facing us. "Why is the set locked?"

He was young, tall, blond, muscled, and dressed in a designer dress shirt that was tucked into equally expensive-looking dress pants, and on his feet were what was surely pricy loafers. On his face was a pair of dark tinted aviators he ripped off as he came to a stop a few feet away from where Zander, Sam, and I were standing.

"Greetings." His teeth were perfect—and all his, not like those Chiclet-looking veneers most famous people were too quick to run out and buy. No, this man took care of his teeth and he deserved to show them off. Despite his rude arrival, he was handsome with a nice smile.

"Paul," Zander said, sighing beside me. "We're shooting the artwork for my single."

Paul bobbed his head, gesturing around us. "I know that."

"She's going to be naked," Zander went on.

Paul's green eyes slid over to me, trailing down my body. "Aware." Impressed, he simply shrugged and faced Zander. "I take it you want me out in the hall?"

"Would you, please?" Zander asked.

Paul sighed, and tucked his aviators into his shirt and went to leave, but not without taking one quick glance at me. A dark brow raised as he boldly checked me out again.

"We'll do the introductions later," Zander assured me. "For now, let's get the show on the road, yeah?"

Natalie was kind enough to step out of the shoot as well, leaving me to my director and photographer. To set the mood, Zander put on some music.

"Any requests?" he prompted as he stood by the speakers.

"Teddy Sykes," I teased.

He peered back at me, giving me a warning look, not a trace of humor on his face. *Whoa.*

"Surprise me," I said with an innocent chuckle.

Soon, the sounds of Ro James filled the room as I went and stood in front of the backdrop. Zander came and helped me out of my robe. Goose bumps were quick to cover my skin as I stood naked in front of Sam and her camera, despite the heat from the lights shining directly on me. Zander went and stood back, getting out of the way.

"Okay, just relax, breathe, get used to the idea," Sam instructed as she squatted down and brought her camera to her eye. "I'm just going to take a couple of test shots for us all to unwind. Zander's going to step in and let you know how he wants you to pose."

I did as told, practicing a few deep breaths before uncovering my breasts and bikini area and tentatively allowing my arms to fall to my sides. Closing my eyes, I took a final breath before channeling my inner model.

Focus, Bia.

Memories of the younger me watching *America's Next Top Model* with my mother came to mind and I got in the zone as I imagined myself preparing for a high-profile fashion campaign.

Zander was strictly professional as he started instructing me on how to pose. He had me arch my back, turn around and look over my shoulder, get on the ground and prop one leg up as I lay back on my arms. He posed me a ton of different ways, and what I liked best was that none of my positions were sleazy or provocative—it was art. All of my essential parts were covered, with only a sense of under-boob or side-boob.

After an hour of shooting, and a full camera roll, we called it a day and I was all too happy to go and get dressed.

"She's going to e-mail me, and our art director will take over from there. I can't wait to see the final product," Zander said to me after I finished getting dressed. He smiled at me, a softness to his eyes. "I can't thank you enough for doing this for me."

I'd gotten paid a stack for my amateur attempt at being a model. I almost thanked him for paying my rent—and then the wording and idea lessened my smile and my mood.

Zander was too busy on cloud nine to notice. "You looked amazing." He soon snuck me a lascivious glance. "But then we both know that, don't we?"

I loved how attracted to me Zander was and vice versa. I could never not feel sexy or desirable with him around, looking at me, studying me, adoring me.

Taking a moment, I stood on my toes and kissed him as my fingers got lost in the hair at the nape of his neck. He closed his eyes and brought his arms around me, keeping me safe in this bubble of us. *Zander.* Everything was new and extraordinary with him. The way he fucked, and there was no touching the way he made love. Kissing him made my soul melt into a puddle of want and need. Zander was romance, poetry, and eroticism, wrapped in an incredibly good-looking package. He was too good to be true, because even his flaws weren't that major.

This was quite the level-up I never saw coming.

"Well, how'd we do?" Paul was waiting out in the lobby, pacing back and forth. He'd been on his cell, but he didn't hesitate to end the call before crossing over to us as we stepped out of the studio.

"She did good," Zander said, flashing me a proud smile. "You should be thanking her, by the way."

Paul was confused, his brows furrowing and his forehead adopting a crease. "For what? She got paid, didn't she?"

Zander frowned. "Because she stepped up and did such an amazing job and killed it in there."

Paul didn't see it this way as he took me in. "It's the least you could do; the guy's writing sappy love songs for you."

"*Sappy*?" Zander repeated, backhanding his chest. "I thought you liked it."

"It's good. Your female fans will eat it up. I like your dirtier records; that's more my vibe." Paul gave me a helpless shrug. "My type of sex is more impersonal. Leave a twenty on the nightstand after a night of just destroying—"

Zander scowled. "Don't be a pig."

Paul blew him a kiss. "Oink, oink, baby." Returning to me, he went on. "Point is, you got my boy whipped. He's defending you on radio shows—which is fine. I support it a hundred percent. But what this team is about, and needs, is loyalty."

"Just because we're friends doesn't mean he's entitled to me stripping off my clothes and posing naked for his single cover," I spoke up. "So, him asking was him coming correct, and him thanking me, is him being grateful, Paul."

Paul's face scrunched up as his lips made an O shape. "Feisty, isn't she?" He nudged Zander on the sly. "Careful, this one bites."

"Watch your words," Zander warned. "I already had to get on Nazanin about *her* mouth."

Paul took a sip of his blue drink I suddenly realized was in his hand, going and looking at me with new eyes. "So, you met, Naz, huh? And you still have your pretty face? Must've been an off day for the ol' lioness, eh?"

His unfiltered approach to Zander had me curious who exactly was in charge.

"Actually, it was the other way around. Bi doesn't take any shit," Zander said with a proud look on his face.

Paul hummed and swished around the remainder of his drink. "Interesting."

"You do know you work for him, right?" I came out and asked.

Paul only smirked. "Yes, just like I know I'm the best. Don't let his little golden boy routine fool you; I'm one of the last few people willin' to work with him." He snuck Zander a glance that had him bowing his head. "Tell her about your old management team? Your assistant?"

Zander didn't look at me and Paul took it as his cue to go on. "Zan here is a complicated artist to manage and deal with. He isn't blackballed, but a lot of people talk and they knew he was too hot to touch." He gestured to himself. "Me, I'm an asshole and proud, I can dish and I can take. Zan tries to get mouthy with me and I'll pop his ass."

Zander clicked his tongue and Paul laughed it off.

"I'm the last one on Zander's side, so trust me, Bianka, I'm not the enemy," Paul concluded. To show support, he reached out and patted my arm. "But I am grateful for you. As we all know, Zan's been in a bit of a rut for a minute, but you, you pretty little muse, have him inspired again. Your idea about Zaturday was a smash hit." He gathered his phone and made a few clicks before bringing up Zander's YouTube account with his latest upload of his cover of Prince's "Insatiable" we'd shot and filmed Friday night. "It's only been, what, two days? It already has almost two million views and people are talking about the notes my boy can hit. Zander deserves to be much further in his career, so we just gotta keep pushing for the best."

I decided Paul was harmless, probably one of those people who didn't sugarcoat shit and just said what was on their mind. I could keep up, and as long as he learned his place with me, we'd be fine. One thing, though, he seemed good for Zander, not an exact yes-man, and not an employee who overstepped their boundaries either.

But then, I wondered what was the story behind Zander and his old management team.

"I'm going to head home. I got a few phone calls to make if

we're going to put together this music video," Paul said. "And be prepared for a radio press run Friday to promote this song, because the world needs to see that pretty mug of yours if you want this world tour to go through. I think Teddy just released something and he's on the circuit, too, so expect the typical bullshit So What questions."

"Oh wow, the music video. What's your plan for that?" I wanted to know.

"Zan's got a cute little idea—I'll let him tell you. Have any clues as to who you want to cast for the female lead? What *look* you have in mind?" Paul asked in a coded manner instead of blatantly just coming out and questioning if Zander was going to use a Black model for his video of "Canvas."

Zander's expression was empty now as he stood beside me. "Try to find me a South Asian model."

Paul nodded and tipped his head towards me before once more hopping on his phone as he walked away.

The lobby was empty outside of the receptionist across the room at the front desk. The large floor-to-ceiling windows on the wall to our right illustrated how night had fallen upon us as the sun was now lower in the sky.

Zander took a step back and stared at me, and I knew something was wrong. "You look like you have a question, as do I. Should you go first?"

Business mode once more.

Fine, I was too curious to let it go. "What's the story with your old team?"

Zander escorted me onto the nearby elevator and blew out a breath before he spoke.

"They dropped me." He peeked at me, ashamed. "I wasn't comfortable performing, or touring—I refused to tour for my first album, and being that the tour bag is massive, my manager didn't like that I was wasting my potential, that I wasn't milking all my opportunities. They wanted me to do movie cameos, guest spots on competitions, and that's just not me. So they walked away.

"I was on my own, and I was angry—a hothead. When I was trying to put together *Damage Control* it was hard finding someone willing to jump in. Paul approached me and just straight up didn't give a fuck about my past. He told me he was willing to get in the ring with me, so long as I was willing to keep fightin' until the end."

Blunt or not, Paul had a heart there. With Zander not ready to tour, he was missing out on major money, which was probably why a lot of people didn't want to touch him. While this was still about business, Paul willing to work with Zander said a lot about him, as if money wasn't the motivator behind his decision.

"And your assistant?" I asked.

"What's there to assist when I'm in a rut?"

Understandable.

"So," Zander went on. "In my life, when I'm crashin' down, the only two people who can get a hold of me and set me straight these days are Nazanin and Paul. My parents allow me to be an adult, so they don't step in, but Naz doesn't care about that. She's like a second mum sometimes. Paul's...what, thirty-three? Outside of the business, he's like the older brother I never had. I do my best to listen to him, because I am grateful he stepped up to work with me when I was on fire."

Zander was from the UK. Here in the States, he had no one. If he ever went on a self-destructive path, there wasn't much to stop him. It was good that Paul cared beyond work, and even though she was in another country, Nazanin stepped up where their parents wouldn't.

I was beginning to question if Zander saw a therapist when our elevator reached our floor and Zander led me towards the exit. Or, he started to, before he stopped and faced me, armed with his own inquisition. "Now, why did you call me your 'friend' when you were talking to Paul?"

Ah, he'd caught that. "Because we *are* friends, Zandy." I

reached out and patted his chest, something that didn't amuse him.

"Bianka."

"What?"

He shook his head. "Why won't you address this as what it is: dating."

"Because you haven't taken me on a date."

Zander blinked. "A date?"

"That's the main component in dating, actually going out and wining and dining each other. Otherwise, we're just friends who occasionally screw around," I pointed out.

Zander folded his arms, staring at me curiously. "So you want to go on a date?"

"Uh, yeah, duh. Court me, I'm worth it."

Zander checked the time on his phone. "Wanna grab a bite and go to the cinema?"

It wasn't extravagant and luxury, but something down-to-earth and low-key. "That sounds perfect."

He took a dangerous step closer, flashing me a dirty smile. "And then can we go home and fuck?"

"Hell yes." I reached out and we high-fived.

Then Zander smiled at me and I smiled at him. And I wondered if he felt tingles deep inside like I did.

I didn't voice this curiosity. Instead, I allowed Zander to take me under his arm as he led me out the back exit where Olson was waiting nearby.

After taking me to a nice discreet restaurant and having a quiet dinner together, Zander made good on his word. We went to the movies and saw a rom-com with Anna Kendrick and Ryan Reynolds, and it was awful. Zander joked about its *White* humor, and his commentary was the funniest thing about the movie.

What really got me, was the ending, that cliché big gesture at the end. It doesn't happen in real life. No man shows up in a limo, or catches you at the airport, or at the train station. In real life, men didn't chase women. They didn't put in the effort to love you.

Love was nothing more than an illusion. Something that was bought and sold in various forms of entertainment from films, television, books—and right in Zander's lane: music.

There were times during the film where I found myself staring at Zander, wondering what the hell I was doing, wondering how could such a prestigious eligible bachelor be so caught up in me. Beneath his bad-boy image and sultry persona, Zander Khalil seemed incredibly sweet, soft, and loving.

Sitting there next to him, I couldn't help but think that maybe, after a lifetime of slight misfortune, I had hit the jackpot on better, on more, and maybe soon to be, *love*. And if love was indeed real, that maybe, it could be us, it could be ours.

On Wednesday, Paul came to show Zander and me the polished images to choose from for the "Canvas" single cover. Zander had played me the studio version, and he was right—when all the production came together mixed and mastered with his vocals, the song was beautiful. His live version was intimate, just for me, but the studio version would take the world by storm come Friday at midnight.

On the glass coffee table in Zander's entertainment room, Paul spread out several glossy images. Each one was more surreal and perfect than the first. With the finishing touches, along with some Photoshop magic, I looked stunning, like a real model fit for a magazine spread.

"These came out so good." I couldn't believe it as I stared between two photos of myself.

"*You* look good in them," Paul complimented.

I felt myself blush. "Can you send me copies? Someday when I get a bigger place, I gotta get these blown up really big so I can frame them and put them on my walls. If I ever have kids, I want to be able to look back and remember this moment."

We were supposed to be choosing the best image for the single, but really, it was so hard to pin it down. I was torn between the image of me lounging in a chair with my back arched and a sheet covering my sex, versus a great black and white shot of my stomach with Zander's hand running along it. That picture was edited to where his fingertips were leaving behind a trail of golden paint. Besides how taut and fit my stomach looked and Zander's hand placement, the nice peek of under-boob made the photo really epic. On one hand, the other picture made me feel like a Greek statue, but then looking at the paint dripping from Zander's fingers, I had to admit, that that was the proper sell for "Canvas."

"This one." I held up the photo. "He's painting me with his touch. The others are just of me—which is nice, but the song is about my body and his touch."

Zander was impressed with my thinking and Paul couldn't deny how well the photo worked for the song.

"Done," he said, gathering the photos and stacking them together neatly. "Now, on to the next piece of business..." He collected his phone and clicked through it before holding it out before him. "Did a little digging and found that South Asian model you wanted. She's Indian, and her name's Shakira Malhotra."

The woman was young and beautiful; she had gorgeous golden-brown skin, long dark hair and her eyes were large and pretty. Paul thumbed through her modeling pictures for us and I had to give credit where it was due; she was sexy in her all her bikini pictures. She had a tattoo of some type of script going down her left side, but even that added to her image. She would look amazing next to Zander.

"Wow," I let out. "That's the one."

While Zander was quick to agree, Paul eyed me skeptically. "How are you okay with this?"

I had *just* met Zander, and wasn't even comfortable calling myself his girlfriend yet; it was far too soon to get clingy and territorial. "It's his job. He's a sexy guy and he needs to play it up in his music videos. He's grown now. Am I thrilled to watch him potentially tongue her down, no, but I trust him to just leave it at the set."

Zander's hand found my knee and he gently caressed it. "The video's going to be very tasteful. I want to show all the angles of love, the cute stuff, the hot and the sexy."

"What's the plan?" I wondered.

Zander spoke with his hands as he began to explain his vision for the video. "So, basically, you have this guy—me—who's at his desk in his little studio flat, and he's trying to draw because he's an artist. Then you have his girlfriend kinda saunter over in just a T-shirt, being all cute. She distracts him, and then the camera pans over to them in bed rolling around under the sheets, as he's cherishing her, caressing her.

"And then, we cut to a shot of them in the shower for the sex appeal, and the final shot can conclude of him back at his desk, looking over his shoulder, and the camera slowly pans up the bed, up the white sheets with her leg sticking out, and she's asleep in bed as he begins to draw."

Zander's treatment for the "Canvas" music video sounded cute and romantic. Most of his past music videos were like mini movies, which if I were being honest, didn't always work for the songs he was singing. Going for a more one-on-one route for his new single would work so much better than a big theatrical piece.

Paul wasn't satisfied with my answer; he went to Zander next. "Can I just ask if *Bianka* inspired the record, why not use her or someone in her likeness for the role?"

Zander peered at me, smiling softly before going back to answer Paul's question. "In the past, some fans complained that too many of my female leads were White, and so with this new album, I definitely want to show more support for women of color. Being that I'm a Brown man, I want my first video to feature a Brown woman. Later on, down the road, we'll use a Black woman for sure, but I think a lot of people are going to like seeing a woman like Shakira be admired and shown in that sort of light."

I loved his vision and his ideas behind the video the more and more he spoke. All I could do was look at Zander in awe.

His cell phone rang and one look at the caller ID had him standing up and excusing himself from the room.

Paul was back in his own phone and I took the opportunity to study him, curious. "Can I ask you something?"

He sent a quick text while responding. "Shoot."

"What made you want to work with Zander, if I may ask?"

Paul appeared thoughtful. "I won't lie, I look at the kid and see a gold mine. If this were Monopoly, that would be one hot property. But honestly, my little sister is a big So What fan and I once got her tickets to one of their shows, but my parents are up in age and couldn't take her. Naturally, that left yours truly being the chaperone. I wasn't too into their sound, but there was one record with an R&B flare that stuck out—"

"'Us or Not'?" I cut in, agreeing that that was the one song from So What that was my jam.

Paul pointed at me. "That's the one. I just remember listening and hearing it and thinking it should've been a Zander solo song. I mean, he really owned that record."

I couldn't agree more. Zander's vocals in that song foreshadowed all that he was capable of showcasing on his debut album. "Hell yeah."

"So, I just knew there was at least something unique about him, something to believe in if you will." Paul sat back and shrugged as if it were an easy decision. "The temper was a red flag, I will admit, but it wasn't enough to just deter me. The problem with a lot of these famous kids is that they were given the world at an early age and don't quite know how to adapt into humility and adulthood. I commend Nazanin for what she does for Zander, because he's been in charge of everything since he was like sixteen or seventeen. He's been allowed to do and say whatever he wants, and sometimes he needs people like Naz, or me, to bring his ass down to Earth.

"People were talking, saying he was a flop, and really, the kid should be just as big as Teddy, if not bigger by now. It's not fair to compare those guys, but let's be real, you can't help it. Vernon's stuff is all right, Oliver's debut was just a clusterfuck of singles, Jac's debut was good, but the real stars are Teddy and Zander. Which begs the question, how does one group get two fuckin' Beyoncés?"

I burst into a loud, terrible laugh, having to cover my mouth to smother it down.

Was Teddy Sykes really that good? "Damn, Teddy's that legit?"

Paul nodded. "Grammy winner for Best Rock Album. The kid's got his own little lane and I admire that. I grew up on the Stones, Guns N' Roses, Aerosmith, and some Mötley Crüe, so I'm liking his solo direction, and how for a young guy he's channeling that era."

I was going to take Paul's word for it, because I already pitied myself for getting into Zander's music. I was not about to go further down the rabbit hole and listen to Teddy, or worse, So What.

Paul checked something on his cell phone before going on. "Anyway, Zander's got the greatest potential, but he's a stubborn ass and we really gotta shoot for the damn stars on album number three so we can get him back into the spotlight. He's gotta tour, he's gotta interview, he's gotta interact. People like mysterious, but they relate to someone who's giving them something to relate to."

I liked that Paul was honest enough to call Zander out on his shit. To truly reach his potential, Zander needed to step up and want it as badly as those hungry upcoming artists who were constantly on the go promoting their YouTube videos and SoundCloud links. "Exactly, that's why I came up with Zaturday. He's gotta keep giving his fans appetizers before they get this album, to ensure them they'll be fed. It's all or nothing now."

Paul was impressed. "Have any idea what this week's song will be?"

Zander had mentioned either "Triggered" by Jhené Aiko or "Rocket" by Beyoncé. Whatever he chose, Zander was going to kill it.

"He's still deciding. The fans will love it no matter what," I assured.

Paul looked like he wanted to ask me more, but then Zander came back into the room, shaking his head.

Paul sat up, on alert. "What's up?"

"We gotta go." Zander grabbed the remote and shut off the TV.

"Was that Naz?"

Zander grimaced, a muscle in his jaw flexing. "We gotta go to LAX to pick up Raj. Naz believes I need an assistant, or someone I—*she* can trust close to me."

Paul whistled and stood to his feet. "So Nazanin pulled an ambush? Gotta love it. Should we get Terry and Dax?"

"No time if we wanna beat traffic; it's rush hour."

Even with Zander's hastiness to avoid linking up with his bodyguards, we still ended up in a bit of traffic. We took Zander's all black Lexus SUV. Paul offered to drive, but Zander got behind the wheel with Paul riding shotgun and me in the second row. He set the destination into his GPS and we hit the road, regrettably having to spend over fifty minutes in traffic to get to the airport.

The airport was a frenzy of people coming and going. That old Miley Cyrus song, "Party in the USA," came to mind at the sight of so many people buzzing around. Young hopefuls arriving to chase their dreams, or seasoned wannabes who were going home as they realized they would never achieve them. So many faces. So many expressions. So LA.

Instead of picking Rajaa up at the loading/unloading zone, Zander drove around the maze of lanes and went for the parking buildings. At Parking-3, he drove to the second level, which wasn't as packed with cars, and found a space and parked.

Paul got on the phone with Rajaa since he was the one going out to find him. "Hey, we're here, where are you?"

Paul jumped out of the SUV and was quick to go in search of Zander's cousin, leaving us behind to wait.

In the rearview mirror, Zander's eyes found me. "I'm sorry about this."

I frowned at his discomfort. "Don't be. He's your best friend, right?"

"Rajaa's nicer than Nazanin for sure," Zander insisted. "She flew back last week upset, and now that you're still very much in the picture, I'm more worried about her sending Rajaa here as a spy.

I unbuckled my seat belt, going and leaning between the driver and passenger seats. "Well then, let's give him something to report back about."

I gave Zander a quick smooch, leaving him wanting more as he came forward and kissed me longer, deeper, slower—in only the way Zander could.

This was just what he needed in the end, to settle his nerves and tension from his phone call with Nazanin.

"He's back!"

The loud sound of Paul's voice echoed throughout the parking deck, pulling our attention out the window where Paul and a young man were approaching the SUV. Together, Zander and I climbed out to properly greet Rajaa. He was a shade lighter than Zander, and he had hazel eyes. His wavy hair was long enough to where he had it in a secured bun at the nape of his neck, and his five o'clock shadow said he hadn't shaved in a day or two. His awkward, trembling smile let me know he was the quiet type, that and the way he simply tipped his head towards us as he and Paul came to a stop in front of us.

"Over ten hours, enjoy your flight?" Zander asked after he went forth and hugged Rajaa.

Rajaa shrugged. "It was okay."

His accent was almost identical to Zander's, just like Nazanin's.

Zander took a step back and gestured to me. "This is my new

girlfriend, Bianka. Bianka, this is my cousin, and best friend, Rajaa Khalil."

Rajaa extended his hand and we shook, and I took in how much larger his hand was than mine, how warm and strong it felt too. Rajaa was also on the tall side, making me feel tiny. "Nice to meet you."

Zander pocketed his hands, liking how things were going and how friendly his cousin was in comparison to his draconian sister.

"Rajaa!" Paul reached over and shook Rajaa's shoulders. "You're my favorite member of the Khalil family, ya wanna know why?"

Rajaa seemed shy under the spotlight. "Why?"

"Because you're the only one of these motherfuckers who isn't crazy."

Zander snorted. "*I'm* crazy?"

Paul deadpanned. "Did you not cancel a tour and jump into a relationship in the same night? Yeah, you're crazy, as crazy as my dick."

"Just say you have herpes, Paul," I jumped in.

Rajaa and Zander laughed and Paul managed to grin. "I might like you."

On the way back to Zander's home, we stopped and grabbed Chipotle. It was one of Rajaa's favorite places to eat in America, and I liked how low-key that was for him, and Zander especially who was quick to co-sign the chain. One of my favorite restaurants to go to growing up was Olive Garden. It was a place my mother and I would go to for a girls' day, and while some called it the basic bitch of restaurants, I still loved the place—or, at least, the idea. I hadn't been to an Olive Garden since my mother had passed.

A lot had changed in five years.

"I'm not here to step on your toes or anything," Rajaa assured me as we all sat crowded around the coffee table eating our food. He was looking at me, holding his hand out for my attention.

"Saad's working on a new album, and I'm just here to help ease the load so the process goes smoothly."

Saad. I liked Zander's family name.

"What do you do?" I asked.

"I'm in uni," Rajaa informed me. "I wanna be an English professor."

"That's cool." English hadn't been my best subject in school, unless we were assigned a book I actually liked, or a topic to write on that I was passionate about.

"What do you do?" Rajaa asked me next.

"I work retail at this clothing store called Angles," I said.

"Oh. Do you dance or sing or anything?"

I shook my head. "My dancing is okay, but I can't sing worth a lick."

"She's just a regular girl," Paul concluded for me.

"That's what I like about her," Zander added.

During this sit-down, I learned that Paul was single and very much mingling after a couple of TMI tales he disclosed. Blunt or not, Paul was fun and funny, and he hadn't lied—he could talk shit but could take it just as well. He poked fun at Rajaa and Zander, and they gave it back to him without missing a beat. I enjoyed myself, sitting there on the floor beside Zander, laughing along with the group. I'd like to think of that moment as before the storm, before the rush of what could possibly happen come Friday when he dropped his latest single, when he finally stepped to the plate to show the world he wasn't going down without a fight. With no pressure, and just a good time amongst us, it was one hell of a night.

Holliston texted me first thing Friday morning letting me know how much she liked "Canvas." It was out for the world to hear and interpret, and I was both excited and nervous for Zander.

A quick browse through Twitter showed mass approval. Everyone was raving about the song and it was currently number one on the all-genres chart on iTunes, as well as their Pop chart. I wrinkled my nose at the classification, but a win was a win.

I was home in bed and today was about promo, pushing the song for others to go out and buy or stream as well. Still, my mind drifted to Victoria.

It didn't feel right to just completely focus on Zander. To celebrate and have fun, with things still messy with Tori. So I gathered my phone and called her.

Unlike before, she wasn't busy as she picked up. "Hello?"

A lump lodged itself into my throat and suddenly I didn't know what to say. "Tori?"

On her end, Victoria chuckled dryly. "The one and only."

"It's been a while. It feels like you've been ghosting me for about a week."

"Never. It's summer, Bia. I'm getting hella clients right now for weddings and events. I'm actually on my way out the door. Look, let's talk Monday. Okay? Just let me have this weekend to gather my thoughts and we'll link up Monday and talk, coffee and snacks on you," Victoria said. She seemed in a rush to go, but I noticed a lack of agitation in her tone. Perhaps she was over the shock of it all—hopefully.

At least she was finally ready to have it out with me. "Okay."

For a moment, she was silent, but due to the sounds in her background, I knew she was still on the line. "I like his new song, congrats. It's one of his best, and it's about you."

I didn't know what to say, because it was hard to acknowledge such a feat. "Thanks, Tor."

"I...I could never hate you, Bianka. You're like my sister. You *are* my sister."

Squeezing my eyes shut, I tried my best not to tear up. My heart had never felt so good hearing those words. She knew me well, and these days, she was practically the only family I had. To not lose her over a man, felt good. Felt safe. "I love you."

"I love you, too. See you Monday."

"Monday."

We hung up and I felt better.

There was no time to dwell. I quickly got out of bed and showered for the day. Zander had advised keeping it simple since I would mostly be sitting around and waiting on him as he did his interviews. So I put on a teal velour tracksuit and placed my hair in a ponytail under a baseball cap. I didn't even bother with a touch of makeup.

It was just early enough to where the drive to Zander's house wasn't a pain. I'd beaten traffic, making it to the Hills in just over twenty minutes.

By the time I pulled in, I spotted Terry, Dax, and Paul already standing outside on his front doorstep. Everyone was ready for today.

Paul was in another expensive dress shirt and dress pants combo, keeping it business, while Terry and Dax were in black tees and jeans.

Dax took one look at me and made a face. "*This* is still happening."

"Don't like it, should've guarded him better," Paul spoke up on my side. He nodded towards me. "Morning. Ready for a long day of promo?"

I hung back away from the two guards as I put my interest into Zander's manager who was growing on me. "That's what I'm here for."

Just then, the front door opened and Rajaa and Zander stepped outside. Zander's mood visibly brightened when he set eyes on me.

"You're currently the number-one song on iTunes," I let him know. "Next stop, Billboard."

Zander played it cool and casual. "Am I?"

"Twitter is hype," I added.

Paul slapped his hand down on Zander's shoulder and shook him a little. "Don't call it a comeback."

Zander loosened up and furnished a smile. "I never left."

"Should we take a sprinter?" Paul asked as he eyed Olson pulling up in a luxury SUV.

Donned under his own baseball cap, Zander shook his head. "Nah, we don't want to attract attention."

Paul sat up front next to Olson; Terry and Dax took the second row; and Rajaa, Zander, and I sat in the third row. The radio was on, and it was a party the first time we heard "Canvas." All of us were hollering, causing Zander to sink into his seat and blush a little.

It was only the beginning for Z3, or *Abstract*, but it felt good to see the first song out, doing good, to hear the radio DJs praise the record and compliment Zander's vocals. With him cancelling his mini tour, some people had counted him out, but this was good for him, to show that he wasn't going anywhere and he was ready to come back stronger than before.

Olson drove to Burbank, the hub and home for most of LA's radio stations. From there, it was like a workout, going from radio station to radio station, getting in and out of elevators, walking from office to office. Zander would go into the studio and talk with the different DJs while we sat out in the lobby. Sometimes Paul would sit with him in some of the interviews in the back.

Through it all, Zander didn't get tired. He was perky right until the end when we hit our final station of the day, Viibe 104.2 FM. Paul went into the studio with Zander for his session while Terry, Dax, Rajaa, and I sat out in the empty lobby across from the receptionist.

I admired how one wall was just a large white smartboard, where a series of celebrity autographs in various colors littered the space. Another wall held photographs from pop stars like Shawn Mendes, Justin Bieber, Rihanna, and Tinashe to rappers like Travis Scott, Vince Staples, and Offset. Viibe 104.2 FM poised themselves as "the urban pop crossover station of the West" and I could see why.

"What are you thinking about lunch?" Terry asked.

"Shit, tacos sound good about now," Dax answered.

Rajaa faced me, his friendly eyes making me not feel alone without Zander around. "What do you want?"

Only one meal was on my mind at the mention of food. "Burger, fries, and a big-ass milkshake."

He smiled and went back to his phone. "Sounds good."

I was just about to add the idea of taking a good nap to the roster when I heard it.

Footsteps were coming down the hall, a collection of heels clicking on the shiny linoleum floor. An army of people entered the area and only one had my full attention as I heard Rajaa swear beneath his breath beside me.

Dressed in a plain black tee and faded black jeans was the one and only Teddy Sykes. Teddy Sykes. Grammy-Award-winning Teddy Sykes.

Holy fuck.

He was with two men, and a woman who was clutching her iPad as if her life depended on it. By her sweater and slacks, I guessed she was his manager or assistant, and the two men in their casual T-shirts and jeans were security.

Either way, this was the wrong place and wrong time to run into Teddy.

"Hello, hello," he greeted the receptionist for all of a second before his eyes zeroed in on Terry, Dax, Rajaa, and me. It was Rajaa that sent a scowl marring his face, Rajaa who he seemed to recognize.

"What's going on?" he demanded to know, facing the woman.

Her nervous gaze flickered over to the receptionist. "Is someone in there right now?"

The woman behind the front desk nodded. "Zander Khalil's doing a little interview. He should be almost done."

The men exchanged looks, wary. "We can wait outside—"

"Nonsense, we'll wait right here," Teddy insisted.

When he spoke, he had a slow, deep voice. The sound of it

made me think of syrup. His English accent was nowhere near as thick as Zander's, but distinct enough all on its own.

"Frankly, I'm surprised he could find his way outside," Teddy mumbled as he eyed the studio door with the tiny window and imagined Zander inside.

"He's got a new song out," one of the men offered with a shrug.

"So, I guess we're on *his* time, then, huh?" Teddy asked the woman with the iPad.

With his back to me, I could see redness on the back of one of Teddy's arms. He'd just gotten fresh ink. On his left tricep, he had a tattoo of crossed arrows, and between each axis was a letter: *J, O, V,* and *Z.*

He turned and faced the window again, not paying attention to the woman's reply.

His lips were pressed into a fine line, while a very serious expression hung on his face as he concentrated on watching through the glass.

Soon, Teddy reached up and raked a hand through his messy curls and found a seat next to me. The crease in his forehead deepened as he took me in, and slowly I watched as a corner of his mouth curled up until a dimple embedded his cheek. A devilish dimple that definitely saw him out of trouble more than a few times.

Teddy Sykes was a charmer. I could tell by the way his brown eyes peered into mine. He was reading me, plotting and planning, in almost a predatory fashion.

"Bianka," Rajaa spoke up. "Want to trade seats?"

That smile broadened as Teddy set his attention on Rajaa, silencing him. I didn't know Rajaa that well, but he didn't seem like the confrontational type, hence his quietly going back to his phone.

I wasn't the most comfortable, but I also didn't want to make a fuss. Like the receptionist said, Zander would be out at any moment. He'd spent a good thirty minutes talking already.

A pretty redheaded girl popped into my head and I knew I couldn't let this opportunity pass me by.

I cleared my throat, anxiously turning my body towards Teddy. "Um, excuse me, I hate to do this, but...could I have your autograph? A friend of mine is a huge fan and she'd never forgive me if I didn't do this."

Teddy coolly shrugged. "Sure."

And then I realized I didn't have anything for him to sign. In my purse, I found a receipt from the local grocery store. How pathetic was that?

"Do we have anything fun to sign, Fiona?" Teddy spoke to the woman with the iPad across the room.

Quickly, she dug around in her briefcase-style bag and procured a magazine. It was a *Rolling Stone*, and upon her coming and handing it to me, I examined the cover. Naturally, Teddy was gracing it in an impeccable closeup shot. His hair was wet and slicked back, and the plain look on his face as he stared into the camera made the image that much more appealing. There was no denying Teddy Sykes was a handsome guy. Movie star good looks, rock star rebellion, and the voice of an angel—or so his fans opined.

I ran my thumb over the subtitle. *Teddy Sykes, Confessions of a Young Rock Star.*

Wow.

I handed the magazine to Teddy. "Her name's Holliston, H-O-L-L-I-S-T-O-N."

Fiona had handed him a Sharpie and he was quick to prop his leg up and lean over to write a little message to Holly before signing his name.

When he handed the magazine back, I read over what he'd written and grinned.

Hey, Holliston :) Perhaps we'll meet some other time and it'll be extraordinary – Teddy Sykes

I opened my mouth to thank him, but the words never managed to escape my lips.

The studio door was open and Zander and Paul were leaving. Zander had been smiling along with Paul at something Eddie had shouted out to them, but all traces of humor evaded them as they set eyes on Teddy. Zander's dark gaze bounced from Teddy to me and back as Paul tried to get a hold of his arm.

Tension set in the air quick. I got high off all the testosterone in the ether.

Beside me, Teddy's smile turned Cheshire as he rose to his feet and we all collectively caught our breath, watching him walk straight up to Zander without a care in the world.

As if it were possible, the waiting area got smaller. Across the room were Teddy's people seated in a row of chairs, while we sat on our side in our seats. The two men on their feet had all of our attention. Watching them, it was like the clash of the titans.

Teddy's dimpled smile was purely condescending as he boldly reached out and patted Zander's chest. "Good to see you, old friend."

At his sides, Zander's fists balled and his shoulders were rising and falling as he got in Teddy's face. Teddy was eating it all up, grinning like a fool as he stood toe to toe with Zander. He was a couple inches taller and not at all intimidated it seemed.

Dax was the first to step in. "Yo, man, we not on that, none of that."

Fiona came and nudged Teddy forward. "Come on, be smart about it, please!"

Teddy flashed Zander a glimpse of his pearly whites as he prepared to step into the studio. "Oh, and congrats on your little song, mate."

It took both Terry and Dax to get Zander to budge and guide him back down to the SUV. All the muscle Terry and Dax had combined let us all know Zander wasn't getting past them. They weren't about to let him do something reckless.

"Put on the *fookin'* radio!" he shouted to Olson as soon as we were all buckled in and on the road. His anger leaked out into his voice, making his accent thicker. He leaned forward towards Olson. "I want to hear 104.2!"

Paul peered back at Zander, rolling his eyes before going and putting on the radio station.

The car was suddenly filled with the sound of Kacey speaking.

"Geez, we got two members of So What with us today. What are the chances?" Kacey asked.

"It must've been awkward in that waiting room," Eddie commented. *"Ya girl came in here shaking a little."*

"Yeah," Kacey agreed. *"What was that like? Because it's been a little...rocky between all of you since Zander left."*

"There's no bad blood in me for anyone. I think the media makes things more than what they are most of the time," Teddy spoke up.

"So, it was, like, a happy reunion for you, then," Kacey encouraged.

"I mean...it's good to see him out and about. We all have our own narratives, and with him particularly, I'm sure we're all anxious to hear his truth," Teddy said. *"I wish him the best. I'm really rooting for him."*

That arrogant son of a bitch.

Next to me, Zander's knee was bouncing and his hands were shaking. "Turn the fuckin' car around!" he practically roared at Olson.

Paul sighed, not even looking up from his phone. "Zan."

Zander stomped his foot. "Just do it!"

Two weeks. Two weeks was how long I'd personally known Zander Khalil and, in that interval, I'd never seen him this angry, this worked up, this volatile. That vein that came out whenever he hit those high notes, also came out whenever he was pissed off.

I had to turn to look at him, catching his eyes ablaze.

His attention snapped to me and then he focused on the signed magazine in my hand and he looked away, shaking his head.

The whole ride back to his house his knee kept bouncing, his body intent on moving somehow.

Olson hadn't been parked in the parking area in front of his house a full second before Zander stormed out of the car, bypassing Terry and Dax and the rest of us. Paul had just enough time to slip Olson two crisp hundred-dollar bills before sighing and following after Zander.

CRASH!

The sharp sound of shattering glass alerted all of us. Together the five of us raced inside to find that Zander had become a tornado of rage. In the entryway of the foyer, there was a small table that held two vases on it along with a plant, and Zander had thrown it to the ground, breaking everything. He was nowhere in sight, but by the light on in the kitchen further down the hall, I could only assume he was out back.

"Jesus," Paul let out. "Rajaa... Okay, everybody take five, Zander's having a meltdown."

This was ridiculous.

I took a step back, not feeling it. "I'm going to go home and take a breather."

Paul eyed me. "Hey, where's your head? This life ain't all sunshine and roses."

I gestured to the glass and dirt on the ground. "Didn't sign up for *this*, Paul."

He pointed at me. "You walk out that door, don't come back. He's got enough people doing that to him, leaving when shit gets too real. He's no fucking Prince Charming, Bianka. He's a hothead, with real issues and feuds right now."

"Paul," Rajaa tried to step in.

Paul didn't back down as he spread his arms out to emphasize the mess we were in. "Welcome to the end of the honeymoon."

"Maybe we should *all* cool down. Why don't you go and check on him?" Terry suggested.

Paul snorted. "I'm not going out there. He snaps at me and I'll punch him in his goddamn neck."

I deadpanned. "Really?"

"I don't condone that shit either, but I'm not walking away from him."

My feelings for Zander were very new, but I didn't want to ends things just yet. "I'm not breaking up with him. I just want to give him space, because I'm not about to watch him act like a fool and treat you guys like shit because *he's* mad."

"Can you go talk to him," Rajaa asked as he set the table upright. "He'll probably listen to you before us."

All four of them faced me, leaving me with the short end of the stick.

Zander was upset, and I got it, Teddy had been an ass. It was because of this I marched down the hall and out the back patio, finding Zander sitting out by the pool on the daybed. He was staring out at the water. His cap lay beside him and his hair was a mess from running his hands through it.

I came to a stop a few feet from him. "I just wanted to see how you were doing before I go."

Zander looked my way, frowning. "You're leaving?"

"Yeah, figured I'd give you some space."

"I'm fine."

I angled my head, studying him. He was calmer now. "Yeah?"

"Yes."

"Well, I don't like the fact that you yelled at Olson, and proceeded to throw a whole tantrum like a child. So I'm going to go."

"Bianka."

I shook my head. "Uh-uh, be mad all you want, but don't take it out on other people and destroy your own shit, that now Rajaa's nice enough to clean up for you. I told you, I won't be your therapist, or your punching bag."

"I'm sorry," Zander said softly. "I'm not usually like this, I swear."

Softening up, I went and stood next to him. "What made you so mad?"

He hung his head. "We've already got tension from me leaving So What, and the things we've been saying back and forth in interviews, so seeing him in person for the first time in years had me on edge. And then he was sittin' next to you and I didn't like it."

"Zander," I sighed.

He looked up at me, serious. "I didn't like it." He wrung his hands in his lap. "And just as I'm tellin' myself to let it go, he decides to take the piss and get in my face, *touch* me, and act like it's all fine. Then he's on the radio being cute, mocking me. It's a good thing they stopped me. I would probably regret hurtin' him of all people." Zander ran his hands down his face. "It's all so fucked up now."

While I understood where Zander was coming from, he almost put himself in a position to lose. Teddy was the golden boy, and Zander was the fallen. He had to move smarter, more calculated.

"Wanna get Teddy back? Cover one of his songs for Zaturday and kill it. You got the better vocals," I told him.

Slowly, Zander managed to chuckle. "That's petty."

"No, that's checkmate: a polite *fuck you*."

He bobbed his head. "I'll do it."

"Good. Get Rajaa to film it and you're set to go."

"You're really leaving?"

"Yes."

Melancholy caused his shoulders to sag in shame. "I don't want you to go."

"I know, and the next time you're mad and about to throw a fit, think about this moment when I'm leaving. When I'm not standing by your bullshit."

He pouted. "Please stay."

I took a step back. "No."

He tugged on my hand, and as much as all of me wanted to go limp and collapse onto his lap where I wanted to be, I resisted and stepped away. He couldn't have me. He couldn't have a reward for losing his temper and being mean.

So, reluctantly, I went to leave.

"I'm scared," Zander spoke up from behind me.

I turned, catching him open, vulnerable. "Of what?"

"That you're really good for me."

He had a way of saying the right thing that snatched my heart into a vice grip. "Don't be."

"You'll be back?"

"Of course, and you'll be good." With a wink, I slipped back into the house.

Terry and Dax seemed to be gone as I walked through the house for the front door. Rajaa wasn't in sight, but Paul had been in the entertainment room when I walked by.

"Hey." He stopped me as I made my way to the front door.

I faced him, giving him a look that asked, *What?*

"You're really leaving?" he asked.

"Yeah, but don't worry, I'll be back."

I had just grasped the knob when he spoke up yet again. "Hey." I turned, finding him watching me. "I like you for him."

It felt good to be admired by at least one person in Zander's life. "Take care of him for me?"

Paul tipped his head. "Always."

It wasn't exactly easy to do, but I went out and got in my car, prepared to leave. I turned on the radio, and it was just my luck, "Canvas" was playing.

Of course.

Hitting the road, I listened to Zander's voice all the way home.

15

WINDOWSILL

Holliston came in to close for the second shift as I was getting ready to get off Saturday afternoon. The sight of her swollen eyes and sluggish movement made me forget all about the *Rolling Stone* I was stashing for her in my bag.

"What's wrong?" I went straight up to her as our coworkers breezed by without a second thought.

Holliston ran her hand through her hair, shaking it a bit for style. "Nothing, I'm good."

Despite her denial, I followed her to the time clock where she clocked in. "Bullshit, Holly."

She went over to her locker and dialed in the combination before opening the door and storing her mini backpack inside and grabbing her name badge she wore on a bright teal lanyard.

"Jake and I got into a fight, and now he wants a break," Holliston said. "I think there's someone else."

She stood there, staring at her locker, willing herself not to cry it seemed.

Sympathy had me going and wrapping my arms around her. "It's okay, Holly. Forget him."

"But I love him." She looked at me with wet eyes. "Why can't he love me back?"

I smoothed back her hair and focused on its softness as I collected the right thing to say. "He doesn't deserve you. One of the biggest lessons we learn in life is to not love people who abuse us without remorse, who use us for their pleasure, and who leave us when we need them the most."

Holliston sniffed. "I'm only nineteen. Promise me I won't be this dumb in my twenties?"

I nudged her. "Nah, we've all played the fool before. It happens. That's what life is all about, growing and learning. I'm twenty-five and just left a really bad relationship for good myself. It only gets harder when you don't try, and that's all you can do."

Holliston did her best to wipe her face and make herself presentable for work. To do my part in lifting her mood, I went into my locker, grabbed my bag, and gathered the *Rolling Stone*.

"Well, it's not much, but maybe this'll cheer you up."

I handed over the magazine and watched as her face morphed into pure shock.

Holliston's mouth fell open. "Oh... My... God." She gaped up at me, her blue eyes enlarged. "How?"

"Zander was doing radio promo on Friday and we ran into him. I sorta figured you'd never forgive me if I didn't try to get his autograph."

Holliston clutched the magazine to her chest. "Thank you. Oh my God. What was he like?"

I thought about how shady Teddy had been, debating if I wanted to defame his image to Holliston. It had been nice of him to sign the magazine with more than just his name.

"Complicated," I decided to say. "I would've gotten a picture for you, but Zander finished his interview and things got crazy."

"How so?"

"Teddy was being snarky and it really pissed Zander off. They had to drag him out of the building before he did something reckless. Even on the way home he wanted to turn around."

"Whoa." Holliston's face suddenly crumbled. "Wait, is that why he covered Teddy's song for his whole *Zaturday* thing?"

He went through with it. *Good.* "Oh, he did?"

"You don't follow him online?"

"God no." I tried to play it cool, like it was totally blasé to be with Zander and I wasn't all that interested.

Holliston wasn't convinced. "Don't pretend you don't like him now."

"Anyway," I pushed forward, "what song did he cover?"

"'Leaving.' It's a sad ballad. He did a really good job, almost better than Teddy, but definitely just as good."

I did a fist pump, feeling proud.

Zander: 1

Teddy: 0

Fuck you well served.

Holliston wanted no part in my revenge scheme as she waved me off.

"Are you going to be okay after this when you get off?" I asked, getting back on track.

Holliston hung her head, nodding stiffly. "Yeah, you kidding? I'm just going to go home and watch *Breakfast at Tiffany's*, the best way to cope."

Holliston was so young, so vibrant and hopeful, I hated seeing her so down. "Hey, the perfect guy is out there for you, someone who'll respect you and treat you with kindness. When you meet him, it'll be *extraordinary*. Next time, no matter what, take it slow, feel him out, because you're the prize. Never forget that."

Holliston gave me a lopsided smile and came forth and hugged me close. I didn't know her too well, but I did know she had a younger brother named Cason, and outside of that, it was them and their parents. Being older, I almost felt like a big sister.

Holliston placed the magazine in her locker. "I'll get it right next time, I will."

So long as she was willing to finally let Jake go, I was in full support.

Holliston smoothed out her hair some more before pulling herself together to face the workday ahead. As soon as she hit the sales floor, she was a whole different person. All of her personal heartache and pain was put to the side as the Positive Holliston came out. I admired her for that. She never really lost herself and got mad or upset enough to let it disrupt her day. Some of us at Angles had our moments where our coworkers had to walk on eggshells around us. Never Holly, though, which let me know she'd be okay, because people like that always looked on the bright side of everything.

When I went on my last break, I pulled up YouTube and gave "Leaving" a listen, first by Teddy respectfully, and then Zander's cover. By the time the last note he sang came out, I was speechless. Really, it was the execution of the bridge, the final chorus, and that falsetto of his that stole my breath away.

I don't wanna fight but you're halfway out the door
To tell the truth I don't think we're going to make it anymore

Lead me to the guillotine
'Cause this'll be the end of me
My heart's in your hands
But you've made other plans

You tell me you're leaving
You must have your reasons
I guess happiness is deceiving
Please turn around
Don't go right now
We can work this out
Don't leave me

Teddy admittedly set the bar and left his mark on the heartbreaking ballad, but Zander's vocals and style did it impeccable justice.

Sometimes, when an artist did a cover, they tanked, badly. Others, they managed to outdo the original by adding that little extra something that made it all their own. I firmly believed Sinéad O'Connor's cover of "Nothing Compares 2 U" was far superior than the Prince original. Sinéad brought an emotional depth that couldn't be touched. Or like the vibe Fugees brought to "Killing Me Softly with His Song" in comparison to Roberta Flack's version.

Other times, a cover could be as good as the original on an equal level. Maxwell's cover of "This Woman's Work" had always been my favorite, until I heard the original by Kate Bush in a John Hughes film and how poignant it was.

And now Zander had covered "Leaving" flawlessly. Both versions were raw and so, so good, leaving it up to debate on which was better.

Regrettably, I looked around before going and purchasing Teddy's version on iTunes.

After it downloaded, I went out and finished my shift with my head held high.

Because Zander acknowledged his wrong and took accountability Friday, I had no problem driving over to his house that evening.

Okay, staying strong and independent aside, I just missed him already and wanted nothing more than to be snuggled in his arms.

God, I'm falling again.

And it was okay.

I got out of the car and made my way to the front door, noting that Zander seemed to be alone because I didn't spot any extra vehicles in the parking area. The thought of being semi alone —there was still Rajaa—made me feel good about having Zander to myself.

He was ready for me, coming and answering the door as soon as I rung the bell.

In a rush of his cologne and radiance, I was immediately immersed in Zander's presence. His dark eyes were covered by a pair of glasses that again just worked for him. The sight of his red long-sleeved top made me want to go forth and hug him, and the added touch of the gold chain around his neck was a nice dash of style.

Without speaking, Zander let me into the house, allowing me to enter the foyer as he closed and shut the door behind me. I wondered what was up as I hung back, waiting for him to say something.

"Hey." I smiled nervously. The house was quiet and sound. "What's up?"

"Rajaa and Paul went out," Zander informed me. "I stayed behind."

"Okay, I see that."

Zander almost seemed to be advancing closer to me in a stealthy way.

"You know, I've been up, thinkin' about yesterday," he said casually and calmly. "I'm aware that I shouldn't have lost my temper, but *you* should've stayed and been supportive. It's not about being a 'therapist,' but rather, being a supportive and caring partner. You should've had my back a little more than just running along."

My hand pasted to my hip, noticing he *was* walking up on me. "Um, excuse—"

Zander shook his head, a hint of a smile on his face, breaking the surface of his impassive mask. "I'm talking." Those two words and the short distance now between us had me going quiet as my back met the wall. "Like I was saying, you should've been supportive all day. You know I've got issues with Teddy, and you were sitting next to him. I didn't like that. You should've gotten up and moved. To make matters more fucked up, you got his autograph."

"For my friend—"

Zander's finger brushed against my lips. My back was against the wall. His other hand shot out and planted itself beside my head as he leaned close, invading my space. "I'm talking, Bianka." Again, I went quiet as he continued. "And let's not forget all that shit you were talking about me being a 'solid five at best' when we were shopping. I've realized I've been lettin' you slide for way too long."

"Zander... Boy, bye—"

He bent down and grabbed me by my legs, picking me up with ease and tossing me on his shoulder. In seconds he was ascending up the stairs, carrying me as if I were as light as a feather. Speechless, I could only watch us climb higher and higher until we were on the second level and making our way towards his bedroom.

Zander set me down on my feet in front of his bed. He sized me up, taking his lip into his mouth in a way that let me know where his mind was. "I want you on all fours."

I fingered along the collar of my shirt, playing coy. "What are you going to do to me?"

Zander came and gently pushed me to where I was sitting on the bed and he was hovering over me. He looked into my eyes and read me, gauging my reaction as he knelt down and pulled off my flip-flops, unbuttoned my shorts, and tugged my tee over my head. This process was slow, full of eye contact, leaving me speechless and wet.

I helped him out of his shirt and tan trousers and lay back on my arms as he stepped out of his boxer briefs.

He came and trailed his hands gently along my body before he flipped me over abruptly, making me assume the position. I had just enough time to process it all before he was inside of me.

"Shit!" I let out at the invasion.

"Not so big and bad now, are you?"

"Fuck you, Zander." I said it to piss him off, and it worked as he slammed his hips into me once more.

Zander came close to my ear, moving my hair out of the way. "I am."

He gripped my waist possessively as he began delivering fierce stroke after stroke.

A hard open-palm slap greeted my ass and I let out a loud whimper.

Zander paused. "Is that too much? Does it hurt?"

Vigorously, I shook my head, consenting to the punishment.

His hand came down hard on me once again, the sensation causing me to bite my lip.

"Say you're fuckin' sorry," Zander ordered.

"No," I protested.

Another slap.

Why did I love this?

As much as I wanted to hold back, to rebel, I was close, and I wanted it to last a little longer. "I'm sorry," I let out.

Zander took me deep, rough, and I loved every second of it as I screamed louder than I ever had before, loved that position better than I ever had before, came harder than I ever had before.

When he finished, Zander collapsed on top of me, coming and kissing my shoulder.

"Don't ever do that shit again," he breathed out.

I was spent, unable to move. "If I ever see him again, I'll be sure to get his number."

In seconds Zander was turning me over and staring down at me. Boldly, I laughed, loving the hint of attitude and jealousy on his face. I moved a lock of hair out of his face and smiled gently.

And then he kissed me and I got it. Understood him completely.

I was his and he was mine.

Zander came and lay behind me, taking me into his tattooed arms and holding me close. I ran my fingers up and down his ink-stained skin, admiring the look and feel of us.

For a while, we lay like that, me massaging his arm and him just holding me. We breathed in sync and just existed.

It hadn't been long, our relationship or what we were building, but already I loved it here. A lyric from The Notorious B.I.G. came to mind, and I couldn't have agreed more; this whole thing felt like a dream. I was in a sexually frustrated funk over my last relationship and here was Zander, *wanting* to please and satisfy me. I was in a lonely mood after seeing my father and brother, and here was Zander, wanting to spend time with me and just be.

This was happiness. This was more.

"Zand?"

"Hmm?"

"You know I'd leave again if you ever went crazy like that again, right?"

"I know. That's why I like you, Bianka."

Because I didn't want him to think I wasn't serious about him or wouldn't hold him down, I went on. "If something ever happened, and the world came crashing down around you, I would be here, no question. I just don't condone *you* being destructive and rude to people who are here to help you."

"I know." He held me closer, letting me know he wasn't upset.

It was quiet again, but it was comfortable. We didn't always have to speak, that was another thing I liked about us; we could just be together without forcing it.

"What's something you always wanted when you were a kid?" I wondered out loud.

Zander didn't hesitate to conjure up an answer. "To make my father proud. My mum, she'll support me no matter what, but my dad, he was just this force, this cool guy in my eye, and I always wanted to impress him and make him proud of me."

"I'm sure you managed that feat and then some."

"Nah, I haven't. I haven't even gone on tour and sold out arenas. I've been slacking in my career and not taking full advantage of this opportunity. He's told me he's proud of me and congratulated me plenty of times, but I know my full potential and I know I could be doing way more than what I am."

I kissed his forearm. "Then you gotta make *Abstract* immaculate and have an amazing tour."

"Paul's in talks right now for the tour to begin next summer for the North American leg and then the top of the year after for the other legs. He wants over eighty shows, but we'll see how it all pans out. It's going to be crazy, but I've been missin' the stage and I'm ready to really give it all I've got."

Maybe it was selfish to think of all the time he'd be gone and how much I'd really miss him then, but I couldn't stop myself from putting it together. As much as it saddened me, I was happy for him, excited more than upset. He would have plenty of material, and so much to prove.

"What about you?" Zander asked me.

A soft smile curved my lips upward. "When I was a kid, there was this store like the one I work in that my mom would shop at. At the checkout counter they used to sell all types of accessories, and there was this water watch I really wanted. Stainless steel with a bubble full of water on the face; some were green, others blue or pink, and I really wanted it.

"My mom kept saying 'Maybe next time, Bia.' Next time never came, because at one point, the store stopped selling them and no one else had them. I used to hold it over her head, about how she never got me the watch. I was only ever teasing, but I could tell in my later years she regretted not getting it for me. Pryor and me, we got a lot of stuff as kids, but we were far from spoiled. But that watch was like the one thing I can really think back on that I really wanted and never got."

Zander came and kissed my cheek. "I'm sure if they were still around your mum would've gotten it for you."

"I know."

My stomach growled, reminding me that I hadn't eaten a proper meal yet that day.

I climbed out of bed and took off towards the shower, where Zander joined me and we made love. His ability to pick me up with ease made me melt. I loved how into me he was, how obsessed I was slowly becoming with him, how electric our spark and energy seemed. Fast or not, I loved us.

After our shower I put on his Green Day T-shirt and some shorts of mine I'd left over and found his phone, getting an idea.

"I'm going to cook some dinner. Why don't you log onto Instagram and go live?" I suggested.

Zander pulled on some sweats and eyed me funny. "Live?"

"Yeah, go live and interact with your fans, be silly, listen to music, just chill."

Zander accepted his phone and mused over the idea as we went down to the kitchen. I put my hair into a bun and browsed his refrigerator for an idea. The sight of fresh peppers and a couple packs of ground turkey made an alarm go off in my head. Stuffed peppers it was.

I washed my hands and rinsed the green, yellow, orange, and red peppers before pre-heating the oven. Zander lit a spliff and sat at the island, going through his phone as I seasoned the meat and found some ready rice.

"Rajaa will be back later," he let me know. "Paul may stop in instead of dropping him off. You think you can make enough?"

I had cut the peppers in half, making a grand total of sixteen. "There'll be plenty."

Zander bobbed his head and sent a quick text message.

When the peppers were stuffed and baking, I washed the dishes I used and rinsed them before letting them air dry.

Zander still wasn't live yet.

"Ahem." I went and planted myself in front of him. "What are you waiting for?"

Zander flashed me a crooked grin. "Don't know how."

I rolled my eyes and snatched his phone, going and clicking on the Instagram app for him and going onto his profile and beginning the live-feed for him.

He hadn't been online for a second before people started jumping on. It was amazing watching his views jump to the thousands in minutes.

"Oh wow," I let out. Me, I never went live, I was obscure with my puny four hundred followers. If I did go live, I highly doubted anyone would click to see me. Plus, I didn't take myself seriously enough to do it since I had nothing to say, and I could easily FaceTime Victoria for a conversation.

Zander leaned over my shoulder to get a good look, prompting his fans to go into a frenzy. My favorite thing ever was whenever a person was flabbergasted or shook, they'd just type a bunch of random letters to emphasize their speechlessness.

I leaned close to read a few comments, super proud of one in particular. "'*Zander is the petty champ.*'" I grinned at him. "Damn right you are."

I set the phone on the counter and propped it against a bowl of fruit. Quickly, I got out of the way so Zander could take over and talk amongst his fans.

"They want to know your name," he said to me, sneaking me a smile. "Can I tell them?"

No one really knew who I was, I was still a mystery. The public knowing my name wouldn't change that, so I shrugged. "Sure."

Zander faced his phone. "Her name's Bianka, and we met on Tinder."

I snorted. "Don't lie."

"Would you swipe right for me?"

Sizing him up, loving what I saw, I wrinkled my nose. "Nah."

Zander snickered. "She kills me." He leaned over and read some of the feedback. "They say you're lucky to have me."

To that, I moved in front of the camera, tossing it a sassy look. "Actually, *he's* lucky to have me. I'm the prize here."

Zander pushed me away and made a face. "So, yeah, I've been dealin' with that. Hope you all are having a safe and nice weekend. You guys liking 'Canvas'?"

Zander talked to his fans for a while and then I got the idea to loosen him up a bit more. I got my own phone and put on some music and stood from the stool.

"Come on, dance, be free," I encouraged as I pulled Zander from his seat.

He cringed, shaking his head. "I can't dance."

"So?"

A dancey hip-hop record was playing and I began moving, staring up at him, goading him to do something. He was shy, smiling at me innocently as I fell into the beat of the song. To do him a service, I turned and whined my waist into his, bending over and twerking on him just a little.

Zander's hands found my hips and he angled his head to peek at me, the biggest grin splayed across his face.

I came back up and kept dancing, bopping around him and nodding my head. "Don't be so stiff, Zand."

We held hands lightly and Zander tried to dance, and it was the cutest thing, seeing him attempting to move in sync with the music. I could tell this was way out of his comfort zone, but it was something I'd never seen myself doing either.

Another first for us.

I went to check on my peppers while Zander settled down on the stool, going back to his fans.

"I'm glad you all are liking this Zaturday thing I'm trying. It was Bi's idea, actually, but it's definitely been a fun exercise and I'm always jonesing to give you guys new music. Next week's cover will be fun, I promise."

"And the album?" I prompted.

"The album's coming along really well. It's going to be a masterpiece," Zander swore to his fans. "I'll be in the studio next week working on a collaboration I'm excited about. This project is special to me. I won't say any more on that, but just know that Z3 will give the best of me and all of me."

In the background, the front door shut loudly and I soon heard footsteps.

"What smells so damn good?" Paul's voice called out as he was coming our way.

Soon, Rajaa and Paul were stepping into the kitchen.

"All right, I'm going to hop off now, but I'll do this again soon. This was fun." Zander waved goodbye to his fans and ended the live-feed before facing his manager and cousin.

"She cooks." Paul was impressed as he came to greet me with a kiss to the cheek.

I shrugged. "I cook."

"She's actually the *first* person to cook for me," Zander announced. "She put together some stuffed peppers that're baking and I'm excited about it."

"I'm not even gonna let him gas me too much because he can cook his ass off," I said. "Shout out to his parents for showing him the way, because he's really good."

Rajaa agreed with a nod of approval. "Have you had his chicken karahi?"

"Not yet, but he's determined," I said.

Paul and Rajaa joined Zander at the island and I sautéed green beans at the stove. It felt normal to be cooking for Zander, to be around Paul and Rajaa like I fit in. Peeking over my shoulder, I found Zander glancing my way as well, sneaking me a smile.

It all felt so...natural.

16

BLUE

It happened Monday.

I had the day off from work so I'd gone to a hair appointment to take out my extensions and get a silk press. But as I stood in front of my apartment door taking in the eviction notice, I regretted coughing up the coins for the do.

What a terrific day to start my period.

Even as I took into possession the folded sheet of paper, reading and rereading the sixty-day notice, I couldn't grasp its meaning. I needed more confirmation as a lump lodged in my throat too big to swallow down. Still, as I looked up and down the hallway, spotting more folded sheets of paper taped to doors, I knew this was all too real and not a prank.

The sound of an old telephone ringing caused me to jump. Someone was calling me, pulling me from my trance.

I gathered my cell phone to find that it was Zander.

"H-Hello?" My heart began to race so much it hurt, and it felt as if I was having a hot flash.

"Hey, I just got out of a meeting with the label. They are loving *Abstract*. We're aiming for a twelve-track record, but I'm feelin' really good about the songs I laid down so far. It's all a time crunch if we're going to make the Dec—"

"I...I can't." I couldn't breathe or focus.

I hung up and went straight to my neighbor down the hall. Of all the people who moved in and out of my level of the building during my time at Lakeside Manor, I'd only spoken to one of my neighbors. A guy somewhat older than me in apartment 1B.

We'd met officially a year before, when I'd been in my own head about to send an angry tweet and he'd greeted me. It went from a simple exchange of hellos to him coming my way and introducing himself, letting me know he'd noticed me for a while and he thought I was cute. His name was Wade, and call me terrible, but I'd been so engrossed in my angry tweet I'd barely paid his compliment any mind—not to mention Rod was in the picture then.

While we hadn't become friends, we'd kept it cordial with hellos whenever we ran into each other. As much as I wanted to run over to the main office building and confront the manager of Lakeside, I didn't trust my temper. Really, the staff in the main office weren't that bad, but judging by our building's maintenance man, I wasn't a big fan overall on their professionalism.

My second year in my apartment they installed a new toilet, and when I complained that the toilet was too far up and I couldn't shut my bathroom door, maintenance came to fix the problem. The resolution? Cutting a hole in my door, sanding it down smooth, and painting it over.

Everything about Lakeside Manor was janky and outdated. This sixty-day notice shouldn't have surprised me, but it did.

Wade came to the door after I knocked a couple of times. He was surprised to see me. I could tell by the way he blinked and bore a small smile. Wade was a much taller Black man, somewhat on the chunky teddy bear size, but otherwise handsome and polite.

"Hello," his deep, musical voice said to me.

My heart ached and I tried my best to keep it together as my shaking hand lifted up the notice. "What's going on?"

Wade's smile diminished as he took in my offending letter. He shook his bald head. "Word is, the owner of this place was back in payments and got bought out. The new owners want to renovate, probably make it a nicer complex or place of business, I don't know. It's a damn shame, though."

It was true.

I had sixty days to find some place new to live.

Stiffly, I offered up a smile. "Thanks. Guess I better go make arrangements."

Wade nodded. "Yeah, for what it's worth, it was nice seeing you around."

I hummed out a response before turning and going back over to my apartment and letting myself in. All at once, everything I owned jumped out at me, my furniture, my TV, my bookcase full of DVDs and Blu-rays, the small collection of books I owned—everything.

Reality started to set in and I knew I was having a panic attack. What was I going to do? Where was I going to live?

A piercing pain shot across my chest as ice seeped into my veins. An ache pulsated in my temple and I feared I'd die of an aneurysm.

The shrill sound of my phone ringing paused my hysteria if only for a moment. Zander was calling me back.

"Zander—"

"What's your apartment number?" he interrupted.

"W-What?"

"I'm on my way over."

My hand covered my face as all I felt was shame. "Please... don't."

"Bianka." I heard him swear on his end as a car door shut in the background. "Something's wrong. Just tell me which apartment is yours."

There was no fighting him. "First floor, 1D."

I piled myself on the couch and froze, my breathing nearly echoing in my ears as I tried to slip into a comforted state of denial. If I didn't think about it, it wouldn't be real. If it wasn't real, it wouldn't hurt. If it didn't hurt, my lungs wouldn't feel like they were about to burst. My heart would beat lightly and my nerves wouldn't have me antsy.

When I heard the sound of knocking on my door sometime later, I knew it was Zander. I could barely bring myself to answer it as I sluggishly got up and crossed the room.

What was left of my dignity fell to my feet as I pulled the door open and realized before it was too late what I had done. From The Residence Hotel, to his own private estate, Zander lived in and was used to the lap of luxury. My building and my space were far below adequate. In my tiny kitchen, I didn't even have a counter. There wasn't room for an official dining room table either, just the small table I'd built with my father after getting it from Target. Even then, there was hardly any room due to my microwave.

I had never felt so poor and pathetic in my life.

Zander didn't seem to outright notice or care as he stood in my doorway, adorn in all black. He was too busy studying me, checking for injuries or error.

"You changed your hair," he said in the end.

My hair. The only nice thing about me now.

"Can I come in?" Zander asked gently.

Could he come in? To see firsthand the sad state of my life?

"No." I started to close the door, and the sad look on Zander's face tore me apart. The wounded hurt in his dark eyes sliced me open. He'd come all this way because he cared.

"I heard about the notice," he let me know. "I get what's going on. There're some tenants outside smoking and talking about it."

Embarrassment caused my shoulders to sag. "Please."

Without asking, Zander stepped forth and hugged me, but I refused to break.

Somehow, we ended up in my apartment with the door closed and there was no hiding who I was and where I lived. My place wasn't a mess or nasty by any means, but there was only so much polishing you could do with a dud of my four very small walls of a home. I never felt shame whenever Victoria came over, even though she had a much nicer home, but something about Zander had me wanting to wave my arms about, as if to distract him from seeing where I lived.

Zander didn't look around long before focusing his attention on me. "Bianka, talk to me."

"About what?"

Zander heaved a sigh. "About the eviction notice and what happens now."

He was only asking because he cared, because he wanted to know if I'd be okay, but I wouldn't, and there was nowhere to go from here.

I hung my head and shrugged my shoulders.

"Bianka." His tone was soft, cautious, as if I were fragile. But you can't break what's already broken. "What are you going to do?"

What was there to do with just sixty days but panic?

"Bianka, please. I'm here," he begged when I didn't respond.

And suddenly I was angry. I knew none of it was his fault, but he was asking very real questions I could not answer. "I don't know! I'm twenty-five, and I still don't know what I'm doing or where I'm going, okay!"

"You're going with me, okay?"

That was just what I needed, his pity and charity.

I walked past him, going and grasping the door knob. "I need to be alone right now."

Zander shook his head, a frown on his face. "You *are* alone, which is why I'm not going anywhere."

It was the truth. The ugly truth. Faithfully, ever since I met her at seventeen, all I had was Victoria. With us on the outs, I had no one.

Try as I might, the tears were coming. Now wasn't the time to break down when I had to get on my shit.

"Go!" I shouted.

Zander stayed planted. "No."

"Leave! I don't want you here!"

His response was another shake of his head, and my rebuttal was a sight full of tears. I fell back against my door as I started to cry and Zander didn't waste time collecting me into his arms and holding me against his chest.

Zander brought me over to my sofa and never let me go as we sat down. His resilient strength let me know he'd hold me all night if he had to.

It was a known fact that rent was high in California. I worked full time at Angles and I still stretched that as far as possible making it work as I lived in the cheap residences of Lakeside Manor. To live elsewhere, I'd have to get a second job, or maybe even a second and *third*. I hadn't gone to college and my meager high school diploma was especially laughable in this predicament. Deep down, I'd always known I couldn't work at Angles forever, especially if I wanted better for myself.

This eviction was a rude awakening, a bitch slap to wake up and boss up—or whatever Rick Ross liked to tweet motivationally.

While I couldn't look at Zander, I could speak, and as I relayed to him my financial troubles and the impossibility of finding my way out of this hole, he listened.

"I already work so much at the store, and now I'm going to have to do double if I'm going to find another place to live," I said. "This place is shitty, but it's all I could afford when I moved out."

"It's not awful," Zander insisted. "I like it."

He was just being nice.

"Will you like me when I'm homeless?" I joked pathetically.

Zander clicked his tongue. "I'm never going to let you go

homeless, Bianka. What about your friend, Holliston? Could you room with her?"

"We're not *that* close, and she still lives at home," I said. "Things are too complicated with Victoria right now to try to ask her. I'm not going to find a place in sixty days, I just know it."

"Don't be so pessimistic."

"I'm being real, Zander." Truthfully, I had one other option. "I just have to call my dad and ask to move back in with him while I figure this out."

Zander's abrupt silence had me peeking up at him, finding his dark brows furrowed in confusion. "Your father?"

"Yes."

"Didn't you claim he doesn't love you?"

"He may or may not, but I know—or I *hope*, he wouldn't let me end up on the street."

Zander held me harder, tighter, closer. "No."

"I have no one."

He blinked, and then he narrowed his eyes. "What about me?"

"No!"

Zander rolled his eyes and released me. He sat up and clasped his hands together, staring out at nothing. "I like everything about you, except your pride. This wall you put up before me grates on my last nerve. Your ego is your worst side, Bianka." He looked back at me, letting me know he was serious. "Here's what I'm going to do, and because I'm not going to intrude, I'll give you two options, but either way, I *will* help you."

"Zander—"

"One, I'm going to go and give you a songwriting credit on 'Canvas.' It's doing really well, and that'll bring in a lot of money," Zander went on.

My eyes watered once more and I choked on a sob. "No."

Zander's stoic expression alerted me to his growing impatience as his nostrils flared. "Two, in thirty or sixty days—hell a week from now, if you can't find a new place to live, you can come live with me."

I hated those options, and he knew I would. "Absolutely not."

I watched as Zander ran his hand down his face. "Bianka."

"All my pride is all I have, please," I begged. "I *inspired* 'Canvas,' but I didn't *write* it, and I won't take your money. I like you a lot, but I can't live with you. It makes me feel like a charity case."

Zander hung his head. "What am I supposed to do? Just watch your demise?"

"I'm going to talk to my dad. He'll understand," I said.

Lindenwood brought on a lot of painful memories and reminders, but I could stomach it. I was strong. I hadn't seen my older brother in three years, but I knew he still came around to visit our father. If he came by, it would hurt me deep, but I could stomach it, I could endure.

"Can I go with you when you ask?" Zander reached back and grabbed my hand. "In support? I won't speak."

I hated how fast my heart was ready to cling to this man, how much of a beacon of hope he was becoming to me.

More tears rolled down my cheeks and I managed to nod. "Yes." I wiped my face up. "I'll just call off tomorrow and go and pay him a visit instead."

"Okay." Zander squeezed my hand. "I gotta go to the studio tomorrow night, but my morning's wide open."

My cell phone rang and I curled up, unable to face anyone else for the day. So I let it ring, and when it died down, it picked back up again.

Zander didn't hesitate to grab it and answer it for me. "Hello ... I'm, uh, Zander ... Hey, Victoria ... Bianka's not feeling well, but I'll let her know you called ... Uh-huh, 'bye." He set my phone back on the table and slid the ringer off. "Can I stay with you? Tonight?"

There was no more fight in me. I'd won in my battle against allowing him to unfairly give me money for his song, and the possibility of making room for me in his home. I liked Zander, I really did, but this was my mess to figure out and solve.

My pride was all I had, as *I* was often all I had.

Together we climbed into my bed in my bedroom, where Zander wasted no time in holding me close. Lying there, safely in his arms, nuzzled against him, I felt a little better.

"I'm sorry I won't let you help me," I spoke up. "I'm not used to anyone having my back. Outside of Victoria, I've always had to handle my shit on my own after my mom died. I don't even get intimidated by men because I'm used to taking up for myself. I used to joke with Tori that I've never met a man whose dick is bigger than mine."

Zander patted my arm, sneaking me a smile. "Well, my dick's bigger."

I bit my lip, so strangely happy despite the impending eviction and the idea of approaching my father. "I mean it, Zander. What you tried to do meant a lot. This isn't easy for me. God, I wish we could've known each other for a little longer before I broke down and cried in front of you."

"Don't be ashamed or embarrassed," Zander said. "We can't forget the night we met I was on a downward spiral. I'm my own worst enemy with my career. I almost lost my shit with Baby and you were there to kick me in the ass about it."

His troubles were different than mine, but I could understand his point. When things were crashing down for him, I had been there for him. In fact, if *he* lost it all in the morning, I knew without a doubt I'd open my door for him until he got back on his feet. Because I was just that type of person when I cared about someone; there were no limits to my giving then. I'd be championing him full force, just like how I was in the process of him working on his album.

It was hypocritical to deny him the same.

"Who's Baby?" I wondered.

Zander's face went blank and he shook whatever thought he'd

been thinking away. "Teddy. It's...it's just a stupid thing from our past. It's nothing."

I didn't push, because it was clear that the topic of Teddy Sykes would be a sore one for a while for him.

Zander let it go as he stared down at me, appearing serious. "I know it's early, but I want to be here for you. I don't mean to be intrusive, but I heard the tone of your voice and it was just instinct to be here. I want all parts of what comes with *this*, Bianka. I want to be someone you can count on. Some days it's sunny, and some days it rains. I promise I'll be here for you during the storms as long as you're with me to see the rainbow."

Poetry this man was, living and breathing poetry. "Okay."

Because Zander knew it all was a lot for me, he didn't say anything more as he continued to hold me close.

My heart was in his hands, and while I still had my pride, I allowed myself to be taken care of that night, to be held and cherished. To not be so lonely.

17

FLIGHT OF THE STARS

Perhaps it wasn't the best idea to call off work Tuesday, considering I needed all the shifts and money I could get, but I wasn't in the mood to face the world. Somehow, I had to get it together enough to go to my father, and I was secretly dreading that.

Zander had laid out some *overly* generous options for me, and maybe I was a fool to turn him down. Make no mistake, I wasn't proud about going to live with my father, but I could never be proud of myself if I took Zander's handout. I was being silly, I guessed, since the eviction was beyond my control, and Zander was only being sincere. It wasn't like I'd caused any of this recklessly.

It was okay to need help.

And even though it was hard to do, it was okay to *ask* for help, too.

I dabbled with these thoughts for about twenty minutes as I lay in bed after waking up and calling off. It was easy to reflect, as I was alone. Zander had been there when I'd fallen asleep, but when I opened my eyes, he was gone.

I knew he was still around, because I could see his shoes on the floor by my dresser and his hoodie was draped across my ottoman.

And then, I suddenly heard him.

"I had some business to take care of ... I'm going to make the session tonight, I promise. I won't keep her waiting..." Whoever Zander was on the phone with must've said something he really didn't like, because he groaned loudly next. "Is it imperative that I go? ... I hate these things ... You know she runs in Piper's circle ... I know, I'll figure it out. I'll see you later, yeah? ... All right, 'bye."

He came back into the bedroom and paused at the sight of me awake. "Morning."

"Hey."

The soft smile on Zander's lips caused any anxiety inside of me to dwindle. "I'm quite disappointed I didn't get a bonnet last night."

Devastated or not, I wasn't about to mess up my hair. Even in all my sadness I'd had the sense to tear myself away from Zander and go into my bathroom and wrap my hair and put on my bonnet. I was sad, but I wasn't about to be sad *and* have shitty hair. I picked a struggle.

The thought of Zander in a bonnet was pure comedy. "We can get you a durag. I'll even get my nails done to match whatever color you get."

"Yeah?"

I'd seen some couples do that, but Zander wouldn't get waves. To tease him, I said, "I'd love you in a durag."

Zander dared to come closer. "You'd *love* me, huh?"

I felt myself shrink and blush. Now wasn't the time for any of this.

I let Zander freshen up first since I wanted to take my time and drag this out for as long as possible until we were out the door. In the end, I dressed conservatively and pulled my hair back into a ponytail. I was playing it clean and safe. Really, I felt like a kid approaching the principal's office, about to defend myself.

Zander's hand found mine and it gave me strength as we

stepped out of my apartment and made our way out to the parking lot. Zander had driven his Bentley, and once inside, I told him my father's address, which he typed into his GPS.

With the destination set, Zander took off for Lindenwood. His phone was paired to his car and some rock band was playing. I wasn't the most educated, but I could tell they were older.

"What is this?" I asked.

Zander looked at me incredulously. "You don't know *Queen*?"

Maybe a song or two, but definitely not enough to know them by ear. "I *know* this is the wrong soundtrack to listen to on the way to the 'Wood." I gathered his phone. "What's your passcode?"

Zander didn't hesitate to tell me. "Four zeroes."

That was the easiest passcode anyone could use. "Really?"

Zander shrugged. "I've got too much going on to remember numbers."

"So you just trust anyone with your phone not to have it password protected?" I asked as I unlocked the device and began sifting through.

Zander made a face as he moved around in his seat a little. "Don't look through my pictures or messages then."

I paused, unable to explain the sudden sadness I felt at his comment. "Why?"

Zander kept his attention straight ahead. "I've got some old pictures I need to delete for one thing, and for two, Paul's got an abrasive way of complimenting you."

My nerves eased up a little bit. For a moment, I feared there was someone else. Of course, there *was* someone else. Jolene Jones. I'd be lying if I didn't sometimes catch myself wondering if he were over her. With his phone in my hand, feeling like hot coal, I felt tempted to spy—except, long ago, before I even got into serious relationships, I refused to be that woman who had to go through a man's phone. I didn't sign up to be a detective, and I wouldn't turn into one now.

That one time with Rod had been painful enough.

Trust.

It was so hard to give, but I trusted Zander enough to not spy on him. "Yeah, well, you better delete anything you wouldn't want me seeing in your photo album."

"Will do." Zander nodded. "It's time to let a lot of things go."

I tapped on his music app and scrolled through his music for the right vibe. "Whaaat?" I stretched out the word, surprised at what I found amid Zander's list. "What do *you* know about Method Man?"

Zander clicked his tongue. "My dad loved all that shit. I'm telling you; I grew up on a lot of different sounds."

I pressed play on a certain Method Man and Redman song and started acting up. Zander let the top down and wind was blowing through my ponytail as my arms shot up and I hollered for extra effect. No matter how much time passed, "Da Rockwilder" by Method Man and Redman would always be a classic—and too damn short.

Being annoying, I leaned over and started rapping Redman's verse in Zander's ear and pointing my finger. Like a true fan, Zander joined me in singing the last line of the song.

I settled back in my seat as the song was over too quickly and laughed. It felt good to let loose and be normal for a minute. It was contagious, I could tell. Zander glimpsed my way, smiling as carefree as I was.

Then he did a double take, his smile lessening a degree.

"What?" I wanted to know.

"Take your hair down," he instructed.

"Why?"

"I don't like how you look right now."

Now I felt self-conscious. "What's wrong with how I look?"

Zander focused on the road ahead. "It's not you."

I scoffed. "What's that supposed to mean? You *barely* know me."

Zander made a face. "You got your hair pulled back and you're wearing white like you're trying to prove you're pure, like you're a good girl or you're worthy. Which is honestly bullshit. There's nothing wrong with you. You shouldn't have to do all this"—he gestured to me—"just to ask your dad for help. I know what you said about your mum, but it wasn't your fault. None of it. If he can't see that, then it's his loss."

I was being defensive and I couldn't help it. It felt like he was attacking me by placing my issues under a magnifying glass.

My lips trembled. "Zand."

Zander didn't back down. "We can turn around right now. I promise it'll be okay if you trust me."

"What if I do move in with you and you don't want me to leave, or *I* get comfortable?"

"Not seeing the problem."

Putty, I felt like putty in his hands. All of this was too good to be true. His generosity and his care were too much for me at times. Only an idiot would think before just jumping in with Zander without looking back to check if there were a parachute or not. "Just...keep going."

Nervously, I smoothed out the material of my pants, plucking up a piece of lint. I wasn't trying hard—okay, I was. But I just wanted to look my best.

Silently, Zander's free hand came into my line of vision as he reached out and took my hand and squeezed. His tattooed hand warmed my freezing cold one. I wanted to be angry at him just then, to push his hand away and be strong on my own.

Damn my pride.

I didn't push him away and he didn't let go.

Not too long later the sounds of Outkast and Killer Mike were bringing us across the threshold of Lindenwood, California. *Home sweet home.*

We drove by a familiar ice cream truck and the sight of old Mr. Harris serving a group of teenagers shaved ice brought nostalgia to me. It was summertime, and nothing beat a frozen treat from Mr. Harris's truck.

I almost felt tempted to have Zander stop so we could get

something, but my belly was too full with butterflies at the idea of eating.

Zander drove to my family home in no time and parked in the same space I'd become accustomed to parking during each of my visits. Those butterflies in my stomach began flapping and nausea was quick to take over.

Easy, Bia, breathe.

"We can go back," Zander said beside me. "If you let me, I'll take care—"

I unbuckled my seat belt and hurried out of the car, refusing to hear him out. I didn't even want to do this, grovel to my father for a place to stay, but anything was easier than leaning on Zander.

I let out easy breaths to calm myself down as I stared up at the house ahead of us. Zander came to my side and his presence gave me strength once more.

"I'll be quiet," he swore.

Looking at him, seeing how sincere and gentle he was, made my heart melt into a puddle of pathetic need.

"This is where I'm from," I let out softly. "This is my home."

Zander took my hand, but really, it was more than that. He took my heart and walked with me up the front walk, up the front porch, and waited beside me as I knocked on the front door.

I should've called, to let my father know I was coming instead of ambushing him. In some families, that idea was absurd, as some families let you know you were always welcomed home without knocking or calling, but my family, or what was left of it, was different.

My father came to the door and naturally he was surprised to see me, and Zander. Perplexity peppered his aged face as he took me in first, and then the stranger beside me.

"Hey, Dad, I...I should've called. I'm sorry, but I need to talk to you," I said. "Especially since I brought someone with me."

With his other hand free, Zander went forth to extend it to my father. "Hello, I'm Zander, nice to meet you."

My father's gaze lifted from our hands to me, ignoring

Zander's offer of a handshake. He questioned me silently at the foreign accent he was hearing, before going and being polite enough to shake with Zander. "Elijah, pleasure to meet you as well. Come in. Let's get out of this heat."

My father led the way into the house and I kept a slow pace behind him, not that Zander seemed to mind as he caught early pictures of my childhood and teen years littering the walls and shelves here and there on the way to the dining room. He smiled at a photo of younger me decked out in early 2000s gear, standing beside my brother as we were in the kitchen posing for the picture. I had hair balls in my hair, a Black-American tradition I couldn't wait to pass down to my daughter along with beads. Pryor was topless in the picture, folding his arms and appearing tough while I stood cheesing all big.

Another picture was of my mother standing on our green lawn out front holding a one-year-old me in her arms while smiling for the camera. The denim bucket hat with the flower on the front was a classic throwback. That photo was the one that Zander got lost in, pausing to study it intently.

"You look just like your mum almost." He turned to me. "She's very pretty."

Yes, my mother was.

Further down the hall to our left we joined my father in the dining room, where he was already seated at the table. He'd pulled out the coloring books, colored pencils, and crayons, as if this counted for our usual meeting.

Zander took a seat next to me at the six-chaired table and said nothing as he'd promised. He didn't grab a coloring book and he didn't ask what was going on. He kept mute.

"So much has changed since we last spoke," I said. "Zander is a singer, and we met at one of his shows."

No response. My father was trying to find a picture to color in.

"We've really hit it off," I went on.

He found his page and smoothed it out.

"Anyway, it's nice to be here."

It felt like I was begging almost, begging him to join me in this one-sided conversation. Or, at the very least, *look* at me. Love me.

My father did no such thing.

Still, I pushed forward. "Hemingway Park is nice, but Lindenwood will always be—"

"Bianka." He paused in what he was doing, staring down at his coloring page.

"Y-Yes?" I asked.

"Are you pregnant?"

My mouth clamped shut. "No."

He hummed, his way of saying, *Get to the point.*

"My landlord got bought out," I began, peeking over at my father, finding him engrossed at the challenge of coloring in a sea turtle. "They're going to tear down my building and so they gave us all a sixty-day notice."

My father went through his colored pencils, trying to find a green. "Uh-huh."

"I don't...I don't think I'm going to be able to find a place in sixty days, on such short notice," I went on. "I was hoping I could come back here, just until I can find an affordable place, or a second job."

I watched as my father's shoulders rose and fell with his heavy intake of breath. He went about shading in his turtle, shaking his head. "What happened to Victoria?"

Squeezing my eyes shut, I willed myself to be strong and endure. "We're not seeing eye to eye right now. If you let me come back, and I can't find a place, I'm sure I could go and live with her."

"And Zander?"

"We just met, and I'd like to be a little more serious before I move in with a guy." I forced out a tortured laugh that no one joined in on.

In fact, I felt Zander turn and face me, study me. His gaze burned my cheek. I was too much of a coward to look his way.

Another heavy sigh came from my father. "If you have no place else to go, I suppose you're more than welcome to come back here. You're going to have to put most of your stuff in storage, but your old room should hold some furniture since it's mostly cleared out."

Painfully, I smiled. It wasn't much, but it was a start. "Thank you."

He nodded and concentrated on his turtle.

Reaching a shaky hand out, I prepared to grab one of my kiddie coloring books to join him.

The sound of a chair scraping against the hardwood floor caused me to look over. I shrank. Zander was practicing the utmost patience as he breathed through his nose and glowered at me. His dark eyes flickered to my father and his face hardened even more.

"Can you excuse us for a moment?" he asked my father in a very clipped tone of voice.

Zander didn't wait for an answer before practically yanking me out of my seat and dragging me back through the house and out the front door.

On the porch, he released me before taking off for the steps. "Let's go."

"Zander." I hung back, wrapping my arms around myself as I tried to hold it together. Something about this place, this house— my home, made me weak and small. Inferior. I wasn't strong enough to say what was buried beneath my heart, and I wasn't strong enough to face Zander's wrath.

He spun around, his blazing hot eyes shooting daggers at me. "Bianka." It was a warning, a hint that he was close to losing his shit.

"It wasn't so bad," I said softly. "He said yes."

Zander narrowed his eyes as a light chuckle rolled off of his breath. "You're shittin' me, right?"

My eyes fell to the chipped paint of our porch. "Please."

"No."

"Zan—"

"No!" Zander roared, causing me to take a step back. He rushed his hands through his hair and tilted his head back to groan, before he calmed down enough to look at me. "You're not staying here."

"I have no—"

"He can't even be a man and look his own fuckin' daughter in the eye when shit is hitting the fan for her," Zander was speaking loudly, not at all trying to hide his current disgust for my father. He walked up on me, hovering over me as he peered down into my eyes. "You did *nothing* wrong, Bianka. Nothing! You don't deserve to feel isolated or like a fuckin' burden—a stain. I won't, I won't allow you to stomach this. It's humiliating."

A sob escaped my lips at the truth of it all. I was embarrassed, couldn't believe my father would treat me like this in front of another person, couldn't believe he couldn't ask about Zander or be interested in my life after all these years. Couldn't believe no one left in my family wanted me.

"I'm sorry," I cried out, shaking my head and squeezing my eyes shut. "I'm sorry I didn't let her know I was proud of her. I'm sorry I didn't tell her she was still amazing. I'm sorry I hurt her."

"She knew, Bianka, she knew," Zander insisted. "Your mum knew your heart and she knew you. We fuck up sometimes, but our mums never doubt us. She knew how you felt about *her*, and she loved you."

For years I'd let my father treat me the way he did because a part of me felt I deserved it due to my own guilt for how I'd rebelled against my mother. I didn't like her job, but I knew she was trying to make a difference, trying to make the world a better place.

"So, please, put your pride to the side and come stay with me," Zander continued. "You don't have to put up with this. I've got you, Bianka. I've got you."

The world was still going on around us in motion, but all I could see was Zander Khalil.

When it felt like I had utterly no one, here he was, standing beside me, willing and waiting to help me pick up the pieces and begin again. My home away from home. How did I get so lucky?

I blinked away my misty vision, refusing to cry over my family ever again. Taking a peek behind me, I knew, deep in my gut, that if I left with Zander, I'd never come back here again.

Closing my eyes, I let a tear roll down my cheek, and I breathed in the last taste of Lindenwood air I'd ever taste again.

My future was in front of me, holding his hand out for me, and what's more, taking me into his arms and keeping me safe.

And I went with him, all the way back home.

18

TALK TO ME

With each mile put between me and my father, I began to finally breathe.

Sometimes you didn't get closure, and that was okay.

I wasn't walking away for Zander. I was walking away for me. The small part of my heart that still felt love for Elijah Leslie was okay with finally leaving him behind because I knew he still had Pryor. And I knew Pryor still had a father. At least there was love there, for the two of them.

Me, I was alone.

Unloved.

I had walked away, but I'd been abandoned long before.

The whole way home I didn't look at Zander, telling myself I would truly cry later when he went back to Beverly Hills.

He parked his Bentley beside my Sentra and slowly shut off the ignition.

"You're coming in?" I focused down on my lap.

It was easy to leave with him, but now in the aftermath, everything felt heavy. Everything felt real.

Beside me, Zander sighed. "We need to talk."

Those words never amounted to any good. "Oh yeah?"

"Inside, Bianka. Now."

Zander liked to get assertive when he was agitated, I noticed. So it was no surprise he was barking out orders and taking the lead in the walk back up to my apartment. He walked so big and strong that I was left sneaking peeks up at him.

I let us into my apartment and kept my gaze on the floor, not ready for this talk he was so intent on having.

"You want to sit down?" Zander asked from behind me.

I shook my head. "No."

"Bianka." His tone of voice was strained, letting me know he was trying to keep his temper in check. I was pushing his patience. Maybe even pushing *him* away.

Finally, I looked at him, finding him very serious and standing erect by the door.

The lyrics of Teddy Sykes's "Leaving" came to mind and I knew right then I would break down if Zander left me too. If this day ended with another goodbye. I was having the time of my life with him, and like I always did, I was fucking it up by being me.

Zander's expression softened. "What are you thinking?"

I couldn't speak. "Just say it, Zander."

"You're about to cry and I want to know why."

"Just tell me what you want to talk about, please!"

He heaved another sigh and hung his head. "We're different, you and me. I get mad at Teddy and break things, and you lecture me and leave. You get evicted from your apartment and I come to your side and you tell me to leave, but I stayed. Your father is a spineless prick and I stood beside you and offered you my hand. I guess what I'm trying to say is, we've got to get on the same team.

"I'm used to leaving when I'm not comfortable or happy. I'm used to people packing up and leaving when they can't take it anymore with me, but right now, here with you, I'm ready to fight. When you're in trouble, Bi, I'm going to fight with you and *for* you. You call it being a therapist, but what else can you ask for in a partner than an ear, than a supportive listener? I've got issues and scars, but I'm not toxic anymore. I'm going to fight for you, but will *you* fight for *me*?"

If someone was keeping score, it did look pretty lopsided. I walked away when it got heated around Zander, and Zander stayed when I told him to leave. I had one foot out the door at the sight of trouble on my end and Zander was being open and honest in his questioning me.

I could feel myself shaking and I hated it. "I'm sorry."

Zander angled his head, studying me, but keeping his respectful distance. "About what?"

"I'm sorry I'm not a normal person from a healthy background. I'm sorry I'm a mess. I collect trauma like a fucking hoarder, and this is the truth about me."

Zander ran his hands down his face. "Bianka."

"I would rather you leave right now than stay here and pity me," I came out and said. "I don't want you to feel obligated to take care of me, to feel bad for me and want to help me because I'm poor. In the beginning it was fun, and you liked *me*, Bia. I don't want that to change. I don't want to become a burden for you."

"Why can't I like you and feel bad that you're in a tough spot?" Zander challenged. "I miss you when you're not with me, when you're here and at work, but I respect the fact that you're in a position that you *have* to work. I won't insult you by telling you if you move in with me you can just quit your job. I won't promise you a fairy tale because I'm no Prince Charming."

Zander just wanted to be my man, to be there if I needed him, and I was too independent to let that happen. To be vulnerable and trusting. The first man I truly let in, hurt me. I told myself I would never be so raw for another person again, and yet, here I was. With Zander, I was doing things I never did before—I was living, young, wild, and free. Zander worshipped my body in ways that left me feeling like a goddess, sought my opinion in ways that made me feel like Einstein, wanted my hand in ways that made me feel like Athena.

Zander Khalil was standing there in front of me, practically begging me to let go of my inhibitions and fall freely in love with him.

And I was scared.

"Everybody disappoints me. I can't take it if you do, too," I let out.

Zander inched closer. "I'm *not* going to disappoint you, Bianka. I'll give you my word on that." Going further, he cupped my face in his palms. "Nobody knows what it's like to be alone more than me. I won't let you go through it."

Tears wet my eyes as I shook my head at the ugly truth. "You have a family. I don't."

Determined, Zander pressed on. "Sometimes you get to make your own family, Bi."

If only it were that easy.

Maybe it could be, if I just took a chance.

"Okay." I wiped my eyes on my arm, leaving behind smeared mascara. "I need you to promise me something, and after that I'll let my guard down and I'll be all in this with you. I'll give you *all* of me."

Zander braced himself. "Done. What is it?"

"When you know deep in your heart that it's over, and you don't want me anymore, you'll look me in the eye and let me know," I said. "I don't want to find out on a blog or social media. I want you to tell me to my face when it's over."

Zander frowned, staring down at the carpet as he slowly and solemnly managed to nod his head. "I will. Promise me the same? Or do I even have to ask?"

"I'll let you know."

Zander peered back up at me. "As for now?"

"I want you, this, everything, so long as you're along for the ride."

The sight of his smile eased up my mood and the feel of his arms soon taking me in against him let me know it was okay to trust him, to fall freely and not worry about the consequences.

His full lips captured mine and I gave mine up to him.

"I would say let's sleep on it, but it feels like someone is squeezing my uterus right now," I joked.

Zander eyed me, catching my meaning. "Need anything?"

I shook my head. "Pamprin and Chill sounds like a good mood for me."

Zander opened his mouth, but the sound of knocking at the door had him chuckling. "I've gotta get to the studio. We should talk about the move-in date later."

Right, because I agreed to live with him. I wasn't sure if I would wait the sixty days, or just chuck up the deuces now and pack my bags, save the rent money and move to Beverly Hills. It was a lot to think about.

"I'll let you know when I'm ready," I said.

Zander nodded, not wanting to push me any further. He went and answered the door, pulling it open and revealing Victoria standing behind it.

Her eyes landed on Zander, her biggest celebrity crush of all time, and enlarged at once. Joy and glee didn't take her. She couldn't have her dream guy because *I* was already with him.

"Victoria, yeah?" Zander was nice enough to hold his hand out, wanting to shake properly.

Tori's attention fell to Zander's tattooed hand and she merely shook her head. "Nice to meet you, Zander."

Zander turned back to me, understanding what this all meant. "I'll call you later." He excused himself out of the apartment and let Victoria in on his way out.

Victoria, despite a little sullenness after seeing Zander, was radiant in her bright colors of blue and yellow. The blue eyeliner she'd used made her makeup really come together.

It had been too long since I'd seen Tori. "Hey."

She made no effort to move, but merely lifted her chin at me. "You two look like you were going through it."

I shrugged. "It's me. I'll always ruin a good thing if you let me."

My best friend perked a finely shaped eyebrow. "You dated a few assholes, Bianka. Don't take credit for their faults and issues."

"I'm difficult," I argued. "Zander sees it, and he wanted to talk."

This Victoria didn't deny as she finally set her purse down and went and sat on my couch, waiting for me to join. "Yeah, there's that." She propped her arm up on the back of the couch and rested her head, eyeing me with disappointment. "You have an amazingly talented and attractive guy and you're being difficult?"

"Can we focus on us first?" I didn't need another lecture about letting my guard down.

Victoria exhaled through her nose. "Let's talk about this eviction. We were supposed to meet up yesterday and you blew me off, and when I called you, *he* picked up and told me you weren't feeling well. I was in the parking lot when I found out why; there was a notice on the ground."

That was another thing about Lakeside Manor, other tenants could be pigs about their trash. We had a row of three dumpsters and it was often full of discarded furniture and other things, and though it was against the policy, when the dumpster was full, some would pile their trash against it. Stray cats were known to linger around the back of the building picking at things they could in the garbage.

I sat back against my sofa and thought of my plight and the day I'd had. "It came out of nowhere."

Victoria frowned with sympathy. "What now?"

"I have nowhere to go, and it's such a short notice so I'd more than likely end up ass-out," I said. "Zander wanted me to move in with him or give me money, but—"

"You and that pride of yours wasn't havin' it," Victoria finished for me. She knew me well, as once Rod had offered to pay my bills for me and I'd declined, something Tori thought was wild. She was just as headstrong and independent as I was, but when a guy wanted to do for her, she had no issue with letting him.

"Right," I admitted. "So I suggested going to live with my father, which Zander didn't like either. He wanted to go with me to Lindenwood today while I asked, for support."

Tori blinked rapidly, completely shook. "Zander went to the 'Wood?"

"Girl." Even I was still tripping over that aspect. Maybe if things hadn't gone sour, I would've been able to show him around, my old stomping grounds so to speak. "Needless to say, my father was my father, and well...I literally have no one now."

A stinging sensation met my arm at the surprise slap Victoria was quick to give me. Hurt hung in her dark eyes, and I knew why before she even spoke up.

"I am pissed at you for lying to me about Zander, I'm hurt that you hooked up with *my* crush, and yeah, jealous too, but I love you like a sister, Bia. If you had come and told me about the eviction, I would've been there for you. I would never let you go without anything. Don't you know that?" She shook her head, annoyed with me. "God, and you sit up here and tell me to my face you have no one like I don't mean anything to you. Like you think I'd really push you to the curb over this Zander shit."

Maybe it was dramatic of me to assume the worst of Victoria like that. We'd been friends too long to just give up on her that easily. "I'm sorry."

"I mean it," Victoria went on. "Your dad and brother are shitty, and I wouldn't have let you go grovel either. I wish you would've called me."

I blinked back tears, happy to know that things weren't too fucked up between us that I couldn't depend on her. "I wish I did too."

"Move in with me. I've got the extra room," Victoria mentioned. "The north side of Hemingway Park is so much better than this side. You'll like it there. We can go half on everything. We should've *been* roommates."

Living with Tori would've been a breath of fresh air versus giving in and living with Zander. It was still new, still fresh.

Outside of my not wanting to be a burden, I didn't want to rush it. "If it won't put you out, it would really mean a lot if I could live with you."

Victoria waved me off. "Just promise me you won't move in just to move out and live with Zander. I'd hate to expect your half of the rent just to be ditched."

"I have been spending the night there, but I don't want to live with him just yet. I like having my own space." I raised my hand, to declare an oath. "I won't abandon you."

Victoria pressed her hand to mine. "Deal. You can move in whenever you're ready."

I took her hand in mine, holding it gently. "About Zander, I'm really sorry I didn't come out before. I wasn't trying to sneak around on you. It all just happened. It was supposed to be a one-night stand, but then he wanted more," I confessed. "I was in a bad mood after seeing my dad, after being rejected from Pryor, and seeing Rod again, and I just wanted to escape."

"But the weekend wasn't enough," Victoria concluded.

"No, it wasn't."

"I can't pretend I don't feel betrayed, because you didn't like him, Bia. You talked shit and judged me for being a Whatter. So, you can't expect me not to feel a way about this. It's going to be hard for me, but I'm not going to throw our friendship away because of it," Victoria swore. "This type of shit never happens in real life, and the fact that it did for you is just crazy, and a little unfair. I can tell he makes you happy. I seen y'all's live on Instagram."

The side-eye she snuck me had me blushing. "I'm trying to help him push this new album and music."

"You're his muse."

I shrugged. "I guess."

"And the sex is that A1?"

I bit my lip, questioning if she could handle the details, and if I should disclose any. We told each other everything in that regard, but this was different. "Not sure you want to know."

She shoved me. "Spill!"

"He definitely lives up to his lyrics." I looked her in the eye, letting her know I wasn't embellishing Zander's abilities. "He fucks so good I want to pay *his* bills."

Victoria snorted, covering her mouth to hide her chortling. "Bianka."

"I'm serious."

"Your body is his canvas," Victoria mumbled. "Wow. He's fucking perfect."

"He's got flaws, trust me, but he's trying to do better, so I guess I have to try to be softer with him," I said. "I don't want to push him away. I like him a lot, and I'm hoping it works, I really do."

"Then let him in and don't overthink it," she told me. "After a string of bad luck, you've finally hit the jackpot. Don't let your fear and ego fuck it up. Believe it or not, Bia, you deserve to be happy."

I deserved to be happy, a truth I hadn't allowed myself to realize and accept. Hearing my best friend tell me made it feel that much better.

It had been a hard day, in some ways, a lot was lost, but in others, so much more was gained. Having my best friend beside me, supporting me, that was all that mattered.

19

BRIGHT

I slept better knowing I had Victoria on my side again. I slept better knowing I had a place to live amid being abruptly evicted.

I returned to work Wednesday and stayed over to get extra hours on top of the ones I missed when I'd called off Tuesday. When I wasn't at work, I was back at my apartment instead of going to visit Zander. I was making the most of my last moments in my first home. It was my first taste of freedom and independence, and though it wasn't much, I was proud of it. It had been mine.

Victoria was being extra hospitable about my coming to live with her. She'd texted me Thursday about possibly getting together to paint and redecorate since her landlord allowed tenants that freedom. It was sweet, but I didn't want Victoria to step outside of herself for me, to break her routine in any way. She was accommodating me enough by letting me move in as it was.

I really loved her for that, for being there just when I needed her most. Sometimes, water was thicker than blood—a painful truth I'd come to know all too well.

My father hadn't so much as called me since Zander and I

walked away from him Tuesday, and I told myself not to care, to put it behind me. To no longer bleed for him.

If the only family I had to my name at the end of the day was Victoria, I was more than okay with that.

It was Friday afternoon and I'd just gotten in from my shift at Angles when my phone rang out a special ringtone. "Chill" by Zander was playing, letting me know Zander himself was calling me.

"Hello?" I slumped down on my bed as I picked up the call, happy to hear from him.

"Hey, you busy?" he asked.

"Just got in."

"Can you come over? I need to see you and talk to you about something. It's last minute, and I apologize, but I've been busy."

Zander had been in the studio all week, also making it easy to just stay home in my apartment. He was dedicated to the process of putting *Abstract* together and I was more than okay with giving him creative space.

"Give me about forty minutes and I'll be there."

I was quick to change my clothes and put on some perfume to pretty myself up before making my way to Beverly Hills. The last time I'd seen Zander I'd been an emotional wreck, and with things finally squared away, I was ready to just fall into place with him and be happy.

Over half an hour later I was flinging myself onto him as soon as I parked my car in his parking area and he came out to greet me. It had only been a few days, but we clung to each other. The taste of his lips and the feel of his arms around me pulled me under a deep spell I never wanted to break. I ran my fingers through his thick, silky hair and reveled in his expensive scent.

"I guess you missed me, too," Zander said as he reeled back and grinned at me.

"If I didn't have to work tomorrow I'd try to spend the night," I said, offering a frown.

Zander took my hand and brought me inside. "Don't worry about it. That's actually something I need to talk to you about."

Inside the house music was playing loudly. Miguel's vocals were easy to recognize after being a longtime fan.

"What's going on?" I shouted.

Zander led me to the source of the music where it was playing from the stereo system in the entertainment room. Paul was inside, having been enjoying his one-man party.

Zander stepped into the room and immediately shut the music off with a remote. "Who can think with it that loud?"

Paul was a sight to see. In the corner of his mouth a joint was hanging out, and in one of his hands was the biggest gold-plated bottle of champagne I'd ever seen. A few buttons of his dress shirt were undone, exposing a glimpse of his muscled, fine-haired chest.

"Bianka!" Paul cheered as he set eyes on me. He opened his arms out in greeting. "Where're your bags? We've got a jet to catch."

This was the first I'd heard of a trip. I looked to Zander for an answer. He merely rolled his eyes at his manager. "I haven't told her or invited her, Paul."

I wasn't invited? "What's going on?"

Paul took a pull from his joint and set the champagne down. "Zander's got the number-one song in the country, that's what. We're going to New York to celebrate."

Zander faced me pitifully. "It's work, not a party. Excuse him."

Paul snorted. "The sooner she knows, the sooner she can pack."

"She's not coming," Zander spoke up for me. "She has a job."

There was no need to be offended, because Zander knew me well. I couldn't just take off for New York and miss work. I needed my job and the money.

Paul eyed me funny. "You are the most honest person I've met out here. Most people would be screaming at a free trip to NYC. I mean, this is America. Who doesn't feel entitled to other people's money?"

Rajaa entered the room carrying a mug of either tea or coffee. He greeted me with a tilt of his head. "Hey, Bia."

"Hey, Raj." While we were still pretty much strangers to each other, I felt a sense of calm around Rajaa for the simple fact that he, like me, was just a normal person dropped into this world of fame and money. Beyond that, it was the fact that he knew Zander as *Saad* that made me most comfortable. He saw his cousin as just family, not this big entity he had to be a yes-man to.

"You done packing?" Paul asked Rajaa.

Rajaa bobbed his head as he sank down on the sectional. "I finished this morning."

"Hope you packed your sense of style, because we're getting you laid," Paul announced. "New York girls are different than the ones here in LA, trust me."

"Paul," Zander warned, taking a protective stance near Rajaa.

Rajaa squirmed a little with all the attention on him. "I'm only here to assist Saad as he works on his album. I'm not in the position to date an American girl, and I'm not trying to have a fling either."

"Not everyone's a pig, Paul," I teased.

Paul faced me. "That reminds me, you and I need to talk, one-on-one."

Zander didn't protest as he settled down next to Rajaa and began sifting through his cell phone. "Be nice," he issued out as Paul began leading the way out of the room.

Paul came past me and made a face at that remark. "Come on, let's use the office."

Curiously, I followed Paul down the hall and over to Zander's private office. It was nothing more than an all-white room with a sheet of glass for a desk over two metal beams. There was a Mac desktop computer on the desk. One wall held a shelf with a few books, ivory elephants, and other decorative pieces, as the other housed black and white portraits of famous people, and the back wall was just a series of windows facing the side of the house. The zebra print fur rug under the desk was a nice touch, making me want to remove my shoes and burrow my toes in the fine material.

Paul shut the door and stood back, narrowing his eyes at me.

"What?" I asked.

He shook his head, soon running his fingers through his blond hair. "You're really staying behind to work that nine-to-five?"

I made a face. "I need my job, Paul. I can't take off for God knows how long to be in New York."

Paul rubbed at his jaw, taking in my words. "Okay. I brought you in here because I need your contact information, e-mail, cell phone—whichever is best to get in touch with you."

I took a step back, caught off guard. "Excuse me?"

Paul delicately placed his hand on his chest. "One, it is important that I have the numbers of everyone in that kid's life. Case in point, the very existence of you. He fell off the grid in LA and came back with you. Second, I'm a manager. Money and career opportunities are my main motivation—you and I could potentially make some cash together."

Money. This was about money. "Did Zander put you up to this?"

"Nah, I'm just a business savvy guy," Paul stated simply. "You came up with Zaturday and his latest video is up to ten million views already. People are eating that shit up like candy. You, my dear, are very important."

I couldn't sell clothes forever. And if my ideas could be worth money, why not? After a moment's thought, I recited my number and Paul typed it into his phone.

"You have my word this is pure business. Terry and Dax told me the story of the slap heard 'round the world, so yeah, you and I are two volatile beings." He gestured to himself as he stared into my eyes honestly. "I failed anger management twice; trust me, I have no intent on getting caught up with another hothead."

I snorted. "How did you fail it twice?"

Now Paul took a defensive stance as he held up a finger to illustrate his point. "First of all, that first time was bullshit. I'm at a restaurant with my kid sister and some asshole hits on her, and I'm like 'hey, she's fifteen,' and you won't believe this fuckface blows it off like it's nothing. All I can say is somehow my hand winds up broken and this guy's missing a few molars." Paul shrugged like it was no big deal. "I don't know how that happened, but I ended up in anger management and it wasn't for me."

Paul was growing on me. "Sometimes people need to be punched."

"Thank you!" he exclaimed, as if I were the first person to see things his way. "Not that *I* hit anyone or anything, but you know, I definitely agree."

To that we shared a laugh. It was always important not to incriminate yourself.

"Does Zander know about this?" I asked, getting back on track. Being a celebrity, I knew his guard was up with outsiders he let into his circle. The last thing I wanted to do was look like I was weaseling my way in just to use his connections to set myself up.

Paul went and opened the office door. "Of course, I talked to him first. I'm his manager, and it's my job to make sure he's solid. No offense, but after the dud that was his last relationship, I'm a little apprehensive. We've got an album to finish and a tour we're planning, so I need his head on straight.

"He actually credited you for his strike of inspiration. He said you called him lazy or something, and it lit a match under his ass. Not to mention there's no denying 'Canvas' is a hit—it's the number-one song in the fucking country. I could kiss you right now I'm so happy."

Call me humble, but I wouldn't take credit for Zander's success. He was Zander Khalil before he met me. I inspired "Canvas," but it was Zander who had it in him all along. Victoria had stayed over a while on Tuesday where I had to eat my words and come out and confess how much I loved *Exposed* and

Damage Control. Vocally, stylistically, uniquely, he was Zander, a phenomenon all on his own. His debut album was pure gold and was totally snubbed by the Grammys. It was such a strong, solid body of work from a new artist who emerged on the scene straight out of a teeny bopper boy band.

Zander was going to New York, the opposite side of the country, and though, I would miss him terribly, I only wanted what was best for him. To see him like he deserved. Blogs and magazines liked to joke that he was the flop out of So What, but really, he was far from it. Teddy was the It guy now, but once Zander stepped on stage on his headlining solo tour, he was going to make anxiety his bitch and show the world who they'd been sleeping on.

I got goose bumps at the thought of sold-out arenas just to hear Zander sing.

Back in the entertainment room, I went and stood beside Zander, taking his hand, and beaming up at him with so much joy and hope. He looked down at me, offering me a smile, probably wondering why I was so happy and giddy, but it didn't matter, I was just proud of him already.

Zander wanted to talk privately so he excused us from the room and led me outside to his backyard. His estate was positioned high up on a hill with a terrific view of the city below him. The sun was setting, and the rose-gold sky above all the lights of the homes, buildings, and attractions below set the tone.

Zander stood beside me, going and taking it all in. "I love coming out here and just looking out at all that. Sometimes, I'd like to think if I had a child, I'd name them Bright. This spot makes me think of so many positive, possible, *bright*, big things."

I loved his reasoning behind the unique name. "Bright Khalil —a little different, but I like it." He was famous, of course he could get away with such a name in the long run.

Zander turned to me, assessing me. "How are things with Victoria? You're set on moving in with her instead?"

When I'd told him over the phone Wednesday afternoon

about my decision to go and live with Tori, he'd been understanding but skeptical given our past drama.

"Yeah, Tori's not the happiest person in the world *I* got with you, but she loves me too much to let it get in the way of our friendship," I assured. "I think in the long run it'll be good for our relationship if I don't move in with you right now."

Zander didn't disagree. "Maybe you're right. Can I spring for the movers? I think you should get on it right away. It was shady of them to leave you guys racing to find new homes, so why not throw them a big *fuck you* by just leaving early?"

The idea of moving soon made me anxious and overwhelmed, but I agreed that it was better to just get it over with than to wait. The notice made mention of waiving rent if we moved sooner than the sixty days.

"If it won't trouble you, you can pay for my movers," I said. It was still hard for me to let him be so generous, but I appreciated that he wanted to do nice things for me.

Zander didn't push and left it at that. "I'm going to New York and I've been dragging my feet about telling you because I know you gotta stay and work. I'll be gone for a week, or maybe two, we're going to shoot the 'Canvas' video and record out there, and maybe hit up a few radio stations to promote the new single since it's doing so well."

His schedule was full and busy, no room for me to tag along anyway, it seemed. He would be working just like how I had to work. Zander's career was a major factor; there was no avoiding what it all entailed.

No matter how much I would've liked to go, or how much I'd miss him, I wouldn't let it show. I didn't want to get in the way of his finally preparing to step up to the plate. "I'm excited for you."

Zander came close and caressed my cheek. "I want to be selfish and beg you to come with me, but I respect you too much for that."

I tried to play it off, to be cool and strong. "It's only a week, right? Go, enjoy yourself. I want you to miss me."

His dark eyes bore into mine and I felt my heart clench at the sight of how serious he looked. Zander turned and gazed out at the city scenery below. "I brought you out here because I have to ask you something, and I know it's a lot, and I'll understand if you say no, but it would mean a lot if you consider it."

"What?" I asked.

I watched as Zander took a deep, nervous breath and stared down at the ground for a moment.

"I've been invited to the Dymond Dinner. Pen posted a video of herself laying out by her pool listening to my song. Apparently, she's a big fan." Zander gave a sheepish shrug, as if it were no big deal.

At once I rolled my eyes. Not *those* Patels. If there was one group of people that annoyed me the most, it was those insufferable Patels. A talentless group of individuals who became famous through the unfortunate passing of their patriarch. Their father was a politician who had been assassinated in the '90s, and a decade later, *they* happened.

There were three of them, two girls and a boy, the children of a White mother, Patsy Hearst, and an Indian father, David Patel. Penelope, Parker, and their younger sister Porsia.

Their parents split up when Porsia was a kid, and Patsy moved on to real estate mogul Jace Hearst, and the two later had a couple of kids of their own—equally intolerable as the true Patels— twins, Piper and Peyton Hearst.

Over a decade ago, a reality show came out of their claim to fame: *Presenting the Patels*, that still ran on the Bravo network. The purpose was to give an inside look on their lives as they navigated years after their father's assassination as well as introducing how totally down-to-earth their family was. None of them had talent outside of being attractive. The show only highlighted how whiny and privileged they all were, and how drugged up Jace was to deal with it all.

Why did I loathe them?

The Patels, Piper and Peyton included, were nothing but a

bunch of culture vultures. It was one thing to appreciate Black culture, but it was another to *appropriate* it and use it as a prop. There were multiple scandals of the girls being accused of stealing ideas from lesser-known Black women to pawn off as their own creations for their Patel brand.

Not to mention the post-and-delete Peyton did when he uploaded a picture of himself sporting a fade haircut with braids on top with the caption: *White boys do it better*. It hadn't been live long before Black social media ate his ass up.

Parker was honestly more low-key. He only hooked up with every model he could from Instagram, and was often seen partying with rappers and ballers to solidify his desperation to be "down" like his sisters.

Needless to say, I didn't fuck with the Patels, which was a shame since Pen married son of hip-hop mogul William Dymond aka Willie D, Owen Dymond, a few years back. Owen Dymond was *the* super producer with a shelf full of Grammys to boast. Any chart-topping hip-hop song that came out in the past twenty years definitely had that Dymond touch on it.

And now Zander had been summoned by them.

It was a known fact that every summer the Dymond Dynasty held a cookout where all the who's who of the music industry and some of the Hollywood elite attended. Blogs and magazines covered it like it was the Oscars, and it was this huge thing. It was to celebrate life, love, Black excellence, and legacy, as well as kick off the summer.

Every up-and-coming hip-hop artist and R&B singer had to feel special to be invited to the Dymond Dinner. Willie D was a legend and his sons weren't far behind. Who was I to step on Zander's toes, even if it meant being near the Patels?

"That's big, huge!" I admitted.

"Yeah, and I'd really like for you to be my date," Zander said. "These things aren't for me, but Paul agrees it would look good to go. I have to show my face. I have to show that I'm still here."

In recent years, momager Patsy Hearst had finagled her way

into putting the Patel touch on the event since Pen pretty much had Owen wrapped around her finger, and Owen was his dad's right hand. Willie was the head of the Dymond empire, but his sons, Owen, Remington, and Galen, pretty much held down the fort these days.

I wrung my hands, suddenly nervous and unsure. Beyond the fact that I wasn't trying to schmooze with people I couldn't stand, I wasn't sure I'd even fit in.

"I'll be in New York, and you'll be here," Zander continued. "Hopefully while I'm gone you can really think about it. It's in two weeks, on the eighth. I understand the pressure of attending. I get it. There's three reasons to say no."

"Three?" I questioned.

Zander began listing them on his fingers. "The Patels aren't for everyone. I get it. So that's one. Two, Piper does some acting and is also good friends with Jo, so I'm certain Jolene will be there. And three, Teddy and Piper also had their thing and he's buzzing right now and he could be there too."

Shit. "You're walking into the lion's den."

"Yeah, tell me about it," Zander commented. "There's going to be enough people there so hopefully certain paths aren't crossed. I'm not counting on Teddy to show up, to be honest. The guy's an asshole, and I'm not saying that to be bitter; I'm saying that because the son of a bitch is a prick. Jo said he and Piper ended badly—word is, *all* his relationships end badly. Hopefully she hates him enough to keep his name off the list."

Despite his golden boy image, Teddy Sykes was drama, I could see that now. One thing about the Patels—they lived on their names being in the spotlight. There were numerous times I'd seen their names trending on Twitter because of some feud they decided to take online rather than a private family group chat.

It was a Dymond event originally, but with Pen now in the picture, she also helped pick who came, with her family's influence. There was no telling who was coming.

Deep down, the idea of going scared me, and *I* wasn't the one with anxiety.

Zander needed me, and I didn't want to let him down.

I gave him an earnest smile as I reached out and held on to his hand. "I promise I'll think long and hard about it."

While Zander was quick to flash a smile, it suddenly dawned on me that if I said yes, this would be my first official event as his girlfriend. Leaving me to question, if I was ready for my debut.

20

FRESH AIR

Zander left Saturday for New York, leaving me behind. Even though he had business to take care of, he made good on his word in providing my moving arrangements.

It happened sooner than I thought. Monday, they showed up prepared to take furniture, and what's more, pack for me as well. I was unprepared and hadn't a clue what to do. For one, Victoria had a pretty much fully furnished apartment. Even the spare room she was giving me housed her makeup kits and extra clothing. It just left me with the task of selling more than half of my belongings since the idea of storage brought on an unnecessary monthly bill.

Victoria was sweet about it, making excuses for me to keep some things to figure out how to work them into the apartment.

She was my best friend, and she wanted me to have some sense of myself when I came to live with her. So, we kept my TVs, the small 32-inch went into my bedroom, and my 43-inch went into Victoria's room as the TV out in her main room was 60-inches—a gift from a past lover.

We kept my air fryer, and I got rid of my dishes. We kept my electric hot comb and hair dryer, and I washed and donated my bathroom towels and a good amount of unused clothing. We kept what food I had, and I got rid of my cleaning tools. I collected my few books and films and made room for them in my new bedroom. It was smaller than my old one, but it made prioritizing that much more prominent.

Zander's crew was practical, patient, and professional. They worked around my schedule, and the man in charge, Sal, even went as far as to help me sell all the things I didn't want and decide what to pitch.

In a record of four days I was moved into Victoria's apartment. When I went to tip the crew for their service, Sal declined, stating that Zander had paid them well *with* gratuity.

Of course he had.

"You think you can get him to pay rent for two months?" Victoria joked as we sat at a table in our favorite club. It was Friday night, and we were having a much-needed girls' night out. The Boot was booming with people, and the DJ was aiming to satisfy with her smooth set. The lights were dim and the vibe was just right. It was the weekend and everyone wanted to unwind and feel good for a moment.

My best friend was joking, but her words made me remember a conversation from a week prior. I stirred my drink with my straw, focusing on the red liquid whirling around and around. As a gift for taking me in last minute, Zander had wanted to pay July's rent for Victoria. It had been the end of the month when my landlord had given us our notices, hence Zander's rush on my moving out so quickly. It was Friday, July third, and I had turned in the keys to my old apartment on Thursday.

"Tori," I warned.

She knew this was a sore moment for me, a lapse in my usual character to let Zander do such a thing. "Kidding, relax."

"The only reason I even agreed is because I do feel like I'm invading your space, and I'm partly sure he wants to get into your good graces." I gave a shrug in an attempt for casual.

Victoria rolled her eyes and settled back into her chair. "Girl, I'ma buy his little album, but the image is soiled. I had to throw my vibrator away."

I choked on my drink. I grabbed a napkin to wipe at my mouth, careful not to ruin my lipstick. "Victoria."

She bore no shame as she simply waved me off. "Too many memories, like, it's done. Besides, H. came crawling back."

Ah H., her most likeable ex. His name was Harold, but he chose to go by *H.* He was the total package: tall, good-looking, respectable, no kids, and he had a great job. In the end, he'd gotten cold feet and broke up with Victoria to chase randoms because he wasn't ready for love.

"Be careful," I warned. "Some people don't realize what they have until it's gone, and some men realize it and think they want it back, but they only repeat the cycle of hurting you."

Victoria pouted. "But he's so good in bed. Look, whatever, trust me, I'm going to break bank before he gets back into these panties."

Vindictive Victoria, gotta love her.

"There's something I need to talk to you about," I brought up as I set my drink to the side. "Zander got invited to the Dymond Dinner and he wants me to be his date."

Victoria's mouth dropped open. "Oh my God!"

I cringed at the thought of it all. The Dymond Dinner was such an extravagant event, and what would little ole me be doing there? "I told him I'd think about it."

My best friend's nostrils flared as she gave me an *oh come on* look. "Bia, the Dymond Dynasty Dinner is like the *royal* meal," Victoria said. "You're nobody if you're not invited."

"I'm happy for him, but I am me, and I wouldn't know what to say or do."

"Say you'll be by his side. This is a big moment, and besides, don't let such hot property like Zander Khalil be alone by all those famous and thirsty chicks."

"That's the thing, he's pretty sure Jolie will be there, not to mention possibly Teddy."

Victoria's lips made an O shape and she soon caught my apprehension. "Drama's on the menu tonight. Didn't you say shit almost went down when y'all ran into Teddy a few weeks ago?"

I thought back to Zander's near brawl with Teddy at the radio station. It had been scary watching them stand toe-to-toe with each other, two powerhouse forces. Zander wasn't a scrawny guy, but there'd been no mistaking the height or size difference. Teddy Sykes was at least six-foot-two, with plenty of muscle to back up that sly taunting he'd been doing.

A quick tap into Google found that in the early So What days, or as fans like to call *fetus* So What days, Teddy had been a skinny little thing, and then he met a gym he really liked around album number three and he just bulked up. There were tons of images of the singer's muscled abdomen that came up when I searched under his name.

Still, I didn't believe it would've been an easy feat for him had he and Zander fought. They probably would've torn each other apart. Zander had been that pissed.

"Let's hope Teddy doesn't get invited. Zander says he and Piper didn't end so well," I said.

Victoria nodded. "Yeah, I remember there being reports that he left her high and dry at some resort getaway, like, he just took off and never called her again. I mean, this is potential Patel/Hearst bullshit, so I wasn't really buying it. Teddy's got a good rep. He's like the sweetest thing out of So What."

Yeah, right, I thought, remembering his going on air and mocking Zander's anxiety and reclusive ways. "Anyway, it feels like if I don't go, I'm letting him down."

"Oh, you are," Victoria was quick to note. "This is huge. Go and hold his hand. If Jolie's going to be there..." She let the idea hang in the air as she gathered her cell phone and rocked to the beat of the latest Tyga record.

I sank back in my seat and sipped on my drink, realizing she was right in the end. This was a big event for Zander, a true test of his social anxiety; who was I to leave him hanging? Paul was going as well, but I was sure Zander would be more comfortable with me there beside him.

I guessed I was going to the Dymond Dinner.

"Aww." Victoria was caught up on something on her phone.

"What?" I wanted to know, being completely nosy and wondering if H. had sent her something romantic.

"Check your Instagram, see what Zander posted."

Oh. "I don't even follow him on there."

Tori deadpanned, her shoulders sagging. "Bianka, quit frontin' like you're not feelin' the kid. Who you tryin' to fool by not following his socials?"

Why did I feel attacked?

I grabbed my phone and clicked on to the social media app and found Zander's page. His latest update was a black and white shot of him in a chair getting a tattoo on the right side of his chest. A closer inspection found that it was a minimalist tattoo of three Xs styled as Roman numerals.

The caption was simple: *In NYC, it was only right to get some fresh ink from my boy @TazTatted #Z3Sessions*

"Looks good," I commented. When Victoria didn't reply, I looked up to find her scowling at something on her screen. "What?"

She gaped up at me. "Check The CelebriTea page. She think she slick."

Her words alerted me, causing me to gather my phone and go on the gossip page's profile. At once, I caught Victoria's disgust.

One of their latest posts was a split image of Zander and Jolene Jones with a caption of: *#ZanderKhalil touched down in NYC this week, and our girl #Jolie was NOT too far behind. #TeaParty, do you think our lil love birds may rekindle that old thang? #ButWhereHisNewBoo*

The post held multiple photos, one of Zander's recent trip to the tattoo parlor, and images from Jolie's page.

The screenshot of Jolie's Instagram story made my stomach sick. It was an all-black post with one word to announce so much more. *Single.* Even worse, her latest post had the location in New York City. She knew exactly what she was doing.

Victoria was right. She was a bitch.

I looked up at my best friend as a frown marred my face. "What the fuck?"

"Have you heard from him today? I mean, that tattoo pic is from yesterday."

The last time I'd spoken to Zander had been on Wednesday, but I'd chucked it up to our both being busy. Him recording, and me moving and unpacking. Now, I wondered...

He intentionally hadn't told me about the trip until the last minute. And he hadn't made an attempt to invite me along. Did he know about Jolie being there?

I stood from the table. "I-I'm getting a migraine. Can we go?"

Victoria nodded, understanding my sunken mood as she was quick to grab her purse and abandon the last of her drink for me.

Everyone was in the club having a good time and all I wanted to do was not jump to conclusions. I didn't want to go to the Dymond Dinner under the act of watching Zander so he wouldn't cheat on me, but now that it was obvious Jolie wasn't about to play fair, I was lost.

My main reason for going to the dinner was to be a supportive girlfriend, but now it felt like a job had to be done.

I could lie and say it was all in my head, but why else would she have gone childish and posted about her current relationship status? Why else post she was in New York City? People only posted their "single" relationship status when they wanted to get a lover's attention.

They had history together, a big one. Could our little budding romance compete?

"Calm down," Victoria insisted as she let us back into the apartment. "I didn't mean to scare you, but now you see why you *have* to go to the Dymond Dinner. Jolie was just posted up with the next dude, and now all of sudden when Zander's making headlines with you and dropping new music, she's single and shouting about it."

I fidgeted uncomfortably from one foot to the other. "Do I call him? Will that make me look like I don't trust him?"

Victoria frowned. "*Do* you trust him, Bia?"

While I stood firm in my being fun, likeable, and good enough in bed to keep Zander satisfied and coming back, it didn't beat the fact that he'd held a very serious relationship with Jolie. Was our newness enough to keep him interested? Could he be trusted around Jolie alone? Did we have enough depth?

This was exactly the kind of stress I did not need with dating someone as high-profile as Zander. He would be on tour, city after city, country after country. The type of anxiety that could come with worrying about him being faithful on the road was not for me.

My mind wandered back to the day he asked to be more. To the day he promised to be faithful to me if I stayed true. If this were real between us.

Feeling a heavy weight set in on my shoulders, I hung my head. "I'm going to wash my face and get ready for bed. I gotta work in the morning."

"Bi—"

I held my hand up, not wanting to talk about it any further, for fear I'd do something emotional like break down. My mind was racing and I kept telling myself I was overreacting.

Still, after my shower, I found myself back in bed sifting through Zander's social media accounts. He didn't post much, but because Victoria was right, I dropped my last piece of armor and followed Zander on all accounts.

It was when following his Instagram account that I caught his page going live. Here in Los Angeles time, it was just after eleven, making it two in the morning where Zander was.

I clicked on his live, finding him in bed in his hotel room. He wasn't wearing a shirt and his chest was shiny from the protective ointment for his tattoo.

"*Wow*," Zander said, leaning close to the screen. "*There're way too many people joining this thing at this hour.*"

He sat up in bed and just stared at the screen, reading the influx of comments. He was breathtaking, something mostly all his followers were commenting on.

Zander yawned. "*I guess I won't be here long. I just wanted to check in on my Zandies. I'm sorry I didn't do Zaturday last week, and I probably won't make tomorrow's. I'm in New York right now recording. I just got back from the studio actually.*" A series of people questioned his recording process and Zander took it as a cue to let them in. "*Uh, tonight we finished a track I'm calling 'Bi 4 U.' It's got this sick beat and guitar, and I can't wait for you to hear it. I'm not sure what the next single will be, but I'm really loving the feedback on 'Canvas.' That's probably one of the records I've made I'm most proud of.*"

The biggest grin stole my lips as I got teary eyed. He was working, and I was beginning to stress over nothing.

"*We also shot the 'Canvas' video this week, too. So be on the lookout for that very soon. This album's going to be amazing. I'm incredibly inspired right now.*" Zander went quiet as he was once more reading comments. "*I just want to promise you that next year we're going on tour, and it'll be the year of Z.*" He chuckled at his own corniness before running a hand through those ebony locks of his. "*I'll be back live again soon, but for now, be safe out there. I love you guys, 'bye.*"

Not too long after the live ended my cell phone lit up with a FaceTime call.

I sank under my comforter, a smile on my face. "Hello?"

"How are you?" Zander's tired voice greeted me, sending

goose bumps across my skin. The sight of his beautiful sleepy face made me wish we were in bed together, snuggled up.

We were nearly three thousand miles apart, but seeing him on the phone, knowing he missed me too, made the distance feel like nothing. Because I trusted Zander, I let all thoughts of his sneaky ex go as I knew that *I* had his undivided attention and that was all that mattered. "Better now."

21

DRUNK

The repugnant smell of broccoli greeted me as I came out of my bedroom after getting dressed after my shower Sunday evening. Angles had been busy that night and now I was ready to sit and relax, save for the odor.

Victoria was sitting on the sofa eating from a blue steam bag of broccoli as she binge-watched *Dexter*. She was in a cute little onesie with strawberries all over its pink material.

"Really?" I questioned her meal for the evening.

Tori shrugged. "You were at work, couldn't decide on takeout, and going out with H. would require talking to him. So, alas, we have broccoli."

I didn't judge my friend as I sank down beside her and she continued to eat from the bag.

"You decide about the dinner yet?" she asked.

"I'm going to go, not because of Jolie, but because I want to support Zander in his moment," I decided.

While we'd FaceTimed Friday night, I hadn't mentioned my decision to join him. I wanted to surprise him when he was back in town. It was Sunday the fifth, six days before the big event.

Victoria paused her episode and faced me, appearing serious. "What are you going to wear, hair and clothing wise?"

That was going to be the big part of the struggle of going. I couldn't afford designer, but the aspiring designer in me knew a thing or two about style, and I was sure whatever I could pull together, be it from Angles or the mall, I could make work. Zander had paid our rent, leaving a little extra money to splurge on.

"First I have to see what he's wearing," I said. "I figured we'd match. I'm not going because of Jolie, but best believe I want to rub it in her face and come to show out."

Victoria made a face as she raised her hand for me to high-five. "Yes!"

A sick smile washed across my face. It wasn't a competition, because I already had Zander, but I did want to show off how good we looked together. "Can you do my makeup?"

Victoria snorted and sized me up. "As if you had a choice otherwise."

Tori was the quintessential girl's-girl, the paradigm of all things feminine. She lived for makeup, nails, hair, and clothing. In a lot of ways, I was her living, breathing doll, as she often would call me up to try new looks on me. I always told her she should start a YouTube channel as a side hustle outside of her makeup gig, because she was that good.

"I think you should wear your natural hair, like a blunt look, you know? Or maybe a few bundles for fullness, but cut short. Don't worry, I got you, girl, we gon' take the spotlight away from Zander."

All eyes on me, I quipped to myself.

"Chill" started playing and I gathered my phone to answer Zander's call. "Hey."

"Hey, you busy?" Zander asked.

"No, I'm just settling down. What's up?"

"I just got back in. You wanna come through?"

Already? He hadn't been sure how long he'd be in New York, but after being gone for over a week, I was almost counting on it being nearly two. "You just flew in? Why didn't you tell me? I wanted to take you out for dinner."

Zander chuckled. "Aww, let's rain check that. Right now I'm just stopping off at the house to drop off my luggage, and then I'm heading to the studio to record. I'd like you to come with me. I want to show you my world."

He was still in work mode, but the fact that he wanted to include me, to show me his process, made me feel special.

"I'll be right there," I told him.

We hung up and I paused, looking down at my T-shirt and shorts. First, I had to change and figure out what to wear. I hurried back into my room and sifted through my closet before finding and settling on a floral print spaghetti-stringed dress. It hugged my curves and was the perfect summer dress. It was short, offered cleavage, and its navy-blue background complemented my brown skin. I was practically glowing after my shower and moisturizing.

I slipped the dress on and brought a choker around my neck for added touch. Makeup was a usual must, but with it being late and Zander being all about business, I decided against it.

"Hey, that was Zander. He just flew back into town. I'm going to see him for a little bit, okay?" I said as I walked back out to the living room and let Victoria know I was leaving.

Victoria put her broccoli to the side as she leaned back to get a look at me. "First of all, yasss, second of all, don't hurt him now."

I twirled in a circle, making the skirt of the dress sway. "You like?"

"I *love*." Victoria gathered her broccoli. "And that's why I'm eating broccoli, so I can keep up with you."

"Stop." I loved being friends with Victoria, the equal benefit of gassing each other up never stopped. "I work tomorrow so I should be back; if not, I'll text you and let you know."

Victoria bobbed her head, went back to her episode of *Dexter*, and gathered her water bottle to take a hearty sip. "Tell him I said hey."

I grabbed my bag from the counter in the kitchen and slipped out the door.

Zander hadn't lied—he was just stopping in to drop off his luggage. As Rajaa let me into Zander's home thirty minutes later, I came to see their bags from their trip sitting in the foyer. The only light on was that of the entrance and down in the kitchen where I could hear the men talking.

"How was New York?" I asked Rajaa as he let me pass him into the house.

Rajaa shrugged. "It's one of those places where there's so much to do, but so little time to get it done. I always want to go here, there, and everywhere when I visit, and yet I never get to. I love the people and the food, though."

New York was one of those places I always wanted to visit. Just being a fan of hip-hop and the reputation New York held gave me an affinity for the state.

In the kitchen I found Zander, Terry, Dax, and Paul scattered around and winding down from their flight.

"Bianka!" Paul greeted me loudly. "She returns! Did you miss me?"

Rajaa rolled his eyes as he went and sat next to his cousin at the island.

"Did you get laid?" I countered playfully.

The guys laughed and Paul narrowed his eyes at my taunting. "Actually, I was too busy keeping the boy scout good and faithful for you. Who do you think got him that nice premium porn package?"

"Classy," I responded as I went over to Zander's side.

Zander brought an arm around me as he eyed his manager. "Watch it."

Paul wasn't fazed in the least. "Mark your calendar, Bi, because in August we've got a date."

"A date?" I repeated.

Paul rubbed his palms together as a devious smile splayed across his face. He tilted his head towards Zander. "MTV called and they want my boy for the VMAs, and he's going to need the prettiest girl on his arm for the event. The world is eating up 'Canvas,' and we have you to thank for it. The video's out Friday, and I can't wait to see those numbers shoot up."

Zander regarded me at the mention of his continued success. "It's going to be my first performance in three years, and I'd really like for you to be there."

"Then I'm there," I promised. I placed my hand on his. "Looks like you should have *two* kids one day, Bright and Courage."

Zander appreciated the gesture as he lifted his bottle of water and made a private toast towards me. "To Courage Khalil."

"A'ight then, Zan," Dax said as he pushed off from where he'd been standing by the sink. "I gotta head out."

He came and dapped Zander up before taking off down the hall for the front door. Terry issued out a farewell as well before following suit.

Zander checked the time on his watch before standing from the stool and facing Rajaa. "You staying in?"

Rajaa nodded. "I'm knackered from the flight."

Zander patted his back and turned to Paul. "Get on some food, okay? We'll meet you at the studio."

"On it." Despite the hour, Paul was still on go as he gathered his cell phone and walked out of the room.

It was nearing midnight and this must've been a casual thing for them to work into the wee hours of the morning. It was nothing for Zander to escort me out to his cobalt blue Maserati and help me inside before joining me behind the wheel.

"Have you given Saturday any more thought?" he asked as soon as we were on the road.

"Yes, I'd love to go with you," I told him.

Zander glanced my way, a mountain of relief lifting from his shoulders. He wouldn't have told me, I could tell, but he not only wanted me there, he needed me there. "Thank you, Bianka."

"Let's just go bask in your much-deserved success right now and have fun."

"Just a heads-up, Naz is flying in. She insists on helping me get ready for it, but really she just wants to be Paul's plus-one."

All of me came to a screeching halt as my head snapped his way. "Wait, so not only is it Patel infested, a potential run-in with your ex, and a could-be fight for you and Teddy; on top of that, we have to deal with your sister?"

To my surprise, Zander chuckled. His perfectly white teeth flashing as he blatantly laughed at my uneasiness. "Easy, that's my family."

"And she wasn't so fond of me the last time we ran into each other."

"Naz is protective, is all. I told her you were here to stay, and yes, her guard's up, but I'm certain she'll come around." Zander's grasp on the wheel tightened. "I don't care about going. I don't want to be famous. I just want to make music I love and stand behind, and perform it. Being seen here and there doesn't really interest me. I like you for me because you're for me, you remind me of Naz, of Paul, not afraid to just call me out and just be here for me. I trust you."

It felt good to hear those words, to know that he liked me best because I wasn't out to be known or become famous. I had nothing to sell or promote off of his name, and he appreciated that.

If only we could be low-key forever.

Thinking further as he mentioned family, I was curious. "I like Bright and Courage, but wouldn't you want to use names from your heritage?"

Zander reached out, placing his hand on my thigh. "Definitely. I think about that sometimes. When I have children, they're going to know their culture, music, films, food, family—

everything. I like *Asad* for a boy and *Amala* for a girl. Courage Asad, and Bright Amala."

I loved the idea of him naming his son *Asad*. Saad and Asad would make a wonderful pair. And Amala sounded so pretty. "I like that."

"When the time is right, I'll probably be as annoying as DJ Khaled when I settle down and start a family."

A smile teased my lips at the memory of DJ Khaled's constant words of affirmation with his firstborn. There was nothing wrong with loving your child and telling them so, and instilling in them the idea of being capable of any and all things. DJ Khaled was the perfect father figure as far as I was concerned.

Zander pulled up to the facility, Platinum Fire Studios, and parked in a lane closest to the entrance. As late as it was, there were other vehicles in the lot as well, letting me know that nighttime recording was popular for other artists also.

Zander was in a simple heather gray T-shirt and a pair of jogging pants, dressed down beside me as he escorted me in.

Inside, at the front desk was a young man bent over a book reading. Zander merely nodded at him in greeting before walking past him towards the corridor of doorways.

"I've got to get a haircut. Outside of that, I'm not too worried about hiring a stylist. I'm sure I got something in my closet." Zander's hair had grown since our first encounter. No longer only short on the sides, it had filled in and I liked it. Especially the way he wore a headband with teeth to secure the longer bit on top back.

I reached out and ran my fingers through his silky locks. "What's the color scheme so I can match?"

Zander shrugged carelessly. "We'll get something on commission brought to the house for you and Naz."

"I was going to buy something from my store, or the mall," I confessed, feeling embarrassed suddenly.

Zander's soft smile warmed me. "Trust me, I get it, but for the sake of my sister and publicist, let's just see what we can pull, okay?"

"Publicist?" I questioned.

"Fran's having a field day spinning all of what's transpired. From cancelling the tour, to this new romance, and to the random single dropping. She's been chewing me out something fierce. She's another one who's insistent on me going to the dinner, to get some good publicity."

Zander was a brand, and it was important that he and his brand looked good at all times. So I was sure that it was imperative that I looked my part Saturday night as well. If I had to wear some ostentatious designer getup then I would do so with a smile. Either way, I was coming to show out with my man.

We walked all the way to the door at the end of the hallway and Zander let me inside first. At once I was immersed in the colors of red and purple.

The private recording suite was lit with neon purple and red lights. A sign on the wall glowed in radiant red as it read *Sin Den*.

There was a desk that stretched the length of the wall with a series of keys and buttons on it, with two plush chairs on wheels sitting nearby. In front of the desk was a large glass window that gave a peek into the next room where the mic was, as well as a daybed where one could lie back and muse over the lyrics comfortably if they wanted. Behind the desk was a leather sofa, and beside the sofa was a large island where complimentary water was sitting and waiting. As well as writing pads and pens for those moments when creative spark hit.

It felt like I was in a world where magic was created and I was Zander's apprentice.

I looked around us, amazed at the realness of it all. "Whoa."

"My producer, Nathan, will be here later, but I just wanted to show you around first," Zander explained. "This is where it all makes sense to me. Where I can expose all that's on my mind, break down every wall I've got built up and be vulnerable. Whenever I'm at my most down and hurt, I come here and I just record. I started working on this album last year and for a while everything was gray and melancholy, but now I see color and I'm living."

He spoke with his hands as he explained his love of this room, of this part of his creative process. I could just imagine him that night we were leaked to the public, the night he came here and wrote "Canvas."

Even further, he sat and explained to me how each button on the mixing desk worked, how to stop and go, how to record while the person in the booth was singing. He was my professor and he taught me all that he knew about the very thing he loved most. The knowledge on his tongue was never-ending and when I got lost, he'd smile giddily and begin to break it down further. I watched with wonder as he spoke, and I took it all in for more than the surface, but for the fact that Zander was happy, full of zeal, ready to work and really do this.

"You should hop in the booth and try singing," Zander suggested as he sat back in his chair and faced me.

"Uh, can't sing," I said.

He threaded his fingers together. "So? Just give it a go. It's you and me here."

Because he wanted me to, I got up and walked over to the door that led into the booth and went inside.

On the wall in the walkway, written in big black script, were the words *Let Your Soul Unwind*. There was no room for inhibitions. You were to leave them at the door and just become completely undone once you stepped up to the microphone.

The light in the booth was bright and fluorescent with a pinkish tint. It rained down on me as I approached the mic hanging from the ceiling.

Back in the control room, Zander looked serious at the desk, waiting on me to do something.

I grabbed the headset and put it on, feeling silly. I couldn't sing. I knew my limits and capabilities quite well.

Zander leaned forward and pressed a button enabling the

talkback system. "Don't be shy." His voice was in my ears through the headphones and I loved the sound and intimacy.

But I couldn't sing.

Butterflies filled my belly as I focused on the black filter and chrome microphone behind it in front of me. It was only Zander and me, but I didn't want to sound terrible.

Zander pressed the button again. "Want me to come in there and *make* you sing?"

Feeling playful, I said into the mic, "Yeah, I'd like to see you try."

Zander arched a brow before pushing back from the desk, standing to his feet, and disappearing on the left. Soon, he was coming into the booth and making his way over to me. Each step he took landed with a thud of his presence. Intimidation seeped into the air and I felt even more inadequate with a *real* vocalist in front of me. I removed the headset and set it to the side.

Zander smirked as he came to a stop. "Sing."

I opened my mouth, but quickly shut it.

He breathed through his nose and came closer.

I felt him behind me, sending the hairs on my neck standing at attention. The smell of his cologne enveloped my senses and I closed my eyes, wanting, wishing for him to take me into his arms.

Zander was in my ear, his lips brushing against my skin. "Bi, the sounds you make when I'm makin' love to you, it feels like I'm hearin' angels sing. You're my favorite song."

My knees about buckled at the tone of his voice and his nearness. Zander Khalil invented sex appeal.

He pressed a gentle, torturous kiss behind my ear, onto my neck, on my shoulder, and I let out a squeak.

His hand snaked around me and pressed low on my stomach. "Sing from here."

Somehow, he'd seduced me into doing it.

Sneaky bastard.

Zander came around me and folded his arms and waited patiently.

I approached the mic with a carefree attitude and started singing the lyrics to "Twinkle, Twinkle, Little Star."

In front of me, Zander looked the least bit satisfied.

"No, no, no." Zander stood back and shook his head. "Your timing is all off."

"My timing?" I questioned.

He angled his head. "You're losing track."

I didn't get it. "Huh?"

Soon, he was coming close and reaching into his pocket. I watched in confusion as he pulled out a velvet box. By its shape, I guessed it housed a necklace or bracelet.

"Maybe this'll help you keep track better." In the next moment, Zander opened the box, taking my breath away.

Inside was a platinum watch with diamonds around the face, but that wasn't what made me gasp, it was the face itself. It was round and protruding, like a bubble.

"I—" I couldn't speak.

Zander handed the watch over. "My first two days in New York, when I wasn't recording, I was searching online for a 'water watch,' and then I even had Dax with me as I scoured a few pawn shops. I did a little digging, and watches with 'bubble' faces came up and I went to my jeweler out there and had him customize a Rolex for me. He thought I was crazy, but I don't expect anyone to get the significance, but you of course.

"I know you've been hard on yourself because of this eviction and what happened with your dad, and I've just been thinking if your mum were here and she could see what I see, she'd know everything you're doing and all that you are becoming is happening right on time."

My lips trembled and my eyes filled with tears. The one thing I'd always wanted when I was a kid, and he'd gone out of his way to design it for me, in homage of my mother, as a sign of encouragement.

My heart burst for him as I stepped forth and brought my arms around his neck and kissed him.

My body belonged to him as it clung against his. I tugged on the waistband of his pants and Zander was quick to lean down and rid me of my panties. We didn't need words as Zander sat back on the daybed and I straddled his lap, needing him in that moment more than ever. Our lips never left each other's as I leaned up and he began sliding his pants down.

An alert sounded in my head and I came out of the heated universe where it was just us two.

"Wait, wait," I said, pressing my hands to his chest.

"What?" His voice was strained as he pulled back from me with a wounded, tortured expression hanging in his eyes.

I wanted this as badly as he did, but still. "What if someone walks in?"

"The door's locked."

His pants came down and I lowered myself onto him. The second we were connected we both mirrored out the same groan of pleasure.

Zander moaned. "I missed this."

"Me too."

My mouth found his as we went at it full force. I wanted to go slow, to savor all of him and the sensation of him inside of me, but it all felt so good. His greedy hands grabbed a hold of me, desperate for our movement to never end.

We finished together, in a loud cry of satisfaction.

Even in the aftermath of my orgasm, I didn't want to leave his lap, to rid him of my body.

I cradled his face in my hands as I wound down from my high. For a moment, all I could do was stare at him as he gazed up at me. Three big words were threatening to spill from my lips as all that I felt for him could only be summed up by one thing: love.

No matter the time we'd been together or not, I knew, without a doubt, that I loved him.

Paul joined the session along with the producer thirty minutes later. I couldn't stop smiling as I sat back on the sofa, and Zander was the same as he kept sneaking peeks at me. Our shared blush was like passing notes.

"Food's on the way in about ten," Paul announced as he looked up from his cell phone and sat next to me. "You ready to work, Z?"

Zander gathered his phone and stood from the chair. "Bring up 'Deeper.' I've been working on the bridge and chorus."

Nathan bobbed his head and faced the mixing desk as Zander went into the booth.

An instrumental began playing and the tone and melody had me intrigued. It was atmospheric with a background beat that was timed well enough for one to clap to.

"Be prepared to be here all night. This kid is a machine that keeps spitting out records," Paul said. "Think we're up to fifty alone for Z3. He's got this one he's rapping on, and I'm going to fight him if he doesn't put it on the album."

I thought of the remix to "The Sound" featuring Drake, where Zander was sing-rapping and Drake was singing. The remix had gone viral the moment it dropped. It was *that* amazing.

Zander was incredibly talented.

After gathering his phone in the booth, Zander began on what was the bridge and chorus of "Deeper."

The lyrics were vulnerable. A call for more, to dig deep, and keep pushing forward in a new relationship. Something I saw myself doing wholeheartedly.

I gave a thumbs-up as a smile split my face.

Abstract was going to be a smash hit. I believed it so.

22

PILLOWTALK

There were fifteen minutes left of my shift Monday, and I was barely holding on. I was beyond tired, and the 5-Hour energy I'd chugged only provided a little burst of energy.

Perhaps it was my rightful punishment for being up all night at the studio with Zander. He'd finalized "Deeper," and cut and recorded another song called "Xs." Every song I'd heard so far sounded flawless.

It was a party in the studio, an exclusive concert where only few were allowed in.

Did I regret being out all night, no, but I knew better.

"You about to go home and have you a good nap," my coworker, Jaliyah, observed as she came up to the checkout counter from the backroom.

"More than likely," I agreed.

"What was you doing all night?"

Only Holliston knew about Zander, as far as my coworkers went. None of them, our manager included, would probably know who Zander was. He wasn't their vibe.

"My boyfriend is sort of—"

The jingling of bells had me stopping to face and greet our newest customer.

Coming in behind a large bouquet of red roses, was Zander.

One look at Zander had Jaliyah's jaw dropping in shock. I wasn't sure I'd ever get used to seeing women zone out over Zander's handsome face.

"Who is that?" Jaliyah demanded to know.

The few shoppers in Angles were also caught up in Zander's appearance.

I stood taller, trying to appear nonchalant. "My boyfriend."

Jaliyah turned and faced me, her jaw showing no sign of closing. "*That's* you?"

"Uh-huh," I responded shyly.

She snuck me a high five just as Zander made his way to us.

"Hey." He handed the bouquet over and tipped his head in greeting towards my coworker. "You've seen my world, and I figured it'd be nice to see yours."

His accent had Jaliyah tripping even further.

Zander meant well, but retail was no match for the recording studio.

I gestured around us. "It's not glamorous."

Zander eyed the sales floor and the clothing Angles sold curiously before returning to me. "But fashion is your niche, so it *is* something. You could be workin' anywhere, but you chose this shop."

Outside of the discount, I did like my job at Angles because at least I got to be close to my dream of being a designer.

"Right," I said as I focused on smelling the bouquet. "By the way, this is my coworker, Jaliyah. Jay, this is my boyfriend, Zander."

Jaliyah blushed as Zander offered her a hand to shake. I should've expanded on who he was, but this was going so smoothly, I didn't want to cause a scene.

"Pleasure to meet you," Zander said to Jaliyah. His gaze

shifted to me, a warmth inside it that made me feel entirely safe. "When can you leave?"

"Now," Jaliyah spoke up for me. "Girl, clock out early. Holliston should be here in an hour, I'll be good."

We were given a courtesy to clock in seven minutes early as well as clock out seven minutes early. I clocked out five minutes before I was due to leave.

Zander was right behind me as I made my way to the employee portion of the parking lot. He saw me to my car and hung back.

"Don't be embarrassed, okay?" He caressed my cheek. His soft touch cooled my nerves and I relaxed. "I should've called."

"It's okay," I insisted.

It was nice to see him in this neck of the woods. Here in Hemingway Park, he wouldn't need Terry or Dax to escort him around. A bunch of screaming fans weren't about to jump out, film, or photograph him in the low-key settings of my neighborhood.

"You wanna see my new place?" I suggested.

"Definitely," Zander agreed.

Ten minutes later we were inside my shared apartment and in my bedroom. Having Zander look around at each and everything I owned made me nervous all over again. He didn't browse for long before turning and looking at me.

"You never showed me your sketches," he pointed out.

Something like panic sent my heart beating hard in my chest. "Zander...they're just a pipe dream."

He narrowed his eyes. "Only if they're not good."

Breathe, Bia, breathe.

I'd never shown anyone my sketches or ideas before. Too afraid to be laughed at or mocked. I'd been obsessed with clothes ever since I was a little girl and would play dress-up. Ever since I owned my first Bratz doll.

With anyone else, I might've rejected the idea of sharing my work. But not with Zander. Not when he'd let down his walls and played me "Canvas" when he was afraid of *my* thoughts.

He'd been nothing but open with me, so, tentatively, I extended him the same courtesy as I crossed over to my nightstand and dug my old sketchbook from the bottom drawer. With shaky hands I handed over the spiral-bound book and stood back to await his opinion.

Zander accepted the book and began sifting through it quietly. A seriousness covered his features as he stood back and leafed through page after page, lingering on each one to really study my detail. Slowly, a corner of his mouth curled up as he neared the middle.

"This stuff...is amazin', Bi." He lifted his head to speak to me. "I like it. I do. It's...urban, it's flirty, it's classy, too, but with your own twist. You'd make a terrific designer."

I bit my lip to keep my emotions in check. I could tell he wasn't bullshitting me. That he really believed in my designs.

He turned the book and tapped at the sketch he'd stopped on. "I really love this idea."

It was a trilogy of looks featuring a blazer dress. One with a mesh back, another that was all mesh with solid borders, and a third that was all solid.

Feeling too much, I crossed over to Zander and kissed him. Chaste, yet deep enough to where I knew it touched below the surface.

"I believe in you," he whispered against my lips. "And if there's anything I can do to help you, I will."

Through a misty vision, I peered up at him, wanting to say those three words, even if they felt ridiculously fast.

But of course, that was the moment Victoria came home.

I heard the front door shut out in the living room. The clunking of Victoria's shoes announced her arrival moments before she poked her head in my doorway.

"Hey—" She stopped, taking in the position I was in with Zander's arms around me in the middle of my floor. Victoria made no attempt to come further into my bedroom. "Hang a scrunchie on the door next time, will ya?"

"Tori, we're not doing anything," I said.

Victoria wrinkled her nose. "Oughta make it a house rule that you can't."

"Hello, Victoria," Zander said cheerfully, trying for friendly.

At once the angst dissolved. "Hey, Zander."

"It's nice to see you again."

Victoria wasn't interested in the pleasantries. She grabbed the doorknob, prepared to leave us be. "Well, at least you're better than Rod." She sized Zander up boldly. "He was never any good to her. Keep that in mind, because if you hurt Bia, *I'll* hurt *you*."

"Yikes," Zander said as he winced. "I thought you were my biggest fan."

Tori snuck him a clever look before she dipped out of the room. "Not when it comes to Bia."

She let the threat and warning hang in the air as she closed the door behind her. Zander peered at me and I shrugged. Tori was my best friend and I was down for her the same.

"You are aware that you're the reason we're in this mess, right?" I questioned as I took my sketchbook back and returned it to my nightstand.

Zander was confused. "How so?"

"You hurt her when you cancelled the show, so out of love for my best friend I went looking for you to call you out," I said. "I was riding for her like she rides for me, so in a way, us being together is all on you."

"Then I have no regrets for what I've done."

It was funny, neither did I.

I was still tired from being up all night so I put on some music and got on my bed. Zander lay back between my legs as I braided the top of his head, trying a new look out of boredom. It was just us, in our little world where no threat could get to us.

"By the way, speaking of 'Xs,' nice tattoo," I mentioned, almost forgetting he'd gotten new ink while in New York.

Zander angled his head, trying to peek up at me. "How'd you know about that?"

I bit my lip, my ego taking a hit. "I...followed you on all your socials."

His dark brows shot up towards his hairline. "Really? What's your handle? I'll follow you back."

It was in his doing this that his fans would find me out. Was I ready for that kind of exposure? Who was I kidding, come Saturday night, the world would know who I was after being photographed officially and formally on Zander's arm.

Before I could second-guess my photos and tweets, I coughed up my info as if it were no big deal.

Zander gathered his cell phone and quickly followed me.

Paying it no further mind, I went back to his hair and Zander relaxed into me, allowing the lyrics of classic LL Cool J to fill the room. Times like this, being together and just connecting one-on-one, when it was all so simple, would be fleeting when he was on the road.

"Can I ask you something?" I said, breaking the silence.

"What's up?"

"For the tour, are you going to dance or do a routine?" I wondered.

Zander made a face. "My biggest love from the So What days was how chill and laid-back we were allowed to be. We were five guys who didn't know how to dance to save our lives, and we weren't about to go out there and make fools of ourselves. We literally went out and had fun being ourselves, and that's what I want for my stage. I'm not interested in the theatrics of dancing and learnin' a two-step.

"We're talking about incorporating lights to make it vibe, but generally I want a chill setting where you can just come and listen to *me*. I wanna play piano and maybe guitar, but no, I'm not a performer like that."

I couldn't see Zander hiring a choreographer and trying to dance. It simply wasn't him. Just like his identity in the quintet.

"What made you sign up for So What anyway?"

Zander appeared thoughtful, a beam of nostalgia in his eyes. "For as long as I can remember, my mum always said I could sing, Naz too, but I just thought they were being nice. Nazanin was online one day and saw this music exec, Liam Lyons, hosting auditions and one was near us. I thought she was taking the piss, but my mum backed her up, and I still wasn't interested. I mean, I was sixteen, who cares about that stuff?

"Then my dad just gave me this look, like he was challenging me, and his little doubt made me give in. The day of the audition we had to get up early, and when we got there, I saw this massive long line and I was ready to just walk away, but there was my dad, silently telling me I probably couldn't do it anyway. I waited all day in line and when it was my turn to go inside to the audition, I was nervous, but I just figured what the hell, and I went for it. I sang 'Love You Down' by Ready for the World."

"Hey!" That song was my jam and I couldn't believe he knew it.

Zander grinned, chuckling at the little sway I did at the mention of the song. "Yeah, I loved that song, and it was the first one that popped into my head when I got in front of Liam and his team. It was weird, as I was singing, they all got this look on their faces; they froze and just all collectively, like, zoned out and focused on me. There was a girl who had her hand on her chest and her mouth was open. That was the moment I knew that my mum and my sister weren't just filling my head up; that was the moment I knew I could really sing.

"A few months later we got the call about going to London to meet with their other finalists. My parents drove me all the way there and that's when we met up with the other boys and their parents."

"Who was the first person you met?" Everything he was saying was probably trivial, but being such a non-fan for so long, everything was new to me. No matter how much time had passed.

Zander sighed, recalling that moment from his youth. "Baby."

"Teddy?"

His mood seemed to shift. "Yeah. I was late, and on the way to the meeting, I ran into Teddy and his dad outside in the hall, and his dad was trying to convince him to go on in."

"Teddy didn't want to go?"

Zander shook his head. "Nah, he was this scrawny little kid, and he was so frightened. I was scared too, and I don't know why, but something told me to give it a go at trying to get him to meet with us. I just told him that there's a reason they called him back, a reason we were all there.

"He had tears in his eyes and he was shaking, but he looked at me and he went, 'There's three other guys in there. They're trying to make us a boy band. The world's going to hate us.' Did I listen to boy bands, no, but it was an opportunity to sing, to do something, and I wanted to see what would happen. I don't know, I just held my hand out, and I said, 'People talk shit all the time, so what.' And he took my hand and we went inside and met Oliver, Jac, and Vernon, and we became a group."

I was amazed by his story. It was Zander who had given So What their name. It was Zander who had pushed Teddy to take that step into going for it. "That's incredible, Zander. I had no idea. I mean, if you didn't go to the audition, didn't end up a singer, or famous, what would you be doing?"

Zander rested into me, taking no time to think over his answer. "I'd probably be drivin' trucks with my dad. I wasn't the best in school and didn't really have any goals at the time."

Chance.

If he hadn't taken the chance to go and audition for Liam Lyons, he wouldn't have been exposed to the life-changing opportunity of joining a pop group.

Just like if *I* hadn't taken the chance to go down that alley to give him a piece of my mind, we would've never met.

"Sounds like you made the right choice in going out for it," I said.

"It was quite a ride," Zander went on, sounding distant now.

"One thing I hated most about being in So What was the image they tried to put on me: 'Oh, he's the bad boy, the mysterious one.' I used to wonder if I was the 'bad' one because I'm Brown. I smoked at the time, but some of the others would drink, like the only one who was 'innocent' was Oliver. *Now*, I can see the mystery angle because I don't talk or like to interview much, but then, it annoyed me. I was the only Brown one in the group, singled out for this idea they had of me. My biggest advice for anyone starting out would be don't let them paint who you are, especially before *you* know who you are."

I brought my arms around him to comfort him as I placed a kiss on his forehead. "Being in So What made you, built you up, taught you a lesson, and it's something you'll always have, despite all the bullshit."

Zander massaged my arm as the tension fell from his body. "Thank you."

There were so many questions I wanted to ask him, and having him there in my arms not wanting to be any place else, I knew I had all the time in the world. For the moment, I let the past go and focused on him, on Zander, on falling even deeper in love with him.

23

DUSK TILL DAWN

I was the talk of the shop Tuesday as Jaliyah filled in our coworkers on how gorgeous Zander was. Holliston, Chekina, and Erin were hanging onto Jaliyah's every word as I stifled my laughs.

"He fine as hell with an accent and everything," Jaliyah was saying.

Chekina and Erin looked at me with new eyes then. I liked that Holliston was quiet about Zander's celebrity status and wealth. It was better for everyone to just see Zander.

When my workday came to a close, I went home and changed my clothes before driving to Zander's estate. As much as I wanted to give him alone time with his sister after she flew in to see him, he was making dinner and wanted me there. So, when I parked my car at the same time as Paul, I took a deep breath and mentally prepped myself to face Nazanin.

Knocking on my window pulled me from my thoughts, finding Paul already out of his BMW and waiting for me.

I was still feeling him out, but I was tempted to form an alliance with him for backup.

I climbed out of the car as Paul stood back to give me space.

He appraised my simple T-shirt and shorts combo before

nodding in approval. It wasn't a surprise to catch him in his usual business attire. At least he made it look good.

"Ready for this?" he quipped, flashing me a kind smile.

Was I? I hung back against my car, blowing out a breath. "I'm not sure what's going to be harder, dinner now, or dinner Saturday."

Paul scratched at his neck, cringing at my angst. "Hard to say. People are going to be on their best behavior Saturday. Here and now, the she-devil has nothing to lose."

It didn't sound like Paul was that big of a fan either. Nice.

"But what the hell, let's get this over with. I'm starving." Paul took the lead and waited for me so that we could walk side by side to the front door. He even went forth to ring the bell for me.

The front door was pulled open and my small joy washed away at the sight of Nazanin standing beside Zander. The lack of enthusiasm she expelled into the air caused dread to settle into the pit of my stomach. As she set eyes on Paul and me, a scowl marred her pretty face.

"Oh, company," she said.

"It's only right, tonight's a family dinner," Zander said.

Nazanin's icy stare went from Paul to me. "So, I take it Paul and Bianka won't be staying long?"

Zander rolled his eyes. "Paul *is* family, and Bi is someone important to me, so they're more than welcome."

Zander let us into the house and I made sure to hang back, not wanting to get too close. Nazanin's rudeness was going to be yet another test of my anger management.

Putting on a peppy persona, Paul opened his arms out in greeting towards Zander's unwelcoming sister. "Nazzi, good to see ya!"

Nazanin wrinkled her nose. "I told you about calling me that, it sounds like—"

"Oh, does it?" Paul feigned cluelessness with a forced laugh. "Can't call it."

"Paul." Zander's one utterance of his name was a warning, as well as the hard look in his eyes. "Let's take it to the kitchen. Dinner's just been finished."

With Zander and Nazanin in front of us, Paul hung back and held his fist out for me to pound.

The corners of my lips curled up as I bumped my fist against his. At least someone was on my side.

The smell of spices and chicken hung in the air and I was ready to eat despite feeling uneasy. Music was playing and upon hearing the male singer's voice, I wasn't able to recognize what language he was singing in. Rajaa was in the room, jubilant and glowing with another member of his family around. Nazanin was near him and even she was smiling.

I stood back in the entrance of the room, suddenly feeling like I *was* intruding on their family dinner. Zander lived in the US and Rajaa and Nazanin lived in the UK. They didn't see him often in person and maybe this should've just been for them.

But then Paul said something that made Zander laugh. Seeing his eyes crinkle and his white teeth flashing let me know that Paul *was* family too. Outside of their professional and business relationship, Paul was like an older brother to Zander, looking out for him and holding him accountable for his actions.

And then there was me.

In the midst of his laughing, Zander looked over and found me. Even more, he reached out for me to join them.

"I know you wanted to take me out, but this was important to me," he said to me as he stood off to the side.

Zander was radiantly happy before me. Who I was to step on that? "It feels good to see you like this. Besides, you've been promising me this chicken for a while now and it's about time you delivered."

Zander stared into my eyes and then he leaned over and pressed a soft kiss to my lips, making my heart ache. "I...I'm happy you're here." He glanced back at his family, taking note of Nazanin suppressing a smile at some expressive story Paul was telling. He returned to me. "Where are we going out to eat?"

Feeling shy, I confessed, "Olive Garden. It's my favorite. My mom and I used to go there for a girls' day."

In total understanding, Zander nodded his head. "Then we'll go on your dime and I might put out."

I bit my lip to stop the huge smile threatening to break across my face.

I did love him, I really did.

The food was done and it was time to eat.

At Zander's six-chaired elegant table in his dining room, we all gathered our seats to get comfortable with the food spread across the tabletop. Zander and I sat on one side next to each other, while Rajaa was at the head of the table on one end, and Paul and Nazanin ended up next to each other across from Zander and me.

Paul and Rajaa had a couple of beers to go along with their meals, while Nazanin and Zander settled on glasses of wine. Me, I opted for a glass of water. If the food was spicy, I would need it.

Before we could dig in, Zander rose from his chair, lifting his glass of Chardonnay. "I just want to take a moment and thank you all for being here, and in my life in general. There are two of you who have been very monumental, and I just want to thank you." Zander eyed his manager first. "Paul came when I was spiraling towards rock bottom. He heard I was a mess but he stepped up anyway. I'm not exactly the easiest client to deal with—"

"Hear! Hear!" Paul raised his bottle of beer in agreement, causing us all to laugh.

"Okay, don't be a prick, yeah?" Zander grinned. "Paul didn't give a shit about the warnings and what other big stars could pull in for him. He saw something in me and believed in me and was willin' to stick it out. He's never given up on me, even when I decided not to do a multimillion-dollar tour. I guess what I'm most thankful for is that you've had every reason to quit or walk away, but you've always held me down and had my back. I love you, mate."

Paul tipped his beer towards Zander in understanding.

Zander turned towards me. "And Bi, in a lot of ways I'm nothing more than a failure, but when I'm with you, you make me feel like a man. Being a creative in a funk is the worst level of hell, but ever since you came into my life, I've been inspired enough to just want to make music with a passion again. What I love most about you is how real you are—you never cared about any of what I have to offer, but for me as an individual. You came up with this Zaturday thing and it's doing exactly what you said it would. You push me when I'm ready to just give up, and I need that in my life. I'm happy to have you."

With all eyes on me, I felt myself shrink and blush as I mouthed a *thank you* and raised my water in the air.

Zander came back to the whole table. "I'm at a point right now where we're embarking on another go with my career. I've got the number-one song in the country and I've been invited to perform it next month on a big stage. Everything's falling into place and I'm finally ready to take full advantage of that, so long as I have you all by my side supporting me. I've learned that family is everything, even found families, and I won't take any of you for granted. To family, life, and just happiness. Salud."

"Salud," we all mirrored as we clinked glasses.

He settled back down into his chair and offered me a kiss to my temple.

It was time to eat.

The food looked good—different from what I knew and was used to, but definitely something I was eager to try. To experience. There was the wok, or *karahi*, filled with the curried chicken Zander had prepared, and a plate full of leavened bread, or *naan* as Zander called it, as well as a bowl of rice for those who preferred that instead. I wanted to try eating my chicken karahi with both, so I scooped a good portion of rice onto my plate before grabbing a slice of the homemade bread.

Zander watched with anticipation and notable pride as I made my plate. He was a renown and twice accomplished singer, and yet this was making his day, I could tell. He made no effort to make his own plate as he was too busy being fixated on me.

Rajaa and Nazanin dug right in, already fans of Zander's cooking, so they wasted no time. Paul was new to the dish just like me. After a few moments of nervous staring, he dug in too.

Zander paid them no attention. His eyes were for me.

I forked off a piece of the chicken with a good amount of sauce and brought it to my mouth for my first taste.

Oh.

The chicken was bursting with flavor—spicy, but not burning hot to where I couldn't taste the food. It was well seasoned, hints of garlic and tomato blended perfectly together. The gravy-like sauce definitely being something I wanted atop my rice.

"I made it mild, just in case," Zander told me. "And traditionally, there're no onions or green peppers in the Pakistani version, but my dad tried it once and I've been a fan ever since."

It was a good call, because the hint of onion had me ready to truly pig out.

The garlic naan was amazing, only increasing my terrible love for carbs. I quickly helped myself to some rice and did a little happy dance. I was really enjoying my food.

Zander squeezed my thigh and began making his own plate.

"So, Zan, what's the game plan for Saturday?" Paul asked.

"The party's in Pasadena. We could either all be driven there, or maybe get a suite nearby and make a weekend of it?" Zander glanced around the table for any objections.

I'd requested Saturday off and Sunday to recover. A weekend away sounded great.

Paul appeared thoughtful before shrugging. "It's the weekend, a potential forty minutes to an hour in traffic if we go that day, so fuck it, let's get a suite."

"Do me a favor and find a nice place and book...a suite with at least three rooms for the weekend," Zander said as he turned to Rajaa. With Rajaa acting as his personal assistant for the time being, he was quick to take his phone out to jot down the info for later.

"I've got a couple racks of clothing being delivered later," Zander announced. His attention zeroed in on Rajaa once more. "You sure you're not coming to the dinner, Raj?"

Rajaa offered a small frown as he shook his head. "I mean, I'll hang out at the hotel, but I'm not trying to go to the event."

Zander went to Paul next. "You sure you don't want me to have them send over some men's clothing? I'm buying."

Paul declined. "The girl at Gucci owes me a favor, so she's pulling something for me already."

Nazanin cleared her throat and narrowed her eyes. "You're not promising some girl your extra ticket, are you?"

"Aww, does Naz want to be Paul's date?" Rajaa teased.

Paul grimaced and visibly shook at the thought. "I'd rather shove my dick in a blender."

Not to be outdone, Nazanin perked up, leaning close to Paul with a smile on her face. "Ooh, can I be the one who does it?"

Paul faced Nazanin and peered into her eyes. "That depends. Can those dainty little hands of yours handle heavy lifting?"

"Paul." Zander sighed and sat back in his chair. "That's my sister."

Paul didn't back down as his eyes flickered to me. "And that's your girlfriend, and I'm your manager. Get a hold of your barracuda over here."

"Actually, Paul's right, Naz," Rajaa jumped in. "You should get to know Bia and Paul more."

After a pregnant pause of tension, Nazanin spoke up.

"So, Bianka, what do you do?" she asked, her dark eyes fixing on me.

I wanted to be petty and respond, *Besides fucking your brother, living my best life!* But there was something elegant and classy about Nazanin that had me on my best behavior, as if one-upping her were impossible. "I work retail."

Nazanin wasn't impressed. "Do you sing, dance, act...?"

"No."

A brow arched. "Are you on birth control?"

Rajaa coughed on his food, going and needing water to calm down.

Paul's eyes enlarged as he paused in his own eating.

"None of your business," I answered as calmly as my temper would allow.

Nazanin looked towards her brother. "I sincerely hope you're being careful."

Nazanin's judgment was misplaced. If Zander cared about getting me pregnant, he didn't act like it.

"Naz." Zander eyed his sister. "I get it, you love me and care, but don't sit there and treat her poorly. I won't tolerate it. I'm sure whatever information Rajaa's been feeding you coincides with who Bi is."

Nazanin pouted. "I don't know what you're talking about."

Zander's gaze shifted to his cousin. "She doesn't text you and ask about Bianka and me?"

Caught in the middle of the dueling siblings, Rajaa shrank. "We talk about a lot of things."

"That doesn't answer my question."

Rajaa was shameful as he focused down at his plate. "I mean, I *am* here to help you, but you know Naz sent me here to spy."

Nazanin huffed. "Am I supposed to apologize? Because I'm not sorry."

An icky feeling of jealousy seeped into me. Nazanin only cared about Zander, loved him dearly to keep a watchful eye on him. Pryor, he would never do that for me.

How could I hate Nazanin for being a loyal and protective sister?

"You should get to know me first," I spoke up. "Instead of making assumptions and monitoring how I manage my vagina."

Paul gaped at me sideways, impressed. He made a show to clap his palms together lightly, as if I'd gained a point against Nazanin.

"Whether any one likes Bianka or not, she's here to stay, because *I* like her. I would hope that would be the most important thing here," Zander said in my defense. "As it is, I wouldn't even have this recent bout of success if it wasn't for Bianka's inspiration."

"I'm sure she's been compensated," Nazanin mumbled as she forked at her chicken.

Zander closed his eyes, taking in a sharp breath through his nose, and I could tell he was trying to remain calm with his sister as he composed himself.

The very fact that he wasn't allowing her to disrespect me meant so much.

For peace's sake, I reached out and touched his shoulder. "Zander, it's okay."

His eyed flashed to me, narrowing. As if to disagree.

My heart swelled, feeling protected.

Nazanin wasn't swayed either way. She faced her brother, and there was no missing the loving look in her eyes as her posture relaxed. "Dinner is amazing, Saad. Dad would be proud. You've got it as down as him."

It wasn't a truce, but a change of subject. So be it.

Dinner went on and I enjoyed every bit of the meal Zander had prepared. After, the doorbell rang and some associates from a boutique in town wheeled in three long racks of women's clothing for Nazanin and me to choose from into Zander's spacious living room.

"If you find something you like that doesn't fit, just come by our store tomorrow and we'll have it fixed for you," a blonde with the nametag *Stassie* told us.

"What are you wearing?" I asked as Zander hung back with Rajaa, prepared to leave the room.

"I've got this Frère burgundy blazer I'm wearing with this black top and black pants. Nothing too crazy."

He left me alone with his sister and I wished he hadn't,

because at least with other people in the room it was easy to contain my temper and not attempt to swing at her.

Still, putting the best foot forward, I went in search for something to wear Saturday.

The Dymond Dinner was an esteemed event, but it was still summer. As I sifted through the rack of immaculate and costly dresses, I wasn't won over by any of it. I wasn't about to wear an evening gown just to hang out at a mansion party cookout.

I was just about to give up when I saw the perfect 'fit. A bandeau top and a long skirt with slits high up in the thighs. The top was black and the skirt was too, but after searching the rack once more, I managed to find it in burgundy, navy blue, and white as well. I grabbed the burgundy skirt and jumped for joy. With the right hairstyle and makeup, I would kill it.

Yasss.

I giddily grabbed the outfit from the rack on a job well done, already mentally planning to call in my hairstylist.

"So you want to work retail forever?" Nazanin again started up with her inquisition as she came over to my rack.

"No, I don't," I said honestly. "But I do like clothes. Styling our mannequins is my favorite part of my job, creating the different looks."

Nazanin studied me, taking in my response and appearing thoughtful. In the end, she merely hummed and went about her search.

"That plum suit would look amazing on you," I threw out. I wasn't a hater. Bitchy or not, Nazanin Khalil was a beautiful woman. This type of event was made for people like her to come and show their grace.

Nazanin plucked the outfit from the rack and examined it. "I have no idea how I'm going to manage makeup and hair for this."

A light bulb went off in my head. "My best friend's going to do my makeup. She doesn't charge too much. She'd slay you." I gathered my phone and pulled up Victoria's makeup page on

Instagram and scrolled through her work. This was right up her alley, and if I could get my friend a little bag, why not?

Nazanin turned so that her whole body was facing me. "That's very sweet of you, Bianka." For a moment, her face softened. "Don't take it personally, my not liking you, it's just my job to protect Saad. Our parents let him do whatever he wants, and yes, he's an adult, but everybody needs a little guidance.

"Ishani was a sweet girl, more, she was family. I got used to Jolene, because at least she has her own career, at least she has a life outside of his bubble, and she had a great deal of his heart. You've heard *Damage Control*. Do I think he likes you greatly, yes; do I think you're endgame, no. Somehow, someway, he and Jolene always find their way back to each other, so enjoy the ride while it lasts, but don't bother buckling up."

She walked on by me and left the room with her head held high.

24

BEFOUR

I felt like Cinderella.

Saturday had arrived and as the hours winded down, I felt like Cinderella approaching her chance to go to the ball. This was probably a one-time thing, as come the stroke of midnight, I would return to my normal status. Partying amongst celebrities wasn't the life for me, but I was okay with that.

Zander had followed me on all social media platforms, and just as I suspected, his fans weren't too far behind in noticing the move. My followers went from four hundred on my Instagram account to well over two thousand. My Twitter numbers spiked as well. Not to mention the DMs I was getting. Most were compliments, some from Black fans bigging me up, and then there were the comments from "Zolie" fans who felt as if I wasn't good enough for Zander. A lot of the hate was borderline racist bullshit, something that made me uneasy.

Not wanting to soil my mood, I ignored the followers, refusing to take any of it seriously.

Rajaa had booked a three-bedroom suite at a five-star hotel named The Residence-Pasadena. It was a luxury spacious unit, complete with a gourmet kitchen with an island and appliances, a roomy living room area, and even a dining room area. There was a second full bathroom, a private balcony, washer and dryer stations, queen-sized beds in the two bedrooms, and a king-sized bed in the master bedroom along with an en suite master bathroom attached.

"Can we live here forever?" I joked as I stood taking it all in.

Zander was on the phone in the kitchen, reading something on his screen.

"Right there with you, Bia," Paul agreed as he came by and rubbed my shoulders. "I love hotels. There's just something about them."

His words made me look at Zander, remembering where it all began. "Yeah."

"Fran just sent me a text," Zander announced as he waved his phone about. "She hopes we have a good time, but she doesn't want any of us to fuck up."

Paul bobbed his head. "We're a classy folk, we'll be all right."

I snorted. "We'll see."

The guest list still had me on edge.

"It's important that Zander networks tonight, people. He needs to mingle. He needs to be seen and heard. Fuck the socialites, just make sure every rapper, every singer, and every producer knows your name by the end of this shindig," Paul instructed.

The itinerary was simple: get Zander in the spotlight.

Nazanin came out of her bedroom and joined Zander in the kitchen. "Did you hire hair and makeup?"

Zander glanced at me before answering. "Yes, Victoria will be here shortly."

Nazanin was confused. "Who?"

"I hired Bianka's friend; she's good," Zander said with a nonchalant shrug.

Nazanin clicked her tongue. "You're kidding me."

I wanted to be small, because I was so damn tired of being the bigger person. Going to a huge event was a blessing, giving me plenty of breathing room from Nazanin—if I could make it that far without punching her in her throat.

"Go natural or don't go at all, your choice," I said.

If looks could kill, I wouldn't be breathing as Nazanin snarled at me. "Don't count on it."

Outside of Nazanin, everything was going great. The "Canvas" music video had been released on Friday, and it had been amazing. Zander's onscreen chemistry with Shakira had sizzled. I would admit, it was hard to watch him hold and kiss her. To roll around in bed with her, and later cling to her during their shower scene. But it came with his job, so I did my best to let it go.

Alongside the "Canvas" release, Zander dropped a Zaturday video early. His cover of Jhené Aiko's "Triggered," along with "My Mine" also by her, had been a double upload to make up for missing two weeks.

Zander's spin on "Triggered" left me swooning. I loved the sound of his voice. I could always get lost in it.

The Dymond Dinner was about the Dymond Dynasty, but it was Zander's night. His rightful step back into the limelight.

My hair was set and ready to go. I'd gone to my local hair salon and gotten bundles installed and cut to my natural length to provide a fuller look. With Victoria doing my makeup, I would be red carpet ready.

My phone went off with a text from Victoria just as there was knocking on the room's door. She had arrived and I didn't feel so crowded in a room full of Zander's team.

Rajaa went and let Tori in and I was quick to go and greet my best friend.

"Nice," she said as she came into the room and took it all in. "Damn near a whole apartment in here."

Victoria set her makeup kit on the table in the dining room before her gaze swept across the rest of the suite. Zander was in the kitchen at the island going through his phone. Nazanin was perched in the chair in the living room, skimming through a fashion magazine, Rajaa was at the island eating a bowl of cereal, and Paul was on the sofa. The news was on the large TV.

Victoria wrinkled her nose in distaste at the scene before her. "Dang, it's so dry in here. Y'all going to a party, turn up!"

"I know." Paul groaned as he lounged back on the sofa. "You tryna smoke up?" He made a smoking gesture with his hand.

Tori turned, intrigued. "Maybe. After I get done with Bia's face at least. Depends on what you got. I heard you White boys be havin' that skunk."

Paul grinned. "Oh, I assure you, my shit's legit."

Victoria sized him up and smiled before turning back to me.

"No, no, you can wait," Zander interrupted. "Everyone knows Remy Dymond has the best weed. If I can wait, so can you."

Paul rolled his eyes and went back to the news.

Victoria shook her head. "Y'all need to loosen up."

She was right. We all should've been having fun, gearing up to go out and enjoy life.

I gathered my phone and scrolled through my music before finding a rap song and playing it loudly.

"Hey!" Victoria squealed as she began moving her body in sync with the beat.

Having my best friend with me, I did loosen up as I began to shake my hips and act silly. Victoria had her phone out and began filming me, hyping me up. I dragged Zander from the kitchen and began dancing on him and rapping along to the rapper's rhymes. Zander was shy, completely not used to this, but I loved that about us, how this whole thing was new for the both of us.

"Okay, I'm about to send that to you," Victoria said as her fingers skipped across her phone's screen. "Put it on your socials and let these people know you coming to wild out and have fun."

Zander brought his arm across my chest as he leaned into my ear to whisper. "Chill, before I take you to the back and we end up late."

I shooed him away and sat down at the table, going and allowing Victoria to do my makeup first.

"You should actually come out with us," Zander said to Victoria. "I could squeeze you in."

Victoria focused on doing my eyebrows. "Nah."

"You sure?"

"Yeah, it's not my scene. *You* just be on your best behavior and make sure Bia has a good time, or else."

"What does that mean?" Paul questioned.

She glanced his way. "He can't sing without his larynx, can he?"

I cleared my throat, unable to believe she'd gone there.

"Hold still," Victoria insisted as she pushed me back into my seat.

"*So this is our trial and error,*" Zander belted out as he headed off towards the master bedroom. "*We gotta find a way out.*"

Victoria was starstruck at his flawless live vocals. I didn't blame her. It still took me by surprise every time he would break out in song.

We let the music play from my phone as Victoria did my makeup.

"You nervous?" she asked me.

"Very," I admitted.

"It's just dinner, and you're with your man, so relax," Victoria encouraged. "He shouldn't let anything happen to you. The same way you won't let anything happen to him."

Right, we were a team. I had Zander's back the same way he had mine.

I laid those thoughts down as my foundation as I gave up my anxiety.

Victoria did Nazanin's makeup and I was extra happy Nazanin wasn't rude about it. She was actually polite enough to be friendly and complimentary about the final product. To go along with her plum pantsuit, Victoria had given her wine-stained lips, and a subtle dusty pink eyeshadow with the perfect sharp-winged eyeliner.

"You look beautiful," I let Nazanin know.

She simply smiled at me, not in the mood to fake it for my company's benefit.

Victoria side-eyed her as she gathered her makeup kit together to go. The mean-mug on her face made me hop into gear before she let loose on Nazanin before I got a chance to.

"I'll walk you to the elevator," I said as we left the suite.

As soon as the door shut behind us, my best friend faced me, gesturing towards the room. "What the fuck is her problem?"

"Don't even get me started."

"If I had not have done a good job, I would've blacked her eye."

Zander had his Pitbull, and I clearly had mine. "I can handle her, trust me."

"Take pictures, okay?" Victoria instructed as we waited for the elevator to arrive to our floor.

"I will," I promised. "You sure you don't wanna come?"

"Girl, I'm not trying to dress up and go and be around them rich bougie people just to eat some barbecue."

"Still, won't be fun without you."

"Yeah, it will. Besides, Zander paid me double my usual rate. I'm going out to splurge."

It was a nice gesture for Zander to do that for Tori. I suddenly realized she was right: I wouldn't have my best friend by my side, but I would have my boyfriend, and for that, I felt invincible.

25

A WHOLE NEW WORLD

The sun was just beginning to descend when we arrived at the estate hosting the Dymond Dinner. Together, Zander, Nazanin, Paul, and I rode over in a truck Zander requested for us. Before we could even get to the house, we were met with a parade of vehicles up ahead of us. It didn't take much to guess that they were all heading for the same location. This area of Pasadena the driver had driven into was filled with nothing but illustrious homes and properties. And of course, the best was for last.

Situated up on a hill was the home for the Dymond Dinner. This wasn't a house, no, it was a manor, a *Dymond* manor. The huge structure with multiple parts to its overall build stretched across acres of land, easily being its own block at the end of the cul-de-sac.

We weren't even inside yet, but if the gushing fountain out front in the middle of the circular driveway wasn't a sign of their wealth, it was the many valet rushing out to vehicles to take off the hands of drivers that was. The valet were taking the cars and driving over to the hangar at the far end of the house. The Dymonds had a separate building for parking for events like this.

"Is this their home, or do they rent for these parties?" Nazanin asked.

"Oh, no, Willie D only likes the best. This is one of their summer spots I read somewhere in *Forbes*," Paul explained. "*He* doesn't even use this place. He lets his kids stay here."

Lifestyles of the filthy rich. I couldn't imagine having the type of wealth where I could just easily lend multimillion-dollar homes to members of my family.

It was our turn to exit our car. Being that Zander was the star, he got out first and insisted on me coming next. He held his hand out for me and helped me out of the car and never let me go. Paul was nice enough to help Nazanin out next.

The four of us stood and faced the steps leading up to the front entrance.

Show time.

"Be on your best behavior," Paul whispered to the three of us.

"Noted. You ready, Bi?" Zander asked me.

I could only manage a nod of my head. Anxiety was back in full force and I suddenly doubted I could even eat with the heaviness in my belly. Still, I played it off as I walked hand in hand with Zander up the steps on inside.

Bright lights shined in the entryway composed completely of white marble and black lacquer railings for the dual staircase. A gorgeous crystal chandelier hung in the middle of the ceiling, shimmery as could be. Straight across from the front door was the far back exit to the party. Music could be heard despite the distance, and I wasn't even fazed by the sounds of Galen Dymond.

This was a Dymond event, so I would've been shocked if they didn't play their own hits. Owen was a producer, and sometimes rapper, Remy was an aspiring rapper, and Galen was the R&B heartthrob. They were a dynamic trio.

We cut across the glossy flooring to the back door and were all immersed in the extravagance of the Dymond Dinner.

We'd walked out onto a balcony that oversaw the never-ending expansive backyard. There was a tennis court with lights, a beautiful swimming pool with a waterfall, and here and there I could make out statues of armless and topless men and women. Talk about extra.

"Ladies and gentlemen, welcome to Shangri-La," Paul mumbled as we all froze, taking it in.

Beyond the pool, pool house patio, and tennis court, was the main yard where a series of tents were set up as well as tables and chairs. The smell of the catering grilling billowed through the air, causing my nerves to ease away as hunger took over.

All at once famous faces started to jump out at me—there was Jay-Z, Usher, Ciara and Russell, Ari Lennox, and not even just famed Black faces; I spotted Ariana Grande mingling about as well as a few Jonas brothers, and Justin Bieber and his wife.

Whoa.

"Network, network," Paul advised as we began our descent into the madness.

People were everywhere—the workers and staff sticking out with their uniforms, and the celebrities because of who they were. Everywhere I turned I could see a group of people hanging out and talking. Laughter and chatter filled the air and I held on to Zander's hand as he ushered us to one of the tents to find us a seat. The trick was, at least in my opinion, to sit near the back or least crowded place. Everyone would want to be near the Dymonds, and with all the attention going in one direction, it was easy to blend in towards the back.

A woman with an earpiece and clipboard greeted us as we made our way up to the nearest tent. "Zander Khalil, right?"

"Right," Zander responded.

The woman turned to her clipboard which was nothing more than a well-designed seating chart and skimmed with her finger for Zander's name. "Ah, you're in tent A, right this way."

There were three long and wide tents with a large collection of tables and chairs spread out. To know that Zander was high-profile enough to be assigned to the first tent said something. As the woman led us to Zander's table, I noticed right away at the largest table was the man himself, Willie D, sitting next to his longtime partner and wife, Tyra. There were three empty seats on either side of them, making me assume their sons and Pen would be joining them. At one of the tables nearest theirs I could see Jace Hearst sitting next to Patsy, whispering in her ear. Another glimpse around and I spotted Piper and Peyton standing and talking to some people they knew, meaning the rest of the Patels weren't too far away.

The tables were fairly big, sitting eight chairs each at them. As we were shown to Zander's table, I suddenly wondered if we'd have it to ourselves, or if we'd have to share.

"They're just about to open up the lines for the food as soon as everyone finds their seats," the woman said to us. "My name's Gretchen. I'm in charge of this station, and I'll be getting you a hostess shortly to take care of drinks."

Paul peered down at Zander, a proud smile on his face. "Your first Dymond Dinner and they got you seated four tables down from the man himself. Look at us. Who would've thought?"

Zander was bashful as he snuck a peek towards Willie D and co. Tent A was clearly full of legends—and the Patels, so it was quite an honor to have Zander be able to make it to be amongst them.

Deep down, exciting or not, I knew none of this was getting to him. I took his hand and squeezed. "This is big for you. Take it all in."

"What's the game plan?" Paul asked, looking at Zander. "We're not trying to get drunk, are we? I wanna smoke out with Remy, but I don't want to get too fucked up."

Zander pulled a face. "You can drop the big brother routine. I'm going to be okay, Paul."

Nazanin heaved a sigh. "He's just looking out for you."

Zander opened his mouth and froze, his dark eyes staring right past his sister.

I followed the direction he was staring and a shiver went down my spine.

Teddy Sykes was crashing the party. Dripping in black, he had on a black blazer, silk V-neck black top, and black pants to match. His silk shirt was unbuttoned, a glimpse of his tanned flesh underneath on display. An assortment of thick banded rings were on his two hands, one on his left hand's thumb, and two on his right hand, his ring finger and pinky. His hair was up in a bun. He was the epitome of a rock star.

"Fuck," I heard Zander mumble underneath his breath.

There were four more chairs left at our table, they wouldn't have...

"If you knock his teeth out, do it quick and run," Paul advised.

Nazanin drove her elbow into his side. "Paul!"

He shrugged. "Or make it look like an accident. I don't know."

"Ay, *Tedday!*"

Peyton Hearst shouted a greeting towards Teddy just as his gaze landed on Zander. This time, there was no smirk, only an empty expression as the tall muscular singer simply went over to Peyton. I was only partly surprised Peyton had saved Teddy a seat, even though he'd ended things badly with Piper. Peyton seemed to still like Teddy. I'd skimmed past countless blogs and reports that the two Hearst twins were always feuding. I wouldn't have put it past Peyton to have invited Teddy just to get back at his sister.

Zander grabbed the pitcher of water that was sitting on the table and was quick to pour himself a glass.

"Jo! Hey!"

Oh, for fuck's sake.

Not to be outdone, Piper Hearst caught Jolie as she was entering the tent and escorted her to the table where her brother and Teddy were sitting. Teddy's eyes ran up Jolie's long legs as he took her in and admired her. The pretty blonde was casual in her gray romper set and wedge heels. Her hair was curled and pinned to the side, and she was glowing from some recent time under the sun. She shook hands with Teddy before taking a seat next to Piper.

"Jesus," I heard Paul sigh. "I'm going to need a couple of shots to make it through tonight."

He wasn't the only one.

Zander drank his water and managed to actually laugh. "I'm the one supposed to be sweating bullets, yeah? So, if I'm calm and relaxed, *you* should be even more so."

"You're calm and relaxed?" Paul challenged.

Zander shrugged, not even glancing in the direction of his enemies. "I've got my manager, my sister, and my girl with me, why should I be anxious? I'm not performing, and we're just here to eat and meet people. You wanna find Remy now and...?"

Paul let it go as he sat back in his chair. "I mean, it, Zan, be on your shit."

Zander held his hands up, flashing a smile. "I am on my shit." He turned and faced me. "Are you good?"

Now that I in fact was in the midst of three of the four horsemen of the apocalypse: Nazanin, Teddy, and Jolie? "Never better."

Zander went to his sister. "You good?"

She rolled her eyes. "I'm great."

"Then we're all good."

It was settled, and not too long later they began ushering people from tent A to go and start making their plates. I hung close to Zander, in case Teddy tried something petty and in case Jolie further wanted to make it clear that she was single. Being that our table was near the back of the tent, thankfully, their table was already through the maze of food by the time we got to the catering tables.

Zander and Nazanin didn't eat pork, so they opted for the grilled chicken pieces. I wasn't the biggest red meat eater, but I also wasn't a fan of ribs all like that, so I didn't mind following in

Zander's lead in getting the chicken. Watching Paul opt for a steak brightened my mood, because somehow, even if I hardly knew him, it was so him.

"What?" he asked as he noticed my staring. "You can get steak at any restaurant in LA, but this, this right here, Bia, is a Dymond steak."

I chuckled as we went back to our seats. "Hope you don't chip your tooth."

Two other couples were seated at our table, new artists in the pop genre and the other in the hip-hop genre. Zander was polite to them and even laughed as the girl dating the upcoming pop star gushed about how much of a big fan she was of So What.

Underneath the table I patted Zander's thigh.

"Excuse me for one moment," Gretchen said into a microphone. She was standing near Willie D's table, gathering all of our attention. "Mr. Dymond would like to say a word to set off the evening, and then we can all continue digging in."

Willie D was just into his early fifties, but he didn't look a day over thirty. Seeing him stand amongst his three sons, all three nearly spitting images of him, made me smile. Black excellence indeed.

"Y'all know I like to talk," Willie joked, causing everyone to laugh. He was known to be that guy at the award shows back in the day who would go on and on during his acceptance speeches. "I'ma keep this short and sweet, though. I just want to take a moment to thank God for being here. I'm fifty-three years old, and a lot of brothers where I'm from ain't make it past twenty. To be able to start a label, break a rapper and R&B singer against all the doubters, to make it here today still relevant after all this time, is something that I can only thank God for.

"I look at my sons and I'm thankful they're alive and healthy. They're all like their old man, hustlers out to make it. Owen got more Grammys than the Beatles, now that's making it!" He raised his glass of champagne in the air and we all mirrored the motion, cheering on Owen. "My son Remy and my son Galen are just starting out and I couldn't be prouder. And my wife, Tyra, I'm thankful for her every day."

All eyes were on each member of the Dymond family, taking them in and admiring them for their legacy and future. They were more than just musical legends; they were big philanthropists as well, often giving back and hosting charity events. Willie was passionate and very much for the people. And what I loved most was that it was real and genuine. Willie and Tyra would donate anonymously, and when tragedy struck, they would even go out of their way to meet with victims to offer comfort. I loved that they never forgot where they came from. They were rich in money, yes, but the equity they had in their moral wealth couldn't be touched.

"What I'm trying to say is, look at the people you brought with you tonight, look at them and cherish them, and most importantly love them," Willie began to conclude his speech. "My wife will be the first to tell you I've been a son of a bitch, but she fought with me the hardest because she loved me that much, even beyond what I deserved at times. Love, love is all we got, and that's something we have to learn not to take for granted.

"So, I want you all to raise your glasses so we can make a toast to just honor love and happiness, because that will always be the way through." He lifted his glass once more. "To love and happiness!"

"To love and happiness," we all chorused in return with our glasses raised.

"Salud." Willie tipped his glass towards our section of tables and towards the other tents as well before taking his seat.

It was only right that the iconic Al Green record began to play next in the background.

The dinner was started and we all began to dig in. Something about Willie's speech really spoke to me, especially about love being all we had. In all irony, love was all I had to give, because of the two of us, Zander came with millions and a life lived through touring the world. What I lacked in money and experience I knew I made up for in my love.

A part of me thought it was too soon to tell him the big three, but another didn't care and just wanted to let him know how much he'd grown to mean to me.

Zander squeezed my thigh and came close to kiss my shoulder. His affection let me know how much Willie's words had gotten to him too.

Love. Love was everything.

26

SCRIPTED

We enjoyed our meals before going and stretching our legs for some socializing. Nazanin abandoned us to go and catch up with Jolie of all people, and Paul had a few industry friends he was chatting with, leaving Zander to me.

"Wanna just walk around? I know I'm supposed to be mingling, but I'm sure we'll meet people along the way," Zander said as we exited the tent and took a glimpse around the Dymond estate.

"Sure," I said.

"Hey!" Paul shouted to Zander before we could get too far. "Be good, Bobby Brown!"

Zander smirked and flipped Paul the bird.

"Zander!"

Before we could leave, a voice shot through the air, and a look over found that it belonged to Pen Patel. She was rushing our way, tugging Owen with her, and despite my feelings, I was still awestruck at being about to meet Owen Dymond.

Owen came and spoke first after shaking Zander's hand. "I finally get to meet you after hearing about you for weeks." He forced an exasperated look that had Pen slapping his shoulder. "My wife's been talking about you nonstop."

Pen blushed, suddenly shy. "Okay, I heard 'Canvas' and became *obsessed* with you. I stayed up all night going and listening to all your stuff, and I had to have you here."

Owen nodded reluctantly. "Yeah, I called your manager and he tried to hang up on me, thought I was pranking him."

Zander laughed. "That sounds like Paul." He reached out to shake Pen's hand. "I'm happy you're liking the record, and thanks for posting that video; it got me a lot of new fans."

Pen was giddy at the sight of Zander and there was something so normal about that. She had been famous herself for years now, yet the sight of Zander Khalil had her fangirling. "I just saw the video yesterday and I loved it."

"Thank you, thank you," Zander told her humbly.

Pen started to say something, but then she suddenly noticed me and how close Zander and I were standing. Putting two and two together, her mouth dropped open. "Oh my God, Zander, she's gorgeous!" She gushed in her extra sweet baby voice. She extended her hand towards me. "Pen."

Zander held me close, proudly. "This is my lady, Bianka."

It was only right to be polite, so I shook her hand and offered her a smile.

"You should put *her* in your next video," Pen told Zander.

He didn't disagree. "I'm workin' on it."

Pen faced me, the friendliest smile on her face. "So what modeling agency are you under?"

That made me laugh. "Oh, I don't model."

Pen frowned. "You should, you're beautiful!" She turned to Zander. "I love how you guys are matching with the burgundy and black. You have to take pictures, you have to."

Owen chuckled and pulled Pen close. "Yo, let them live, okay?" He tossed Zander a helpless look. "My brother got this record he trying to put together with Saadiq, you should hit him up. Rem's been on the lookout for a solid singer, and we can't just stay in house with Galen."

Zander's eyes lit up at the offer. "Oh, wow, I'll definitely have to link up with him. Thanks for considering me."

"Nah, wifey's been playing your albums and I'm impressed. Leave that pop shit alone and you could really take over the R&B game. Weren't you in that boy band?"

Zander kinked up his nose and nodded silently.

Owen tapped his chest. "Bet you if you stick with the R&B route you'll get a Grammy. You got something in your sound that's unique, it's urban, it's foreign, it's American influenced. You got it." Owen appeared thoughtful as he looked around the party. "But listen, this a party. We won't get into all that now. Hit up Remy and we'll talk later."

Zander promised and Owen and Pen left us alone.

"Holy shit, Owen Dymond wants to work with you." I took a step back and examined Zander and couldn't believe how he wasn't freaking out. "Oh my God, what if you get a Grammy next year?"

Zander stepped forth, hovering over me. "Bianka, if I win a Grammy for 'Canvas' or *Abstract* I will fucking marry you."

My mouth dropped open and my heart throbbed. Even if he wasn't serious, the idea that he didn't mind saying it out loud made me feel full. We hadn't known each other long, but to think of this being *that* real, to have a future with rings? I didn't know what to say as my feelings consumed me.

Zander stared into my eyes. "What?"

I should've let it go, but I didn't want to get my hopes up. Didn't want to believe in someday. "You'd marry me, just like that? You can see us together in six months?"

Zander's brows furrowed as he took a step closer, frustration arresting his handsome features. Soon, he grabbed my wrist and steered me over to a quiet spot in the yard away from the cacophony going on. With his back to the party, he peered down at me. "Yes. This isn't a fling to me, or a game, Bi. Don't you want us to work?"

"Yes," I admitted breathlessly. I didn't want to feel desperate for love, but what I felt for Zander was scary. The fact that he was all in with me, was almost too good to be true. "I just... I'm falling heart first here, and I'm scared that I'll hit the ground and crack."

Zander shook his head as he came forth and brought his arms around me. The Dymond Dinner was long forgotten as his entire focus was on me. "We're in this together. Hand in hand. Heart in heart. You fall, I fall. Yeah?"

I bit my lip to stop myself from being dramatic and crying—because this was an A-list event! "Okay, you're the first man to meet my father, and as you can see, I don't know if there will ever be a bridge there. If this goes the distance, and it's time for *me* to meet *your* parents, will they treat me like Nazanin?"

Zander looked off, appearing thoughtful as he raked a hand through his hair. He returned to me, an earnest expression in his dark eyes. "My family is very close and protective. At first, my parents didn't want to meet Jo; they were too loyal to Ishani. We grew up together. She was my first everything. Naturally, Shani was a big part of our family. I know my mum and Naz still keep in touch.

"My mum's a lover. She's super warm and welcoming. My dad...he can be reserved, but if he knows I'm serious about you, he won't question it. You've made me happy and open when all I wanted to do was freeze up. My parents will love you."

I let the sound of cackling in the distance distract me and keep me from breaking down right there. Nazanin was one thing, but it was nice to know the battle wouldn't extend to his parents.

Zander reached out, thumbing at my jaw tenderly, smiling just a little. "Your folks never met your boyfriends?"

I shook my head. It was too late by then. "I didn't really date all like that. In high school I hung out with some guys, but Rod was my first real, serious boyfriend."

"Until he fucked up," Zander was quick to note.

"They always do," I said bitterly.

Zander heaved a sigh as he ran his knuckles up and down my arm. He searched the party, tension lifting from his shoulders. We would be okay. "Let's take some pictures and make some memories."

There were photographers set up to take guests' pictures against a vivid green artificial hedge, as well as a photobooth station nearby.

We waited our turn before taking our place in front of the hedge. Zander stood behind me, going and placing his arms around my waist and angling his head to where he was staring at me. The heaviness in his eyes had me blushing.

"Beautiful!" The photographer had already taken our photo.

Zander wasn't paying this any mind. He leaned closed and kissed my neck, holding me tight. I smiled for the camera, trying to keep it together. He posed with me for a few more photos before letting the next group take their place in front of the lens.

The party was still going on, but neither of us cared. I stood and snuck Zander a kiss and melted when he brought his arms around me.

"Zander, my man." Remy Dymond materialized next to us, going and greeting Zander with a pat on the shoulder. "We're about to go smoke out, you tryna come?"

Zander released me. "Uh, yeah, you're okay on your own, Bi?"

I was nervous, and alone at a party where I knew no one, but I didn't want to spoil this big connection for him. "Of course, I'll be fine."

"I got this record I'm tryna put you on, 6LACK on it too, it's easily gon' be a smash if you touch it," Remy said.

Zander bobbed his head. "Send it over with the open verse and I'll see what I can do. If not, I'm sure you and I could get in the stu' and cook something up."

"Ah man, heard you. Say less." Remy held his hand out and I watched as he slapped palms with Zander before pulling him in for a quick pat on the back. And then Remy noted me, smiling all friendly.

Zander's arm came around my waist naturally and Remy noticed.

"Damn, I can't even just look?" Remy joked.

Zander wagged his finger. "No. Did you not drop that song with Galen about stealing girls, mate?"

Remy's grin was all telling. He coolly licked his lips, eyeing me with a sheepish shrug. "You know what they say."

"What?" I wondered.

"Dymonds are a girl's best friend."

His cute little joke made me laugh. "Oh my God, stop!"

Remy was handsome, yet pretty, too, with his dark facial hair against his brown complexion. He was smooth, a lady's man according to hip-hop blogs, but respectful to say the least. It wouldn't be hard to imagine him stealing girls with his wealth, looks, and rapping skills.

Remy laughed and started backing away. "A'ight, man, let's go."

He took off and met up with a group of men, going and waiting on Zander to leave me.

Zander came and stood in front of me, a gleam in his eye. "You look so fucking good, Bi."

Remy was waiting, but Zander was only interested in me. "Thank you."

He was in my ear. "Say the word and we can go find a room."

My knees went weak and I leaned away. "Zander!"

"I'm ten seconds away from taking you off somewhere and pushing that skirt up."

I moved some of my skirt out of the way, giving Zander a nice peek at my naked thigh. Taunting him. "Oh yeah?"

Zander's amusement was deadly. "Don't say I didn't warn you."

I chanced a look around us. No one was paying us any

attention. Remy included as he was lost in conversation with his friends.

It wasn't the time *or* the place, but...

"Do you think we can be quick?" I asked, unable to contain my smile or excitement. My hands were shaking. I was getting such a rush at the thought of sneaking away with him.

That half grin I loved so much spread across Zander's face. His focus locked on me. "Yeah?"

"You only live once, right?"

In no time, Zander had my hand and was dragging me towards the back patio, making excuses as we meandered through the crowd. He was walking with such determination I had to cover my face to hide my laugh.

"Ay! Zander!"

Behind us, Remy was flagging Zander down, looking at us incredulously as we got farther and farther away.

This was crazy. Remy was waiting on Zander, and Zander was intent on finding us a corner to hook up in. Not only that, this was a high-profile event, one his publicist explicitly told him, and all in co., not to fuck up at.

I strained my arm, almost pulling away. "Zan, he's—"

Zander turned, reading my face and pausing, before going and flashing Remy a cool smile as he held up a finger, illustrating for him to wait. Even in the distance, I could see Remy's brows furrowing in confusion. Zander wore no shame as he quickly walked me over to the back patio.

"Do you really want to keep him waiting?" I whispered.

Zander's fingers grazed my waist as we climbed the steps and slipped back inside the house. "I *need* you right now."

The look in his eyes, the desperation and total want, caused a flame to ignite between my thighs. Something was building between us that neither one of us would be able to control if we let loose here and now.

Getting a hold of the nearest host, Zander halted, his hand

squeezing mine. "Hey, mate. Where's the bathroom?" he asked patiently and nonchalantly as he rocked on the heels of his feet.

The young man grinned politely, eager to help. "There's three on this floor. The nearest one is right off the kitchen."

Zander tipped his head towards him. "Thanks."

Guests were still arriving as we ambled by them on their way to the backyard. Workers were here and there, escorting people where to go to use the bathroom, or helping women in high heels on their way to the exit to wait for their cars. Others were merely standing around, enjoying the AC. It was quieter inside, which explained the little groups of people in huddled circles having private conversations.

"Let's go to the second floor," I suggested as soon as we were out of earshot.

The back staircase to the second level was vacant, and as we reached the second floor, the coast was clear.

Still, I had just enough time to look around before Zander snatched me into the closest room he could find.

"Uff," I let out as my back immediately met a wall.

We were in a bedroom, judging by the size, a guest room. The canopy bed, night tables, dresser, and TV were telling of this room being for guests rather than for an actual resident of the home. Nothing personal stood out. And the plain gray and white bedding held no charisma or particular taste.

Zander stood back and shimmied out of his blazer. "Move your skirt a little. Matter of fact"—he eyed the garment and licked his lips, his eyes ravenous—"take it off."

"Zander!"

Growing impatient, he helped himself to sink to his knees before me and found my zipper. He gazed up at me, the eye contact making me hotter than the threat of the impending act alone.

Beneath my skirt, I wasn't wearing underwear, something that caused me to cover myself at once when he slid the material down my legs.

Zander peered at my hands, and then back up at me, arching a brow. "Another first?"

The door was locked and the party was still going on, oblivious to our stolen moment for a quick rendezvous. I tucked some hair behind my ear, managing to nod my head. "Yes."

Zander removed my hands from shielding myself. "Good, I want to be a part of all your firsts from now on."

He came forward and swept his tongue from my entrance to my clit before sucking it into his mouth.

My eyes slid shut and I released a cry. "Zander!"

"I love it when you sing for me." Zander's eyes flashed toward me, a darkened gleam in them.

I couldn't speak. I couldn't move. All I could do was endure his skilled tongue melting away all my hesitation as I leaned back against the wall. I propped a thigh on his shoulder as he kissed me like this would be his last meal and he intended to savor every bit of it. Nice and slow. Languid and firm. I needed this more than ever as my fingers lodged into his hair. My mouth fell agape as I started to twitch.

Zander was on his feet quicker than I would've liked, undoing his pants and picking me up effortlessly. Once we were together, joined into one with my legs locked around him, keeping him in place, we groaned out in a combined melody of pleasure.

We had to make it fast, and I hated it, wanting it to last forever. I would never get tired at the feel of Zander inside of me, of him wanting me, needing me, worshiping me.

I clawed at his back when I was close, biting on my lip to keep my whimpers at bay. His own muffled gibberish was buried in my neck.

It was a race, it felt like, one where we came in first together. As much as I wanted to linger against him, resting and breathing in sync, I didn't make a fuss when he released me and took a step back.

"There's a bathroom in this room." I suddenly noticed a door to my right leading into a private bath.

Zander picked up my skirt. "Let's get cleaned up."

Just the sight of him near me made me want to forgo the party all together and hop into bed.

I accepted my skirt. "I'll use that bathroom, you find another."

Zander pouted, coming closer and kissing me softly, chastely, deeply, before reeling back and meeting my eyes. "I...I'll see you downstairs."

I let him leave the room before I pulled myself together and freshened up in the bathroom. His stutter kept replaying in my head. Had he been about to say *I love you*? I was still questioning timing on my end, whether or not it was too soon. It didn't matter, though, as I knew I loved him more and more as each day passed.

Out in the hall, I breathed a sigh of relief on a job well done. It felt like we'd just committed an illustrious heist, or some other secret caper—

I jumped at the sight of Jolie rounding the corner up ahead of me in the hall. In fact, I froze all together.

The closer she got to me, the more her perfect smile broadened. "Bathroom?"

It took me a second to figure out what she meant. The guilt from my hookup already sinking in. "Um, couldn't find it."

"This place feels like a maze, right?" Jolie chuckled before going and trying the scene of the crime, almost at once turning back to me. Could she tell? "Nope, that's not it."

She went on in search of a bathroom and I quickly went back downstairs and out to the party, desperately in need of some fresh air. She was *so* pretty up close in person.

Zander was nowhere in sight, leaving me to believe he'd caught up with Remy. I let it go and decided to go and grab me something to drink. With my accidentally bumping into his ex still fresh on my mind, I was suddenly hot and parched.

There was a bar under the portico at the pool patio and seeing the colorful iced drinks was tempting me to try one. I made my way in front of the bartender and ordered me an Electric Smurf.

The cup had just touched my hand when a figure saddled up beside me.

"That looks good." Jolie came and leaned against the counter casually, smiling my way before flagging down the bartender and ordering the same thing.

I took a sip of my drink. "It is good."

Jolie angled her head. "You have wonderful taste."

Something told me to walk away, but like an idiot, I stayed planted where I was. "Thanks."

The bartender gave Jolie her drink and she stirred its contents with her straw before leaning close. "I think we should talk."

"About what?"

Jolie eyed me funny. "Don't play dumb, Bianka. Woman to woman, we should talk about Zander."

"I have nothing to talk about." I started to walk away, soon way too aware that she was following me.

"I just thought you deserved a heads-up." Jolie brought her straw to her lips and took a sip of her drink. "Mmm, you *do* have good taste."

My temper was rising and I did my best to keep it in check. "What do you want?"

"I think you should be careful, with Zander. He's a lot to deal with. *I* should know." Her little laugh she let out was totally fake. What's more, she reached out and placed her hand on my shoulder gently. "The beginning was fun, but then he got clingy, demanding to see me all the time, wanting me to skip filming just to be up under him. It got way too intense for me.

"His codependency was so overwhelming. I started to feel... suffocated, and our relationship felt like a chore. In the end, I had to get away." Jolie frowned, trying to sell it more. "I don't want you to go through that. No woman deserves to be put in that position."

Stiffly, I clapped my hand on my arm since holding my drink

made the task of clapping my hands together impossible. "Bravo. You're really going for that Oscar gold, huh? You almost had me, except, wait, you didn't."

Jolie dropped her nice girl act and stood straight, pursing her lips. "I was trying to be nice."

"And I'm trying to walk away. Have a good night." I turned my back on her and started in search of the direction Remy had instructed. I'd rather catch a contact high than deal with this.

"It'll never be you," Jolie announced from behind me. I turned back around, catching a mean smile stretching her pink lips. "I get it, right now, it's new and fun, but at the end of the day, you're just a new feel, and you know men, they'll always end up dying to try something new, but when they get bored, we all know where they end up. He left Ishani for me, and he'll do the same with you."

Composing myself as best as I could, I marched right up to her face. "The only reason I'm not breaking that new nose of yours, is because I don't want to embarrass him."

Jolie stepped up to me, fearless, smirking as if I were nothing more than a joke to her. "Sweetie, I posted a picture with another man and Zander cancelled his whole tour. This is *my* game of chess we're playing, not yours. If you think you matter to him, you're sadly mistaken. You have his dick, but I have his heart. You're the girl he's fucking, and I'm the woman he'll marry...*if* I let him."

To brag about my hookup with Zander made me feel dirty suddenly, as if she were right and I was just someone he was sleeping with, versus her being someone he actually loved.

In seconds, Jolie's whole demeanor morphed into light and friendly as she peered past me. "Peyton! Hey! Hugo was asking about you for his upcoming campaign." In a move to be nonchalant, she nudged me out of the way as she went over to Peyton Hearst.

My hand was shaking and I couldn't hold on to my Electric Smurf. I set it on the bar and I tried to calm down my impending panic attack. Nazanin said they were endgame, and Jolie wasn't about to back off. Did Zander like me enough to tell her to go fuck herself?

I didn't know what to do with myself. I was out of my place amongst all these A-listers, and not in the mood to fake a smile. Against all my might I was shaking, unable to let Jolie's poisonous words go. Around and around they circled my thoughts, leaving—

Up ahead of me, at the hedge to take pictures was a group of pretty, young, rich people. Piper. Remy. Zander. Peyton. Galen. Jolene Jones.

"Fame" by David Bowie was blaring through the speakers, causing some attendees to sway to the iconic song. The group at the hedge were too caught up in each other to notice. They were all laughing and smiling, and Jolie was right next to Zander.

I waited for him to move, to stop smiling, to stop looking so damn happy to be around her.

He didn't.

A lump lodged in my throat. *Oh.*

I did *feel* dirty just then.

Doing the best that I could, I jostled away from the crowds, finding a place to be alone. The empty gazebo at the edge of the yard. A string of lights decorated the top of the roof, and once inside I found that there was a nice view of the mountains of Pasadena. It was a breathtaking sight, if only I could catch my breath. Even the stunning angel statue nearby couldn't lift my spirits.

Footsteps sounded behind me and in seconds Teddy was coming up beside me, going and looking at the view as well. Gone was his bun, letting his curls rein free.

He admired the view. "In some ways, the view from the top is the most haunting."

The calmness of his voice intrigued me. "Why?"

"Because the fear of falling back down can eat you alive. When you're at the bottom, the only place to go is up. You're hungry, you're passionate, and you've got a goal and vision. At the top, sometimes it feels inevitable that you're bound to tumble back down."

His fear honestly took me by surprise. He was the most beloved member of a multi-platinum selling boy band. Probably the world's biggest boy band to date. He was set for life with a bright future ahead of him as his rock star turn was a massive success. "You're Teddy Sykes. You're planted here and rooted deep. Nothing can take you down."

Teddy regarded me, his brown eyes studying me deeply. "I'd like to apologize for our last encounter. It wasn't my best."

"Yeah, when you acted like an asshole."

Teddy's response was a dimpled smile. Even more, he leaned close to say, "I may be an asshole, but at least I make it look good." He reeled back and winked at me, tossing me a crooked grin.

That sinful dimple was his Get Out of Jail Free Card.

A chorus of chuckling had me looking over, catching Zander and Jolie together once more. She was in his ear, smiling all big as she spoke. She pulled back just a bit, gazing at Zander who broke out into a huge grin, mouthing something I couldn't read. Nazanin was around, looking on with a satisfied grin on her face. Cameras were flashing and Piper was instigating more and more group photos.

Worse, in another second, Jolie's hand captured Zander's, he didn't pull away, and she took him with her easily as she smiled back to him, ushering him somewhere away from the group.

But...he's mine.

My heart tore in two, and then in two more, and then it disintegrated deep in my chest, falling to ashes to never be collected again.

In his deep, husky voice, Teddy stepped closer to me and started singing the lyrics of "Jolene" by Dolly Parton, rubbing salt on my wounds.

I faced him, unable to hide my hurt. "Why do you have to be like this?"

At once he stopped, a seriousness taking him from boy to man. "Like what?"

"Such a bastard!" My chest was rising and falling and I feared I'd do something lame like cry. There was nothing I could do in this situation. I'd already lost.

Teddy's forehead adopted a crease as he appeared thoughtful. "I won't be staying long. I didn't want to come."

I wiped at my eyes, embarrassed to hear my voice crack. "Then why are you here?"

There was that grin again as well as a simple shrug. "Because I was hungry."

For that I was able to release a pained laugh. "I'm sure there are easier ways to get food than this."

Teddy opened his mouth.

"Oh no, not happening." In a blur, Paul was coming and seizing my arm and taking me away. "You got split-ends, Theodore!" Paul shouted back as he ushered me down the path from the gazebo.

I struggled against Paul, trying not to cause a scene. "Let me go."

Paul did no such thing as he excused his way through the crowd and had us back up the patio steps and into the house.

He let me go once we were alone, safely away from Teddy. "Let's take five."

My lips trembled and my eyes watered. "I gotta go."

Paul sighed, watching me. "Bianka, the only reason I'm with *you* right now is to keep myself from going and ripping Zander's head off."

I'd already seen enough. When presented with an invitation from his ex, Zander hadn't declined. He'd gone away with her to do God knows what.

I let out a sob, going and staring up at the ceiling to keep it together. "It's not fair."

"He's a fucking idiot." Paul handed me his Gucci pocket

square to dab my eyes with. "He knows better than this. She's going to be his downfall."

"I'm going to go."

"Bia— Okay, just let me walk you out to the car." Paul took me under his arm and led me back to the front door.

I didn't bother chancing a look behind me, at the world I was leaving behind, at the world I never belonged in anyway.

27

Paul saw me out to the valet so our truck could chauffer me back to the hotel. The party was still going on without us, but we didn't care. It had long since lost its splendor and glitter.

"They say, 'Be all that you can be,' and he decides to be a prick," Paul said as he hung in the window as I sat in the back seat. "Go figure."

I wanted to laugh, but my heart hurt too much. This one was a low blow, even if it were my fault. "Thank you, Paul."

Sympathy tugged on his face; his green eyes sad for me. "I'm sorry, Bia."

"Me too."

The driver pulled off and out of the driveway, making his way back to the The Residence-Pasadena. Unlike on our way to the dinner, the sun was down, and it was dark out. But my heart was darker. It pounded violently in my chest and I choked on air as I struggled to breathe.

What really stung, was that I'd let my guard down. For so long I kept everybody at an arm's length, and Zander had been no different, except he wanted in, just to use me up and break me.

Just to have somebody to pass the time until he could get back into Jolie's good graces.

Rajaa was in the suite when I got in, laying back watching TV.

"Hey, Bia, back so— What's wrong?" He sat up, examining me, worry crossing his face.

Rajaa had always been nothing but nice and accepting to me, and for that I fought my urge to scream and not take my pain out on him.

I went for the master bedroom. "I wasn't here."

Rajaa was confused. "But—"

I closed my door on him and pressed my back against it. At the loud interruption of "Chill" I could finally cry. As much as I wanted to break down and pile myself on the floor, I kicked into autopilot and began collecting my things to go, all the while ignoring the repeated sound of my phone ringing.

I just wanted to be gone, as soon as possible, but I didn't want to make my exit dressed all pretty. I didn't feel like I looked, and for that I was quick to slip into the bathroom and take off my makeup and wash my face.

My phone pinged again and again. A single look showed me a stream of notifications from social media. I was being tagged in photos of Zander and Jolie. Fans openly mocking me for being a rebound. Others showing support in my embarrassment.

All I saw was the look on Zander's face. The smile he held in a candid. Jolie's back was to the camera, but there was no missing Zander's joy. Ten minutes went by as I scrolled through my phone and I kept going back to that single photo. In real time, the whole world could see the ending of Zander and me play out as he was back in the grace of his ex.

As if my heart could take another dive.

My hands gripped the edge of the counter, willing myself to calm down as I practiced breathing normally. *It'll be okay, Bia. Just get as far away from here as you can.*

In the bedroom, I sifted through my bag to find something to put—

The door shut, and in my peripheral vision, I saw him go and rest against it.

Zander.

I hoped and prayed with all that I had that he didn't come close. I didn't trust myself or my emotions. I was on my last seam, ready to tear into pieces.

Zander was quiet, taking in my bags on the bed and my state of packing up. "I looked for you at the party. Paul gave me shit about Jolene and told me you left. You wouldn't answer my calls. And now I come back to you packing up to leave."

"Fuck you, Zander." My voice wasn't strong enough to properly yell, to really let him have it.

Zander blinked, angling his head. "Fuck me?" He looked away and bobbed his head. "Why don't you be an adult and tell me what the hell is going on? If this is about Jo—"

I couldn't do this anymore. Not after seeing him with her in person. "Did you fuck her in New York?"

All at once Zander stood before me expressionless. Cold. Distant. His hands were in his pockets and his erect posture and straight face had me feeling weaker and more inadequate.

He suddenly chuckled, a mean grin on his face. "I told you what I did in New York."

"It sure as hell was hard to—"

"I'm talking, Bianka," Zander cut in, his tone clipped and detached.

How dare he. How dare he stand there while I was breaking inside because of him. All of me was in pain, bleeding, and he had the audacity to go cold. "Fuck you, Zander!"

He pinched the bridge of his nose. "There is no Jolene for me. But you see her standing with me and that means I fucked her? I saw *you* standing with Teddy, but am I in here questioning you? Especially after what he's done?"

I was standing with Teddy. I hadn't gone off with him. "Fuck you!"

Zander didn't yell or get angry, instead he was eerily calm. His expression shifted to neutral, no longer holding the fire in his eyes he'd held for me just an hour before.

Tired and defeated, Zander's shoulders sagged as he heaved a sigh. His gaze fell to the floor. "I've always been nothing but honest with you. More honest than I've been in a long time." He studied me, his eyes lingering on my clothing. "You...you look beautiful tonight, right now, and you're walking away from me. Fuck you, Bianka."

Without another word, he turned and left the room, shutting the door behind him.

What hurt the most was that he didn't even slam it. He didn't give me any emotion at all. He just up and left. Quietly, and all at once.

28

Victoria was the greatest. She collected me up late Saturday night when I returned to her in pieces. She let me cry on her shoulder, and she rubbed my back to soothe me like a mother to a child. She didn't bask in my failed relationship with Zander. She didn't rub it in at all.

I didn't deserve her kindness, but I was grateful for her support.

Zander had left the suite, leaving Rajaa befuddled as he'd been in the living room while we fought—no, *I* fought. Zander just walked away.

He hadn't called when I returned to Hemingway Park, and I hadn't reached out either.

Just like that, the ride was over.

Sunday came and went as I hid myself from the world, refusing to leave the comfort of my bed. Victoria didn't let me suffer alone. She was quick to come crawl under the covers and lie with me. We didn't speak at all Sunday, but it was enough with Tori being there.

By the time Monday rolled in, I migrated to the living room to be sad and depressed in some new scenery.

"You going to work?" Victoria asked of me. She was in the

kitchen making coffee, probably preparing to get started on her appointments.

Was I going to work?

I was due in at Angles at noon, but I still felt gloomy.

As I sat on the couch in the living room, I brought my knees to my chest. "I should. I need the money."

When Victoria didn't respond, I turned to catch her engrossed in her phone. Her mouth hung open as a look of shock covered her face.

"What?" I asked.

Slowly, Victoria peeled her eyes from her screen. "N-Nothing."

It was such an obvious lie. "Tori."

"Bia, you don't want to know," Victoria warned.

She was acting strange, making me cautious. "Did something happen?"

My best friend managed to nod her head and frown. "Bianka."

"Am I going to find out regardless?"

Apparently, there was no denying this as Victoria bobbed her head once more. "Yeah."

"Then what is it?"

After a moment's pause, Victoria crossed over to me. She handed me her cell phone and it all became clear. There was a blog pulled up, The CelebriTea, and there was a photo of Zander and me with a big tear in between us. There was also a circular photo of Jolie nearby as well.

Ah.

———

The CelebriTea

Your Source for All Celeb News

Jul 10

DEBUT DUD

Over the weekend our favorite hip-hop clan, the Dymond Dynasty, held their annual Dymond Dinner where notable faces like Nas, Rick Ross, and La La Anthony were seen in attendance. What had most of us here at the tea table shook was spotting Zander Khalil at the meal. He didn't come alone, as his recent love, *Bianka*, was his date for the evening.

The two showed up hand in hand in a matching assemble of burgundy and black, looking stylish and decadent. After snapping a few hot and totally dreamy pics against a green hedge, the two were seen whispering sweet nothings in each other's ear—but things didn't stay so sweet.

Not too long into the evening our man Zan was seen cozying up with his ex, Jolie, standing close to each other in group photos where Jolie was clearly all up in Zander's ear winning him back. Bianka was nowhere in sight. A close source says she was seen leaving with none other than former So Whatter Teddy Sykes.

Ironically, hours before the event, Bianka uploaded a video of her getting ready and dancing on Zander, and the two seemed in such good spirits. We haven't seen this much emotion out of Zander since he first went solo!

Reports are saying that Zander and Jolie have in fact rekindled their once simmering flame, and Bianka is out the door. Jolie was quick to repost an image of the two together on her Instagram story with the added quote "Back as it belongs." We checked and she's even following Zander again.

Yikes! Looks like what would've been a dashing couple debut, ended up in a very awkward swap. What do you think, Tea Party, did Zander make a good call spinning the block? Is Bianka giving anybody else groupie teas going from Zandy to Syko? Let us know your thoughts, spill below!

———

There was a screen recorded video of me dancing on Zander before we'd left for dinner. There were several images of us together at the party, including the photos the photographer took.

I got lost staring at those, admiring the happiness on my face, and what looked like love in Zander's eyes. Had we made it, perhaps I would've saved a couple of the photos and used one as my lock screen. For years, Victoria's lock screen was of Zander, and even the first two digits of her passcode to her iPhone were made of his initials.

My heart broke even further at the screenshot of Jolie's Instagram story, where she'd marked her territory and claimed her place in Zander's life once more.

I didn't know what to believe, though. The blog reported that I'd left with Teddy, that I'd gone from Zandy to Syko, as Teddy's fan base were known as *Sykos*. Either way, it wasn't true. And if that part wasn't true, how much more of the report was fabricated? Zander himself hadn't confirmed or denied anything —yet.

Now I sounded desperate to hold on when I should've been wiser and let it all go.

"Well?" Victoria asked as she sat beside me. "What do you think? I mean, what really happened, Bia?"

It was a simple question, but in truth, I could barely answer it. It had all happened so fast, spiraling toward a pain I still couldn't stomach. I tried to paint the picture for Victoria as best as I could, being completely honest in case *I* was wrong in any way. I told her everything, except for our moment in the bedroom, wanting that last nice piece of heaven to be just for us. When I finished, she still held no judgment against me.

"Fuck him," she stated simply.

"I don't know, Victoria. It's different between us, it's... deeper." *Deeper*, the only word to describe my short romance with Zander Khalil. I let him in, I let him pick me up and hold me down, I was ready to go to bat for him, I allowed myself to fall in love with him. "We were supposed to be having a weekend fling, and instead I ended up crying over my family, and he held me and he made love to my body and my soul.

"I let go with him, I tried new things, I wasn't so bitter and jaded, I was happy. And now all I wanna do is throw up and cry."

Victoria reached up to wipe at my eyes. "You can still be happy. Don't let Jolie or Zander ruin your joy; you're much bigger than that. Maybe you both need some space right now to clear your heads, if it's meant to be...well, you know how that goes. For now, maybe you should block his socials and number, just to take a moment and focus on yourself."

I hadn't even looked at my phone since I'd come home from the hotel. Paul had called and texted me, but I hadn't been in the mood to carry a conversation or respond.

My mood wasn't the best, but Victoria was right—I had to free my mind and focus on myself. Suddenly, going in for my shift at Angles felt completely appealing.

"Guess I'll be going in to work after all." I stood from the couch and headed into my bedroom, going and finding my phone to check its battery charge. Upon grabbing my cell, I found dozens of notifications on my screen. People were tagging me on The CelebriTea's post about my split with Zander, others were DMing me support, and there was even a text and missed call from Holliston.

Block it all out, Bia, I coached myself as I took a deep breath.

I went to wash my hands of it all, even if it meant either giving Zander his proper time to cool down as well, or leaving the two lovebirds to reconnect. Only, on every social media profile I had, when I went to try to unfollow Zander, *he* was still following me.

It had been a day, and I didn't know what to think of it. I was probably overthinking, finding an excuse to be hopeful, or maybe it meant The CelebriTea was full of bullshit.

In the end, I tossed my phone to the side to go and get ready for work instead.

As if a follow meant anything anyway.

29

I DON'T WANNA LIVE FOREVER

"Maybe we should have a girls' night out, I mean, if you want," Holliston suggested Tuesday while we were styling mannequins on the sales floor during the shop's downtime.

She was trying to cheer me up, and I appreciated her effort. Three days without seeing and speaking to Zander had me down. I wanted to just get over it, but love was tricky that way. I couldn't even unfollow him online. And my dreams, like my thoughts, were invaded by him. Every time we were in bed together, every time he cooked for me, the times I cooked for him, the nights shared in his arms or holding him.

My hands felt lifeless and lonely without his to hold. My lips felt dry and cracked without his to kiss. My time felt wasted without him to share it with.

"I don't know, Holly, I've got a depression nap scheduled for when I get off," I said.

Holliston's face deadpanned, her blue eyes narrowing. "Really?"

"I need about three to five business days to recuperate and get over this."

Holliston shook her head and pulled her cell phone from her

back pocket. She was still sporting her Teddy Sykes case on it. "If you don't want to go, it's your loss. I hear that new Chris Evans movie is so good. Reviews are saying it's the best romance of the year."

Only Holliston. She was such a hopeless romantic. I thought it made her naïve and cute. In the long run, though, any guy would be lucky to have her. She had a heart and soul made to love, and I just hoped the right guy won her over in the end.

"Not my vibe," I told her. I wasn't big on romance movies; my taste was more drama, dark, or thriller. In my reading, I was the exact opposite: I loved a good love story in written form. But now wasn't the time for any of that. Too triggering.

Holliston looked up from her phone and I wasn't sure she even heard me. "Whoa."

"What?" I prompted.

"Zander."

Her response caused me to gather my own phone and sure enough, my notifications were going crazy. A glimpse through Twitter found why, Zander had finally broken his silence.

His last tweet was a link to a YouTube video where he'd done a cover of Rihanna's "Kiss It Better." Even more, there was another link to his website where he'd uploaded a new song called "Pride & Failure." The cover art was a gritty black and white photo of him smoking in the studio. So moody and artistic. Only Zander.

What really snatched my breath right from my lungs, was in the photo he was wearing a simple T-shirt to the untrained eye, but I could recognize that Yin and Yang tee for as long as I lived. My heart leaped to my throat, threatening to end me. He was wearing my shirt.

I pressed play on the song and immediately was lost in its tone and lyrics.

Your pride and my failure, consumes all of me
It's up and it's down, and it's hard to breathe
It's not right, it's not fair, I don't want you to leave
I will stay, I will fight, I'll give all of me

Tell me what are you running for
Is there anything I can do more
Tell me is this really the end
Can't we go on and pretend

I'm gonna hold, I'm gonna hold on
I'm gonna hold, I'm gonna hold on

Remember it just like yesterday
Right before you went away

We were going on
Going strong
Suddenly, it went wrong
No more holding you, touching you
Kissing you, loving you, nothing

Tell me what are you running for
Is there anything I can do more
Tell me is this really the end
Can't we go on and pretend

I'm gonna hold, I'm gonna hold on
I'm gonna hold, I'm gonna hold on

Now you wanna go
And I say no
Then it's fuck you
But I love you
Can we stop

Don't run and hide
Run and hide
Don't run and hide
Run and hide

Tell me what are you running for (What are you running for)
Is there anything I can do more (Can I do anything)
Tell me is this really the end (Is this really the end of you and me)
Can't we go on and pretend (Can we go on)

I'm gonna hold, I'm gonna hold on
I'm gonna hold, I'm gonna hold on
Gonna hold on
Gonna hold on

Drop your pride, I'll drop my failure
When I'm with you, I'm much better

It was when I listened to the bridge that my eyes started to water. His high note on "hide" left me speechless. That unreachable falsetto of his showed the rawness of what he was feeling. I was truly at a loss for words as I stood clutching my chest.

Zander *wasn't* with Jolie.

It was so painfully obvious that this song, "Pride & Failure" was about me—*us*.

His words echoed in my head, about how when things were going bad for him, he found himself in the studio to find his way. He hadn't gone back to Jolie, no, he went where it all made sense to him and put it all into this song.

My cell phone rang and I found Victoria calling.

"Hey," I answered, my voice shaky.

"So, I take it you heard?" she asked.

I let out a breath. "I don't know what to say."

"Shout out to him for putting homegirl in her place," Victoria started. "But, seriously, Bia, this is heavy. Like, you can hear how hurt he is on this song, and the sound of him begging? *Girlll*."

The bell to the shop went off and a couple of women entered to browse around. I couldn't get caught up in my emotions and feelings now, I had work to do.

"I mean, the blogs say he *finally* unfollowed her, too. She had this coming trying to be cute, now look at her, dress like a clown, get treated like the circus."

Her bluntness made me laugh. "Good riddance."

"I know it's tempting, but I think you should take your time and evaluate before going back. See if this is really what you want. The CelebriTea called you a whole groupie over bullshit speculation. This spotlight shit ain't for everybody, and I can't beat up the whole world for you, but lord knows I'd try."

I loved Victoria Raymond.

I let her know this before hanging up and getting back to work. My heart and head were in the clouds, and for the first time in days, when I smiled, it didn't hurt.

Tori was right. I needed time to myself to focus and think. I caught Holliston at the checkout counter ringing a customer up. "Hey, about that girls' night out, you're on."

30

CRUEL

It took a lot of convincing, but I managed to persuade Holliston into going out for our girls' night. She was only nineteen, and otherwise a good girl who followed the rules, but getting her to come out to The Boot was a feat.

Victoria kept sneaking looks her way to make sure she was really there. But indeed, she was, dressed demurely for the occasion at that. She was wearing a T-shirt tied into a little knot at the side along with some black ripped jeans. The black Converse sneakers on her feet made me chuckle. Holliston was the cutest.

She was sitting at our table drinking a virgin daiquiri, seeming out of place. It was a chill kind of night for the club, offering a lounge vibe with the smooth Erykah Badu record that was currently playing at a moderate level. Holliston wasn't moving along to the song. She was out of her element, but she was here for me.

"Wanna dance?" I leaned over and asked her.

Her eyes enlarged. "Oh no."

Victoria laughed. "C'mon, you gotta loosen up."

Holliston was shy. "I grew up on Fleetwood Mac, Eagles, and Tom Petty. I don't know a thing about *this*."

"*Who?*"

Victoria's confusion caused Holliston to reel back and gape at my best friend. "Oh my God."

Victoria came to me next. "Who?"

I chuckled. "I think I know like one Fleetwood song."

Victoria tipped her drink towards Holliston. "Sounds good."

Holliston smiled. "This place is cool, though. I'm having fun. We should do this again. No boys allowed."

"Unless they're buying us drinks." Tori lifted hers in the air to signal a toast.

As I reached for my glass, I caught my phone lighting up. It had been like that all day since Zander spoke and dropped "Pride & Failure." The emotional ballad had garnered me thousands of new followers, tags, and comments on my social media pages. It was overwhelming, but I was flattered.

"To finessing these fellas like dummies for free drinks," I joked as I toasted with the girls.

Holliston giggled as she clinked her glass against ours. A man had tried to buy her a drink and she'd turned him down, staying loyal to Jake.

Rookie.

"How's H.?" I asked Victoria, curious how her love life was going.

Tori shrugged. "Groveling. I love to see them sweat."

Holliston's auburn brows furrowed. "What did he do?"

"Waste my damn time the first go-round we were together. Now that he sees the grass ain't greener, he's crawling back."

Holliston appeared thoughtful, but said nothing as she sipped on her drink. She needed to leave Jake alone.

"Geez, Bia, you're popular today." Victoria spotted my glowing notifications. "Any word from your boy?"

After sending those tweets and dropping the song and cover, I hadn't heard from Zander.

I grabbed my phone up to scroll through my notifications in case I missed a call or text. I was even prepared to send a cheeky little *fuck you* text if he hadn't.

Only, as I thumbed through my screen looking for Zander, I noticed countless tags on a post by The CelebriTea. I thought it was just Zander's new song, but comments started jumping out at me.

sowhat4ever Omg! This is crazy!
16m   107 likes   Reply

ExposedByKhalil Yikes! He needs HELP
1h   734 likes   Reply

zeddyzolo Connect the dots, you know @JonesJolie is behind this
8m   23 likes   Reply

TeddysBanana How could she leak this?
9m   59 likes   Reply

janiarose i can't look at him the same after this
5m   76 likes   Reply

Leaked?

I opened my phone and clicked on one of the comments, going and being led to The CelebriTea's page. Sure enough all of the commotion was not about the song, it was about a leaked video of Zander. An *anonymous* leak I read from the caption: *Oops, someone sent in an anonymous video of our guy #ZanderKhalil high. The unseen woman in the video doesn't sound pleased with the singer either. We here at the tea table hope things are okay. This is NO joking matter.*

Oh shit.

I pressed Play on the video and sure enough it opened up to someone filming a mirror where a couple of lines of cocaine were cut. A rolled up hundred-dollar bill lay beside the mirror. What really hurt me, was I could hear him. Somewhere offscreen, Zander was singing loudly. The person filming walked off, going and finding Zander and showing his face. His hair was different, messy, and he was topless—skinny, but otherwise energetic. He was shaking, giddy, singing some song by Usher as he smiled towards the camera.

"You're a fucking cokehead," a woman's voice spoke up. It was distinctively female, but low enough to where one couldn't place *who* was speaking—although it wasn't too hard to assume. What's more, her White finger appeared onscreen as she pointed at Zander accusingly. *"Like, you're really disgusting."*

Zander wasn't offended in the least; he wiped at his nose, once, twice, three times before buzzing about and singing more of "U Don't Have to Call." He came closer to the camera and reached out, being silly as he tried to swoon the woman.

The clip ended and my face twisted in anguish.

This was a low blow.

"What? What's wrong?" Victoria asked, concern washing across her face.

Holliston peered my way as well, a look of worry etched on her face too.

I blinked back tears. "I...I'm ready to go home."

31

FOOL FOR YOU

I couldn't sleep.

After we got in from The Boot, I'd gone to my bedroom to obsessively watch and *re*-watch the video. I read so many comments my eyes started to hurt after a while through reading with my blurry vision.

As dawn called for a new day, I found myself tired, but unable to rest.

Celebrity exposures and leaked images and videos happened all the time, and now I could truly *feel* for those it happened to.

Zander.

There was probably no way to prove it was Jolie, that bitch, but as the day settled into Wednesday, I rejoiced in the aftermath of her wake. Everyone was shook and in complete shock from what I could digest, but no one was shaming Zander or judging him. Even The CelebriTea were being gentle on the subject.

———

The CelebriTea

Your Source for All Celeb News

Jul 14

ZANDER KHALIL EX-POSED?

What seemed like a cozy little reunion for Zander Khalil and Jolene Jones turned out to be a fantasy when Zander took to his Twitter account to clear up rumors. After clarifying that he and his *Chasing Love* star ex were not rekindling their relationship, Zander dropped a sizzling cover of Rih-Rih's "Kiss It Better," as well as a new song on his website called "Pride & Failure," which many are speculating is about his recent partner, Bianka.

Shockingly, while most of us at the tea table were swooning and hoping for Zianka to be okay, shit hit the fan when a leaked video of what appears to be Zander high on an illegal substance took the internet by storm.

An unknown woman can be seen in the two-minute video mocking the singer and calling him out on his habit. Neither Zander nor his team has spoken up about it.

Many Zandies are claiming that the video looks old, and we can only hope that is the case, and our favorite "The Sound" singer is doing better in recent times.

After watching Zander struggle with fame and scrutiny, we've been delighted to see him stepping out and taking charge in his career, and can only root for him further as we await his third release.

Staff writer: Jackie

Comments (2,493)

ProudZandy
Drug addiction isn't something to mock or belittle. Instead of recording, she should've tried to help him.

paris_uber_music
Let's be real, it's time to cancel J*lene J*nes.

sykoteddybear
Lol, like, what did she expect to accomplish by leaking this? Half the industry is on something asjjsjsjs.

xxhayleyxxduh
After years, Zander is finally happy, out and active, ready to tour and be seen. And this leech tried to manipulate a situation after breaking his heart, he tells her to kindly fuck off, so she retaliates by exposing his addiction? #JolieIsOver.

*Michele03_*
I just want to hug him, because I know this is probably really triggering for him.

sincerelyjaymess
We've lost so many amazing entertainers to drug addiction, and now we've reached a low where we can't handle rejection so we expose REAL issues and make light of the seriousness of addiction?

beyoncesbackupsinger
I'm legit disgusted right now, like I'm really shaking.

plantbasedlyfe
Someone drop her addy, I just wanna talk.

———

What really caused my heart to throb the most, was the surprising tweet of support from Teddy.

I placed my phone facedown after that.

Victoria entered my room after knocking on my bedroom door. She approached me cautiously, unsure how I was dealing. After crying the whole way home, she knew to give me space when I'd gone straight to my bedroom.

"Hey," she said gently. "What's up?"

Zander's team denied the video was proof *he* was on coke, but they also stated the video was old. His much thinner frame could attest to that, not to mention the absence of his new *XXX* tattoo.

Now Victoria wanted to know how I was holding up. So many thoughts were running through my head, tiny ones where I was thankful we'd broken things off and I wasn't attached to this scandal. Those thoughts were small and selfish, no match for the piece of me that didn't care about how risky it was dating someone of Zander's stature. I wanted to be there for him.

He hadn't said a word about this leak or about the song.

I placed my hand to my heart as I got out of bed and began pacing around, my head racing. We were going through a fight, but truly, it wasn't over, not by a long shot. He'd said *fuck you* and walked away, but he'd promised me at a time before that when it was over he'd look me in the eye and tell me so.

Zander hadn't done that Saturday night.

Swallowing, I faced my best friend. "How are you feeling? As his biggest fan?"

Victoria frowned. "I didn't know he used coke."

Because it was private information he'd disclosed to those closest to him. If Zander had have gone back to Jolie, I would've been heartbroken and upset, but I wouldn't have exposed him like this. Done something so treacherous to get back at him. What did I have to gain by hurting someone I loved? All night I cried for him, because I hated to see this happen to him.

I hugged myself and heaved a sigh. "He told me, but he said it's been almost three years."

"I can tell. He was so skinny in that video," Victoria said as she came and sat on my bed. "This had to be during the *Damage Control* era because he didn't even have some of the tattoos on his left sleeve yet."

Old news, the video was old news.

"Bia," Victoria spoke up. "What are you feeling right now?

I bit on my thumb, contemplating my next move.

Maybe...maybe I should call him. A text was so impersonal at a time like this.

That tiny selfish part of me noted I could just walk away and clean my hands of this messy life before I got in too deep, but my heart had already waded away from the shallow end weeks ago.

In the end, as I lifted my head to face my best friend, I knew my fate. It was something I'd wanted to do the moment I'd heard "Pride & Failure." The moment I had seen the leaked video. The moment we left the club.

Zander's voice was in my head as I crossed my room, going and grabbing my purse. *I'm going to fight for you, but will you fight for me?* he'd asked me.

Yes, Zander, I'm coming. I'll fight.

I tried to listen to the radio, but I couldn't because they were discussing Zander. I couldn't listen to music from my phone because my shuffle was still on *Exposed*.

I drove in silence to Beverly Hills, racing against traffic to get to the man I loved.

Now wasn't the time to get emotional; now was the time to be strong. I had a lot to say, and lord willing, I wasn't leaving Zander's estate until I said it.

It was no surprise to catch Paul's BMW as I pulled into the parking area in front of Zander's house and parked. Of course he'd be here for Zander. Outside of being his manager, he was his most loyal supporter. Someone Zander definitely needed in his corner right now.

In the rearview mirror, I found my reflection. I was trembling, unprepared and totally scared for what the future threw at me— at *us*, but there was no turning back. For my whole life, I'd been a fighter. My mother had raised me to be. Pryor broke my heart when he walked out on me, but I fought and forged on. My father broke my heart when he strung me along to keep up appearances, and begrudgingly, I cut him off and forged forward. Fighting was all that I knew how to do, but somehow, with Zander, I'd rebelled against him.

He was the only person outside of Victoria who had fought *for* me.

A glimpse at the watch on my wrist could attest to that. It could've been any other girl, but it was me.

And to think, it started with a slap.

A sad smile formed on my face and I managed to gather myself together enough to get out of the car and be a big girl and march on.

I went and rang the doorbell, not knowing what to expect on the other side. Nazanin would probably never accept me, but I was here, and I wasn't going anywhere so long as Zander wanted me. This was our ride, and even if it rained or stormed, I was ready to ride along with the top down. No inhibitions or regrets.

Paul came to the door. For the first time, he was undone in a simple T-shirt and jeans. His hair was a mess, and he looked tired.

A woman's loud voice could be heard in the background. "I don't care if we have to get the fucking CIA to hack into her phone, I want proof that Jolie is behind this. I am going to bury that bitch."

Whoa.

Paul blew out a breath, his shoulders rising and falling. "So, that's us, what's been new with you?"

Everything was in chaos and somehow he managed to lighten my mood.

"Hey, Paul, can I come in?" I asked.

He opened the door wider and allowed me into the front foyer. Coming out of the living room was a brunette on her cell phone. The pissed-off expression on her face let me know not to get on her bad side, because she was raging internally by the looks of it. She sized me up, going and holding the phone out of earshot. "Bianka, right?"

I nodded. "Yeah."

"Perfect timing." The woman slipped back into the living room, once more on her device. "I'm spinning this story the best that I can, but I want her head on my desk by midnight."

Paul shook his head. "That's Francel, Zan's publicist. Not the person you want to piss off, trust me. I've had my balls handed to me a few times for letting Zander do some stupid shit in the press."

"Can we prove it was Jolie?" I wondered.

Paul shrugged. "Everyone's saying this was an anonymous submission into some blog, but it's not hard to put two and two together. Fortunately for us, no one's got their claws out." He made a claw with his hand along with a striking gesture. "Except Fran of course."

Footsteps sounded down the hall and a look over found Nazanin coming our way. Her sleek dark hair was pulled up in a ponytail and she too was dressed down in a T-shirt and pair of shorts. She folded her arms as she came to a stop just short of us. Skeptically she took me in, silently questioning why I'd shown up.

Sister or not, she wasn't getting my respect any longer.

Against Paul's attempts to hold me back, I marched straight up to Nazanin and got in her face. "Well? Happy? This is what you wanted, right? Team Jolie for the fucking win, right?"

Nazanin lifted her chin and pursed her lips. "I had no idea."

"Fuck you, Nazanin."

She arched a brow. "Spare me the foreplay, Bianka, I'm not my brother." She uncrossed her arms and threaded her fingers together, hanging her head in shame. "I was wrong to have judged you, I see that now. Saad is the only sibling I have, and it's my job to protect him. I've always had my guard up with outsiders, and now I see that sometimes the snakes can already be within."

"Leave her alone."

Coming down the steps, Rajaa had his hard gaze fixed on his cousin. "She's one of the best things that's happened to Saad. Isn't it obvious now?"

Nazanin stepped back. "Immensely." Her dark wounded eyes peered into mine, searching it seemed. "I'm sorry, Bianka."

We had finally established our truce. It was a shame it took such poison like this to get there.

"You're either going to get to know me and love me or not, either way, as long as Zander does, I'm good," I let his sister know. I turned to Paul, done discussing it. "Where is he?"

Paul raked a hand through his hair. "Out back. Word of advice, the guy's been pissed since Saturday. When he found out about her posts online... I've never seen him that mad. And now this."

"There's not much I can do, but I'm here." I gestured at myself.

Together the three of them let me go as I descended down the hall, past the kitchen, and out into the backyard.

At the edge of the yard he stood. Staring out at the city and taking in this night.

Bright. He'd said the hillside of his house always made him think of bright and positive things. Now was such a moment to be radiant.

Slowly, I made my way over to him, hoping for the best, but willing to accept the worst. "Hey."

Zander pulled his attention from his staring, facing me. His mood didn't lift, yet the sight of him took my breath away like always. He, like the others inside, appeared tired and drained. The five o'clock shadow covering his jaw and the dullness in his eyes were evidence of the past few days for him.

"How are you?" I asked in a small, uncertain voice.

A corner of Zander's lips quirked up. "Swell."

He was being sarcastic, but his word choice wasn't lost on me. He was using my lingo.

As if I could love him any more than I already did.

I bit my lip, trying to stay calm. "Nice word."

Zander gave a lazy shrug. "Learned from the best."

Short and quick responses. He was closed-off, and rightfully so. So much had happened.

"I thought long and hard about coming here," I confessed.

Zander lifted his hooded eyes up to mine. "You don't want to be here?"

I clasped my hands together, wanting to tell the truth. "Honestly, no. I'd rather be pulling up on Jolie so I can kick her ass, but I don't know where she's staying."

Zander snorted. "What are we going to do with you, Bianka?"

"Love me," I said softly, because it was all I could bring to the table, and he knew that.

"I do, but can *you* love *me*?"

"I've loved you since you freed me from my father, ever since you got me this watch."

"Then why did you run?"

"Because...because I thought you were still into Jolie. She got into my head and I thought...I thought I didn't stand a chance, especially after you went away with her."

"Why didn't you fight for me like I fight for you?" Zander questioned.

"I'm not going to fight over a man who wants to go," I argued, shaking my head. "I can't be that person again."

Zander appeared wounded, his shoulders sagging further. "I was wrong, okay? I should've never left you alone. You should've been right by my side the whole night. I was taking a picture with Remy and Galen, and Peyton and Jolene walked over and I should've moved, but I didn't want to be an asshole. A while later I'm taking the piss with my sister and the guys and she comes to stand next to me.

"She asked me if I was happy and all I could do was smile at the thought of you. I told her I was absolutely happy. Happier than I've ever been."

My heart ached at the revelation. "Zander."

Zander shook his head in shame. "I saw you with Teddy and I got upset, I won't lie, but I was with Jo and I figured why cause a scene? It was just one night of bullshitting. We could get through it. But then she had my hand, she wanted to talk, and I just—I should've stayed where we were."

"Yes," I agreed. "You should have. She made it very clear she could have you whenever she wanted, and how was I supposed to feel seeing you together immediately after she said it?"

A muscle in Zander's jaw tensed, a flash of anger coating his eyes. "She's a terrific actress then. She was in my ear, she was being friendly, and it didn't do anything for me. I told her I was happy with you, and she was smiling and calling you pretty. Then the next thing I know, we get back and you're gone, and Paul's yelling at me for being with Jo. I just booked it to the hotel, just to see you running—again."

"Nazanin wanted you together, Jolie was in my head bragging about taking you back, and then you looked so happy to be around her and you didn't put up a fight when she had your hand, and I just couldn't deal."

Zander shook his head. "I love *you*, Bianka, okay? And it hurts when you run instead of talking to me. I would've rather walked into a screaming match than to see you there packing your bags to go. I ask you what's wrong and you hit me with a 'fuck you.'"

I let out a pained laugh. "I thought that was our love language."

Zander rolled his tongue over his upper lip, trying his best to fight his smile. He peered out at the city once more. "I left and went to the studio. It was the only way to communicate how I felt. I turned off my phone and just stayed until that song came out solid. On Tuesday I got word of Jolene's posts, and Naz was telling me it wouldn't be so bad for me to take her back.

"I didn't know she was talking shit to you, but after seeing her posts I could tell she wasn't being genuine when she was complimenting how good you and I looked together. I've never wanted to bash her, but to play with my emotions…that's a level of disrespect I won't tolerate."

He could've said much worse in his tweets, but he hadn't. Still, it'd been enough for her to lash out with the leak. "Do you remember? That video? Being recorded?"

Zander bobbed his head. "I can't prove it's her, but honestly, I'm not trying to fight her either. She had her little moment, and I'm done."

Being the bigger person was for the birds. "Zander."

He faced me. "I love *you*, Bianka. Can't that just be enough? Three years ago I was making bad choices, choices I no longer entertain. She wanted to bring me down, but I've already been there, and I'm not going back."

"Nobody's judging you," I let him know. "So many people are pissed at her and showing you support. Even Teddy."

Zander quietly stared at me for a while, taking in my words. His career could've been in jeopardy, but he didn't care. He was ready to forge forward and keep going. His resilience made me love him more. Jolie's petty move hadn't worked, not in the least.

"I'm here because I love you," I told him. "I have no idea how this is going to work with you going on tour and me figuring my shit out, but I just know I love you. Not the idea of you, or your image, I love *you*, Zander.

"I love you for you, just like you love me for me. You're the only person outside of Tori who's ever fought for me, and I'm willing to do the same for you. For *us*."

He came closer, softening up with each step. Gently, with his thumb, he wiped at a stray tear that had fallen down my face. "Promise?"

"I swear," I let him know. Wherever this went, I was willing to fight, just like he had for me. Fuck the blogs and terrible exes; all that mattered was us.

Zander searched my eyes and I could see his guard lowering. "What now?"

Tangling my fingers with his, I stared up into his eyes, feeling my heart lift up. "Now, we face the world, together. But first"—I went closer, standing tall to reach his lips—"we've got some making up to do."

Zander leaned down and met me halfway, bringing his arms around me as his mouth met mine.

32

GOLDEN

I didn't mind standing in line; it made the moment authentic.

Victoria didn't think so.

My best friend wasn't shy about letting me know she wasn't feeling my decision for the night.

"Bia, you have an inside advantage, and yet we out here with the locals." Victoria gestured around at our current place at the front of the line where we were waiting to get into The Warehouse. It was Friday night and the doors were just about to open. We had been the first to show up due to my insisting.

Call me sentimental, but since we were bringing it all full circle, I wanted to do it right.

Ten minutes ago, an all-black Cullinan had driven by, and no one had noticed. Which was good, they weren't supposed to.

I beamed over at my impatient friend. "Not too long ago I was in your shoes."

She sized me up, blatantly. "And we both know how that turned out."

Right, my current status as the girlfriend of this generation's best R&B vocalist and ex-So What member.

The doors officially opened and we paid our way inside, another thing that had Victoria shooting me an attitude.

It was Friday night, the people entering the venue were here to unwind, dance, and enjoy their weekend. I was still a little shaky following the leaked video on Wednesday, but I had some pretty incredible people in my corner willing to stand tall against any attack coming my way. The blogs and social media were still tearing Jolie a new one, even if she denied being involved. Whether or not Francel could prove it, it wasn't about to stop Zander from releasing an amazing comeback album in the winter. From what I'd heard of *Abstract*, it was going to be a solid body of work.

The album would be released sometime after the official Grammy deadline, but Zander and his team were still shooting to submit "Canvas" to be recognized. If not, there was still the Grammys in the year to come. Zander had so much talent, I was willing to bet my life on it that he'd end his career with a few on his shelf.

"You owe me a drink." Victoria pouted.

I rolled my eyes and went and shelled out for her to have something to sip on while we enjoyed the show.

Once the Sex on the Beach hit her hand, she took a moment to study me and my attire, shaking her head. "God, who are you and what have you done with Bia?"

My oversized Zander T-shirt and combat boots felt even more fitting for the occasion.

I elbowed Tori on the sly. "Jealous?"

She sipped on her drink. "Low-key."

It was hard to believe after all the years of her being a Zander stan, that I'd be the one in a relationship with him. That I'd be the one who had pulled this night and event together.

It was funny how time changed.

"Okay, where's the DJ? Where's the music?" a woman asked as she breezed by with her friend. "I didn't just pay ten dollars to stand around waiting."

The lights in the room dimmed, managing to quiet those also questioning what was going on. The lights dimmed and soon a purple tinted light took over the ambiance of the venue as the stage lights came to life.

All eyes turned to watch as the curtains opened, revealing a lone figure at the microphone.

Beside me, Victoria sighed helplessly as she set eyes on Zander. "Finally."

All around me women gasped and then screamed with excitement at the man on stage, the man about to perform for the first time in three years. The man who had taken his place at the top of the charts. The man set to go on an impressive world tour come next summer. The man who had made a stan out of me.

Zander took in the moment, soaking in the applause and admiration before him. Then he grinned that sexy ass half grin of his and I felt my heart melt. He gripped the microphone, prepared to speak. "Well, hello."

Screams echoed out in response, making a big smile split my face. We'd talked greatly about his next move following his scandal, Francel and Paul all ears on any idea I had. I could laugh at myself for the irony in the situation. Francel and the others were worried, and Zander just wanted to sing and continue promoting his album.

We all sat together in Zander's living room—Rajaa, Nazanin, Paul, Francel, Zander, and me. They all were curious and eager to move on, to make this go away and restore the momentum behind *Abstract*.

While they were brainstorming and throwing out ideas, it hit me.

"So what," I'd spoken up, catching all of their attention. "Some crazy shit went down on Wednesday, but so what? The show must go on, and Zander should show that he's not going to hide." I faced him, reaching out and grasping his hand. "Why don't we take this back to the start?"

The others had thought I was crazy for this idea, but seeing Zander up on stage facing a room full of people hyped to see him, I knew my call had been right. Celebrity scandals were a dime a dozen, and this wasn't about to break Zander's spirit or drive. I wouldn't let it.

Jolie didn't deserve his reaction.

You didn't feed a rumor, you let it starve and die out.

"I was supposed to perform here a month ago, and at the last minute I psyched myself out," Zander spoke into the microphone. "A lot has happened since then, but it feels good to come full circle. There are some things in the media going on about me, and I'm sure you've all got your thoughts. Someone tried to ruin me, but guess what, I'm still standing. It's only really over, and you're truly defeated, when you give up on yourself. I'm not goin' out that way."

The club roared with support and praise, drinks raising to the air to salute Zander in their full loyalty.

"I appreciate all the messages and support I've been getting; it means a lot. Had this been some time ago, I don't think I would've made it, to be honest," Zander confessed. "I wasn't at my best before, but I've got some wonderful people in my corner. People I want to thank for being solid from the beginning and helping get me here. I'd like to thank my sister, Nazanin, because she's tough as shit, but she gives a damn the hardest and I'll always be grateful for that. In ways, she's saved me from myself."

Nazanin was tiptoeing around me, still apologetic for her rudeness before, but I was hopeful we could find a page to get on. I'd FaceTimed with Zander as he spoken to his parents and they hadn't batted an eye at the idea of me. It was only natural that at some point, Nazanin would come around as well.

"I'd like to thank my manager, Paul, because he's never been afraid to square up with me, and I'm a tough son of a bitch to deal with," Zander admitted, causing the room to ripple in a wave of laughter. "I love him like a brother, and I'm grateful too. I'm also very, very grateful and indebted to one young woman who entered my life by one brutal bitch slap.

"I know you're in here somewhere, Bianka, and I hope you

know I love you, and I'm never going to stop driving as long as you're riding with me."

Victoria nudged me, leaning close to whisper. "This could've been me."

I stuck my tongue out at her tauntingly. "What's not to love about me?"

She pretended to think it over and I laughed as I shoved her.

"There's one more person I have to acknowledge before I start," Zander continued. "I know we've got our issues, mate, but I seen the tweet my brother Teddy Sykes sent out in—"

Before he could even finish his sentence fangirls all around screamed at the thought of a possible reunion of the *Zeddy* brotp. Zander wasn't quite ready to mend that bridge, but hearing him mention Teddy's show of solidarity was a small start.

Zander grinned, standing back from the mic for a moment and just taking in all the love and support being thrown his way. His anxiety would be a lifelong battle, but here today, he wasn't afraid, he was ready to take the stage and own it.

He came back to the mic and held on to it with both hands, his eyes searching out and somehow finding me where I stood by the bar with my best friend. A gleam passed through his eyes. An unspoken *I love you* passed from him to me. "It's good to be here tonight, Warehouse. Who wants to hear a song?"

The melody of "The Sound" came through the speakers and the crowd went wild.

SLOWER

HOLLISTON & TEDDY'S STORY

1

THE MOMENT I KNEW

He should've been here.

The night was winding down, and there was no sign of him. I sat alone at our table, a lonely party of one. Waiting. Fingers crossed. Hoping.

Tonight, I wore a special dress to feel more grown up. A powder-blue lace skater dress, the color so light it was almost white. It was short, my legs were bare and visible. It was flirty, my cleavage was on display. In this dress, I was woman.

Only now I was freezing. The draft in the restaurant too much to ignore. I couldn't sit here any longer. I couldn't even lift my gaze up from the table as I was too embarrassed to make eye contact with any of the hostesses walking by, the ones who were shooting me pitying looks. It was going on two hours, and I was sure they were questioning why I was still holding out. He wasn't coming.

It was a bitter pill to swallow. My host, a young man named Ben, had been so gracious enough to light a candle when I told him it was my birthday. The long stick of wax had long since melted down to half its original height, the desperate flame still burning. A symbol, if you will, for my holding on for my boyfriend to come here.

October tenth, my twentieth birthday. My first step into my twenties, and he said he'd be here.

It was Jake's idea to come to LA for my birthday, to make an experience of it. He rented a motel room and made reservations at this nice restaurant, and yet, he hadn't shown up at the room, nor was he answering my calls or texts.

This moment was supposed to make me grown up, but all I wanted to do was go home and cry. I couldn't, though, because then my mother would know. My father too, and then there was Cason.

My two best friends, Anya and Lindsay, knew this would happen. They both told me countless times to just let Jake go, but did I listen? I clung to Jake because outside of my home he was my constant, my mine, my piece of the universe I collected for myself to have and to cherish. My first serious boyfriend. My first time ever in sex. I was all virgin when I met Jake Jennings, and once we were together he took care of that, gave me all those things I'd read about in books and seen in films. Only, it wasn't as pretty as the movies made it seem, wasn't as dreamy as the books wrote about, wasn't as swoon worthy as the songs went on about. It was bitter.

Bitter.

Much like the glass of water I was babysitting as I waited.

The heavy smell of food in the air didn't excite my hunger. I was in a restaurant, but I felt empty and full at the same. Quite a paradox, I know.

"Miss?"

Ben was back, balancing a tray of dirty dishes on one shoulder, while leaning my way with the other. "Hate to do this, but..." The sympathy and condolence on his face were hard to miss.

I knew this was coming. There was only so much time they would allow me to hog my table. It was Saturday night, date night for many, and I clearly wasn't on a date.

Just another lonely heart beating alone.

Slowly, I pushed away from the table and stood to my feet. I didn't like to wear heels, but in this moment, thankfully, I was steady on all six-inches. "I'm sorry about this." I couldn't look at him, but I wanted to let him know I felt terrible for wasting his time.

Ben frowned. "Oh, honey, you're fine."

Ben was being sweet, and even though I'd only gotten my water, I pulled out a bill from my wallet and laid it on the table as a tip before stiffly hanging my head and walking on by. No one was looking at me, but I felt like I had an audience as I shamefully walked to the exit, out into the night.

Sheltered, and maybe just a bit naïve, I knew nothing of LA, of a life outside of Hemingway Park where I was from. Panic and anxiety didn't take over, a reprieve of sorts, as the hurt of it all was too much for my heart already.

Goose bumps prickled my pale arms and I shivered as I hugged myself on the way to my parked Kia Forte. I climbed inside and went into autopilot, my shaky hand reaching over and shoving my key into the ignition as I grasped the steering wheel with the other.

I should've seen this coming. When he didn't show up to the motel. When he was over an hour late for our dinner. When he didn't pick up the phone. When he was distant even before all of this.

Jake and I, we were on and off, but I knew, deep down, we'd get better. We'd find a page and just write our own story our way. It didn't have to be perfect; it didn't have to make sense to anybody but us. This love was our very own.

October tenth, my birthday. Jake used to call me his "perfect ten" because of this day, and now, as I followed the GPS back to the Stargaze Motel, I began to realize that perhaps he had written another heroine for his love story. A true flawless beauty who was indeed...*perfect*.

Tears filled my vision and I did my best to keep them back so I could get to my destination safely. With all that my family had been through, I couldn't be selfish and hurt myself.

Even more, as much as I was hurting, I would stay the night at the room. No, I couldn't go home. Going home was admitting failure. Going home was facing the reality of it being over and done. Going home meant coming cl ean about what happened, and I couldn't bring myself to utter those words.

It's almost sad how when people hurt us, that we get so caught up in our feelings for them, we're willing to protect them to the end. To not let them suffer. To not let them get in trouble for their wrong and what they've done to us. As if an odd sense of guilt takes over at the thought of holding them accountable.

My father hated Jake, Cason even more, and yet I was ready to pretty up an excuse for him, so that they wouldn't think any less of him.

I felt like a child for how excited I'd been when I'd arrived at the Stargaze earlier that evening to find a bouquet of roses sitting on the table by the door. They'd been delivered with a card from Jake, citing, *10 + 10 = 20. Happy birthday, Holly, now you're twice the perfect ten – J*

The Stargaze was located in downtown LA, it wasn't the prettiest or most fancy motel. As some of the bulbs in the sign out front were broken. The letter M was half lit up looking like a lowercase H, and as I drove into the lot, it only glowed with the phrase *Starze hel.*

When Jake spoke of coming here, I immediately turned him down. If we *had* to spend my birthday in LA, I would've rather done something memorable. According to social media, Teddy Sykes was in town, and even if it were a bit stalkerish and wasteful, I would've rather hung around places we could've potentially ran into him for an autograph or photo-op.

Or, if I were living on planet Earth, I would've much rather settled down with a frozen pizza and my favorite movie than do something so showy like this, but Jake had aspirations and wanted this lavishness. He dreamed of becoming an actor someday, and while he worked a series of various temp jobs, he was constantly on the go about auditions. He'd once landed a commercial for Mountain Dew, and was quick to tell anyone who would listen about it.

Jake didn't have the most money, and neither did I, but I liked to think that I wasn't needy, that I didn't ask for too much. And it was because of this, that I felt that maybe it was okay to go along with this weekend getaway, maybe it was okay to be pampered.

It wasn't lost on me why he chose this motel, as Teddy Sykes himself had once stayed here with his touring band and I'd obsessed over the photo he'd posted to his Instagram for how down-to-earth he'd been to choose such a place, like they were slumming it on their come-up. As if a member from a previous best-selling boy band could ever truly *slum* it. Established in 1963, the Stargaze Motel held a history of hosting various up-and-coming rock stars and bands in its quarters. I thought it was kind of cool that Teddy had stayed here for the legacy of it all.

But then Jake didn't show up to the room he'd booked. I told myself not to think anything of it, and so foolishly I'd driven to the restaurant he'd booked for dinner and sat there like an idiot for two hours.

The Stargaze wasn't the biggest establishment, but as I did a quick sweep across the parking lot, I didn't see Jake's Volkswagen. He wasn't here.

He wasn't coming.

It was my twentieth birthday, and I was cold and alone.

I got out of the car and made my way over to the steps that led up to the second level of rooms. Down on the far end from my room, a party of some sort was going on, loud raucous music was blasting and I could faintly hear women squealing and men laughing. The door was ajar and the curtains were opened, happiness on full display as I could see inside. Nobody paid me any attention as I slipped into my room.

The first thing I noticed was the vase of flowers on the door side table, and just the sight of them lit the fuse of my heartache.

In one swinging motion I shoved the vase to the floor and released a loud cry. Of course, I was weak, though. The teal vase didn't even shatter, it simply landed with a *thud* and sent those thorny roses in a wet mess across the carpet.

I'd failed yet again.

The room wasn't big at all, only housing a full-sized bed with an ugly olive-green bedding, a dresser with a TV, the table by the door, and the bathroom with a tiny closet next to it. Standing alone in this foreign place, my world started to spin as the walls seemed to be closing in on me. My hands started to shake and I couldn't calm down no matter how hard I tried.

Shower. Clean. I needed to get clean. I needed to wash this night completely away.

With each step I took towards the bathroom, a piece of me fell off until I found myself crumbling in the tub. I still had my dress on. I didn't care as I turned on the water, hoping the shower would wash me away. Maybe as I circled the drain would the pain finally cease.

Sitting there in the middle of the tub with the hot spray of water raining down on me, I hugged my knees to my chest and allowed myself to finally sob.

Stupid. Stupid girl.

Lyrics to my favorite song by my favorite singer came to mind, depressing me more, picking at this fresh wound and bleeding me dry, making me—

"What the fuck?"

A voice cut through the fog in my head. A foreign voice. *In* my motel room. Beneath the sound of the shower, I could hear hefty footsteps walking around out in the bedroom, each step landing heavy and sending a sudden terror in my veins.

The sound of the bathroom door squeaking open as the knob twisted made me squeeze my knees closer to my chest. With nowhere to go, I felt my heart race with panic. Behind the frosted curtain a dark figure appeared, massive and tall, wide shouldered —and definitely not Jake Jennings.

My mouth fell open, but not a sound came out as they approached the shower.

A hand reached out and tanned fingers curled around the curtain before yanking it back.

He appeared suddenly, in all the steam, like an angel of darkness, coming to take me away from this place. He was Hades and I was Persephone, fit for the claiming.

Slowly, my vision adjusted—or so I thought. My eyes were playing tricks on me. Because *who* I was staring at couldn't in fact be there. There was no way *the* Teddy Sykes was standing in my motel room. In my bathroom.

Seconds ticked by into minutes and there he remained, hand on the curtain, peering down at me. Dressed in the darkest shade of navy blue with his T-shirt along with black jeans, he was very real. Teddy Sykes, tall like I'd seen in pictures. Long unruly golden-brown hair I'd dreamed about running my fingers through. Same tattoos I'd imagined running my fingers across. Gorgeous face I fantasized kissing. And deep dark eyes I wanted to stare into. There was no mistaking the stranger in my bathroom was indeed Theodore "Teddy" Sykes. Almost as if I'd conjured him up.

In my blurred vision, Teddy was as serious as could be as he stood over me, taking me in.

"Where is he?" he asked calmly in his English accent.

He? Did he mean Jake? Did he know Jake? "I don't know."

Frustration peppered across Teddy's face as he took a step back, examining me further. He sniffled, running a thumb over his dark and thick eyebrow. I watched in sheer confusion as he fished a buzzing phone out of his jeans and he gazed impassively at the screen before answering the call.

"What the fuck did you do?" he snapped into his phone. "Waiting for *me*? What about the girl? ... What girl? The one in the tub..." Teddy quieted down and began to listen to whoever had called him, his eyes bouncing from me to out into the room.

As if it hit him, he froze, running a hand down his face. "I'm in the wrong fuckin' room."

He hung up on the caller, I could tell by the way he simply pulled the phone from his ear and shoved it back into his jeans without issuing a farewell or further explanation about the series of events.

Teddy pushed those two big hands of his through his hair, the light glistened on the two platinum bracelets on his wrist. He blew out a breath and swore so deadly and sweet, his accent wrapping around the offending words so delicately.

Without another word, he turned to leave and I let out a sob.

This wasn't real. No, it was just some cruel nightmare bent on destroying me further. First Jake ghosted me, and now I was meeting Teddy Sykes of all people? Teddy Sykes who was just going to walk out the door without a goodbye. No way was life this awful. This had to be a dream, some horrid, terrible dream. Some—

The water shut off and he was still in the room. I could feel him standing over me again, staring down at me.

A warm hand grabbed a hold of me until I was standing. A white towel came into my vision and Teddy stood back, giving me room to step out of the tub. The material of my dress weighed me down now as I tried to towel off. Outside of the heat that had been my shower, I was colder than before, shivering even.

Teddy studied me further, his eyes starting at my head and ending at my bare feet. His hand reached out, capturing the pendant of my necklace I wore around my neck and fingering it. "What's the L stand for?"

I sniffled. It could only mean one thing now. "Loser."

A flash of annoyance coated his brown eyes. "What does it stand for?"

"*Lucky*. Sometimes I think about getting a kitten to name that, to remind myself to always shoot for luck, for positivity, for something good. It's silly, I know, especially considering."

Teddy stood back, quizzical. "Considering what?"

My gaze fell to the floor. "I don't feel so lucky."

I walked by him out of the room, going back to the bedroom and finding the door wide open. The night wind caused me to freeze even more. No, Teddy hadn't materialized out of thin air, he'd walked right in.

"The door was open and I thought this was another room." Teddy came out of the bathroom and threw a hand towards the roses on the floor. "I saw the flowers, the heels, and heard the shower and...I don't know."

Buzzing from his pocket caused him to once more gather his phone and the sight of it made me all too ready to end this night.

I went over to my purse and found my own cell phone, feeling nothing at the discovery that Jake hadn't responded to any of my attempts to gain communication. No, only a missed text message from my coworker, Bianka, and another text from my mother awaited me.

The phone was out of my hands before I could even unlock it. I had just enough time to catch Teddy's angry eyes on me as he again rudely just cut his call short.

"What are you doing?" he demanded to know.

The tone of his voice and the anger on his face sent me stepping back. "I just wanted to call my mom."

I just wanted this night to be over. To no longer exist. To no longer matter.

He must've thought I'd meant to record him, snap his picture or something, because relief washed across his face as he went to hand my phone back.

And then, in total embarrassment, he noticed my phone case. The phone case I'd customized online from a photo of him singing up on stage during his fourth tour with his old boy band, So What.

"You're...a fan." It was a statement, not a question. A painful realization on both our parts.

I hung my head, allowing my shoulders to shake and the tears to fall. I finally got to meet him, and I wasn't ready, was emotionally devasted, had no words to say.

Teddy's black boots came into my sight and I peered up at him, finding him holding my phone out.

He seemed frustrated the longer he stared at me.

"W-What?" I let out.

Teddy frowned. "I've never seen an angel cry."

Pitifully, I managed to chuckle. *Angel*? "You're too kind."

Serious again, he said, "I'm not nice."

His attention shifted around the room and he ran his hand behind his neck. "I gotta...I gotta go. Are you...?"

Teddy cut himself off, returning to me and just looking on. He swore once more and went and shut the door, latching the chain lock before turning and facing me. "Who were you expecting?"

"My boyfriend," I told him. "He's not coming."

"How do you know?"

Wasn't it painfully obvious? "I waited for him at the restaurant, and he never showed up. Didn't call. Didn't text. He's not coming."

"How long did you wait?"

I looked over at Teddy, confessing my shame. "Three hours."

He blinked. "*Three* hours?"

"Happy birthday to me." I regretted this the moment the words left my lips. To voluntarily make myself look even more pathetic made me cringe.

Teddy was quiet as he remained against the door. Helpless even. He was a somebody, with places to be and people to meet. The last thing he needed to do was spend another second in this crappy motel room with the lonely heart down the hall.

He glimpsed at the window, probably imagining just walking away, before coming back to me. Those brows furrowed and his lips drew into a firm line. "Get dressed. Turn on the tele. I'll wait here. Maybe he'll show up."

"You don't have to do that," I insisted.

Teddy made a face. "I know that. You don't have to be reckless and leave your bloody door open, either."

He raked a hand through his hair and paced for a bit, his eyes once more flickering towards the door. He seemed to bounce even, unsteady with standing still.

"It's okay, I'll be okay," I told him.

On any other day, I would've been more creative, thinking of a desperate reason to keep him here, but now, I wasn't at my best, not fit to properly meet him.

Teddy looked at me, the mental debate to leave or stay clear on his face. "What's your name?"

"Holliston."

At once, he angled his head, seeming to see me with new eyes suddenly. "H-O-L-L-I-S-T-O-N?"

"Yes. My friend, Bianka, met you a few months ago and you signed—"

"A magazine," Teddy concluded. "Get dressed, you'll catch cold."

Maybe he didn't want me to see him leave. It wouldn't hurt today, not any more than Jake.

I found my bag and fished out my night clothes I'd stowed before I left home. In the bathroom, I slipped on a T-shirt and a pair of shorts. I took my time, so he could leave as easily as he'd come. I ran a brush through my hair, fixing the mess it had been in after I'd rubbed my towel through it. In the mirror, my blue eyes stared back at me, a sadness so deep I could drown in it. Teddy Sykes was in my room and I couldn't even grasp it, cling to an ounce of happiness. I used to joke with Jake, Anya, and Lindsay that though I was devoted to my boyfriend, Teddy Sykes was my one true hall pass—that person you were allowed to hook up with despite your current relationship status.

Now here he was and I couldn't feel anything.

Jake sucked me dry on this day of all days, this day that was entirely mine. This moment in time where I would forever look back on turning twenty alone and cold. This moment where love died.

I hugged myself close as I walked back out to the room, stopping short at the sight of Teddy sitting at the foot of the bed, flipping through the channels. He didn't seem satisfied with the options before him as he kept flipping absentmindedly.

"You stayed," I spoke up.

He nodded. "I did."

I went and crawled under the blanket, both tired and wide awake. Teddy's presence sent me on alert, he smelled good, and I could *feel* him too.

"Thank you, Teddy, for being here," I said. "I thought about this moment a thousand times—I never thought it would actually happen, especially not like this, when I look...like *this*."

He didn't turn around as he settled on some adult animated cartoon. "You looked lovely in that dress, probably even more so before you got into that tub. You're even pretty when you cry."

He didn't say any more, and I didn't either.

I bundled up underneath the blanket and looked on at the TV, watching, but not seeing, hearing, but not listening. Waiting, but not expecting Jake to show up.

ACKNOWLEDGMENTS

It started with a tweet. I can't start this off without thanking the girls who saw a certain tweet I sent and encouraged me to write this novel (iykyk). Without you, this book wouldn't exist.

I'd like to thank the following people for having a hand in making this book possible.

Erica, thank you so much for WANTING to work on this book with me. Your enthusiasm from the very beginning made this journey that much more fun. Your support and belief made *me* feel more confident in this story. You are one of a kind and I can't stress that enough.

Zahra, I was so nervous to reach out, but once I did, your warmth made me feel safe and comfortable. Even with just the synopsis you were onboard and that meant a lot to me. Thank you so much for being an excited cheerleader.

Mary, you created the best cover for this book. You nailed what I was going for right away. I am in LOVE with this cover.

And last, but not least, all the readers who've had a hand in supporting Zander & Bianka's story in its rough stages. Thank you so much!

Before I go, I just wanna say for anyone who relates to Bianka's story involving her family that you're not alone. It's completely OKAY to walk away and put yourself first. For a long time society has told us that family matters and we must be loyal to this unit, but unfortunately, sometimes family is the one who hurts you the most. And it's okay to protect yourself first. It's okay to choose YOU. Sometimes we have to find our own family and that's okay.

Until my next release,

B.

ABOUT THE AUTHOR

Britney July is a dreamer from the Midwest who grew up camped out in her local library gorging on books. Now as an author, she endeavors to write fun and steamy edge-of-your-seat romances that leave you devouring page after page and emotionally undone.

When she's not writing, Britney can be found watching films, as her second love is cinema. *Deeper* is her first novel.